A Woman on the Knife's Edge

Hearts and Sails Book 4

Alina Rubin

Publisher: Hearts and Sails Author Services

ISBN: Paperback 979-8-9855378-8-8

Cover Design: GetCovers

Editors: Betsy Judkins of Maine Woods Editing and Carrie Krause of Get Carried Away Editing

Dedication

To all medical and pharmaceutical workers, including my dear husband, Vitaly, who strive to discover new cures while ensuring patient safety and well-being. And to Elanna with all my love.

I would love to know what you thought of A Woman on the Knife's Edge! You can write a review at:
Amazon
Goodreads
BookBub

Be the first to know of new releases by subscribing to the newsletter at alinarubinauthor.com
I love hearing from my readers! Please connect with me!
Instagram: Alina.Rubin.Author
Facebook: Alina Rubin Author

Ella's and Jamie's first meeting occurs in the prequel novella **Hearts by the Sea**

Read for free!

An innocent game brings unforeseen consequences

In the idyllic setting of the English coast in 1800s, Jamie Flowers experiences his first infatuation when he meets Ella Parker, a mysterious girl with a troubled past. As the two rehearse *Romeo and Juliet* together, they decide to sneak out for a midnight swim. But their plans are abruptly halted by a shocking revelation, and Ella is soon gone. Left with a broken heart, Jamie searches for her... and himself. With unexpected twists and turns, Hearts by the Sea is a story of first love, secret codes, and self-discovery.

Read for free!

ALINA RUBIN

Contents

Chapter 1

Plymouth, October 1812

Jamie's whisper swirled over and over in Ella Parker's head, pushing out all other thoughts.

"I'm sorry. Ella, I am so sorry."

Heat traveled from her hairline down to her fingers, which grasped the needle and thread.

How could I have been so stupid?

"Dr. Parker? You must suture."

Her assistant Tyler's voice jarred Ella, and she blinked. The patient in front of her, carpenter's mate Mr. Wilkinson, was hemorrhaging from his calf. Just hours before the *Neptune*'s planned departure, the unfortunate man became injured while repairing a railing. Her second assistant, Sully, held the patient's shoulders, while Tyler restrained the leg. The injured seaman, however, was no longer fighting their grip. Blood loss made him faint.

The heavy air of the sickbay and the metallic scent of blood rushed into Ella's nostrils, making her head spin. Her vision blurred.

"Are you all right?" Tyler's voice sounded as if it came from a tunnel. "You look like you are about to swoon."

The pitches and rolls of the ship made her stomach lurch, and bitter bile shot up her throat.

What's wrong with me? I haven't been seasick in years, and the ship hasn't even left the harbor. And I've seen rivers of blood after battles.

Tyler's hand touched Ella's elbow. "Do you want me to take over?"

His question cut through the fog of her vision. The crimson blood pooling around the deep gash, contrasting with the patient's ashen face, struck her senses. If she hesitated any longer, she risked losing her patient. But her hands trembled, and her knees weakened.

If she were working without her assistants, she'd somehow push through this awful sensation and close the wound. But she had Tyler by her side. While she was in France, caring for British prisoners of war, he'd proven to be more capable than the surgeon Captain Grey had hired in her absence.

My hands are shaking. I will be too slow. It's better if Tyler sutures.

She passed the needle threaded with catgut to Tyler and forced her tongue to respond. "Yes, please take over. I'm not feeling well."

With his deft hands, Tyler crafted neat stitches just as she'd taught him.

What happened to me? I proved to these sailors that I belong on the ship by being strong. But I don't feel strong today.

When Tyler finished suturing, he looked up at her. "Do you approve of my work?"

Ella checked the patient's pulse. It was regular, and a bit of color had returned to the injured man's face. "I much approve."

Breathing hard, she dipped her hands into water from the basin to wash off the blood and threw off her apron. The wide eyes of her assistants followed her as she dashed from the sickbay. Her legs hurried up the ladder. On the deck, she paused and leaned on the railing, filling her lungs with the crisp autumn air. Larger warships stationed at Plymouth port surrounded the sloop-of-war *Neptune,* the ship she'd belonged to for three years. The only place where she was accepted as a surgeon. She'd overcome the sailor superstition against women onboard and proved her skill.

I've worked so hard to belong here. But I can only belong if I'm doing my job. I haven't been myself since Jamie's rejection. If Jamie is on this voyage, I won't be able to perform to the best of my abilities. My mistake may cause somebody's life.

With her teeth clenched, she marched toward the captain's cabin. At her knocking, Captain Grey's voice bid her to come in. She pushed the heavy door open and stomped inside.

"Sir, I—" She stepped back with her mouth gaping.

Captain Grey sat at his desk; a faded chart of the Spanish coast spread in front of him. Jamie Flowers and his best friend Conor Leach, both in midshipmen's uniforms of navy and white, flanked him. Only two weeks ago, the *Neptune* rescued Ella, Jamie, and Conor, along with several captured sailors, after their imprisonment and near death in France. But the culmination of their adventure, what should've been Ella's happiest moment, proved disastrous. She disembarked at Plymouth, where the ship had stopped for repairs and supplies, and avoided everyone from the crew until today.

Jamie's cornflower blue eyes pierced Ella. The uniform highlighted his tall, graceful form. His straw-blond hair framed his handsome face, no longer gaunt or pale.

Ella's fists clenched. *It's thanks to me that he's alive and looking well.*

Captain Grey tore his gaze from the chart. "Good day, Dr. Parker. Did you come to report on the state of your patient? How is he?"

Feeling Jamie's eyes on her, Ella swallowed. "Mr. Wilkinson will be fine. He lost a significant amount of blood and requires rest, but he will be able to return to his duties in a couple of days."

"Good." The captain made a note in his journal. "Does the dispensary have sufficient medicines for a six-month voyage? We are sailing to bring supplies to our troops in Spain. They are giving Napoleon a proper thrashing. Then we'll patrol the Spanish coast."

"Aye, sir. I inspected the medical inventory earlier this morning, and we are well stocked."

Captain Grey added a note to his journal, then shifted his gaze back to the chart. "If that's all, you are dismissed. These gentlemen and I have much to accomplish before the sailing, and I'm sure you do as well."

Her gaze shifted between the captain and the door.

I must tell him what occurred. What's more important, my pride or my patients?

She forced herself to turn around. "Sir... I must speak to you alone."

Captain Grey grunted. "Can it wait until tomorrow? As you can see, my officers and I are discussing our course, and then we sail on the evening tide. Or do I need to know this before we sail? You need more bandages? Are men ill? What is it?"

Ella opened her mouth to speak, but a bang on the door halted her tongue.

"Sir, Lieutenant Drake Landon reporting for duty," a boisterous voice rang.

"Glad to finally have you aboard, Mr. Landon," the captain answered.

A tall man, about twenty-five years old, with a thin mustache and dark eyes, walked in.

"Sir, I'm immensely pleased to sail under your command." He saluted the captain with a fist to his forehead. His eyes glanced over Jamie and Conor as if they were part of the modest furniture of the cabin. Then they focused on Ella and squinted with keenness.

"Will we have the pleasure of sailing with your beautiful daughter?" he asked Captain Grey.

Something about his voice made the hair at the nape of Ella's neck stand.

"My daughters are home, attending dancing lessons or practicing their musical instruments." Annoyance seeped through the captain's voice. "Please meet our ship surgeon, Dr. Ella Parker, who was about to report something important when you came in. Please go ahead, Doctor."

Four pairs of eyes studied her. Her face heated.

I've worked so hard to be here. But my first duty is to do no harm.

As she searched for words, Drake Landon puffed out his chest, ran his finger over his lips, and winked at her. Immediately, Jamie and Conor snapped their necks toward him, like hounds catching the scent of an outsider.

The captain's eyes seemed to bore into her mind.

"Sir, I don't think I should join you on this voyage."

"You are telling me this when we are about to sail?" Captain Grey's hands hit the desk. "Why in the world?"

"Sir, I know what this is about," Jamie spoke. "And it's entirely my fault. Dr. Parker should remain. I resign."

Captain Grey grunted. "I was hoping to avoid speaking of what happened, but I see it's unavoidable. Mr. Leach, why don't you show Mr. Landon his cabin? I must speak to Mr. Flowers and Dr. Parker privately."

When Conor and Drake left, the captain stared at Ella and Jamie with his lips drawn into a line. "I don't have time for lovers' quarrels."

"That's why I resign," Jamie repeated.

Ella considered whether Jamie's absence would ease her worry.

What happened in the sickbay wasn't normal. Something must be wrong with me.

"Sir, when caring for Mr. Wilkinson, I didn't feel well. My assistant Tyler Monk stepped in."

"What's wrong then? Do you have a fever?" Captain's eyes widened.

Sweat ran down between her shoulder blades. "I don't believe that my body is ill. And yet I'm unwell."

My instructor in medical school, Dr. Miller, would call it female hysterics. But I've seen men break down in a similar way.

Jamie bit his lip and stared at the deck.

Captain Grey clicked his tongue. "If I hadn't taken the *Neptune* for repairs, the damages we sustained last voyage would put all our lives at risk. You must do the same for your sake and those of your patients. I hate losing you, Dr. Parker, but you must leave the ship. You need time to heal from the trials you overcame in France. My wife and daughters will extend their friendship to you. Please know that I've valued the service you've given to the men, and I'm sure they will miss you. They are busy with sailing preparations, however, and won't have time to say goodbye. I wish you well on their behalf. I will appoint Mr. Tyler Monk as the surgeon. He proved himself capable in your absence. I hope to see you again, recovered and ready to work."

What have I done? Did I destroy everything I've worked for?

Her chest squeezed as she thought of the friends she'd made. Especially the shipboys she treated and tutored.

The captain checked his pocket watch. "Time is short before the sailing. Please give Mr. Monk whatever instructions he needs and collect your belongings. I'll order the coxswain to lower the boat and take you to shore."

"I wish you the happy life you deserve. And again, I'm sorry," Jamie mumbled, still staring down.

You wish me happiness, Jamie, but you are the one who broke me.

"Safe voyage, Mr. Flowers. And you, Captain Grey." She flew to the door so they couldn't see the tears that had formed in her eyes.

Chapter 2

At sea, February 1813

Jamie's hammock swayed with the pitches and rolls of the waves, lulling him to sleep. After spending the cool night on his feet, as required of an officer of the watch, his body craved warmth and rest. Conor snored in the hammock next to his. Even though it was morning, no daylight seeped to the orlop deck, below the water line, making it easier to pretend that it was nighttime. Besides, Jamie had learned to sleep at any opportunity, and the system of the watches and bells was as ingrained in him as the multiplication tables that his older sister, Caroline, liked to test him on.

Should I write to my family when we return to Plymouth? His jaw tensed, and he rubbed it to loosen the cramped muscle. *Most likely, they read of my imprisonment in the naval papers. Since they know about my illness, they must've determined that I died in France and perhaps have already stopped grieving for me. I would've died there, if not for Ella.*

An image of Ella came to his mind. She was before him on one knee, her raven locks tossed by the wind, her eyes reflecting the sea. So brave of her to break the social rules and propose to him. If only he could accept.

His heart hammered, reminding him why he'd forced himself to say, "I'm so sorry, Ella."

If I'd told her about my heart, she'd pity me. Conor'd behave the same way. I'd lose my love and my best friend.

Dr. Miller said I would die by the age of twenty. I will be that age in six months. Since I left home I found adventure, friends, and Ella, just as I planned. I'm ready for death when it comes.

"Mr. Flowers! Mr. Leach!" a high-pitched voice called, and a lanky figure entered the berth.

"Tobby, is that you? What do you need?"

The thirteen-year-old shipboy limped as he approached Jamie's hammock. The boy seemed a few inches taller since their days of imprisonment in France.

"You must come to the deck!"

Jamie shushed him. "Don't yell. Mr. Leach is sleeping."

"Not anymore." Conor yawned and swung his legs down to sit. "This better be important. Did the captain call us?"

"Aye, sir. I mean, no, sir. I mean, the captain didn't call you. But it's important."

Jamie put his hand on the boy's shoulder. "Breathe. Then tell us why we're needed on deck. I assume Lieutenant Landon is there. Did he call for us?" If Drake wanted them, it would likely be to give them an unpleasant, even useless task and to criticize them as they performed it.

Tobby sniffled and took out a white handkerchief. Jamie was pleased to see the boy remember Ella's lessons in manners and use the hankie instead of his sleeve to blow his nose.

"It's Mr. Olson. Mr. Landon ordered the bosun to flog him."

Jamie groaned and shoved his arm into his uniform coat. "I'm sure it's over some nonsense. Captain Grey almost never flogs the men. You were right to wake us, Tobby. Now hurry to the captain and tell him. We'll try to delay the punishment until he intervenes."

Tobby sprinted away as well as he could with his limp, and Jamie hastened to the ladder. Conor's arm caught him on his elbow mid-stride.

"Jamie, are we right to interfere? Landon has the authority to punish anyone below him. That includes us. By involving the captain, we'll be snitches."

Jamie faced his friend. "Landon must be stopped. We can't let him hurt an innocent man. Especially Olson. He's an excellent carpenter and a friend to everyone. And he survived such horrors while being enslaved in the colonies."

They climbed up to the deck, where the morning sunlight, reflected by the sea, made them squint. The winter chill seeped through their midshipmen's uniforms. Tobby hurried to the captain's cabin, while Jamie and Conor joined the crowd of men at the bow. The men parted for them.

One of the men whispered to Jamie, "Please help, Mr. Flowers. It's unfair."

"I will try," he whispered back and stepped in front of the gathered men, Conor next to him.

A chill much colder than the morning breeze ran down Jamie's spine. Carpenter Owen Olson was tied by his arms to the grating. His whole body trembled, whether from the cold or fear, Jamie couldn't tell. An array of faded scars crisscrossed the seaman's brown back.

Drake Landon, with the gold buttons of his lieutenant's uniform shining in the sunlight, scanned the men with his eyes blazing. His gaze lingered on Jamie and Conor for a moment. "Let this punishment be a lesson to everyone. He failed to salute me when I came to inspect his work."

"I meant no disrespect, sir. I was sleepy and didn't see you," Olson pleaded.

The fear in Olson's voice made Jamie's heart ache.

Drake leered. "The whip will wake and warm you."

Jamie filled his lungs to make his voice boom with authority, even though he had none over the lieutenant's command. "Mr. Landon, a word if you please."

He stepped to the railing and waited for Drake to approach him. Conor dashed to his side before Drake swaggered over.

The lieutenant glared at Jamie. "What is it, Mr. Flowers? Do you have a problem with how I discipline the men? Before you begin, I want to remind you that the captain has given me the order to punish anyone how I see fit."

Jamie swallowed. "I know that, sir. But you may not be aware of Mr. Olson's history. He's an escaped slave. Those scars on his back were given to him by his owner. A man who suffered that much deserves mercy. If you insist on disciplining him, you could choose a different punishment. Or bring the matter to the captain's attention and let him decide how to punish Mr. Olson."

Drake's face flushed. "Do you dare to teach me, Flowers?"

Conor's fists clenched. "You're just trying to show how tough you are. I know because I used to be like that too. But flogging that man is going too far."

"Stop before I order you to join him." Drake ran his tongue over his teeth and bellowed to the bosun. "Twenty lashes for Mr. Olson! And put your full strength into them or I will have you flogged for not doing your duty."

The bosun raised his thick arm, and the cat-o'-nine-tails swished through the air. Olson screamed as the whip sliced red lines into his back.

"One," Drake yelled.

Another lash cracked amid heavy silence. More streams of blood. Another cry of pain that turned Jamie's gut inside out. "Two!"

The men stared down at the deck, and a few shipboys sobbed. The whip tore at Olson's skin, his moans and Landon's counting following each blow. With each lash, Jamie's heart sped faster, constraining the air in his lungs.

Break now. Without Ella, I've had enough of this life, he told his heart.

"Stop!" The captain's voice came before Drake announced the tenth lash. The bosun froze the whip in the air before it could add yet more slices to Olson's decimated skin. A collective exhale came from the men.

"Sir, this man's punishment is twenty lashes." Drake's voice seeped with false surprise. "We are only halfway through the count."

Captain Grey cringed. "Our bosun has exceptional arm strength. His flogging can strip flesh to the bone. We need our best carpenter to keep this ship sailing."

Tobby limped to Jamie with tears running down his cheeks. "The captain was sleeping and didn't understand me at first. We are too late."

Jamie put his arm around the boy. "You saved Olson's life. His back will heal."

Captain Grey's brow knitted as he studied Olson's back. "Someone take Mr. Olson to the surgeon. Mr. Landon, please see me in my cabin. Everyone else, get back to work." He stomped away, and Drake hastened after him, giving a hateful look to Jamie and Conor as he went.

Most of the men dispersed. The bosun untied him and was saying something, but Olson stared at the grating, seemingly oblivious to his words. With a sigh, the bosun stepped away. A couple of men crept toward Olson, exchanging glances. Jamie reached him before they did.

He put his hand on the seaman's shoulder, careful to choose a spot that hadn't been welted or cut. "Olson, let's go see the surgeon."

Olson turned to face him. His eyes were cloudy and his lips shook. His face was fixed with painful intensity.

"Sir, I'm sorry. I won't run away again."

Jamie's eyes widened. "Run away? What are you talking about?"

"He doesn't know what he's saying," Conor whispered. "He must think he was beaten by his master."

Tobby sobbed. "What's wrong with him?"

Jamie shook his head and spoke louder, staring into the seaman's eyes. "Olson, you are a free man. A sailor. You have friends here."

Olson's expression stayed dazed.

"It's too bad Ella isn't here. She would know what to do," Conor muttered.

"Sir, let us try," one of the men said. "Perhaps he'll follow us below to the sickbay."

After several attempts, they got Olson to put his arms around two men. With slow strides, they led him away. Tobby blinked hard, as if trying not to cry, then hobbled away. Jamie and

Conor remained, both staring at the grating where Olson had been flogged.

"Do you think he will recover?" Jamie asked Conor.

Conor ran his hand through his hair. "Let's hope so. I don't want to think about what will happen to him if he doesn't."

Steps thundered behind them, and they turned to face Drake. The lieutenant's face was flushed, and Jamie wondered if he received a reprimand from the captain.

"I know it was the two of you who sent the shipboy to snitch on me. You will pay for it."

The menace in his voice made Jamie's insides freeze, but he forced himself to sound calm. "Why did you do this to Olson? The flogging broke his mind."

A mean grin appeared on Drake's lips. "If his mind is so fragile, he doesn't belong at sea. I did it because he must show me respect. As do you. Besides, there are so little diversions on this ship. Had that girl-surgeon remained here, I'd know what to do with my time. But since there are no women or other amusements, the best fun I can have is getting a rise out of you. Now get out of my sight." He crossed his arms and grimaced.

Conor balled his fists, and his lips moved as if to say something that would surely get them in trouble. Jamie's muscles clenched, but he grabbed Conor's arm and pulled him away. "He's toying with us. If we play into his hand, he'll take it out not only on us but on our friends. Don't argue with him. Let's go see how Olson is doing."

Thank goodness Ella is far away from Drake's clutches, Jamie thought as they descended to the sickbay.

Chapter 3

Plymouth, April 1813

Prostrated on the narrow bed, Ella stared at the crack that ran through the ceiling. Morning sunlight streamed through the window, but the promise of a bright spring day failed to cheer her. Her body craved sleep, but she refused to close her eyes. If she did, Jamie would haunt her dreams again.

The door creaked, and the aromas of porridge and coffee floated from the tray Matilda carried in. The midwife's gray hair were woven into a tight braid. Her lips tightened, making her wrinkles more visible. "Why are you lying like a log and staring at that old crack?"

Ella sighed. "This crack makes me think of the rift inside my chest. My heart is broken. And yet, it's beating, keeping me alive. How can that be?"

"Stop this nonsense." Matilda put down the tray with a thud. "Even I know that a heart doesn't shatter like a vase. Mine ached when Lindsey died and when my brother Joseph perished. But

I got over my grief by working myself harder, delivering babies and healing women with my herbs."

Matilda brought a chair and sat down next to Ella's bed.

"Ella, I'm trying to be understanding. You are just shy of twenty, and heartaches hit hard at that age. But six months of your gloom is too much. A man didn't want to marry you. So what? You are better off."

"It's not like that!" Anger bubbled through Ella's veins, and she bolted upright on the bed. "I was so sure of his feelings that I got down on one knee and proposed. Can you imagine? My crew watched me do it. And he—"

"Refused you. Yes, you've told me." A rueful smile appeared on Matilda's lips. "I repeat: You are better off, and work is the best remedy for your sorrow."

"I do work—I prepare the medicines. And I help around the house."

"You don't visit patients."

Ella groaned. "I can't be trusted with patients. Memories come to my head, and I cry like a child. If I shed tears while cooking soup, it doesn't matter. But if I lose composure when examining a patient..."

"So that's why the soup was salty last night." Matilda rose and crossed her arms. "My herb shop is not a warship. Women understand another woman's sorrow. When Lindsey died, I cried with my clients. They knew my pain. And I knew theirs."

"But how could you help anyone in such a state?" Ella threw off her blanket and stood.

A shadow crossed Matilda's face. "I'd have a long cry on someone's shoulder, then dry my tears and get to work. Enough. It's almost ten, and we're still prattling. Today, you will visit a patient."

"But what if I'm... unwell?"

There were mornings she couldn't summon the energy to leave her bed. Days she had no appetite. Nights that left her sobbing into her pillow.

The midwife rolled her shoulders. "Ella, stop thinking that you are ill. You are capable and resilient. Cure yourself with the work you love. Take one of my clients; I just received a note from a Mrs. Landon. She lives in the best part of town, judging by the address. Get yourself cleaned up and see to her."

"Mrs. Landon? That name sounds familiar for some reason."

"This woman never sent for me before. Her note says to keep the visit private and to ask for her maid Sarah when you knock on the back door."

"Sounds mysterious." Ella bent over a basin and splashed some water on her face.

Matilda snorted. "Secrecy is common in my business. Many women don't want it to be known that they need a midwife or an herbal healer."

"It's driving me mad why that name sounds familiar." Ella ran a comb through the her raven locks that grew past her shoulders. The years of disguising herself as a male medical student were behind her, and her hair was growing back to its former glory.

"Then find out. And afterward, visit Mrs. Grey and her daughters for dinner. I'm tired of making excuses for you."

Matilda is right. I've been hiding from people too long, Ella told herself as she got ready to go out.

Chapter 4

Mrs. Landon's three-storied house boasted Doric columns and decorative cornices. Coal smoke from tall chimneys lingered in the air. Servants in uniforms swept the front steps and washed the window sashes. Ella walked past them to the back, where several women cleared dead leaves from flower beds. None of them spared her any attention.

I should write to my caretaker and ask how spring cleaning is going, she thought as she watched the servants' activity. *It's been four years since I inherited my father's wealth and land. But I don't miss that life at all.*

Ella's thoughts buzzed as she knocked on the back door.

A wide-shouldered, heavy-chinned woman in an apron covered with soot opened the door.

"Are you the new cook?" the woman asked, crossing her thick arms.

Ella answered, fidgeting from her stare, "No... I'm here to see Sarah."

"What for?" The large servant leaned forward. Ella stepped back from the onion smell on her breath.

If Mrs. Landon wanted to keep this private, she's likely afraid of servants' gossip. I must be discreet.

"Can't you fetch Sarah?"

The woman's gaze lingered on Ella's medical bag. "What's in there?"

She'd be suspicious of my surgical set.

"Medical herbs." Ella rolled back her shoulders. "I sell medical herbs. Sarah asked to bring something for her... dyspepsia."

The large servant grunted and closed the door in Ella's face.

Ella adjusted her shawl as she waited, unsure if the servant was returning with Sarah or turning her away.

After a few minutes, the door opened, and an older woman with silver hair peeking from under her bonnet emerged in the doorway. The large servant Ella saw before stood behind her.

The older woman hacked into her fist and rubbed her chest. "Yes, this woman is here for me. I've been coughing all week, and I'm too old to walk to the healer's shop."

Ella gave a conspiratorial nod. "Yes, I've brought ginger and peppermint."

The large servant tilted her head. "She said the herbs were for dyspepsia. That's not a cough."

"Ah yes... that too." Sarah shot a puzzled glance at Ella. Reading her confusion, Ella folded her hands on her stomach.

Sarah cringed and grabbed her abdomen. "Nothing worse than having a cough *and* a stomachache. Please tell me you have something to make me better."

Ella offered her hand to help Sarah straighten. "The same ginger and peppermint should help with those symptoms as well. Where can I show you how to take them?"

"Come to my room."

Sarah coughed and pressed on her stomach as she led Ella past the other servant. They reached the back staircase and climbed up to the top floor. Narrow cells, each containing just a small bed, lined both sides of the hallway. Sarah ushered her into one of those tiny bedrooms and closed the door.

"Hilda reports everything to the mistress." Sarah sighed and pointed for Ella to sit on the bed. "I'm sorry about all of this, Mistress Pesce."

"My name is Dr. Ella Parker," Ella said, sitting down on the hard bed. "I work with Matilda Pesce."

"My mistress wanted this to be handled with secrecy." Sarah's lips turned down.

"I will be as discreet as Mistress Pesce would be. But who are you hiding me from?"

Sarah pressed a finger to her lips and whispered. "Sound travels through these walls. Keep your voice quiet. I'm hiding you from Mrs. Landon."

Ella blinked. "But the note said I'm to see Mrs. Landon."

The servant woman inhaled. "There are now two Mrs. Landons. Dowager Mrs. Georginia Landon, the owner of this house. And my mistress, Mrs. Lillian Landon, the wife of Mr. Arthur Landon, her older son. I've cared for her since she was a child, when she was Miss Lillian Davis."

A daughter-in-law is keeping secrets from her mother-in-law.

"Let me check if someone's watching her. The dowager has eyes and ears everywhere. Poor Mistress Lillian had no idea what trouble she got herself into by eloping with Mr. Arthur." Sarah bent her head.

The maid left and soon returned, with her finger to her lips, motioning for Ella to follow her. "My mistress is pretending to be sleeping. I'll stand outside the door and keep everyone away from her room," she said as she led Ella down the back staircase to the floor below.

Their feet sank into the luscious carpet, and jasmine perfume scented the air. Sarah opened a door and gestured for Ella to come inside.

Ella stepped into the room and looked around. The vast bed seemed too large for the petite woman who was curled up under the embroidered blanket. She peeked from under her eyelids, pretending to be asleep. After a few seconds, she opened her hazel eyes. Standing next to the bed, Ella noted the young woman's pale cheeks and dark crescents under her eyes.

"Mrs. Landon, I'm Dr. Ella Parker. Mistress Pesce sent me."

The young woman blinked. "Did you say Parker? A few nights ago, I dreamed of a lady in a very fine dress. She was a little older than you but had your resemblance, the same black hair and green eyes. She introduced herself as Lady Parker."

That sounds like my mother. How?

Ella stared at the young woman. "You said this happened in a dream?"

"A childhood memory perhaps." Lillian frowned and moved a chestnut curl off her forehead.

"Are you disturbed by your dreams... or memories? Is that why you called for a healer?"

"No, it's something else." The young woman sat up and threw off her blanket. Her shoulders were covered by a loose white nightdress.

"I have long wanted to speak to a woman skilled in medicine. For years I've suffered headaches and lack of appetite. My parents had me examined by several physicians, and they agreed my ailment is of a nervous nature."

"But you disagree?"

Lillian sighed. "I don't know. Four months ago, I became nauseous, and my monthly courses stopped. I vomited a few times. When I told my mother, she grabbed her chest and called my father. Unfortunately, a month before, my little sisters spied me kissing a stable hand and told our parents. It was only a kiss, but my parents no longer believed me."

"They concluded you were with child. Did they fetch a midwife to examine you?"

"They didn't trust a midwife and insisted on a family physician. But I refused. The thought of being examined by that unpleasant old man just to prove my innocence made me furious. My word should've been enough. I craved to speak to a female healer, but my father doesn't trust such women. I still remember how, when I was seven years old, he tried to prevent my mother from calling on a midwife when she was about to give birth to my twin sisters. Instead, he invited a surgeon, supposedly a famous man, who was taking a holiday in our town. That surgeon said he would open my mother's belly and remove the babies. I was listening at the door and almost fainted. I believe my mother did as well. Thankfully, she delivered my sisters without that dreadful surgery."

Ella patted Lillian's back and pushed down her own memories of stepping into her mother's birthing room as the doctor sliced into her mother's abdomen to save her brother. Unfortunately, the surgeon couldn't save their lives. Her eyes brimmed with tears, but she wiped them and focused on Lillian.

"I'm here for you, and I will do what I can. You said that before your marriage, you had had headaches, loss of appetite, nausea, and vomiting. Your monthly courses stopped. Your parents concluded you were pregnant even though you know that's not possible. Do I understand you correctly?"

Lillian nodded. Ella lifted the young woman's hand, so small that it looked like a child's, but before she could count her pulse, Lillian spoke again. Her voice quivered. "My parents said I've shamed our family. They sent me here, to Mrs. Landon, so she could use her connections to find me a husband. My supposed condition was to stay a secret from her or she'd refuse to help me. I was to marry quickly and quietly. Mrs. Landon found me a widower three times my age. I was devastated. And ill. As the wedding date approached, my nausea became more frequent and my headaches, even more agonizing. Mrs. Landon assumed it all to be prewedding anxiety. As did my parents, to whom I wrote. They insisted that even if I'm not pregnant I must go through with the wedding. The widower was wealthy and influential in society. Then Arthur saw my anguish and came to my rescue. That's how he put it." Her hand touched her colorless lips.

"He suggested you elope with him?"

Lillian nodded. Tears ran down her face. "Yes. His mother was pressuring him to marry a wealthy woman he didn't like. He said he preferred me."

"When was that?"

"Two months ago. But please understand, there's no chance that I'm pregnant."

She lifted her hand to wipe her eyes. The sleeve of her nightdress shifted and revealed a purple bruise on her arm.

"How did you get this bruise?" Ella's stomach clenched. "Did your husband—"

"No. This happened yesterday. I was in the music room, playing the pianoforte. A headache came on, and that's all I remember. I must've fallen and hit my elbow on the stool. Sarah was with me, and she helped me get up."

Ella bit her lip. "Was that the first time you've fainted?"

Instead of an answer, Lillian covered her face with her hands.

Worried, Ella tried again. "Have you fainted in the past?"

When Lillian lowered her palms, tears ran down her cheeks. "I fainted right after the wedding as well. Arthur became so angry, even though I couldn't help it. He canceled our travel plans and returned to his mother's house with me. She watches every move I make. I'm scared."

Ella scooped Lillian into a hug. Lillian put her head on Ella's chest and let Ella hold her. Ella's eyes wetted.

This woman needs more than a healer. She needs a friend.

"I remember now," Lillian whispered. "I said that I was scared, and Lady Parker held me in a hug just like you are. She told me, 'Don't be scared, little one. Hold this doll.' I took the doll but said that I'm a big girl, four years old. She answered, 'Then you are the same age as my daughter. She also cried when I gave her a jab. But ten minutes later she forgot all about it.' And then she poked my arm. Why would she do that?"

Ella's heart expanded far beyond her rib cage. "My mother in-oculated you against smallpox. She was brilliant and brave. Despite being born an upper-class woman, she traveled to work-houses, orphanages, and even prisons and asylums to inoculate children and adults. I always wanted to meet someone she saved from that horrible illness."

The young woman hugged her tighter. "Please call me Lillian. And if you allow, I will call you Ella. You are the friend I've been praying for."

Chapter 5

Ella was still holding Lillian when Sarah peeked in. "Dowager Mrs. Landon and your husband are coming up the stairs with the doctor." Lillian startled, and Ella dropped her arms.

"Why are they coming now?" Lillian whispered and wiped her tears. Her pupils were wide with fear.

"What's happening?" Ella stood from the bed.

"It's likely Dr. Miller, the physician my mother-in-law prefers. He makes me so uneasy."

The Dr. Miller who taught me in medical school?

Voices floated from the hallway. Sarah informed the visitors that young Mrs. Landon was sleeping, but a vexed woman's voice commanded her to leave. The melodic baritone of the next speaker made Ella's neck heat. "Why don't I come another time? Rest is imperative for the patient."

My esteemed professor. What is he doing here? He should be at the hospital in Churcham, performing his innovative surgeries.

Lillian touched her face. "Where can I hide you?"

"Hide me? No, my friend." Ella took Lillian's hand. "You must assert your authority. You may choose who examines and treats you. Although, I have the highest regard for Dr. Miller."

Even though he wanted me gone from medical school.

Beyond the door, a woman's voice spoke with gravity. "Doctor, she sleeps all day and cries all night. She barely leaves her room. When she does, it's only to play her pianoforte. I read somewhere that musicians are prone to melancholy."

"She's a hysterical lunatic." The deep male voice that said those words could chill water to ice.

"Was that your husband?" Ella's eyes widened.

Lillian shivered and pulled her blanket to her chest. "He was charming before the wedding. But then... he became so cruel."

Ella touched her shoulder. "You deserve diligent care and kindness."

Lillian squeezed her eyes shut and grabbed her head with her hands. Her face became as white as her nightdress. "My head hurts."

"Lie down. I'll do my best to make them go away." With her shoulders squared, Ella opened the door.

"Please quiet your voices. The patient isn't feeling well."

A woman past her youth but not old, in a burgundy dress and with her hair up, gaped at her. The rose scent of her perfume floated toward Ella. A well-dressed, blond man at her side jerked back. He reminded her of someone.

He looks like that new lieutenant on the Neptune. *What was his name? Drake... Drake Landon. Arthur is his brother!*

The third person who stood by the door she knew well. Dr. Miller scratched his trimmed beard, a gesture she often saw him make when she was his student. His brow knitted as if he was trying to sort out if he knew her. Ella didn't blame him for his confusion. Aside from two occasions before today, she'd always appeared before him dressed as a man. The memory of Dr. Miller telling her she must leave medical school caused her stomach to clench.

"Who are you, and what are you doing in my house?" Dowager Mrs. Landon spoke first.

Ella lifted her chin. "I'm Dr. Ella Parker. The young Mrs. Landon summoned me to examine her."

A smile of recognition appeared on Dr. Miller's lips.

Now he will tell them how I pretended to be a man to receive medical knowledge. I will be put out.

Dr. Miller leaned forward. "In that case, your daughter-in-law is in excellent hands. Dr. Parker was my most talented student."

Ella gaped. *Did I hear him right? The Dr. Miller I knew refused to admit that I belonged in medical school.*

"That's preposterous." Arthur Landon twisted his lips as he pointed at Ella. "Get out of this house."

No. I will do all I can for Lillian. She's ill, scared, and friendless. And she remembers my dear mother.

Ella planted her feet wide.

"As Dr. Miller said, I studied in medical school and was one of his pupils. After that I was a ship surgeon and saved sailors from wounds and illnesses. I've also apprenticed with a midwife and studied medicinal herbs. But most importantly, the patient wanted *me* to examine her. With all due regard for Dr. Miller, I request we respect the patient's preference. And right now, she needs quiet and rest. She has a headache."

Dowager Mrs. Landon stepped back and gestured for her son to approach. While they conferred in hushed voices, Dr. Miller's gray eyes peered into Ella's as he extended his hand.

"It's a pleasant surprise to see you here, Dr. Parker. I must admit I didn't recognize you at first. Your accomplishments are impressive."

Ella's muscles jellied as she accepted his handshake. She mumbled a thank you.

"No, thank *you*. I've followed your career by reading the naval papers. It was easy to guess that the ship surgeon Alan Parker was you, since that was your alias in medical school. You've surprised me more than any other student I've taught."

Ella's heart fluttered. *I must be dreaming.*

She was still smiling when she returned to Lillian's bedside, but Lillian's bloodless cheeks sobered her.

"How's your head?"

Lillian massaged her temples. "Like a nut being cracked."

The door opened, and dowager Mrs. Landon, Arthur, and Dr. Miller walked in with Sarah behind them.

Ella folded her arms. "The patient needs rest and a compress for her headache."

The dowager glanced at Dr. Miller, and he nodded. After Sarah rushed away with instructions to bring supplies for treatment, the older Mrs. Landon set her hands on her hips.

"What do you think ails my daughter-in-law?"

Ella straightened her back. "I haven't done a full exam. If you would give us some privacy, I will do my best to determine that."

Mrs. Landon raised her hands. "It's hysteria. Her maid has confirmed that several reputable physicians have examined Lillian and concluded that she's suffering from nerves."

Lillian curled into a ball. "Why did Sarah tell her that?" she moaned to Ella.

"And now, after she entrapped my son and lied to me, the guilt is eating her alive and her nerves are shattered further. Am I right, Dr. Miller?"

Dr. Miller scratched his cheek. "It's clear to me that the patient is under much distress. She's agitated and upset—"

"She's always agitated and upset," Arthur cut in. "Cries like a spoiled child."

Ella's blood boiled. *How could Lillian marry that insufferable man?*

The doctor made a clicking sound with his tongue. "I will prescribe a calming tonic."

"I won't drink your tonics." Lillian bristled. "I don't trust you. I want Dr. Parker to treat me."

The dowager stared at Dr. Miller. "She's acting like you mean to poison her, Doctor. Isn't that a common symptom of paranoia?"

Dr. Miller pursed his lips. "It can be. But there could also be other explanations. Maladies of the nerves take time to diagnose."

"What are you paying him for, Mother?" Arthur's large hands fisted tightly. "Get a physician who—"

"Arthur, you forget yourself!" Mrs. Landon grabbed her son's elbow. Her lips stretched into an apologetic smile. "My son is heartbroken over Lillian's illness. He didn't realize how serious it was. But it's not his fault. She kept her symptoms a secret from us."

This family will suck all the life out of Lillian.

Sarah returned carrying a tray with tea, a jug of water, and folded cloths for a compress.

"Thank you, Sarah." Ella dipped the cloth into the water.

"I have some questions for you, Doctor." Dowager Mrs. Landon tilted her head toward Dr. Miller. "Let's speak in my study. Sarah, please show the woman healer out."

Ella, who pressed a wet cloth to Lillian's forehead, avoided eye contact with the dowager. "I'm tending to my patient."

The older woman's lips curled. "Her maid can care for her supposed headache. Please leave us."

As Ella's lips moved to form a rebuttal, Lillian shook her head. "They won't leave me alone while you are here. They only trust Dr. Miller's advice. I'm sorry about all this."

"Don't be sorry. Send for me if you need me." Ella straightened. "I will show myself out."

With her head up, Ella walked past Lillian's mother-in-law and husband. Dr. Miller's voice made her halt. "Dr. Parker, I just want to say... the things I said to you the last time we met... I made a terrible mistake, and I'm sorry."

Ella's jaw dropped, and she stared at her professor until the dowager cleared her throat and pointed at the door.

Chapter 6

Jamie's legs moved with difficulty when they stepped off the gangplank. After months at sea, the stillness of the ground felt strange, as did the sight of green April grass. They'd been docked here for two days, but Jamie had no chance of leaving the *Neptune* until this morning, busy with ship repairs as he was. His nose took in the stench of dirt and horse manure, but those odors were faint compared to the familiar smells of the sea and of people crowded in one place. The port was busy with tanned sailors, loud peddlers, dirty children, and women of all ages and positions.

Jamie gently tugged on Olson's arm. "Olson, do you recognize this place? We are in Plymouth."

The seaman's back was bent, as if he carried a heavy sack, and his head was perpetually bowed. His arms were covered with scratches, not only from the day he was flogged, but with new ones he inflicted on himself later. Saliva ran down his chin and his gaze was cloudy.

A heavy feeling in his whole body made Jamie sigh. *No, he recognizes nothing.*

Jamie put his right arm around Olson, careful not to put too much pressure on his healing flesh. While Ella's former assistants tried their best to care for him, Olson seemed to prefer Jamie as his caregiver. In his left arm Jamie carried Olson's sea chest, light with only a few meager possessions. No names or addresses of the carpenter's family were found there for Jamie to write to about Olson's fate.

"Come, my friend. The captain is waiting for you." He led the carpenter toward a hackney coach with covered windows. Captain Grey stood next to it.

The captain's face was as solemn as if someone had died. *In a way, it is like a funeral.*

A man jumped off the driver's seat and opened the door. "Ah, another mind lost to the trials of the sea. What a sad fate."

Captain Grey's Adam's apple bobbed. "Perhaps it's only a temporary condition. The poor man may recover his wits."

"There's little hope for that." The driver accepted the sea chest from Jamie's arms. "I've been working there for over a year. Few people ever leave an asylum better than when they arrived."

Jamie's shoulders fell. "Is there anything that can be done for him?"

"He's fortunate to even have a place. The demand is high. You may eventually get him a nicer cell with a window, better food, or a softer bed." The driver shrugged. "But it'll cost you."

"I'll do what I can," Captain Grey muttered and thrust his hand toward Olson. "Mr. Olson, thank you for your many years of faithful service. I hope you get better."

Olson's arms hung at his sides and didn't lift to take the captain's hand. His eyes stayed vacant and without a hint of understanding.

With Jamie's help, the driver pushed Olson inside the coach. The carpenter, large and strong enough to fight them off without much effort, did not resist as they maneuvered him to sit inside. Another man was seated there, with ropes ready in his hands.

"Don't tie him up!" Jamie exclaimed. "He won't hurt anyone."

"It's for his safety. And mine," the man said as he secured ropes around Olson's wrists.

The carpenter allowed himself to be tied without protest. His passiveness gave Jamie a sinking feeling. *Olson does not know what's happening to him.*

When the coach drove away, Jamie staggered to Conor and Tobby, who watched the scene from a short distance away. Tears ran down Tobby's cheeks.

"Where did they take him?" Conor asked.

"Plymouth Public Asylum for the Poor."

Conor pressed his hand on his stomach. "That's a horrible place. The stench there—"

"You know it?" Jamie's mouth rounded.

"No... I only heard." Conor wiped the sweat off his forehead.

Tobby sobbed. "He taught me how to make toy ships."

"It's all Landon's fault." Conor clenched his fists. His eyes were large with fury. "I will—"

Jamie grabbed his arm. "Keep your voice down. I already told you. Neither you nor I can challenge Landon to a duel because he's our direct superior. Such duels are forbidden. And thank goodness for that because Drake Landon is a daring and ruthless duelist."

Conor exhaled through his teeth. "I cannot stand him. He must pay for what he did."

"I agree with you, but there's nothing we can do about it."

Captain Grey approached them with a solemn expression and scanned their faces. He reached for his money purse and tossed a few coins to Tobby. "Here, lad. Get something to eat for you and your friends." When Tobby limped away, the captain rubbed his forehead with his fist. "Sad business, gentlemen, but we must put it behind us for. Get back to your duties. In the evening, please visit me at my home. I have some news to share."

"Aye, sir," Jamie replied in a monotone voice.

When the captain walked away, Conor gasped, and his eyes glistened. "I believe I'm getting a promotion."

Chapter 7

Ella sipped chamomile tea sweetened with honey to relieve the dryness in her throat.

Captain Grey's wife, Mrs. Gertrude Grey, offered another piece of apple tart, but Ella declined. With the hostess's coaxing, she'd already put away a dinner of chicken with vegetables and a couple of servings of the dessert. She hadn't eaten this much in months. Meeting the Landons had exhausted her, but Mrs. Grey and her daughters were such pleasant company she felt guilty for not visiting them until this evening.

"While I was tending to the patient, Dr. Miller came. He was my professor in medical school and is probably the best surgeon in England. Back when I disguised myself as a male student, he found me out and told me to leave the university. But today, he spoke to me as a colleague. Said he was wrong about how he treated me. I'm still afraid that I was dreaming."

"That's wonderful!" Bella, the elder daughter, seated on Ella's right, clapped her hands. "But who was the mysterious patient you visited? And what ails her?"

"That I can't tell you." Ella bit her lip, thinking of Lillian's pale face and pleading eyes.

On Ella's left, Cecilia, the younger daughter, put down her cup so hard tea splashed. "Why should you be in such awe of some shortsighted professor who tried to make you leave the university? You're a great surgeon in your own right. Father's told us about all the wounded and ill you've saved on his ship. He said you are the finest surgeon who ever sailed with him."

Ella's cheeks heated. "That's nice of Captain Grey to say that. But I was only doing my job."

"You've proven many doubters wrong." Mrs. Grey's smile brought out her dimples. "And I'm glad that you are attending patients and finally visiting us. We were worried about you."

Bella put her hand on Ella's shoulder. "When I heard of how Mr. Flowers refused your proposal, I cried."

"And I said that Ella will make him thoroughly regret his refusal." Cecilia twisted the linen napkin in her hands.

Ella held hands with both sisters, then smiled at Mrs. Grey. "I'm sorry for staying away and making you worry. Your concern means much to me. How have you been?"

"Keeping busy," Mrs. Grey said. "I've joined a charity board, and that has proved to be a significant amount of work. And I ensure my daughters keep up with their dancing and painting lessons, despite all the protests from Cecilia."

Cecilia rolled her eyes. "Dancing is a bore. I'm taking fencing lessons from an excellent teacher. When Mr. Flowers returns, I will challenge him to a duel for how he treated you."

Mrs. Grey pressed her hand against her heart. "You've lost your mind! I regret ever allowing those lessons." She sighed as she gazed at Ella. "I agreed to them as a compromise to get Cecilia to go to social events and behave appropriately."

"And I've kept my end of the deal." Cecilia grimaced, but then her lips stretched into a grin. "Ella, you should join. Then you could fight in the ship battles or duel your enemies. Bella will be your partner at first, and eventually you can spar with me."

Ella's mouth rounded as she shifted her gaze to Bella. "You fence as well? I assumed you preferred more traditional pas-times."

Bella's cheeks became rosy. "Cecilia needed a sparring part-ner."

"Oh, don't sound like such a martyr." Cecilia poked out her tongue. "You squeal and hop for joy when you score a hit."

The elder sister's cheeks reddened deeper. "It can be quite exhilarating."

Mrs. Grey lifted an eyebrow and poured everyone more tea. "I have a better suggestion. Ella should join us for the ball."

"That's a lovely idea!" Bella exclaimed. "Ella, you must come. There will be dancing and card games. Cecilia and I are preparing a special entertainment to raise funds for charity."

"Except they refuse to tell me what it is." Mrs. Grey grinned at Ella. "It's in two weeks at Mrs. Landon's beautiful home."

The same dowager Mrs. Landon I've met? She'd throw me out.

"I... I'm not sure it will be appropriate for me to come." Ella scratched her cheek. "I don't have an invitation."

"Oh, don't worry. I'm helping with the planning, and Mrs. Landon gave me several invitations to distribute at my discretion. I will happily chaperone you along with my daughters."

That will show that haughty dowager who dismissed me from her home. And perhaps I could assist Lillian in some way.

"Please say yes." Cecilia sighed. "Then we can suffer together. Besides the boredom, that house makes my skin crawl. The two sons were embroiled in scandals involving dueling and gambling. And their mother finds pleasure in matchmaking between naive young girls and men three times their age—"

"Cecilia!" Mrs. Grey gasped. "You don't speak that way of a respectable family that fought bravely for king and country. The father tragically died in the war, and the sons are brave officers. The youngest, Mr. Drake, is your father's lieutenant. And Mrs. Landon is a saint, heading wonderful charities that ease suffering. Ella, you may be interested in The Women's Sanctuary, her biggest project. It's a special hospital only for women. In fact, I believe Dr. Miller runs it."

"I'd love to learn more about it." Ella nodded.

"Knowing that Mrs. Landon is involved, I'm scared to think what that place could be like." Cecilia shivered. "Mother, how can you call that horrible woman a saint? Do you remember that girl she introduced us to, Lillian Davis? She planned for her to marry a sixty-year-old widower with five children!"

Ella's ears pricked at Lillian's name.

Mrs. Grey sipped her tea. "Cecilia, it was an act of kindness and a special favor to the young woman's parents. Lillian had no dowry and little prospects. Mrs. Landon's matchmaking offered her an auspicious future."

"I liked Lillian." Bella stirred her tea back and forth. "Her piano playing was beautiful. A sensitive, talented girl like her should only marry for love."

Cecilia's eyes blazed. "The thought of marriage to that old man made her ill with anxiety. She barely ate and needed to lie down to nurse her headache. It should be a crime to torment a girl like that."

Ella grabbed another tart and chewed it without noticing the taste. "When was this?"

Mrs. Grey frowned. "I believe it was three months ago or so. I haven't heard about that engagement again, so I assume Lillian returned home. She's from a small town in Cornwall. It's very unfortunate she didn't marry. Most likely, she'll end up a spinster her family cannot support. They have two more daughters, not of age yet."

No. Instead Lillian eloped with one of Mrs. Landon's sons.

"It's not right, Mother." Bella stared at her hands. "Marriages should be for love. Like you and Father."

"Few people are that fortunate." Mrs. Grey touched her elder daughter's shoulder.

Ella's heart echoed dully. *Jamie, we could've been a love match.*

Excited voices sounded from beyond the room, too far away for Ella to make out the words.

"Well, I should get home before dark." She rose.

As she threw on her shawl and Mrs. Grey and her daughters bid her goodbye, a servant woman rushed in.

"Mrs. Grey! Your husband is home!"

Cecilia jumped to her feet, almost knocking over her chair. Bella was more graceful as she rose, but just as much happiness shone on her face. "He wasn't sure when he could come home. Some business with the Admiralty," Mrs. Grey said to Ella as she smoothed her dress and fixed her cap. When the captain entered, she rushed into her husband's embrace, and the girls followed suit. Ella slipped toward the door, trying to leave unnoticed so as not to disturb the family scene.

"Dr. Parker, you don't need to rush out." The captain's voice halted her at the threshold. "It brings me joy to see you well and keeping company with my wife and daughters."

Ella returned and took his large hand. "I'm glad to see you as well, sir. Is the crew healthy? I trust Mr. Monk has performed adequately as the surgeon."

"Yes, he has, and the crew is mostly in good health"—the captain's smile waned—"except for one man whose fate gives me severe grief."

A stone lodged in Ella's chest. *He must mean Jamie. He's wounded. No, worse. He's dead.*

"Who is it?" Mrs. Grey asked. "If he's at the naval hospital, I'll send a basket with food."

Captain Grey shook his head. "It's Mr. Owen Olson. And he's not at the hospital."

"What's wrong with Olson? Is there something I can do for him?" Ella asked.

The captain's arms hung loose at his sides. "I'm afraid there's nothing you or anyone can do. He lost his sanity. A fate perhaps worse than death."

"No!" Ella's throat clenched. "Where is he? I must see him."

"Plymouth Public Asylum for the Poor." Captain Grey's gaze was on his muddy boots.

Bella wrapped her arms around Ella. "We'll go together and see him. Right, Mother?"

Mrs. Grey jerked back. "No. You and your sister are not to go there. I don't want you to suffer from nightmares."

"We'll find a day to get away and take you with us," Cecilia whispered in Ella's ear.

Ella's heart squeezed as she walked out to the street. *Olson was a dear friend. I must try to see him.*

Chapter 8

A servant ushered Jamie and Conor into the sitting room of Captain Grey's house. Conor shifted his weight from one foot to another as he scanned the embroidered cushions and pillows. "I should've removed that stain from my collar before coming."

Jamie, who made a habit of caring for his own clothes as well as the captain's when he had been his servant, adjusted his neck scarf. "You look fine. The stain isn't noticeable. Sit." He sank into the sofa cushions while Conor perched on the edge.

"It's an impressive house. Much larger than the one I grew up in," Conor said.

Captain Grey's home was relatively modest to Jamie's eye, but it was adorned with lovely touches. Jamie's stare lingered on the paintings that decorated the walls. "That seascape reminds me of my sisters' watercolor paintings. My older sister Caroline likes to find the exact shade to paint the sea. She came up with over thirty color combinations to show all the vagaries of the weather."

Conor blinked. "Was your home as large as this one? Why would you ever leave?"

A painful lump squeezed Jamie's throat. He shrugged to avoid an answer.

Conor's gaze darted among the figurines on the fireplace mantel, the linen tablecloth, and the volumes in the bookcase. His hand leafed through the book left open on the table, its pages filled with mathematical formulas. "Look, this is basic trigonometry for navigation. Do you think the captain is reading it?"

"Probably not. He learned that years ago."

"Then who? Does he have a son in the navy?"

"No." Jamie smiled. "He has daughters. I've met them. Both are pretty."

Conor's shoulders jumped and his hand brushed the wrinkles off his waistcoat. "I should've removed that stain from my collar. But soon enough I'll be ordering a lieutenant's uniform."

Jamie's eyebrows rose. "Did the captain recommend you for the lieutenant's exam? And isn't that done after six years at sea?"

"Technically I have six years because my father wrote my name into the ship's books. I believe this is what this meeting is about. Captain Grey will tell me to prepare for the exam."

"Then why would I be invited?"

Conor scratched his chin. "Hmm. I'm not sure. But what I am sure of is that the answer to this problem is wrong." He picked up a pen that lay next to the book, dipped it into the inkwell, and corrected the answer. "This one is wrong as well."

Jamie shifted in his seat. "Perhaps you should ask permission before writing in someone's book?"

At that moment, Mrs. Grey entered the room with Bella, and Jamie and Conor rose to greet them.

"Mr. Flowers, it's a pleasure to see you again. And good to meet you, Mr. Leach. Captain Grey stepped out for some quick business but will be back soon." The captain's wife smiled at them as everyone sat. "We are so relieved you've return from your imprisonment in France unharmed."

"My friends and I knitted warm mittens and scarves. Did you receive them?" Bella's gray eyes dashed around the room, avoiding meeting Jamie's.

She's Ella's friend and likely knows what happened with Ella's proposal.

Jamie bowed his head. "That was extremely kind of you. I'm afraid your gift never reached us, but Mr. Leach and I are thankful for your concern."

"If you have a scarf left for me, I'll happily accept one. It would go well with my new uniform." Conor flashed a smile at her. "I will be a lieutenant soon."

Bella pursed her lips. "I'll see what I have left. But we are no longer knitting scarves. We are practicing our dancing for the charity ball."

"A ball? Then I hope to receive an invitation. I happen to be an excellent dancer." He bowed.

Jamie rolled his eyes. *Tomorrow he'll confess to me that he's never danced in his life and beg me to teach him.*

Bella glanced down at her dress. "I don't think you want to go to this ball. I'm no longer sure I want to go."

Mrs. Grey crossed her arms. "Of course you and your sister are still going, and Dr. Parker as well." She smiled at Conor. "I'm glad you dance, Mr. Leach. The hostess was worried there wouldn't be enough partners for the ladies in attendance. I have two invitations left, and they will be for you and Mr. Flowers."

"But, Mother..." Bella's cheeks flushed burgundy. "Ella doesn't want to..."

Jamie's chest tightened as if strangled by a belt. *Ella will be there, but she prefers to avoid me. I can't blame her.*

"If Dr. Parker wants to avoid my company, I will not force it. Perhaps it's better I don't attend."

Bella exhaled. "I'm sure you could find better diversions that evening."

Her mother threw her hands up. "Oh, stop that silliness. It's the biggest event of the year in one of the largest ballrooms in Plymouth. If Mr. Flowers and Dr. Parker prefer to avoid each other, they can easily do so. If, on the other hand, Mr.

Flowers has something to say to her, this could be a perfect opportunity."

It may be my last chance to see Ella. Before my heart gives out.

Mrs. Grey tilted her neck toward Conor. "I'm counting on you, Mr. Leach. Think of the young ladies in need of dance partners. Will you come and bring Mr. Flowers?"

"It will be my pleasure." He puffed out his chest and winked at Bella. "Which dance will you save for me?"

Bella tightened her lips and leaned away.

Why does he have to be such a boasting fool? Jamie shook his head. *It's his habit to use bravado when he's unsure how to behave.*

The rug rustled, and Cecilia marched in. "Ah, that's where I left it!" she exclaimed and grabbed the trigonometry book off the table. "Excuse me for not staying for the conversation. I must solve these mathematics problems. If I don't, I will not get any sleep."

Her mother caught her hand. "Cecilia, you are to greet your father's guests properly, Mr. Flowers and Mr. Leach."

She clenched her jaw as she stared at Jamie. "My friend's enemy is my enemy."

Bella froze with her jaw open, then used her hand to close it.

"Cecilia, you've lost your mind." Mrs. Grey rose. "Apologize at once. Mr. Flowers is hardly Dr. Parker's enemy. In fact, I've invited him and Mr. Leach to the ball."

Cecilia's eyes flashed like two daggers. "How could you, Mother? After what he's done to Ella?"

"You are being melodramatic. Now apologize and sit down to converse with our guests while they await your father."

"I won't apologize." Cecilia took a step toward Jamie. "If I were a man, I would challenge you to a duel."

Jamie bit his lips to prevent them curving into a grin and glanced down at the floor. Conor chuckled into his fist, and Cecilia gave him a murderous glare.

"That's it. No more fencing lessons." Mrs. Grey crossed her arms. "Apologize this instant and leave us."

"I'm happy to leave. I have trigonometry problems to solve," Cecilia muttered as she lifted the open book. Her jaw hung open, and she gave a scathing glance at everyone in the room. "Who has written in my book?"

Conor shifted in his seat. "I only meant to help. You made the same mistake in each problem."

"I didn't ask for help!" Cecilia shut the book with a thud. "Do you think me incapable of learning trigonometry? I'd challenge you as well."

She stormed from the room.

Bella gave a side-glance to Conor, then rose. "I apologize for my sister, but you shouldn't have written in her book. We both enjoy mental challenges and don't need answers to be given to us." With her straight back turned to Conor, she sauntered away.

Mrs. Grey sighed. "I'm sorry about their behavior. Cecilia had always been wayward, and Bella often follows her lead. Let's speak of something more pleasant. Mr. Flowers, your parents and sisters must be relieved by your return from capture. Have you seen them?"

"No, ma'am... Between the voyages there was no chance to visit."

His heart pinched. *I will never see them again.*

"Then I hope you've written a detailed letter about your ordeal. And you, Mr. Leach? I met your father a long time ago, when he sailed with my husband. Is he away at sea?"

"Yes, ma'am. He's the captain of the *Southern Star,* sailing in the West Indies."

"May he return safely." She folded her hands in prayer. "I don't believe I've met your mother. Is she in Plymouth?"

"No." Conor's voice was low, and he rubbed the back of his neck.

"Where does she live?" Mrs. Grey narrowed her eyes. "As a captain's wife, I support other women as they await their husbands. I want to write her a letter."

Sweat beaded on Conor's forehead and his hands trembled. "No. My mother... I don't know... I mean... she's dead."

Mrs. Grey brought her palms to her lips. "I am so sorry. I did not realize."

Jamie put his hand on Conor's shoulder. "Nor I. You never told me, but I assumed she died together with your brother and sisters."

"Yes. They all died in one week." Conor averted his eyes. "Typhoid."

"How terrible." Mrs. Grey sighed.

Uncomfortable silence dominated for a moment. When the screech of the door and pounding steps sounded, a collective sigh of relief resonated through the room.

Conor and Jamie stood at attention as Captain Grey marched in wearing his uniform. Jamie studied it for buttons to shine or creases to press. He was no longer the captain's servant, but the habit remained. He noted several faults for the new servant to fix.

The captain's green eyes lit as he approached his wife and kissed her outstretched hand. They beamed at each other and stared into each other's eyes a moment too long.

Conor's cheeks reddened.

The captain turned and scanned Conor's and Jamie's faces. "I must give you some unpleasant news, gentlemen. Let's speak in my study."

Jamie followed Captain Grey, whose back, usually straight and proud, slumped. Jamie exchanged glances with Conor.

"Perhaps this is not about a promotion," Conor whispered.

Chapter 9

"Half pay. I can't live on that," Conor muttered as they descended the stairs of Captain Grey's house. "How can there be a no commission for us when my promotion was right in my grasp?"

"It's better than nothing. The crew will be paid their wages and sent home," Jamie replied, following his friend.

Conor's mouth pinched. "The men will return to their families. I have no home or family to return to."

Mrs. Grey greeted them at the bottom of the stairs. She tilted her head as she studied their faces. "I venture a guess that the *Neptune* is docked for the foreseeable future."

Jamie sighed. "Yes, madam."

"That's unfortunate news for young men yearning for promotions. But I rejoice for families that will have their fathers and husbands home. And sons." She smiled at Jamie, then touched her throat as her gaze shifted to Conor. "If there's anything I can do..."

"You are truly kind, Mrs. Grey. But I won't be a nuisance to you or the captain." A vein on Conor's forehead pulsed.

"I hope you attend the ball. Amusement would do you good. Dancing, cards... young ladies." She handed them invitations printed with elegant letters.

"Thank you, Mrs. Grey." Jamie bowed.

Conor's drooping head lifted, and his eyes regained their shine. "Did you say *cards*?"

When they stepped outside, Conor turned toward the main street instead of the port.

"After news like that, we must have a drink. Let's go to the Cooked Goose."

Jamie scanned the street, lit by oil lamps. Seamen and officers staggered toward various inns and saloons. "We are not the only ones with that idea. Taverns will be crowded. Let's go to the ship and get some sleep. Tomorrow we'll need to pack our belongings and decide where to go."

Conor scoffed. "What's for you to decide? You are going back to your parents."

Jamie's shoulders fell. *I can't go back home. Not if I'm to die in a few months.*

"I think I could use a drink after all."

"Then you are paying." Conor grinned.

When they stumbled inside the noisy dining room of the Cooked Goose, a cheerful fire warmed their faces. The aromas of roasted mutton and onions mixed with the less pleasant odors of sweat and unwashed bodies. All tables and barstools were full, taken by seamen or workpeople. A rosy cheeked, plump woman dashed from one table to another, bringing trays of food and tankards of ale. Jamie remembered her name was Jenny.

This is where I ate the day I arrived at Plymouth. I met Tobby when I sat at the table over there.

As his gaze shifted to the table, he stepped back in surprise because Tobby sat in exactly the same chair, across from Ben, another shipboy. Tobby slumped and clenched his belly, while Ben cringed and held his head.

Jamie rushed to them. "Are you sick? What did you eat?"

"I think it's what they drank." Conor pointed at the glasses with dark liquid remaining at the bottom. He brought a glass to his nose. "Rum. What a waste."

"Didn't Dr. Ella tell you to stay away from strong drinks?" Jamie put his hands on his hips. The misery on the boys' faces softened his indignation. "I will take you outside. Fresh air will make you better."

"Digby is completely senseless." Conor pointed to the boy seated at a large table. Digby's head drooped so low that his nose touched a dirty plate. The sailors at his table chuckled, watching him.

Jamie rushed to the table and shook the lad by the shoulder. "Digby, get up. You need air."

The diners laughed as Jamie helped Digby to his feet.

Jamie's blood boiled. "Did you get him drunk? He's only a boy." He scanned their faces, looking for familiar ones, but these men were not from the *Neptune*.

Digby took a couple of shaky steps, clenching Jamie's arm. Then his knees buckled, and he collapsed in a heap.

"Dear Lord." Miss Jenny put down the tray she carried and rushed to Digby. "Did someone give him rum?"

"Must be those fellows," Conor said.

"We meant no harm," one of the men said. "The lads looked old enough. They've been sent home but have no home to go to. They needed to cheer up."

Jamie sighed. *Tobby and Ben are orphans, and Digby's father is in jail. Like Conor, they have no home. And where will I go?*

Miss Jenny spoke to Conor. "Take the lad downstairs. He can sleep on the bench by the stove."

Conor swung Digby's scrawny body onto his wide shoulders and carried him away.

Jamie motioned toward Tobby and Ben, whose faces were sickly green. "These two look like they won't be able to hold their drinks inside them much longer," he said to Miss Jenny.

"I'll take them down as well and have someone look after them." She approached the table. "Come, boys. If you are going to be sick, please try to hold it a little longer. I'll get some bowls."

Tobby and Ben moaned and clenched their stomachs as they staggered toward the steps, Jenny's hands on their shoulders ushering them along.

Conor returned and sat at the table the boys had occupied. "When I was their age, I held my liquor better," he said when Jamie sat across from him.

"Of course you did. Like that night you lost your money at cards and then almost choked on your vomit." Jamie's lips tightened. "Why do you brag so much? Like when you said that you are a great dancer."

Conor blinked and drummed on the table. "I wanted to impress Miss Bella. Did I overdo it?"

"I'm afraid so."

Miss Jenny brought them tankards of beer. "Those boys are violently ill from that rum. Dr. Parker would be furious."

The image of Ella's scarlet cheeks and tightened lips came to Jamie's mind.

Conor exhaled and sipped his beer. "You are right. I boast, and I don't know why."

Jamie lifted his tankard. "I think it's because you are afraid of people knowing the real you. But you are a good person. A loyal friend. A survivor who overcame a tragedy, losing your mother and—"

"I lied about that."

Jamie put down his tankard. "What? Your older brother and little sisters dying in one week—that was a lie?"

"No. That is true." Conor paled and gulped his beer. "But my mother didn't die with them. She... she's likely dead, but my father and I don't know for sure. We don't know where she is."

"How can that be?" Jamie leaned in.

Conor's cheeks burned and his chin trembled. "It's all my fault. She left... she left to search for me."

Jamie's eyes rounded. "Why?"

Conor dropped his chin to his chest. "Two years ago, when Father was away on one of his voyages, I met these men. They took me to a tavern and got me drunk." His eyes shifted to the table where Digby had sat, and his shoulders tensed. "I woke up in some dirty flat with a terrible headache. I wanted to leave, but they said I owed them money for my drinks and food. When I said I couldn't pay, they offered to let me play cards with them to win some money. They taught me how to play."

"I can predict what happened. You lost, and then you owed them even more. How long were you with them?"

"Two months."

"Two months?!"

Conor shivered. "I know how that sounds. But at that time... my life was miserable. Just Mother and me sharing a small room we rented. She cried day and night, grieving for my siblings. And those fellows... they were scary, but they were fun as well. They offered me a place to sleep and told me I could make money playing cards against rich fellows. After I paid my debt, I could make more for myself."

Heat rose to Jamie's head, and he gulped his beer. "Have you thought how worried your mother was? Not knowing where you were and what happened?"

"I dreamed I would return with pockets full of chiming coins and my mother would be pleased." Conor rested his head on his fist.

"And what happened instead?"

Conor averted his eyes. "One night... something told me I must return home. That feeling didn't leave me all the next day, and in the evening, I made up my mind. I was stupid enough to tell those men that I was leaving. They grew hostile and reminded me of my debt. I promised to return with the money and ran to the street. They caught up with me and beat me. I crawled home with my ribs broken, spitting up blood, and praying that my mother would care for my injuries. But when I finally made it home, she wasn't there."

"What happened to her?"

"I still don't know. The neighbors said that a month after I left they saw her walking down the street, looking unkempt and dirty, her eyes staring into space. A coach almost ran her over, but she kept walking as if she didn't see it. That's the last anyone saw of her. The landlady was planning to collect our possessions."

The tankard handle almost broke from Jamie's tight clutch. "They didn't report her missing?"

"No. They thought they should mind their business. My father returned two days after I did. He cared for my injuries and searched for her. Before he left on his next voyage, he hired a man to keep looking for my mother and asked Captain Grey to take me on the *Neptune*. Father was furious with me and thought the sea life would make me a better man."

"You did become a better man. A man your parents would be proud of. Someone I'm honored to call a friend."

"The honor is all mine. I was thinking to ask you, would you let me come to Dorset with you? Perhaps I can find some work there."

"I'm not returning home."

A wide grin lit Conor's face. "Let's look for a merchant ship to take us on. And while we search, we could get a room here, at the Cooked Goose. The place is cleaner than most, and the food is the best in town. We'll find a way to afford it."

A bell rang in Jamie's head.

"Ella rents a room here, upstairs. This is where she lives between voyages."

Conor scratched his cheek. "I take it you don't want to be her neighbor. We can find another place."

Jamie inhaled a deep breath. "It's time I spoke to Ella."

Conor leaned back. "Are you thinking to accept her marriage proposal?"

"No. But there are things I need to say to her."

I will tell her about my diagnosis. Conor should listen as well. It's time they knew why I couldn't marry the love of my life. They will pity me, and everything will change between us, but... Ella shouldn't suffer.

Jamie put coins on the table and rose. "Come with me."

As he led Conor up the stairs, his heart hammered.

Conor spoke in his ear, "You remember that Ella said she never wanted to talk to you again, right? Are you sure about this? She's a woman, but... do you recall how she whacked that scoundrel Vignon on his head with a candleholder?"

"If that's what Ella wants to do to me, please don't interfere. She's right to be furious," Jamie muttered as he walked down the corridor. There were two doors in front of him.

"Do you know which door?"

"No, but there's only two."

Jamie knocked on the first door. There was no answer. He tried the knob, and the door swung open. Nothing but bare furniture was inside.

He tried the other door. No one answered, but a quiet rustle sounded from inside the room. Conor's hand touched his shoulder. "Perhaps Ella doesn't live here anymore."

"I just heard her."

It's now or never.

He pushed the door open. "Ella, are you—"

His question died on his lips. A young man, slightly older than him, slumped over a desk that was lit by candles. He raised his head from the book he was reading.

"I'm sorry, we were looking for... someone else." Jamie exhaled.

The young man rose. He was of a small height, with black hair. His dark eyes studied Jamie and Conor, and his face tensed. "Yes, I heard you. Why are you looking for Dr. Parker?"

Conor ran his hands over his hair. "We... thought she lived here. We didn't mean to disturb you."

He yanked Jamie's shoulder, but Jamie remained rooted. "Do you know where she is?"

The man approached them, his eyes peering at Jamie. His lips formed a thin line.

"You haven't answered my question. Why are you looking for her?"

Jamie widened his stance. "Since you seem to know where she is, would you please tell us? Then we'll leave you to your reading."

"Dr. Parker doesn't want to be found." The young man crossed his arms. "That's why she moved out of these rooms. She doesn't wish to be troubled, especially as unceremoniously as this. I suspect you or your friend may be the reason she feels that way."

Jamie's eyes dropped, and the young man nodded, as if confirming his guess.

"Come, Jamie. We can find a room somewhere else," Conor called.

Jamie put on a friendlier tone. "Please tell me how I can find her. I mean Ella no harm. Quite the opposite."

The man rolled his eyes. "Dr. Parker. That's the proper way to address her, unless you are a close friend, which I have the honor of being. I won't tell you her whereabouts. Leave her alone."

Determination ebbed from Jamie. "If you see her, please tell her—"

"Dr. Higgins! Your help is needed." Miss Jenny was walking toward them. The room's occupant stepped past Jamie to meet her.

"What is it?"

"Two boys are violently sick from drinking rum. Another one, a bit older, is sleeping like the dead. Would you please see to them? They are in the kitchen."

"Of course." The fellow ducked back into his room. He emerged a moment later with a worn medical bag and dashed down the corridor to the stairs.

Miss Jenny gazed after him, then frowned at Jamie and Conor. "What are you fellows doing here?"

"Nothing. We didn't mean to bother him. We are leaving," Jamie muttered and gave Conor a light shove.

Conor flashed a smile. "Miss Jenny, my friend and I wondered if you have a room for rent. That one seems to be free." He pointed at the first door.

Chapter 10

When the coach stopped, Ella opened the curtain to view the gray stone building. It looked as miserable as she feared. Cracks snaked up the facade. The narrow windows were barred. The prominent sign hung at the door: Plymouth Public Asylum for the Poor.

"Why are the patients called lunatics?" Bella's voice quivered. Her cheeks were pale, and she kept rubbing her abdomen.

Ella wrinkled her brow, trying to recall her Latin studies in medical school. "*Luna* means *moon*. Falling sickness and other forms of madness strike during the full moon."

"Is tonight a full moon?" Bella's neck craned toward Cecilia.

Cecilia frowned. "No. It's not for a week and a half. Haven't you been doing the moon chart to predict the tides?"

"I got distracted by all the ball preparations." Bella bit her lip. "We should be with the dancing master right now."

"Then go practice your minuet." Cecilia grimaced. "I cannot believe you still want to go to the ball after what Father told us about Mr. Landon. And Ella will not want to go because Jamie Flowers may be there."

Ella's heart sank at hearing his name.

"Ladies, I don't have all day," the driver called. He'd been standing by the door, waiting for them to exit. "Or would you prefer I take you somewhere else?"

"No, we are where we need to be," Ella replied as she lifted her medical bag and her basket, loaded with fresh bread, apples, and jars of jam. The sisters had brought socks, hats, and scarves they knitted for the British prisoners of war.

They climbed out of the coach and walked toward the asylum shoulder to trembling shoulder. Ella knocked on the heavy door, and a portly man with a red face answered. His breath reeked of alcohol when he yawned.

"Visiting day is Thursday," he muttered. "But I can take your baskets."

"How kind! Please deliver them to Mr. Olson." Bella extended her arm to give him the basket. "Thank you, good sir."

Cecilia smacked her sister on the hand. "Are you a child? He'll take them for himself."

"But we cannot return on Thursday. We have a fitting that day. For our ball gowns..." Bella said the final words with her neck drawn in like a crab's.

While Cecilia scorched her sister with her gaze, the man moved to close the door. Ella grabbed it to stop him.

"Wait! I'm a surgeon visiting a patient."

"Surgeon?" He ogled her. "I don't know you. Speak to the superintendent first. He'll come in an hour or two." He pulled the door to close it, but Ella stuck her foot in to prevent him.

"Will this allow us entrance?" Ella put a few coins in the man's wide hand.

The man shoved the coins into his pocket. "I'll ask the superintendent when he arrives."

He closed the door in front of their noses.

"Now I feel foolish." Ella's head dropped. "He'll likely wait for us to give up and leave."

"Let's all bang on the door and demand to be allowed in," Cecilia suggested.

Bella blinked rapidly. "I don't think it's a clever idea. They may think we are... you know... insane."

Ella shifted her feet as she considered their options. Returning on visiting day seemed like the most reasonable choice. She was about to make that suggestion, but the clop of hooves halted her. Two gray horses pulled a black carriage with touches of gold.

"Perhaps the superintendent is here early," Bella said. "We should ask him directly and appeal to his kindness."

"Or his wallet," Cecilia added.

The driver opened the door, and Dr. Miller emerged with an energetic step.

Ella froze with her mouth open.

His head jerked back as he glanced in her direction, then he approached her with a grin. "Good morning, Dr. Parker. We meet again. Are you here to visit someone?"

A warm feeling spread in her chest at his greeting. "Yes, my friends and I visiting a patient. But we've been denied entry."

"I believe I can help you." He rapped on the door. "I'm here to inspect the women's gallery."

The same man who had barred them from entering swung the door open for the well-known physician and surgeon. "Dr. Miller, we were expecting you later today," he muttered. "The superintendent isn't here yet."

"I'm afraid I cannot wait for him. Please take me to see the female patients. And these ladies will come with me as well. They are visiting someone in that ward."

Ella swallowed to relieve the dryness in her throat. "Actually, sir, our friend is not in the women's gallery. He's a sailor, Mr. Owen Olson. He arrived a few days ago."

The attendant's shoulders jumped. "Ah, that man. He's been moved to one of the private rooms. They are beyond the women's gallery. This way."

As they followed him, Dr. Miller tilted his head to Ella. "Your friend must be wealthy or have influential friends. Private rooms are expensive and difficult to secure."

"It must be our father," Bella said with a hand on her heart. "He's good to his men."

Cecilia raised an eyebrow and lowered her tone. "Apparently you neglected not only the moon chart but our household ledger as well. We cannot afford large expenses, especially with our father on half pay."

"I wonder who it could be then." Ella frowned. "Olson has no living family."

Drafts blew through the broken windows, making her shiver. The attendant took a key from his belt and unlocked the door, then ushered them inside.

The stench of sweat, vomit, and human waste made the Grey sisters cover their noses, but Ella was used to it. The hospital and the sickbay often smelled just as bad. The tiny cell contained ten women, but a ship had crowded places as well. It was the nakedness and the chains that made Ella flinch. The women were covered by blanket gowns that provided little dignity. Their feet were bare. They sat in various positions, chained by an arm or leg to the wall or a chair. Some muttered, one laughed, and another wept, but most remained quiet and made no eye contact. A female attendant spoon-fed a thin woman some kind of gruel that ran down the patient's chin. When the woman opened her mouth wide, Ella gasped; all her teeth were missing.

Some doctors think that when teeth rot, the decay can spread to the brain, so they pull them.

Cecilia took Ella's hand. "Look at her. Is she dead?"

Ella's eyes followed where she was pointing. A child lay on dirty straw, her blanket tossed to the side. Bones showed through translucent skin. The poor creature was likely too weak to stand up, and yet her leg was secured with a heavy chain. Ella's trained eye registered the shallow undulations of the rib cage.

As she bent over the girl to check her pulse, Dr. Miller's hand touched her shoulder.

"Allow me. Your friends can't take much more."

She turned to Bella and Cecilia. Bella held her stomach as her face took on a greenish hue. Cecilia swayed on her feet like she was about to faint. Ella grabbed her friends' hands and led them out of the ward.

"Get fresh air," Ella told them. "I'll go on."

The sisters exchanged looks and shook their heads. Ella dug into her medical bag and handed Cecilia smelling salts. Then she nodded to the attendant who was watching them. "Please take us to see Mr. Olson."

The gloomy corridor the attendant shepherded them through echoed with screeching and weeping. They ascended a winding staircase and came to another corridor. The air was easier to breathe thanks to fewer foul odors, and bigger windows illuminated their way. The attendant stopped by one of the doors, selected a key from his ring, and unlocked it.

"Shout if you need me."

Holding her breath, Ella stepped in. To her relief, the room was of a decent size. Instead of benches and straw pallets, this room had a chair next to a table and a bed, where shirtless Olson sat. From what Ella could see, he wasn't restrained. He was staring down, mumbling to himself, and didn't raise his head to look at his visitors.

Ella's knees were weak when she approached the carpenter. "Olson, it's me, Dr. Ella. I'm your friend, remember? I removed a fishing hook that was stuck in your hand, and you taught me sailor curses."

Olson appeared not to hear her.

"Olson, these are Captain Grey's daughters, Miss Bella and Miss Cecilia." The sisters came to stand next to her. "We brought you warm clothing and food. Are you hungry?"

She lifted the bread from her basket, hoping to tempt Olson with the aroma. Olson showed no reaction.

"Bella, do you see those terrible scars on his shoulders?" Cecilia's hand hovered over the lines and swellings on his skin.

The elder sister touched her throat.

"Those are from the beatings he received when he was enslaved in the colonies. He escaped his owner, snuck onto a British ship, and gained his freedom," Ella explained, but then she blinked and inspected Olson's back and shoulders. "There are many new scars. Recent ones."

"Lieutenant Drake Landon did this to him." Cecilia stomped her foot. "He ordered this poor man beaten. Father tried to stop him, but he was too late."

"Not only did he suffer physical pain from the beating, his mind broke from the strain of his memories." Bella dabbed the corners of her eyes with a lacy handkerchief.

Ice traveled down Ella's veins. "The Landons are a family of vipers."

"We're not attending their ball." Cecilia crossed her arms.

Ella nodded. "I wish you'd told me about the flogging. I'd make a special salve to treat a few stubborn sores that had not healed. But what I have with me will help as well."

She rummaged in her bag and removed the ointment, which she rubbed on Olson's back, shoulders, and arms. The man didn't react in any way.

While she was working, the sisters unloaded their baskets and found places for the clothing and the food.

"Perhaps we can make the room more cheerful," Bella said as she folded the shirts and scarves into a neat stack. "A flower bouquet or a painting. Or what if you bring your violin, Cecilia, and play for him?"

"Don't you see how useless that will be?" Cecilia's hands bunched the scarf she held. "His mind is gone. Do you think a few daisies or a picture of a tree will change that?"

Bella bowed her head but then raised it high and set her jaw. "We should at least try."

All three of them sighed as they left Mr. Olson's room and then retraced their steps out of the oppressing walls of the asylum. Dr. Miller's carriage still stood, waiting.

Bella's hand touched Ella's elbow. "Ella, do you think that Mr. Olson's mind cannot recover?"

Ella shifted her weight from one foot to another. "Physicians have been trying to cure madness for centuries. But it presents in so many ways. The cures are usually ineffective and may cause more suffering to the patients than their illness."

"But we shouldn't give up trying or there will never be progress. Right, Dr. Parker?"

The deep, male voice came from behind, and Ella spun around.

Dr. Miller had removed his hat and was rubbing his nearly bald head. A man behind him carried a large bundle in his arms. Ella had to look twice before she realized he was carrying the girl they'd seen, wrapped in a blanket. The girl's eyes were closed, her cheeks bloodless.

"Where is she being taken?" Ella stiffened. "The morgue?"

The Grey sisters trembled.

"Not yet." Dr. Miller rolled down the sleeves of his jacket. "There's still a chance for her to survive, but not in such dreadful conditions. Unfortunately, many asylum residents are tormented not only by their insanity, but also by lung illnesses, skin inflammation, head lice, or as appears in the case of this patient, starvation. I'm taking her to The Women's Sanctuary. I'd love to tell you more about that remarkable place but now is not the time. Perhaps we'll meet again soon." As he entered his carriage, Ella spied the girl lying on the velvety seat. But then Dr. Miller closed the curtain, and the carriage sped away.

They climbed into the waiting coach. As it jostled on the cobbled road, they sat in silence, occasionally interrupted by Bella's sniffling.

"Poor Mr. Olson. And those poor women. They should not be reduced to such an undignified state. Something must be done." Bella sobbed.

Ella stared down at her hands. "I became a healer to save lives. But I've never learned how to save minds. It's considered almost impossible."

"But there has to be something…" Bella chewed her lip.

Cecilia flicked her gaze up. "Are we going to sew bonnets for insane women instead of knitting scarves for prisoners? Or will you join some ladies' committee like Mother and plan a charity ball with *saint* Mrs. Landon, whose son caused Mr. Olson's madness?"

Color returned to Bella's cheeks. "No. You were right. We must not go to that ball. Even if they have the most beautiful ballroom, so perfect for the minuet we've practiced. And all those handsome gentlemen in attendance. We absolutely mustn't go. Do you agree, Ella?"

Ella pressed her fist to her forehead. "That dreadful ball is the last thing on my mind right now."

Bella nodded solemnly. "I will tell Mother."

"What excellent timing." Cecilia leaned toward the window. "There's Mrs. Landon's carriage standing here, at our house. Looks like our mother is entertaining a visitor."

Chapter 11

Ella glowered at the maroon carriage with its two white horses. She was still shaking with rage over what Drake Landon did to her friend Olson. The thought of running into Drake's mother made Ella's fists ball. She was about to bid goodbye to the Grey sisters and walk home, but Cecilia clenched her hand.

The younger sister's nostrils flared. "That woman must learn what her son did. And Mother must open her eyes to what a monster she's befriended. Let's tell them!"

Ella and Cecilia marched toward the house with Bella speeding behind them and shouting reminders for her sister about acting civil with guests, even ones they loathed. Cecilia hissed at her and swiveled her head to stick out her tongue.

As they entered the antechamber, a soft, mournful melody floated toward them. Each note carried the weight of unspoken emotions that made Ella's breath catch. The pianoforte wept with heartbreaking grief.

"It must be Lillian playing. Strange; we thought she had returned home to her parents. I wonder what happened," Bella whispered. "She's a marvelous musician."

The fuse in Ella's chest, about to explode from righteous anger, extinguished. Her heart quickened with the desire to hug Lillian's thin shoulders and ask her what troubles were making her play with such profound sadness.

As they stood spellbound, Mrs. Grey came out to them. Her jaw dropped. "Goodness, how you look and smell! Where on earth have you been?"

Cecilia put her hands on her hips. "Mother, we visited the asylum where Mr. Olson—"

"What? After I forbade you?" She covered her mouth with her hand. "Upstairs to your rooms, both of you! After you change and our guests leave, we'll have a serious talk." Her gaze shifted to Ella, and she touched her throat. "Ella, it was good of you to visit Mr. Olson, but you shouldn't have taken my daughters with you. They are far too impressionable to visit such a place. But I'm glad you are here. Mrs. Landon is eager to speak with you. Bella can lend you a clean dress. Please go with her and change."

"No, Mother." Bella's voice quivered as she locked hands with Ella and Cecilia. "Some things cannot wait. We will speak with Mrs. Landon right this minute. She must learn of the tragedy her son caused."

As they walked into the music room followed by Mrs. Grey, who seemed to have lost her ability to speak, Cecilia caught Ella's eye and whispered, "You should check Bella for a fever. It's most unlike my sister to appear in front of guests in a dirty dress."

At the pianoforte, Lillian lifted her hands off the keys and folded them on her lap. Her back rose and fell as she caught her breath.

Dowager Mrs. Landon reclined on the sofa with her head tilted. "My dear, must you exert yourself to such a degree when you play? Surely Dr. Miller wouldn't approve."

Lillian slammed the keys with an open palm, making a disjointed chord. "I'm tired of hearing what Dr. Miller would or wouldn't approve of."

"Temper, temper, Lillian. What will our hosts think?" She rose and grinned at the Grey sisters and Ella. The exaggerated grin seemed to freeze on her lips. Lillian also smiled, the warmth of that smile growing as she gazed at each sister and then Ella. Her cheeks, however, were thin and pale.

Bella made a quick curtsy. "Mrs. Landon, we apologize for appearing in front of you in such a state, but we had the most disturbing morning. We visited the mental asylum where Mr. Olson—"

"How valiant of you!" Mrs. Landon folded her hands on her chest. "I could never step inside such a place, but I spoke with the superintendent. Was the poor man moved into a private room?"

Ella opened and closed her mouth. "You know what your son ordered done?"

"Of course I do, and we both feel terrible about it. Drake never meant for such a thing to happen. And I apologize about how I treated *you*, Dr. Parker. Please forgive my confusion. Now that Mrs. Grey and Dr. Miller have told me all about you, I'm overjoyed that Lillian has made such a wonderful friend."

Ella's head reeled. *Mrs. Landon knows about what Drake had done to Olson, and she was the one who paid for a private room in the asylum? And she's happy that I'm Lillian's friend? What is happening?*

Cecilia cleared her throat. "The ball... we simply cannot—"

"Cannot miss it." Mrs. Landon beamed at Cecilia, who seemed to be at a loss for words. "We will raise money to benefit The Women's Sanctuary, which hired Dr. Miller as their chief physician. Those funds will allow Dr. Miller to take on more charity cases and to give the impoverished patients better accommodation."

"We saw Dr. Miller at the asylum today. There was a girl who was near death. He said he would take her to The Women's Sanctuary," Ella said.

"He will save her life and sanity." Mrs. Landon's eyes sparkled. "It's a progressive institution dedicated to curing minds. You all must come to the ball and help me convince my guests to donate generously to this cause."

Lillian rubbed her temples.

Is she having another headache? Ella worried.

While Mrs. Landon boasted about the ball, Ella walked up to Lillian.

"How are you feeling?" Ella asked quietly.

Lillian took her hand. "My head hurts again. The medicine Dr. Miller gave me helps a bit. He also brought another doctor to see me, Dr. Quail. I'm sorry I didn't send for you, but there's been no time. Mrs. Landon is introducing me to her friends before the ball. We've been making several visits a day. We just came from Magistrate Harrow's house and are hosting several of Mrs. Landon's friends after this."

Why is Mrs. Landon taking Lillian on all those visits? It's enough to exhaust anyone!

Mrs. Landon's voice hushed them. "I already shared the happy news with Mrs. Grey, but I still haven't told you! You remember that Lillian came to stay with me intending to get married. While I looked for a suitable match for her, my son Arthur noticed this charming country girl and proposed. They married quietly and without any fuss. So romantic!"

She came up to Lillian and embraced her. Lillian accepted the hug without enthusiasm, but Mrs. Landon showed no notice.

"The ball will be the perfect occasion to announce the marriage. Can you believe that Lillian has never been to a fancy ball? Please help her feel more comfortable with the guests." She gestured to Lillian. "Lillian, aren't you excited your friends will be at the ball?"

"Yes, please come. It would be lovely to have you." Lillian smiled, but her hand went to forehead. "May we please go? My headache is becoming worse."

"Is there anything we can offer?" Mrs. Grey asked. "Tea, water?"

The dowager answered before Lillian. "Nothing cures headaches like fresh air. Would your daughters be so kind as to escort Lillian for a brief walk outside while I speak to Dr. Parker? Only five minutes will be enough and then we'll go. Lillian needs to take her medications and rest before a dinner with several friends of mine."

When Lillian left, her gait unsteady, holding onto Bella and Cecilia, Mrs. Landon sighed. "Please sit with me, my dear ladies. You better than anyone will understand my burden. Mrs. Grey, you've raised such lively, spirited girls. Have they always been of robust health?"

Mrs. Grey's lips pinched as she sat to Mrs. Landon's left. "Overall, we've been blessed. Are you speaking of Lillian? She looks painfully thin and pale."

"Yes." Mrs. Landon folded her gloved hands in a steeple. "Poor dear. And poor Arthur. It's a bleak future for a young man with a sickly wife. Dr. Miller is most concerned about her."

"What was his diagnosis?" Ella asked.

"Her illness stumps even him. And what's worse, Lillian refuses to take her medicines and overtires herself with her music and reading."

Mrs. Grey leaned toward the dowager. "You're gracious to care so much for her. Ella, what do you think ails Lillian?"

Ella touched her face. "I don't want to guess without a full examination. If Dr. Miller refrained from giving a diagnosis, it must be because he needs to continue observing the patient. But I think Lillian needs more rest."

"What a clever young woman!" Mrs. Landon clapped her hands. "Dr. Miller said that. But there are some things that have given me terrible anxiety, and I'm still debating whether to discuss them with Dr. Miller. I prefer to confide in you. Dr. Parker, would you please tell me, can disorders of the mind pass from parents to children?"

Ella shifted on her seat. "Why do you ask that?"

"Well, like I said, it's a concern that worries me a great deal." Mrs. Landon wrinkled her brow.

"Are you saying Lillian's mother or father is suffering from insanity?" Mrs. Grey touched her throat. "I thought you knew her parents well."

"I do!" Mrs. Landon's eyes brightened. "I attended a boarding school with her mother, now Mrs. Davis. Her husband is a proper gentleman, a landowner, although his property is derelict and unprofitable."

"If Lillian's parents are of sound mind, I'm confused why you are worried about hereditary illnesses." Ella shrugged.

Mrs. Landon cocked her head. "That's because you don't understand a mother's heart. Not everything is logical. I only hoped you could give me an answer that would stay between us. Perhaps I should ask Dr. Miller. He will probably know better."

Ella squirmed. *Any medical pamphlet about mental maladies will give her an answer. I'm not harming Lillian by confirming what most people know.*

"Many illnesses of the mind run in families. Diseases such as melancholy, mania, and the falling sickness may be passed on to one's children."

"Thank you, my dear." Mrs. Landon squeezed Ella's hand and grinned. "This was extremely helpful. I hope you keep this little talk confidential."

The sisters and Lillian walked in. Bella's and Cecilia's cheeks had regained a healthy color, but Lillian's remained blanched.

"I hope you had a lovely walk." Mrs. Landon wrapped her arm around Lillian's shoulders and smiled at Ella and the sisters. "We are looking forward to seeing you at the ball."

The sisters exchanged glances, then nodded. Ella swallowed.

Mrs. Landon is up to something. I must attend for Lillian's sake. Even if it means I will see Jamie there. Her heart skipped a beat.

Chapter 12

When the carriage stopped by the Landons' house at around eleven at night, Ella threw back her shoulders. *This time I'm a guest and coming through the front doors.*

A servant in red livery helped Mrs. Grey, Bella, Cecilia, and Ella disembark, shielding them from the rain with an umbrella. As soon as they entered the house, a different servant took their coats and boots. The women changed into dancing slippers.

"Will you finally tell me what surprise you have prepared and what you brought?" Mrs. Grey asked her daughters when Cecilia passed her bundle to the servant. Mrs. Grey was wearing a pale-yellow dress, which made her look younger and allowed Ella to glimpse the stunning beauty who charmed the brave sea captain.

"Mother, if we tell you, it would not be a surprise." Cecilia rolled her eyes. The lavender dress and elegant updo gave her a more sophisticated and womanly appearance.

They were announced by a butler, who ushered them into a large ballroom filled with guests. Ladies and gentlemen, many of them navy or army officers, conversed among themselves. The music of violins and pianoforte floated, mixing with the conversations. Gold chandeliers illuminated the room, reflecting in champagne glasses that the servants offered to the guests. Ella spotted her friends Marietta Wyse with her husband Lieutenant Jack Wyse, Henrietta Fillips, and Veronica Allen and waved hello to them.

Bella's face had a dreamy expression as she glanced around the ballroom. Her cobalt-blue dress revealed the curve of her shoulders and her long neck.

"Isn't this a marvelous ballroom?" she prattled to Ella. "How lovely it will be to dance. And so many gentlemen are attending."

Ella scanned the faces of the uniformed officers. Jamie wasn't among them. That should've been a relief, but Ella's feet curled inside her dance shoes.

Why isn't he here?

Her side vision caught Arthur and Drake Landon, who stood by the wall with wineglasses. Drake raised his eyebrow and said something to Arthur while pointing at her. Ella turned her back on them.

Mrs. Landon approached Ella and her companions, holding Lillian by the hand. Lillian's gown, white as fresh snow, emphasized her paleness. She seemed even thinner, and she had dark crescents under her eyes. Ella wondered if she suffered from insomnia.

"How lovely to see you, ladies!" Mrs. Landon gave them a wide smile. "I hope you will have a wonderful time, and I can't wait for your entertainment number. Enjoy some champagne!" She waved over a servant with a tray, and everyone but Lillian took tall wineglasses filled to the brim. The hostess frowned and handed a glass to Lillian. "You must drink with us, my dear. I want to propose a toast. To my daughter-in-law! To you, Lillian!"

As the bubbles tickled Ella's throat, her eyes lingered on Lillian, who took a tiny sip.

"No, Lillian, that won't do!" Mrs. Landon touched Lillian's arm. "Tonight, leave all your worries behind and enjoy your first ball. A night of fun could be curative! Am I right, Dr. Parker?"

"If we don't overdo it." Ella locked eyes with Lillian, who finished the glass.

"You heard the doctor!" The dowager threw her head back, laughing. "I won't let you drink too much. Would you excuse us, ladies? We must greet Magistrate Harrow."

When Mrs. Landon whisked Lillian away, Mrs. Grey glanced at her daughters and Ella.

"I will introduce you to the ladies I've met through my charity work."

As Mrs. Grey led them around the room and spoke to the finely dressed women, Ella caught a glimpse of Lillian from the corner of her eye. There was another champagne flute in her hand, and again she raised it in a toast and drained it. Just as Ella considered approaching her and discreetly warning her to stop drinking, two figures appeared in the doorway, distracting her.

Jamie's and Conor's uniforms glistened from the rain, and their hair was damp as they stepped in. Jamie's gaze locked with Ella's for a heartbeat, and a rush of heat rose to her face. She took in his blue eyes and the dimples on his cheeks, and her heart sped up.

Silly heart! He doesn't love you.

She broke eye contact and glanced at Conor, whose shining eyes were ogling the young ladies. He grinned at Bella and Cecilia, but then his gaze shifted to Lillian. He froze with his mouth open.

The music changed, and the hostess announced that the dancing was about to begin with the minuet. Ella crept to the wall to hide behind the women waiting for partners, but Mrs. Grey caught her by the hand.

"Where are you going? It's proper for a young lady to stand with her chaperone while gentlemen are looking for dance partners."

Ella hunched to avoid notice as she stayed with her friends. A couple of young officers approached Mrs. Grey and introduced themselves. She, in turn, introduced Bella, who bounced with excitement, and Cecilia, who pouted. The gentlemen escorted the Grey sisters to their positions for the dance.

The skin of Ella's neck itched, and when she turned, she caught Jamie's gaze on her. He shifted his feet as he studied her from across the room.

She crossed her arms and turned to Mrs. Grey. "I won't dance with Jamie Flowers."

Her chaperone raised an eyebrow. "Are you sure, my dear? I've noticed he's been looking at you. Perhaps reconciliation is possible?"

"Absolutely not." Ella jerked her head and added in a whisper. "I cannot stand another heartbreak."

"Then let's make sure you are far too busy dancing with other men to even think of him. Who would you like as your partner?"

"I don't want to dance. I prefer to observe."

"None of that." Mrs. Grey tapped her arm with her fan. "I'd give much to trade places with you for one evening. Youth flies by before you know it. You will dance."

Mrs. Landon's shrill voice sounded nearby. "Lillian, why aren't you on the dance floor? Your husband is waiting for you to start the minuet."

Lillian's unsteady gait made Ella wonder just how many glasses of champagne she'd had. Preoccupied with her friend's well-being, Ella was startled by Mrs. Grey's touch on her shoulder.

"Did you hear me, dear? You have a partner for the minuet. I believe you know Mrs. Landon's younger son, Lieutenant Drake Landon."

Drake Landon stepped up to her and bowed. "Miss Parker, I'm delighted to have your first dance."

Ella jerked back. "Sir, I'm not dancing tonight."

"Nonsense!" Mrs. Grey interjected, and nodded to Mrs. Landon, who walked toward them.

The hostess beamed. "Ah, Dr. Parker. I asked my son to invite you. As I told you, it was never his intention to cause that poor sailor's misfortune. Please give him an opportunity to win back your good opinion."

Lacking the will to argue, Ella allowed Drake to lead her to middle of the room. He reeked of cigars and a musky cologne, and his eyes darted among the ladies taking their positions.

When her eyes met Jamie's for a moment, her heart sank into the pit of her stomach. To hide her anxiety, she put on a smile. "Do you enjoy dancing, Lieutenant?"

Suppressing a sigh, she watched Jamie turn on his heel and follow Conor to the card room.

Drake's lips sneered. "No. Most of the women my mother invited are too unsightly even for my unassuming taste."

Her chin dropped, and she leaned away from him. "I'm relieved to know that you do not fancy me. Because I loathe you."

"I said *most*. The way your eyes blazed just now made your face much more interesting."

He left her between Bella and Cecilia and took a spot across from her. As the music started, Bella's eyes shone even brighter, while Cecilia tapped her foot to the measured rhythm.

Lillian and Arthur started off the minuet. Arthur glided with the music, while Lillian faltered through her dance steps. After their hands detached, Lillian stumbled back and collided with Bella. Muttering apologies, Lillian trudged to the end of the procession. Arthur glared at her and curled his lip. As onlookers raised eyebrows or whispered to each other, sour champagne crept up Ella's throat.

"I almost feel sorry for Lillian," Drake whispered to Ella as he took her hand to prepare for their turn. Everyone's eyes were on Bella and her partner as they moved with wonderful grace. "Arthur was under pressure to marry well. He wished to spite our mother and to have a wife he could control. That slip of a girl satisfied both of those requirements. But he didn't expect her to embarrass him in public."

"How cruel," Ella whispered back.

Drake shrugged, then composed his expression, as it was their turn. With a bow, he led Ella to the middle of the dance floor. They took two elaborate steps forward. Drake was in sync with her, and she matched his movements with ease. Her breathing relaxed.

As she turned away from Drake, her eyes scanned the room for Jamie.

Jamie and I never danced together.

The thought dropped like a pebble in a river. She continued the turn, looking for him. The fabric of her dress tightened, and her neck snapped back to see what was happening. Drake's foot was on the hem. Ella spread her hands to stop her turn, but the momentum carried her, and she tripped over her feet. Her behind hit the floor and her legs flew forward. In a shocking breach of etiquette, her ankles peeked from under the ripped hem. Drake flashed a wide smile before taking on an expression of mock horror, offering his hand to help her stand and muttering apologies. His head was bowed as he led her to the tail end of the dance procession.

"You planned this!"

He concealed his mouth with his hand. "Seeing your ankles was worth it. This ball is no longer a bore. I'll try my luck in cards, and then we can dance again."

Ella glared at him. "Never."

Chapter 13

Ella gulped water to calm herself after the disastrous minuet. Mrs. Grey approached her and patted her back.

"Are you all right, dear? Such a shame to fall like that."

The next dance was playing, a quadrille. None of the dancers were familiar to Ella.

"I'm fine." Ella composed her face so as not to show the fury that stormed inside her. "Mr. Landon made me trip to rile me. I won't give him the satisfaction."

"I'm sure it was an accident and he feels terribly." Mrs. Grey gave her a weak smile. "I wonder where my daughters are."

When the dance finished, the hostess came out to the middle of the room and waved her arm. The guests grew quiet.

"This ball is not only for merriment, but also a chance to fulfill our Christian duty. Several ladies have volunteered to show their talents to support The Women's Sanctuary, an extraordinary place of healing. Please reward their efforts by donating generously. The first performance will be by Miss Bella and Miss Cecilia Grey."

Following a burst of applause, a few huffs rippled through the audience. The loudest gasp was from their mother, who clutched her chest. The sisters circled the room dressed in breeches, stockings, and shirts and carried fencing foils. The audience stepped back as they stood across from each other.

Cecilia's voice boomed with vigor. "In the spirit of charity, my sister and I offer a friendly match to show that we can dance with blades as well as fans."

"And if our duel amuses you, perhaps you might be moved to offer your support to the ill," Bella finished.

Their speech drew thunderous applause.

With Cecilia's exclaimed "On guard," they began their swordplay.

Moving with natural grace, the sisters danced from one fencing maneuver to another in a series of lunges and retreats. As one foil got close to touching its mark, the other parried it. Metal clashed against metal; each clink resonated in the still room.

"What do you think of this?" Mrs. Grey fanned herself.

Pleasant heat radiated through Ella's chest. "They are marvelous. And the donations are pouring in already." She pointed at the donation box on the table adorned with flowers. A queue of guests was filling it with envelopes and coins.

"I suppose you are right. Although I'd rather see them with needles suitable for knitting."

Cecilia scored the first point when her foil's dull tip touched her sister's chest, prompting applause from the spectators. Ella's attention shifted to Lillian, who stood across the room, next to her husband and mother-in-law. Arthur was speaking to Lillian, and her face crumpled. She massaged her temples as she replied. Dowager Mrs. Landon patted her shoulder and passed her a glass from a servant's tray. Ella feared it was more champagne.

Ella's toes curled in her dance slippers. *Lillian needs to go lie down in her bedroom. This party will make her ill. Arthur is upsetting her, and her mother-in-law is giving her too much to drink. No wonder she's getting another headache.*

Another round of applause erupted, this time for Bella, who scored by striking Cecilia's side. With their match tied, the sisters made elaborate bows, first to each other and then to the appreciative audience.

The two, flushed from their exercise, came to stand by Ella and Mrs. Grey.

"How did you like our surprise?" Bella wiped beads of sweat from her forehead.

Mrs. Grey rocked in place. "I suppose this sport improves agility and balance. But now, please change back into your dresses."

"Oh, Mother..." Cecilia scoffed, but Bella tugged her by the hand as she hurried to leave the room.

"You were terrific," Ella called after them.

She scanned the crowd for Lillian, hoping to speak to her and persuade her to rest. But that was not to be, as Ella spied her being dragged by the hand by Mrs. Landon to the pianoforte. Coldness rushed up Ella's spine at the sight.

"After such a… spirited performance, we need something soothing. My daughter-in-law, Mrs. Arthur Landon, will play the pianoforte. Please give her your full attention. She practices almost all the hours she's awake. I'd say she's obsessed. So please show your appreciation for her effort by donating to The Women's Sanctuary."

Lillian, sitting on the bench, pulled her neck in like a turtle as the audience applauded. But once her fingers touched the keys, her face relaxed. The melody, fragile and mournful, put the audience under a spell. Ella's heart fluttered as Jamie reentered the room with Conor.

Jamie, how can I teach my heart not to race when seeing you?

Conor froze mid-step, and his lips parted in a silly grin when his gaze landed on Lillian at the piano. Jamie led him toward the wall and whispered something in his ear. Then he made his way around the room toward her.

Panic rose in Ella's throat, and she squeezed her eyes shut. *No, Jamie, don't torment me. Don't make me burst into tears in front of all these people.* On weak legs, she hastened out of the ballroom.

Chapter 14

Each step Ella took as she rushed out of the ballroom resonated like a punch in Jamie's chest.

She said she never wanted to speak to me again. I can't blame her for being angry.

He shifted his attention to Conor, who still gawked with his mouth ajar at the woman playing the pianoforte. Once again, they'd walked in too late to catch the hostess's announcement, but he suspected that this young woman was connected to the Landons. His friend barely blinked as he stared at her.

Jamie returned to Conor and whispered in his ear. "After how much you've won at the card table already, I doubt anyone will play with you. Let's go home and get a good night's sleep. You said you are meeting someone tomorrow."

Conor didn't seem to hear.

Arthur Landon stood beside the pianoforte. His narrowed eyes darted between the woman playing and the spectators. When his gaze lingered on Conor, his lip curled. Jamie tugged on Conor's sleeve to get his attention, but his friend stood like a statue, seemingly spellbound by the music. Or more likely, the musician.

The young woman finished playing, and her hands and shoulders drooped. Sweat poured from her forehead. The audience applauded, but she stayed seated, perhaps requiring a moment to rest.

"I will speak to her," Conor said and, before Jamie could stop him, strode to the pianoforte. Jamie hastened after him.

When they approached, the woman at the piano was speaking to Arthur.

"Please find Sarah and ask her to make me the tea that the doctor prescribed."

Arthur grimaced. "Why can't you go find her yourself or ask another servant?"

She massaged her temples. "I asked before but still no one has brought me that tea. The servants are busy with the guests. Please, Arthur."

He walked away scowling.

She must be Arthur Landon's wife. Conor should not get involved.

These thoughts whispered in Jamie's head, but before he could get his friend away, Conor bowed to the woman.

"Miss, is there something I can help you with? My name is Conor Leach, and this is my friend James Flowers. And I want to say that I'm awestruck by your playing. Your music has left a great impression on me." Conor's babbling and the interest glowing in his eyes were more than apparent to anyone who would look at him.

The young woman blinked as if having a tough time following the thread of Conor's rapid speech. But she must've caught the last line because she gave a tentative smile.

"Thank you. You are too kind. Do you enjoy music?"

"More than anything." Conor's eyes glistened. "At least, starting today. I will attend every concert I can."

What a fool! Jamie resisted slapping his forehead with his palm.

The woman's smile grew warmer. "I'm flattered to be such… an inspiration. For your newfound love of music, I mean. Perhaps I could also inspire you to make a donation? The cause is dear to my heart." She nibbled her lip as if regretting the expression she'd used.

Conor's grin stretched from ear to ear as he handed her one of the money bags he had won in cards.

Jamie's stomach churned. *What are you doing? We could use that money. But if Ella had asked me… I'd do the same.*

She opened the bag and gaped. "That's very generous, sir. Mr. Leach, is it? Thank you. Many will benefit from your kindness."

The hostess was walking toward them with her face pinched. The young lady flinched and rose.

"I'm sorry, I'm a bit tired. I should get a little rest. It was nice meeting you, gentlemen."

"Likewise," Jamie jumped in. "We are going home and—"

"Is there anything I can fetch for you? Something to eat or drink?" Conor jabbered before Jamie could complete his bid goodbye.

The hostess clutched a gem on her necklace as she came closer.

"Um..." The young woman swayed on her feet. "I am thirsty. Water would be nice."

"Lillian, must everyone here run errands for you?" Mrs. Landon threw up her hands. "First you send Arthur for your tea and now one of our guests for water. We have servants to do these tasks." She snapped her fingers at a valet who carried a heavy tray. "A glass of water for Mrs. Arthur Landon." There was a purposeful emphasis on each word of the name.

"Mrs. Arthur Landon?" Conor echoed, staring at the young woman. The smile waned from his lips, and his cheeks paled.

"Yes. Did she forget to tell you that?" Arthur shoved Jamie as he approached Conor. "I was at the other end of the room and saw everything. The attention you paid my wife did not escape my notice, sir."

***

After rushing through several corridors, Ella was lost in the vast house. Initially she wanted to find her way to the garden or some other quiet place, but she gave up on that idea.

It was silly of me to run off. I should've stayed with Mrs. Grey.

She was trying to find her way back to the ballroom when she stumbled upon the glass doors that led to the library. The candles flickered, casting a warm glow on the room, and a cheery fire crackled merrily in the hearth.

She slid inside, settled on the sofa, and lifted the book that she found there. To her surprise, it was a recently published medical journal opened to a piece written by Dr. Miller. Her esteemed professor described his visit to an asylum and its horrendous conditions.

Unfortunately, some of my colleagues still believe that fear is the key to treating diseases of the brain, such as the falling sickness. Upon my recent visit to a public asylum, I came across a woman held in a dark room, tied to her bed. The attendants forced medicines into her mouth that loosened her bowels severely. She screamed as she soiled herself, but no one would bring her a chamber pot. The physician in charge told me that the patient must be sufficiently scared for the brain to heal itself. Such cures are worse than the feared falling sickness that brought the patient to the asylum.

Ella sucked in her breath. *How awful. But who was reading this and left it here?*

She read several more accounts of similar nature.

Heavy footfalls made Ella raise her head from the article. Drake walked in. A cigar was in his hand, and his breath smelled of spirits.

"I was looking for you."

***

Arthur's face was crimson as he stepped nose to nose with Conor. "Sir, I ask you again. What did you mean by showing such attention to my wife?"

Lillian clutched her hands. Tears poured from her eyes. "Arthur, please stop it."

The elder Mrs. Landon stepped between Arthur and Conor, waving her fan as if she were trying to extinguish a fire with it.

"I didn't know she was your wife. She looked upset, and I asked if there was anything I could do to help," Conor spat.

Jamie cringed and shook his head. The dowager squinted at Lillian and tightened her jaw. *You caused this,* her expression seemed to say.

The temperature in the room seemed to increase by several degrees. Guests broke off their conversations and stared at the scene.

Jamie cleared his throat. "Mr. Leach meant no harm. His question was perfectly polite. And his donation was benevolent, without any hidden meaning. If we must speak of this further, perhaps it should be done privately."

Mrs. Landon touched her son's shoulder. "This must be a misunderstanding, Arthur. Your wife made a mistake by encouraging Mr. Leach's attention, but let's not overreact."

"This is not my fault!" Lillian wrapped her hands around her head. "Please, Arthur, stop it."

"You wanted his attention." Arthur's finger jabbed Lillian's blanched cheek. "And now you want everyone else's attention as you cringe and moan from your endless headaches. Why don't you swoon for a more dramatic effect since you are determined to embarrass me? You are a disgrace. Sickly, drunk, and making a fool of me in front of everyone."

"Don't speak to her that way!" Conor stepped in between them with his arms wide.

Oh Lord! This will not end well. But Conor is right. No one should speak to a woman like that.

"You tell me how to treat my wife?" Arthur roared; spit sprayed from his mouth.

Conor lifted his chin. "Stop it! She doesn't deserve such treatment."

"How dare you?" Shaking, he ripped off his glove and flung it at Conor. "Sir, I'm challenging you to wash the insult with blood. Send your second in the morning to speak to my brother."

Jamie grabbed Conor's hand. "Let me handle this," he mouthed.

Conor shook off Jamie's arm and lifted the glove. "I accept with pleasure, sir."

I can't let Conor fight this duel. It's madness.

The hostess closed her fan and pointed it at her daughter-in-law. "Look what you've done, Lillian! Look what you've done."

Lillian crumpled to the floor. Conor and Jamie stepped toward her but then froze in shock. Her body arched and convulsed, as if possessed by some horrible demon. Saliva dripped from her clenched lips. The guests gasped and spoke among themselves in hushed whispers.

"Falling sickness." Someone gasped. "She's a lunatic."

"Such people must be kept away," another voice said.

"Fetch Dr. Miller, quick!" the dowager yelled to the servants as she put her hand on Arthur's shoulder.

Conor turned to Jamie with his eyes wide. "She needs help. Where's Ella?"

Chapter 15

In the library, Drake plopped next to Ella on the sofa. The alcohol on his breath made her wince, and she slid her body away from him, hiding her face behind the medical journal.

"What's that you are reading?" He snatched the pages from her grasp. "Ah, some boring medical nonsense. Shouldn't a woman read sappy novels about love?"

She attempted to rise, but his hand pushed her back down. He grabbed her by the shoulders, pulling her closer. Ella writhed, trying to free herself, but he was too strong. She kicked him, but the soft dance slipper had a negligible impact on his boot. Her eyes searched for something heavy she could use to smack Drake on the head.

The door flew open, and Drake shifted away from her. Jamie stood on the threshold, taking in the scene. His face blanched, and his hand went to his throat.

Sweat poured down Ella's back. *Jamie, it's not what you think!*

Drake spoke before she could. "What are you doing here, Flowers? Can't you see Miss Parker and I are busy?"

"I was looking for *Dr.* Parker. The young Mrs. Landon is unwell."

Ella bolted to her feet. "Where is she?"

"In the ballroom." Jamie started walking, and she followed, with Drake behind them. "Conor and her husband got into an argument, upsetting her. She collapsed."

"Is she shaking like she's possessed?" Drake asked.

Ella turned on her heel. "I thought her headaches made her faint. Are you saying that Lillian is having epileptic seizures?"

"I don't know what it is, but she had a fit after the wedding, and Arthur said it was something out of a nightmare. That's why Arthur brought her home. He wants our mother to help him annul the marriage."

"So they are scheming behind her back? Outrageous!"

Jamie led her out of the corridors into the ballroom, where a cluster of guests surrounded someone. Ella wedged her way between the gawkers. Lillian's limbs flailed as she thrashed on the floor.

Ella knelt and put her hands under Lillian's head to prevent her from injuring herself. She hadn't witnessed such fits before, but Dr. Miller spoke of them in medical school.

Lillian's skirt became wet, and the stench of urine emanated from her.

"Oh, that's revolting!" Arthur flinched and pinched his nose.

Ella's blood boiled. "She can't help it!"

"What's happening to her?" Conor asked in a shaky voice.

"She's having an epileptic seizure," Ella answered and peered at Arthur. "She had one before?"

Mrs. Landon answered instead and addressed not only Ella but the guests who ogled the scene. "Yes, she's had at least two such fits before. Unfortunately, she hid her condition from me when I welcomed her into my home. One of her many lies."

Guests gasped and whispered among themselves.

A chilling realization hit Ella. *She must be building a case for annulment. That's why she provoked Lillian's fit and ensured there would be credible witnesses.*

Lillian's jerking seemed to slow, and Ella hoped the fit would abate.

"Ella, what can we do?" Concern in Jamie's voice enveloped her.

Conor, wide-eyed, swayed on his feet. "Should she be carried to her bed?"

Arthur planted his legs wide. "I suppose that task would interest you."

"He did not mean to imply..." Jamie winced, and his ears turned red.

"Get out of my sight."

Conor stepped toward Arthur with his fists clenched. "Is that what you're thinking about when your wife is ill?"

Ella's insides quivered as she met Jamie's gaze. "Jamie, take Conor home. This is not the time for an argument."

Lillian lay still. After a few seconds, her eyes blinked open. "What... what happened?"

A smile brightened Conor's face. "She's better."

"Yes, she is. Now we should leave." Jamie pulled Conor by the elbow and ushered him out of the room.

Ella caressed Lillian's limp arm. "Lillian, you had a seizure. Do you know what that means?"

Lillian nodded. Her voice was little more than a whisper. "Dr. Miller said..."

"Dr. Miller will be here soon." Dowager Mrs. Landon wrung her hands as she turned to her guests. "This is why The Women's Sanctuary is a vitally worthy cause. It cares for patients with illnesses like the falling sickness. I apologize for ending the evening early, but what you've seen should inspire greater donations than any act."

The guests expressed sympathy to the hostess and eyed Lillian with disapproval and disgust as they left.

Seething, Ella addressed Arthur and Drake. "You must carry Lillian to her bed. She's too weak to walk."

Arthur jerked back with a cringe. "She reeks of urine." His gaze hopped from one servant to another, as if deciding which one he should ask to carry Lillian.

"Ella, don't leave, please..." Lillian muttered as Drake lifted her and carried her out.

Ella straightened and glanced around the room, where only a few guests remained. Cecilia paced with a thoughtful expression, and Bella sobbed into a handkerchief.

"Ella, will you come home with us?" Mrs. Grey asked. "Our carriage is waiting."

"No. Lillian asked me to stay. I will care for her."

As Ella exited the ballroom, Arthur's voice reached her as he spoke to the butler. "When Dr. Miller comes, take him to my mother's study."

Ella's breath hitched. *What are they planning?*

Chapter 16

Once the maids finished washing Lillian and dressed her in her nightgown, they left to attend to other duties. Only Sarah remained in the corner. The servant kept her eyes to the floor and was biting her lip, as if holding back tears.

Ella sat on the edge of the bed and reached for Lillian's hand to count her pulse. It was rapid.

Lillian sobbed. "Dr. Miller, he tried to warn me. He said if I worked up my nerves, my symptoms would get worse. But Arthur and Mrs. Landon insisted I attend the ball."

"Drake said they want to annul your marriage to Arthur. I believe they are trying to use your illness as the reason."

Lillian's fingers touched her pale lips.

Sarah's knees hit the floor. "I have something to confess. Your mother-in-law made me tell her... why you don't resemble your parents. She said that if I didn't speak the truth, she would accuse me of stealing, and I would rot in jail."

"They know?" Lillian's shoulders shook.

Ella rubbed her forehead. "Mrs. Landon said you told her many lies."

Tears formed at the corners of Lillian's eyes. "She thinks I lied to her about my parents. But I learned the truth just before I came here. When my father suspected me of being pregnant, he bellowed to Mother so loudly that I could hear him from his study. 'The day our daughters were born, we should've sent her back to the orphanage where we found her. I told you she was nothing but a useless burden, eating the little we have for our family. And now she's brought shame upon us.'"

A strained moan escaped Sarah's throat. "They should've told you a long time ago. They adopted you because they lost hope of having children of their own. To let you find out the way you did..."

Lillian massaged her temples, and Ella asked her to rest and tell the story later. But Lillian shook her head. "I've kept this to myself too long. Imagine this, Ella. Before they put me into the coach to bring me here, my father said I was not his daughter and that he'll have nothing to do with me. My mother gave me a stiff hug and said I must get married before my belly grows and not reveal my condition to anyone until a few weeks after the wedding. Once again, I swore I wasn't pregnant, but she didn't listen. Instead, she said something like, 'Lillian, you don't remember the blessed day when we first met, but I cherish that memory. I know you love us, and I think of you as my daughter, even if my husband does not. But we must protect our family's reputation. Please don't return. Start a new life with the husband Mrs. Landon will find you. She's doing us all a great favor, and you must be thankful.'"

Sarah sobbed. "I'm sorry for revealing your secret to Mrs. Landon. I cared for you from the day Mr. and Mrs. Davis brought you into their home. What a joyful day it was. You were a clever, spirited four-year-old child. I've never seen Mrs. Davis so excited... But two years later, when she became pregnant, after all this time, and with *two* babies... well, it was a miracle nothing could top. Not even the love of a sweet child they adopted."

Ella took Lillian's hand. "When you told me that you met my mother, I wondered where that had happened. Most likely it was at an orphanage. She visited many to inoculate the children from smallpox."

"But all this means to my mother-in-law is that my parents must be lunatics. And I might've inherited their affliction and may pass it on to my future children." Lillian covered her eyes with her palms.

I wonder what Mrs. Landon and Arthur wanted to tell Dr. Miller.

Ella's chest squeezed so tightly she had to rub it. "After all you've been through, it's no wonder you rushed into a marriage with Arthur. Your choices were so few. And the falling sickness... your despair is making it worse."

"I know." Lillian swallowed. "But what can I do? I would be happy to be away from Arthur, but where will I go?"

Tense voices sounded from the hall.

Lillian bristled and pulled the blanket to her chin. "Ella, stay here, please. I beg you."

Ella stroked her cheek and stood as the door opened. Arthur, his mother, and Dr. Miller stepped inside. Dr. Miller carried the bag Ella remembered from the time he was her instructor, while Mrs. Landon held a rolled-up paper.

Mrs. Landon pointed to Sarah. "Go pack your mistress's belongings."

"Where are we going?" The maid pressed her hand to her heart.

"She has no need of you anymore. After you finish packing her bags, take your own things and leave this house."

Sarah departed the room in tears.

"You can't fire my maid!" Lillian clenched her blanket.

Mrs. Landon raised her eyebrows. "I can because I've been paying her wages. Mr. Davis hasn't sent the money he promised. And how you repaid me for my kindness!"

Arthur sneered. "All of Plymouth now knows you have the falling sickness."

What a horrible man. I pray Lillian will be free of him and his family.

"Because you wanted everyone to know." Lillian closed her eyes. "Fine. If you want to use my illness as grounds for the annulment of our marriage, so be it. I want to be rid of you as much as you want to be rid of me."

"Excellent." The dowager gave Ella a wolfish grin. "I'm glad you are here, Dr. Parker. Please be a witness."

The wine and morsels of food churned in Ella's stomach. *What part do they want me to play?*

Mrs. Landon unrolled the paper she was holding. "Dr. Miller and Dr. Quail signed this document that declares you insane. This gives us grounds for annulment. Alas, the process will still take many months. Those months you shall spend at The Women's Sanctuary. We will incur significant costs to maintain your comfort at that fine institution under Dr. Miller's expert care. I hope you see how kind we are by not sending you to the public asylum."

Lillian's face froze, her lips parted.

Ella's heart skipped a beat. *Epilepsy is dangerous and incurable, but Lillian is not insane. It's cruel to treat her as such. But without a caring family, she'll be confined.*

"No, please, not that," Lillian whispered after a couple of minutes of silence. "Allow me to go free. Perhaps I can convince my mother to take me back..." Tears flooded her face.

Mrs. Landon glared at Lillian. "There's no chance of that and you know it. Your maid revealed the secret that you are an orphan with no parents known. Mr. and Mrs. Davis had enough of you. What a mess you've caused. And you have only yourself to blame." She faced Dr. Miller. "My and Arthur's duty here is done. Take her away from my house."

Arthur bared his teeth. "Tie her up well so she doesn't escape."

As he exited the room after his mother, he slammed the door, startling both Lillian and Ella.

Ella was watching Dr. Miller. *What does he intend to do?*

Dr. Miller sighed and removed a handkerchief from his pocket. "Mrs. Landon, please dry your tears."

"Don't call me by that name ever again!" Lillian hiccupped as she wiped her face. "I'm Miss Lillian Davis. Oh dear, that's not my name either."

The doctor wrinkled his brow. "I will call you Miss Davis. I won't ask my assistants to tie you up. You will be safe and comfortable at The Women's Sanctuary."

Ella swallowed. Images of Olson and the starved child from the public asylum twisted her insides. *What kind of place is this Women's Sanctuary?*

"I don't believe you!" Lillian climbed out of bed and stood. "You are that surgeon who wanted to cut into my mother's belly to remove her twins. I recognized you. After your visit, she and I couldn't sleep—"

She screamed as her shaking legs buckled. Dr. Miller caught her by her shoulder. With Ella's assistance, he helped Lillian sit.

Dr. Miller sighed. "Yes, it was indeed me. I'm sorry I caused you such distress back then. I only wanted to help. Perhaps Dr. Parker can reassure you?"

Ella took Lillian's hand. "Lillian, you need diligent care. That's even more important than dissolving your dreadful marriage."

Lillian buried her face in her hands. "Do what you want with me. I have no strength to fight. And since two physicians and my husband think me insane, disputing is useless anyway."

Dr. Miller opened his bag and retrieved a small vial and a spoon. "You must rest. Laudanum will help you sleep."

Lillian winced as she swallowed the medicine, but soon her face relaxed and her jaw went slack. She fell back on the bed.

Dr. Miller removed a strand of hair from her drooling lips. "So young and so much suffering."

A warm sensation spread through Ella. *He used to have a cold demeanor and showed little empathy to patients. But he's became caring. He's profoundly changed.*

His deep voice resonated in Ella's chest, as it had when she'd been his diligent student. "It's almost morning. I will call my assistants to carry our patient into the coach. Would you like to come with us, Dr. Parker? I'm sure you are tired, but you'll find The Women's Sanctuary fascinating. And your presence would reassure Miss Davis."

She stood on the balls of her feet. "I'm most eager to come along."

Chapter 17

The first rays of morning bled through the window, yet Jamie was already dressed to go out. He couldn't sleep after the ball. The visions of Drake leaning to kiss Ella and worries about Conor's duel tormented him.

When he threw on his coat, he turned to Conor, who slumbered on his narrow bed.

"I'll return soon."

Conor's eyes fluttered, and he yawned. "Where are you going this early?"

Jamie rubbed his forehead. "To get you out of a duel with Arthur."

At his words, Conor gasped and bolted up. "I'm fighting that scoundrel. He made his wife so miserable she became ill."

Jamie raised an eyebrow. "You think she will be happier if you kill her husband?"

And if you get killed... No, I won't allow it.

Conor winced. "No, I don't want to add to her suffering. But... There's no way forward for us, is there?"

"For you and Lillian Landon?" Jamie's eyes widened.

"There's something about her that makes me want to dry her tears and make her smile."

"Come to your senses. She's a married woman. And she's terribly ill."

Conor's shoulders fell. "You are right."

"I will bring your apologies and ask to withdraw the duel."

Conor nodded. "Fine. But don't let them think that I'm scared. If there is another provocation..."

Jamie waved his hand as if to swat an annoying fly and opened the door.

"Jamie, wait!" When he turned, Conor was hugging his knees. "Please ask if Lillian is feeling better."

"Such interest may be misinterpreted. Drake or Arthur may think—" Jamie's muscles tightened.

"Jamie, please." Conor's voice dropped. "Find out if she's all right."

***

As the carriage left the city gates and jostled on the unpaved road, Ella cushioned Lillian's head from the bumps. Lillian slept, covered with a thin blanket. A bundle of her belongings lay at her feet. Dr. Miller assured them she wouldn't need much, as clothing would be provided.

Dr. Miller closed the curtain, leaving a sliver to catch the dim light of morning sun. He leaned back on his seat across from the women. His assistants, two strong-looking lads who had brought the sleeping patient to the carriage, were up front with the driver.

Ella checked Lillian's pulse and listened to her breathing. As she did that Dr. Miller leaned toward her.

"How is our patient?"

"Her pulse is steady now." Ella bit the inside of her cheek. "The Landons completely exhausted her with that ball and their behavior."

Dr. Miller rubbed his chest. "I cautioned the family that exhaustion, adverse emotions, and excess of strong drinks could trigger a dangerous fit in young Mrs. Landon. They've done everything I implored them not to do. There's a positive aspect, though. Now the patient will be fully in my care, and I can treat her properly."

A draft seeped through the window, and Ella fixed Lillian's blanket.

"Treat to ease the worst of her symptoms and ensure her safety, I presume. She cannot be cured, right? Not from the falling sickness."

"The dreaded falling sickness." Dr. Miller clicked his tongue. "Sufferers are treated as if they were raving mad. Thought to be possessed by the devil. Yet I wonder if I, or perhaps we, can do more than keep Miss Davis safe and comfortable."

Ella waited for him to say more, but he turned to the window and moved the curtain. The bright rays of the May morning entered the carriage. "We are at the gates of our destination. I must arrange for the patient to be taken to a room and put to bed. And then, perhaps you'd like a tour of the facility?"

"Absolutely! I'm not sleepy at all."

Dr. Miller offered her a hand as she climbed out of the carriage. While he gave orders to his assistants, Ella admired the stately building with white columns. The trees and bushes next to it were neatly trimmed. A woman in a gray dress swept the front steps.

"As you can see, the building is new and well cared for." Dr. Miller came to stand by her. "And inside... You've visited the public asylum. How would you describe it?"

Ella shivered from more than just the cold breeze. "People tied to beds and chairs. Screaming, yelling, and other horrible noises. Patients forced to eat and sleep in overcrowded rooms, unable to care for themselves and neglected by caretakers. That poor girl who almost starved to death..."

"The things you describe are what I found in public and some private asylums I've visited. The suffering of patients inspired me to put aside teaching and surgery and dedicate myself to The Women's Sanctuary."

The attendants carried the sleeping Lillian on a stretcher. A young woman in a modest gray dress and a white apron opened the door for them. She was about twenty-five and would've been pretty if not for the dark scars on her right cheek.

"Good morning, Dr. Miller. Who is the new patient? And do I put her in the East Wing or the West?" She smiled at the older doctor but gave a side-glance to Ella.

"Good morning, Miss Burke." The doctor nodded to her. "Our patient, Miss Lillian Davis, will be housed in the East Wing. Please make sure she receives the best room available and has someone keeping an eye on her. And I'd like you to meet Dr. Parker."

Miss Burke looked around as if trying to see someone besides the three of them. Then her eyes bulged. "Oh, you mean..."

"Yes, I'm Dr. Parker." Ella laughed. "I understand your surprise. Pleasure to meet you..."

"Miss Lavinia Burke, the Sanctuary's matron." Dr. Miller tipped his head toward the young woman. "She does a marvelous job of supervising workers and ensuring the comfort of all the patients. I've known her since her childhood. She was the brightest girl in the orphanage where I treated children. That orphanage then suffered a fire, and Lavinia saved several children, leading them to safety. After that, I hired her as my domestic servant and later gave her a recommendation for her first job as an attendant in a public asylum. When The Women's

Sanctuary was built, I recruited her as a matron. She became a pillar of this institution."

Miss Burke's cheeks flushed, making the scars stand out more.

Ella's heart fluttered. *He values and appreciates the work of women. It's incredible how much he's changed.*

"I will give Dr. Parker a short tour. Miss Burke, would you please arrange breakfast for us? After you attend the patients, of course," Dr. Miller said.

When Miss Burke darted away, Ella noticed that his eyes twinkled.

"Dr. Parker, would you indulge me in a little game? Close your eyes and let me lead you inside. As we walk, please think of all those terrible things you remember about the public asylum."

Ella closed her eyes and gave the doctor her arm. "Lead the way, sir!"

They walked for a short while, and Ella's feet sunk into a soft rug. The scent of baking bread wafted in the air. Someone was humming a song mingling with a whisper of a feather duster. There were no odors of dirt or bodily fluids that had so offended Ella in the public asylum.

"Open your eyes!"

They stood inside a vast parlor furnished with chairs, sofas, and a pianoforte. Drawings decorated the walls. Someone's knitting was left on the sofa.

"It's lovely. Do many patients use this room?" Ella asked.

"Yes. We encourage all our residents to enjoy company or leisurely pursuits. Many of them draw or play parlor games. Some knit or do embroidery. We have yet to have a skilled musician among the patients, but several play simple melodies. And when the weather is pleasant, we encourage the patients to stroll the grounds or tend to the gardens. Right now, the residents are getting ready for breakfast, but by late morning, this room will be full. Miss Burke keeps the schedule as to when the ladies of the West or East wings should gather here."

"The East and the West wings?"

"Oh, I forgot to explain." Dr. Miller tapped himself on the forehead. "Paid patients live in the East Wing. They receive the best rooms, food, and anything else we provide. Our charity patients are housed in the West Wing. Those are women of lower classes, often suffering from malnutrition and other maladies they've acquired from neglect or, at times, outright cruelty of the carers. Most of the East Wing ladies prefer to avoid them, and thus we use a schedule for this room."

"Who owns this place? It seems well funded."

"I'm one of the owners and also the chief physician. Someday I hope to open a similar facility for men."

"And who are the other owners?"

Dr. Miller pulled on a loose thread on his sleeve. "I'm not free to say. They wish to be anonymous."

Strange.

Ella glanced at the drawings, books, and the pianoforte. "I'm glad Lillian will enjoy some rest here. But will it improve her condition? Or do you have something in mind to treat her?"

Dr. Miller tugged on his beard. "I have a few ideas, but I want to observe her some more. Now, let me show you the dining room."

Delicious smells floated in the air as they approached the vast, brightly lit room. Five women in brown dresses were eating at one large table covered with a white tablecloth, some of them fed by attendants. Two women, dressed like the patients, poured tea and gave out bread.

"Those are our West Wing patients, those who are well enough to eat with others. Some even help with breakfast duties," Dr. Miller explained. He pointed at another table. "And these are the East Wing ladies. Their meals will be lavish today because Mrs. Landon sent leftover delicacies and desserts from her ball. But Miss Burke ensures that the food is always satisfactory."

The table he indicated was occupied by five women in dresses of assorted styles and colors. Two chatted with each other, two had vacant gazes as they chewed, and another was singing a bawdy song while the attendant struggled to get a spoon into her mouth.

"How many patients are there?" Ella asked.

"We currently have ten patients in each wing. Some dine in their rooms."

"I imagine this must be the case with anyone... dangerous to others." She shuddered.

"None of our residents are violent. As a private institution, we choose whom to treat, and I accept only patients who won't hurt others."

A plump young woman walked in and curtsied to Dr. Miller.

"Good morning, Doctor. Miss Burke sent me to tell you that the new patient is awake. She refused breakfast and is crying. Other patients are having a fine morning. Except... I forgot."

Dr. Miller tapped his foot. "Constance, you must try to remember. If Miss Burke sent you to tell me, it must be important. Is someone not feeling well?"

Constance bit her lip. "I think that's what she said."

"Who? Is it Ginny again? A stomachache?"

The young woman's face brightened. "Yes. That's it."

When she left to help with breakfast, Dr. Miller frowned. "Constance is not our brightest attendant, but she's meticulous at cleaning and a kind soul. And a childhood friend of Miss Burke's. They came from the same orphanage. Why don't you check on Miss Davis, and I'll see to Ginny, my youngest patient."

He led Ella to the wide stairs and up one floor. "The East Wing is on the right. I believe you'll find Miss Davis in the second to last room. After you comfort her, you can find me in the West Wing, on the other side of the floor. Ask for Ginny's room."

Chapter 18

Ella had no trouble finding Lillian's room, as her weeping resonated through the corridor.

"Go away, you ugly witch," Lillian shrieked when Ella knocked.

"It's me, Ella."

"Oh, I'm sorry. Please come in."

Walking in, Ella looked around the spacious, well-lit bedroom. A window faced the garden, which featured blooming trees and a gazebo. There were no bars to obscure the view. A table by the window boasted a plate of boiled eggs and ham, a steaming cup of tea, and a dish with oranges and grapes. Someone had already hung Lillian's clothes in the closet.

Lillian, wearing a clean dress, was sitting on the bed. "I didn't mean to call you a name. I thought it was that horrible Miss Burke again. I finally got rid of her."

"Why is she horrible?" Ella sat next to Lillian. "From what I observed, she's a capable matron."

"She runs a madhouse." Lillian hugged the blanket tighter. "Haven't you read about places like this, where the commissioners found patients who were beaten and starved? Some had been trying to prove their sanity for years, and that only led to more abuse by the staff. I read about one woman who was tied to her bed and forced to soil herself. She had fits, like me."

"I read that article as well. You left it in the library. This is not a place of horror like what you read about. Look around this room. Won't you be happier here than in your mother-in-law's home?"

Lillian sighed and walked over to the window. After staring at the view for a few seconds, she picked up a grape from the plate and put it into her mouth. "The garden looks pretty."

"It's a beautiful home. Why don't you eat some breakfast and then ask someone to show you around?"

Lillian sighed. "I guess I have no choice. Please visit me often. I have no friends in the world but you."

When Lillian sat down to eat, Ella hurried down the corridor into the West Wing. Shrieks and grunts echoed through the walls. As Ella neared the door the noise came from, she ran into Constance and another attendant carrying trays with dirty dishes.

"I'm looking for Ginny's room and Dr. Miller," she said.

"Oh, that's poor Ginny you are hearing," Constance replied. "Two doors further."

Ella entered the indicated room and glanced around. A sour odor hit her nose. Dr. Miller stood by the bed where a scrawny girl with disheveled ginger hair moaned as she rubbed her belly. Ella recognized the child Dr. Miller saved from the public asylum. Yet despite the vomit on the girl's face and dress, Ella noted a serious improvement in Ginny's conditions in the three weeks since she'd seen the girl. Ginny looked like a sick twelve-year-old girl, not a skeleton. Her room was smaller than Lillian's and the furniture looked older, but fresh flowers in a vase brightened the atmosphere.

"I give her nothing but beef tea or gruel," Miss Burke was saying as she washed Ginny's face with a cloth. "She had a few good days until last night, when she became agitated and bit me as I put her to bed." Miss Burke rolled up her sleeve and showed a red mark. It stood out among paler scars, similar to those on Miss Burke's face. "And this morning, a bellyache again."

Dr. Miller put his hand on Ginny's forehead. "No fever. The illness must be of nervous nature. Something troubles the patient, and her digestion becomes upset. I will increase the dose of her calming draught."

"Did Ginny say what distressed her? Why she bit Miss Burke?" Ella asked.

Miss Burke coughed into her fist as if hiding a grin. Then she looked at the patient with pity. "Ginny doesn't talk, only grunts. Some disease in her childhood left her feeble in the head and incapable of hearing or speaking. But we are getting along." She patted Ginny's hair. The girl shook off Miss Burke's hand. Then her face scrunched and she whimpered, arching her back.

Ella's chest pinched. *Poor girl. She's hurting and can't communicate her needs any better than a baby.*

"May I examine her?" Ella asked. "I can do it when you change her out of her dress."

"Ginny hates being examined." Miss Burke winced. "She scratches, bites, and kicks like an angry cat. We usually need several people to hold her down so Dr. Miller can check her belly."

"Yes, I don't think it's necessary." Dr. Miller waved his hand. "I examined her the last time she had a stomachache. Her abdomen was tender and bloated. But the pain goes away in a few hours."

Ginny drew her knees to her chest and pointed to the floor with a grunt. When Miss Burke frowned, the girl grabbed her hand and pointed again.

Miss Burke narrowed her eyes but then smiled. "Oh good, Ginny. You've remembered how to ask." The matron knelt and retrieved a chamber pot from under the bed. She glanced up at Dr. Miller. "I will let you know if she improves. Your breakfast is waiting in the dining room."

If Ginny learned to show that she needs the chamber pot, she can learn other gestures to communicate, Ella contemplated as she followed Dr. Miller. *But first, her stomach pains must be cured.*

"Doctor, did I understand correctly that Ginny's on a strict diet of beef tea and gruel? Is it possible that the attendants offer her other food or she takes it from the dining room? Perhaps eggs, milk, or baked goods are upsetting her digestion."

Dr. Miller frowned. "I don't think so. The staff is well aware of Ginny's illness and watches her diet carefully. Miss Burke feeds her all meals to ensure the child eats and gains weight. As you saw, she's done a marvelous job."

"Then it could be... I once treated a shipboy who came down with severe abdominal pain every few days." She sighed shallowly, thinking of Tobby's scrunched up face. "It took me a while to correctly diagnose his illness. It turned out to be intestinal worms. The boy grew up in an orphanage, exposed to filth. Once I treated him with medicine made from eucalyptus, he quickly improved."

"It's worth a try."

He opened the doors to the dining room Ella had seen earlier. By this time, it was empty of patients. A couple of working-women swept the floor.

Ella and Dr. Miller sat at a table bursting with tea, bread and butter, cheeses, and appetizing tarts. She sipped her tea; the cinnamon and honey were sweet on her tongue.

"How is Miss Davis? Were you able to calm her?" Dr. Miller asked as he buttered his roll.

"Yes. She's seeing that The Women's Sanctuary is not as terrible as she feared. But she could be lonely here."

"Her story is heartbreaking. I'm shocked that Mr. and Mrs. Davis were so cruel to her. I'd believed them to be kind, caring people."

"It's quite a coincidence that you treated Mrs. Davis and met Lillian before, especially considering that her home was in a small village in Cornwall, far from where you lived or practiced."

He pursed his lips. "It's a long story. But yes, I saw Miss Lillian in her childhood, when she seemed happy and healthy. It's sad to think how much she's been through. I'm glad she has you as a friend. It's one of the reasons I have a proposal for you."

"A job proposal?" Her heart sped up.

"Yes. I want to make things right. You must've been extremely disappointed with how your university experience ended. I dismissed you just for being who you are. You deserved that diploma more than any other student."

I cannot believe I'm hearing this! He was adamant that women cannot be surgeons.

"It was disappointing to leave the medical school without a diploma." She leaned in. "But learning from you was a privilege. The knowledge you gave me allowed me to pursue medicine."

Dr. Miller regarded her with affection. "Do you remember the offer I gave you after you took your exam and astonished the professors with your knowledge?"

"You wanted me to become your apprentice and protégé. But you had a condition. While working with you, I had to continue disguising myself as a man. Sir, if that's what you're thinking, my answer is the same."

"No. I'm not asking you to hide who you are. I want to offer you the opportunity to work by my side. I would welcome you as a colleague in treating the patients in this facility." His eyes twinkled. "You and I can do great things together, Dr. Parker."

Ella had to remind herself to breathe. "I-it would be an honor."

"Please don't give me your answer yet. Take a day to think about it. If you accept, you would have to live here and commit yourself to the patients and the research that I will entrust you with. You won't have much time to visit your friends or former patients. I think it would be best if you told them you are going to be away for a while."

"I must consider this and speak to my friends. I will return tomorrow with my answer and the medicine for Ginny."

"Very well. I will be anxiously waiting."

Perhaps I should tell people I'm returning to my estate in Newcastle. That will avoid all kinds of questions. Only Matilda should know where I am, and... Oli Higgins. Although he mayn't take it well after how Dr. Miller treated him in medical school. What should I tell Jamie?

Her thoughts remained on Jamie as Dr. Miller escorted her to the coach.

Chapter 19

The young valet led Jamie through the long corridors of the Landons' house. Servants rushed about their duties, tidying up after the ball.

"Mr. Drake is rarely up at this hour," the valet said. "I told him you are here. Let me show you to the sitting room."

When they approached a half-closed door, dowager Mrs. Landon's voice echoed in the hallway.

"From what you've described, my dear, I agree. Your stepdaughter is not of sound mind. You will need two physicians to confirm, but I'm rarely wrong about these things. I hope you convince your husband that The Women's Sanctuary is worth the cost."

The servant halted. "I'm sorry, I didn't realize Mrs. Landon was receiving a visitor. I'll take you to the library instead."

Jamie's blood boiled as he remembered seeing Drake with Ella in the library. Trying not to listen to Mrs. Landon's loud praising of the sanctuary, he followed the valet.

When they stepped into the library, Jamie asked. "Could you please tell me... is Mrs. Arthur Landon feeling better?"

The servant shifted on his feet. "I'm not sure I'm allowed to say..."

"I'm not asking you to reveal any secrets. I was there when she had a fit last night. Did she recover? Is she up and about this morning?" Seeing that the servant stared at the floor as if hoping a hole might open up to hide in, he removed a coin from his purse. "Please. I'm asking for a friend."

The lad accepted the coin with shaking hands. "Thank you, sir. Last night, the doctor—"

"What are you blabbing about?" Drake burst into the room. Arthur stomped behind him.

The servant shuddered and dropped the coin. It clinked as it hit the floor and rolled under the sofa.

"You've bribed my valet to divulge information." Arthur's eyes bulged, showing the whites. He snatched the servant by his collar. "What did you tell him, rat?"

"Nothing, sir. I..."

Arthur's palm struck the servant's cheek with a resounding smack. Jamie felt sick to his stomach.

"Please calm down, sir. I have no interest in your wife and simply inquired about her health," Jamie said. "Your servant did nothing to warrant a slap."

A vein pulsed on Drake's forehead. With a bellowing "Out!" he shoved the servant toward the door and came nose to nose with Jamie. "Why are you spying in our house?"

Jamie's hands clenched into fists. As his gaze stopped on the sofa where Drake had sat so close to Ella last evening, his muscles tightened like a drawn bow.

"I'm not spying. I'm here about the duel. Perhaps there will be a second duel if you continue to speak to me like this."

"What did you say?" Drake's eyes blazed.

How I would love to shoot that scoundrel. And I can. He's no longer my superior.

A stomp made everyone turn. Dowager Mrs. Landon stood at the door with her face pinched into a grimace. "There will be no duel."

"Mother, we are—" Mrs. Landon's glare cut Drake off.

"I repeat. There will be no duel. It was all a misunderstanding caused by Mrs. Arthur Landon." She dropped her head. "But we must forgive her. She's terribly ill, as we all saw."

"His friend and he—" Arthur started, but his mother cleared her throat loudly.

"Showed kind concern." She put her hand to her heart. "It's understandable."

There's something false about this woman, but I'm glad she's here to stop this pointless duel.

"Mr. Leach didn't mean to cause an argument," Jamie said.

"I'm sure of that." She beamed at Jamie. "Mr. Leach's donation to The Women's Sanctuary was extremely generous. Such a nice young man. I hope we can resolve this disagreement."

Jamie's shoulders relaxed. "Yes, madam. If Mr. Landon will withdraw his accusations, the duel will be called off."

She turned to Arthur and stared until he reddened and mumbled an apology. "It's all Lillian's doing. She's not worth risking my life for," he added under his breath.

Coward. I'd give my life for Ella. Or Conor.

"Thank goodness this is settled." Mrs. Landon fanned herself with a hand. "Good day, Mr. Flowers. And you can reassure Mr. Leach or anyone else who asks that Mrs. Arthur Landon is getting the best care. The best our money can buy."

***

Relieved that his mission had succeeded, Jamie had a spring in his step when he returned to the Cooked Goose. He found it half empty. The hour was too late for breakfast and too early for dinner. Miss Jenny had taken pity on Tobby and given him a job, and he now swept the floor with a serious expression.

"Tobby, how are you?" Jamie asked the boy. "Is Miss Jenny making you work hard?"

The lad stopped sweeping and stretched his shoulders. "Compared to the ship, this is not bad at all. And I get to eat more. But I miss the other shipboys. They ran off."

Jamie tossed him a coin.

"Lucky day!" Tobby exclaimed as he caught the coin. "Dr. Ella gave me plenty just now."

"She's here?"

Tobby pointed at Ella, who sat in the corner with her back to them. Across from her was Dr. Higgins, his brow knit and lips tightened into a line.

"They are arguing about something," Tobby whispered. "Well, not exactly arguing, but not agreeing."

"It's not nice to eavesdrop." Jamie slouched as he walked toward the stairs to his room.

Ella's voice rang behind him. "Don't you see, Oli? It's an opportunity of a lifetime."

Dr. Higgins scoffed. "Ella, people don't change like that. Remember what he said about working with a woman by his side? Or about me being a Jew?"

Jamie forced himself not to listen. He was halfway up the stairs when Ella called his name. Immediately, his heart fluttered, then sped wildly. He turned and approached her table.

Ella bit her lip. "Do you know each other?"

"We're neighbors," Dr. Higgins answered, keeping his eyes focused on her. "Ella, would you like me to escort you back to your lodging? I hope you speak to Matilda and then sleep on your decision."

"Thank you, Oli, a walk with you would be lovely. I have more to tell you about that remarkable place." She stood and faced Jamie. "Jamie, I'm going away... back home to Newcastle. I will be away for half a year or so."

Jamie's breath and blood froze. *My heart won't last another six months. It's the last time I'll see her.*

"You've decided then?" Dr. Higgins raised an eyebrow as he placed coins on the table.

"Yes. It's what I want." A smile trembled on her lips as she studied Jamie. "I leave tomorrow. Please say goodbye to Conor for me and to everyone from our crew when you see them. Are you planning to stay here in Plymouth or go home?"

"I don't know." His voice sounded strange to his ears.

"Well, when you see your parents and sisters, please give them my regards." She took a long breath, then dipped her head. "Goodbye, Jamie."

"Safe travels." His lips spoke the words on their own.

Paralyzed, he watched her hug Tobby. She turned her head one more time and gave him a quick nod before leaving the dining room with Dr. Higgins.

My love, I will never see you again. When you return from your trip, I will be dead. Be safe and happy.

Chapter 20

In her bedroom, Ella stuffed her trunk with dresses, bonnets, and medical books. She also packed a medicine for Ginny. Her hands were folding a pair of trousers as she considered if she should take them or leave them behind.

I won't need to disguise myself.

The thought made Ella grin.

Matilda's voice murmured behind her. "What are you so happy about? Do you really think that pompous doctor sees you as his equal? He's likely hiring you to take notes for him."

Ella spun around to face her friend. "The Dr. Miller I knew wouldn't trust a woman to pen his notes. He has changed. Most of his staff are women, and he treats them with respect."

"Men like him don't change." The midwife crossed her arms. "What did your friend Oli Higgins say?"

"Oli also thinks that Dr. Miller is incapable of changing." Ella glanced at her hands. "He has his reasons. But I disagree. I've changed since I left my wealthy but lonely home. Others can change as well. Especially a genius like Dr. Miller."

Matilda scoffed. "I'm more inclined to believe that a cat can become a dog than a man like that would treat a woman as his equal."

Ella closed her trunk and locked eyes with her friend. "Matilda, this is bigger than me. This is a step for all women who want to be doctors. How can I refuse? And I already care about the patients, especially Lillian and Ginny."

Matilda left the room and returned with a rag doll in a tiny red dress. "I had a client with a deaf daughter. That child always carried a doll. It helped her show what she needed. This was Lindsey's doll. Take it for Ginny."

"I can't." A lump formed in Ella's throat. Lindsey was Matilda's adopted daughter. She had wanted to be a surgeon and helped Matilda's brother, Dr. Pesce, but died of consumption she caught from a patient.

"Lindsey would want that child to have her doll." Matilda sighed. "And she'd want to heal her. You are right, Ella. This is bigger than you. Show Dr. Miller what you are capable of."

Ella kissed the midwife on both cheeks. "If anyone asks about me, tell them I returned to Newcastle to check on things there."

"And Jamie Flowers?" Matilda stepped back and peered into Ella's eyes. "Will you leave without learning why he refused you?"

"I saw him today." Ella shivered as a cold sensation spread through her. "I told him I'm leaving. I admit, I wanted him to say something... I don't know. That he has some feelings left for me. But he..."

"He did nothing to stop you?" Matilda brought her hands to her lips.

Tears fell from Ella's eyes. "He... wished me safe travels. Matilda, it's better that I'm going to a place where nothing reminds me of him. Each time we meet, I keep hoping that he will say that he regrets his refusal. But..."

"Oh, my dear." Matilda caressed Ella's arm. "Perhaps you do need some distance from him. I give you my blessing to explore this new path. But please, keep your eyes keen and your wits about you. Among people who have lost their minds, that's especially important."

"I will." Ella smiled at Matilda through her tears.

***

With his legs heavy as sandbags, and his mind on the image of Ella walking out of the tavern and his life, Jamie ascended the stairs. As he stepped into his room, his forehead collided with Conor's nose.

Conor didn't seem to notice the pain as he mumbled an apology and shot down the stairs.

What trouble is he getting himself in now? Jamie thought as he chased after him.

He caught up to Conor when he stopped to hail a coach. "Where are you going in such a hurry?"

Conor stared at him as if he had just noticed him. "The man searching for my mother sent a note. There's a woman been brought to the Plymouth Public Asylum whose appearance matches my mother's."

"I'm coming with you."

Jamie was about to propose walking to save money, but Conor's face made him reconsider. Besides, a coach stopped, and the driver nodded to them to get in.

"Are you all right?" Jamie asked instead. They were jostled over the cobblestone road, and Conor's knuckles were white as he gripped his seat.

Conor blinked, not hearing or understanding Jamie's question. "That place is horrible," he finally said. "And the note said that my mother is severely ill." His face crumpled.

"You don't know if this woman is her."

"It's her." Conor rubbed his chest as he glanced out the window. "How is Lillian? Is she feeling better?"

Jamie sighed. "You mean Mrs. Arthur Landon. And don't you want to know about the duel first?"

"Don't call her by that awful name. And no. Please tell me about her and then about the duel. If she's not treated well by her husband, I still want to send a bullet into him."

"Stop it already!" Jamie threw up his hands. "Her mother-in-law said she's getting the best care their money can buy. She probably has the best physicians and caregivers attending her."

Conor sat back on his seat. "That's a relief. I was worried Arthur would send her away to an asylum. But if she's recovering at home, I could—"

"Forget about her." Jamie pointed his finger at his friend. "Arthur has withdrawn the duel, but any attention from you will provoke him. She's a married woman dealing with a serious illness."

"Something tells me I won't forget her that easily." Conor closed his eyes. "My father met my mother when his ship sank. He was one of a few survivors to reach land by boat, and her family gave them shelter. It wasn't logical for him to marry a woman living so far away from England, a fisherman's daughter. He was betrothed to a woman back home. Yet after he returned to England, he couldn't forget her. He broke his engagement, arranged for leave, and found a ship going to the West Indies. It took him nearly a year to return. He didn't know if she would be waiting for him—she had a suitor her parents wanted her to marry. But she was waiting, and they wed the day after he arrived."

Jamie rested his hand on Conor's shoulder. "That's beautiful. And I'm sure something like that awaits you, but with a different woman."

"You are right. I should be thinking of my mother."

The coach stopped at the Plymouth Public Asylum for the Poor. Jamie's gaze swept over the sign and the bars on the windows, and a thought flickered through his mind.

"This is where Mr. Olson is confined. We should see how he is faring. After we find your mother, that is." He added the last part as he sped after Conor, who had already paid the driver and was rushing toward the heavy door.

A portly man tried to block Conor's way, babbling something about a visiting day, but quieted when Conor put silver in his meaty palm.

"Is there a woman who recently arrived by the name of Marie-Louise Leach? Or perhaps someone who doesn't know her name?"

"No one by that name. But there's one we don't know the identity of. She won't last long with her fever."

Conor's head dropped.

Jamie patted his shoulder. "It may not be her."

They strode through the dim corridor behind the attendant. He brought them to a door, which he unlocked before walking away. Jamie and Conor found themselves in a crowded cell where half-naked women were chained to the walls or chairs. One of them cackled, and the hideous sound bounced off the walls. Another tossed on the straw, likely from a fever, muttering nonsense. Embarrassed by the nakedness and sickened by the smells, Jamie stared at the dirty floor.

"Is she here?" he whispered to Conor.

Conor made a step toward a woman who shook in a bout of fever, peering into her face. The woman moaned, then muttered more gibberish.

"No, that's not her. Thank God. This woman looks awfully ill." Conor shook his head.

An attendant, a hard-looking woman in her forties, walked in with a jug of water.

"Don't get too close to that one if you don't want to catch her fever," she said as she filled a basin with water.

"She needs to be at the hospital, not here," Jamie said.

The attendant shrugged. "Does it matter where this lunatic dies? She's delirious. Doesn't speak a word of sense. Not even her name."

"It's not delirium." Conor's head snapped to the attendant. "She's saying she must go home to care for her children."

Jamie and the attendant stared at him wide-eyed.

Conor exhaled a long breath. "She's speaking Portuguese." He said something to the woman, and she responded in a raspy voice. "Her name is Inês Ana da Conceição."

The attendant spat on the floor. "A foreign vagrant. Too stupid to learn English. Now I must go to the superintendent and explain."

When she stomped out, Conor's chin trembled. "That's what people said about my mother. I was ashamed of her for not speaking English. But I was a ten-year-old boy when we sailed to

Plymouth and felt at home here from the day we arrived. She, on the other hand, missed her village and grieved for the three children she lost."

"I never suspected that you weren't born in England. Although when we were imprisoned in France, I noticed that your French was flawless," Jamie said as he led Conor out of the gallery to the corridor, where the air was slightly less pungent.

Conor shrugged. "My siblings and I were born in a fishing village in Trinidad and spoke French Creole, some Spanish, some English, and some Portuguese we learned from my mother. She knows some English words, but she forgets them when she's anxious. I'm afraid that she's suffering like that woman, speaking her native tongue that people here take for nonsense."

Jamie's throat was parched. *Not speaking the local language is a dreadful reason to lose your freedom.*

He put his arm on Conor's shoulder. "We'll keep looking for her. Perhaps we can do better than the man your father hired. Let's make a list of places she could be and visit them all."

"There are worse asylums than this one. Just the thought makes me sick." Conor covered his mouth with his palm.

"I will go with you."

"You would do that for me? Don't you want to enlist on a merchant ship, like we planned?" Conor peered at him.

"This is important. You've won enough money for us to live on for a few months. Let's take that time to find your mother."

This quest will make him forget Lillian Landon. And help me not think about Ella these last few months of my life.

Steps thudded through the corridor, and the man who had greeted them appeared, followed by two women. One woman held a basket that seemed heavy for her, and another carried a violin case.

"Is that Bella and Cecilia Grey?" Conor asked. "What are they doing here?"

Jamie squinted in the dim light of the lantern the man in front carried and recognized the sisters. Despite their pinched faces, their steps were fast and determined.

"Mr. Flowers and Mr. Leach!" Bella exclaimed. "Are you here to see Mr. Olson?"

"Yes, we are," Conor answered before Jamie opened his mouth.

Right. He can't say that he's looking for his mother because he told them she's dead, Jamie remembered.

"Then why are you standing here?" Cecilia shrugged.

Bella sighed. "Please excuse my sister. When our mother taught us manners, she was out climbing trees. It's kind of you to come. We've been visiting Mr. Olson regularly."

A pang of guilt tightened Jamie's throat. It hadn't occurred to him to visit the sailor until today.

Their guide was already continuing along the corridor, and the four of them followed.

"Your friend is popular," he said as he brought them to the open door. "There's a physician visiting him."

"A physician? That Portuguese-speaking woman needs one," Jamie said, but the man had already walked away. They entered the cell, which looked more like a room. Not only was there a bed just for Olson and cheerful light from the barred window, but there was a vase with flowers and pictures of ships on the walls. Jamie guessed that the Grey sisters had brought those touches of comfort.

Those gifts, however, did not appear to calm Olson. He pressed himself into the wall, every muscle taut with fear. The short man before him stooped and clicked his tongue. When he swiveled his head, Jamie recognized Dr. Higgins.

"You know him too?" Jamie blurted out.

"Dr. Parker asked me to look after Mr. Olson. I thought to check on him before my hospital shift, but I'm afraid I can't do him any good. He's obviously frightened of me." The young doctor dropped his chin to his chest.

"Why did Ella ask you to visit him and not come herself?" Cecilia crossed her arms.

Dr. Higgins rocked in place. "She... is going away to her home in Newcastle for a few months. Are you Miss Bella and Miss Cecilia Grey? She was planning to write to you before leaving."

This was not news to Jamie and yet his limbs felt heavy. The sisters stared at the floor.

"Perhaps we can try to put Mr. Olson at ease while you go with Conor and help a woman in the grips of a fever. The people here thought her to be insane, but Conor recognized she's speaking Portuguese. He can translate for you."

Dr. Higgins lifted his case and followed Conor.

After they left, Bella gave Jamie a timid smile. "I hope we can coax Olson to let Dr. Higgins treat him. I believe the cuts on his back hurt. But he doesn't react when we speak to him. We even tried music but to no avail." She gestured at her sister's violin.

"Let me try. On the ship he responded better to me than anyone else." Jamie stepped forward. "Olson, do you remember me? Jamie Flowers? I came to visit you."

Olson's shoulders relaxed and his breathing became more audible. Jamie gave him his arm and eased him into sitting on the bed. But when he touched Olson's shirt, trying to remove it, Olson bristled.

"Perhaps you should try some music, Miss Cecilia," Jamie suggested. "Olson used to love listening to the fiddle."

Bella murmured that Cecilia had already played all her partitas, but Cecilia slapped herself on the forehead.

"How could I be so stupid? I should've played jigs or bawdy sailor songs." And to her sister's dismay and Jamie's surprise she played "Sally Brown." Olson stared at her as she played and didn't protest when Jamie pulled the faded shirt from his shoulders and uncovered horrible scars and an open sore that oozed blood.

When Cecilia got to the end of "Spanish Ladies," Conor and Dr. Higgins returned.

"Hopefully that poor woman will pull through," the young physician said. "We've arranged for her to be transferred to the hospital, recorded her complaints for the doctors, and sent a note to her family."

"Then I hope you can help Mr. Olson as well." Jamie pointed at the sore on the sailor's back. "Miss Cecilia charmed him with her musical skills."

Cecilia grinned and played "The Maid of Amsterdam."

Dr. Higgins bent to wash the ulcer with vinegar, and Jamie held Olson by the shoulder. When the music sped up, Olson belted out the words to the chorus in his full voice. "I'll go no more a-roving with you, fair maid!"

Bella's face became redder than a cherry, but Jamie, Conor, and Dr. Higgins roared with laughter. Cecilia put down her fiddle and doubled over, holding her belly.

When everyone recovered from their bout, Jamie asked Dr. Higgins, "He remembered the song. Does it mean that his mind isn't gone, and he will recover?"

Dr. Higgins paused as he applied a thick poultice. "I'm relieved that he has a private room and receives extra food and benefits from your visits. But I'm afraid that between those visits he slips back into madness. He needs more interactions with people, ideally in a home environment. Then he may regain his wits."

Bella and Cecilia exchanged concerned looks.

When the visit was over and the sisters left in their carriage, Jamie and Conor began walking home. Both men's steps were as heavy as their thoughts.

"May I join you, gentlemen?" They turned, and Dr. Higgins caught up to them. "I'm going the same way, toward the hospital."

"We'll be glad to have your company," Jamie said. "Your timing today was most fortunate."

"My visit would've been a waste if not for the ladies and you both. I have to say, you've impressed me. Perhaps I misunderstood Dr. Parker."

"We started on the wrong foot. I hope we'll be friends, Dr. Higgins." Jamie offered his hand.

The young doctor shook Jamie's hand and then Conor's.

"Please call me Oli."

Chapter 21

When Ella's coach stopped at the gates of The Women's Sanctuary, the guard greeted her.

"Dr. Parker, I will take care of your belongings. Ask for Miss Burke, who will show you to your room."

Ella took her medicine bag and left her large trunk for the guard to carry in. After thanking him, Ella sped toward the building, but then she halted.

I'm no longer a student in a hurry to class.

She smoothed her skirts and walked with her back straight, taking time to wipe her boots and to greet the cleaning woman.

In the hallway, Miss Burke walked briskly with a frown on her face. When Ella greeted her, she nodded.

"Dr. Parker, your room is ready. It's at the end of the East Wing. I'm sorry I can't show you there right now. I'm on the way to Dr. Miller's office to ask if he could give Ginny some grains of calomel. Her stomach is hurting again."

Ella dug into her bag. "I have the remedy for worms. I'll give it to the patient."

Miss Burke fidgeted. "I should ask Dr. Miller first. And Ginny will not take the medicine without me."

"Dr. Miller already said that we should try the worm treatment. And I have an idea how to befriend Ginny."

"Befriend? But Ginny can't—"

"Let's not argue while a patient is hurting." Ella marched toward the stairs, and Miss Burke hurried after her.

Moans and grunts pierced Ella's ears as she approached Ginny's room. Once inside, she found the girl curled on the bed and hugging her stomach. A tray with an empty bowl and a cup stood on the table.

"What did she have for breakfast?"

"Only tea and porridge as usual." Miss Burke sighed. "I fed her myself. And she had nothing for supper. Threw her spoon at me when I brought her broth."

Ella sat down next to Ginny's bed and patted the girl's back. "Ginny, do you remember me? I have something for you."

Ginny curled into a ball, and Ella removed the rag doll from her bag and put it on the pillow near Ginny's face. "Look, it's a doll. I understand if you don't want to play now, but you can hold your new friend while we give you some medicine."

Miss Burke touched her lips, perhaps to hide a smile. "I'm afraid Ginny doesn't know how to play with dolls. But it was a sweet thought. I think I better get Dr. Miller."

Ella's neck heated. *She's laughing at me. It used to hurt when men doubted me, but it feels worse coming from a woman.*

Ginny's sobs ceased. The girl lifted the doll, stared at it with her mouth open, and then hugged it to her chest.

"I believe she's familiar with dolls." Ella grinned at the matron.

"Well, that's nice. Now, I'll hold her down, and you slide the medicine into her mouth. She can't put up too much of a fight."

If only she could understand that we are helping her.

"Let me try something." Ella pointed to the doll's mouth. "Look, Ginny, your doll is thirsty."

Ella fetched the teacup from the table. She pointed again at the doll's threaded mouth, then brought the cup to it. With a shriek, Ginny grabbed the teacup from Ella's hand and, mimicking the game, brought it to the doll's lips.

"Oh, how clever, Ginny can play tea party with a doll." Miss Burke grinned. "But I believe the priority should be on relieving—"

Ginny pointed to her mouth and grunted.

"I think she's telling us she wants a drink," Ella said. She took the teacup from Ginny's hands and filled it with water from the jug. Ginny gulped the water in two sips, then brought the empty cup to the doll's mouth.

I can learn to communicate with her.

"Let's show we are giving the medicine to the doll. Then perhaps Ginny will drink the remedy."

Ella poured the medicine and, after offering it to the doll, brought it to Ginny's lips. Ginny opened her mouth and swallowed the medicine, wincing at the taste.

She then pretended to examine the doll's belly, and Ginny allowed Ella to palpate hers, whimpering at Ella's touch.

"What a good patient." Ella caressed Ginny's arm and turned to Miss Burke. "Her belly is bloated and tender. I bet she has worms. Please keep me informed on her progress as the medicine takes effect."

Miss Burke grin was unnaturally wide. "Yes, Dr. Parker."

She doesn't like another woman in charge of her. Well, she'll get used to it, Ella thought as she walked to Dr. Miller's office.

When she knocked, Dr. Miller bid her to come in. He sat at the desk. A bespectacled young woman slouched in a chair across from him. She did not look up when Ella stepped in.

Dr. Miller nodded to Ella. "Dr. Parker, I would like you to meet Miss Spencer, an East Wing patient."

Ella greeted her, but Miss Spencer didn't answer. Her bleary eyes were fixed on Dr. Miller. "Sir, I insist that I'm sane. Please tell this to my father."

"I've already written to your father. Unfortunately, you are not well at all. I'm afraid your stay here will be lengthy."

Ella's skin tingled. *Must she stay here if she wants to go home? Perhaps she's more ill than she appears.*

Miss Spencer hugged herself. "How long must I be here?"

"I cannot tell. But if you want to get better, you must stop spitting out the sleeping draught. I assume that's what you've been doing to stay awake and write." He opened a drawer and lifted a thick stack of pages.

"My stories!" Miss Spencer reached out for the crumpled pages. "Please give me back my manuscript."

Dr. Miller closed the drawer and locked it. "Miss Spencer, you are showing compulsory behavior. And your stories reveal disturbing fantasies. If you want to recover and return home, you must take your medicines and stop writing. Otherwise, I will have to try other methods. Now, I suggest you take a walk in the garden with the other patients. Fresh air and exercise are beneficial to you."

When Miss Spencer left, Dr. Miller invited Ella to sit. "What do you think of this, Dr. Parker?"

Ella folded her palms in a steeple. "Miss Spencer appears sane. Sad, but she has a reason. She wants to go home."

"Where she would speak to imaginary people and write at all hours. Her father found her crying hysterically over the death of a character she'd made up. She maintains that the people in her stories are real to her. This is why illnesses of the mind are tricky to diagnose. Insanity takes so many forms."

"What will you prescribe if she won't take medicines?"

"There's a treatment I'm experimenting with. It shows promise, and dowager Mrs. Landon has raised a great sum to make it available. But there are risks. Hopefully Miss Spencer won't need it." His shoulders tensed but then he relaxed his posture. "How was your morning? Did you find your room comfortable?"

"I haven't seen my room yet. I gave Ginny the worm treatment."

"Let's hope it works. Have you seen Miss Davis?"

"No. How is she?"

He rested his chin on his fist. "She had a seizure yesterday after dinner. One of the attendants was with her and prevented any serious harm."

"Is there anything we can do to ease the symptoms of her epilepsy?"

"You believe Miss Lillian has epilepsy?" The doctor peered at Ella.

"What else could it be?"

He drummed his fingers on his desk. "One time I saw such fits caused by a different condition. A boy... It was about thirty years ago. Unfortunately, I cannot remember in which journal I recorded my observations. I've had so many over the years."

A sensation reminiscent of butterfly wings brushed against Ella's skin. "May I read your journals? I'd love to learn from your vast experience. And I will find the case you are referring to."

"Hmm. Some of what I've written is of a personal nature, and I never meant for anyone but me to read it. But then, it was ages ago..." Dr. Miller went to his bookcase and removed stack after a stack of notebooks and loose papers, mounding them on the table. "These are all the notes about my patients, hospital and private, year by year. You are free to peruse them in your free time, which will be limited."

Ella took a deep breath to steady herself. *Every case Dr. Miller encountered is in these notes! Lack of rest or sleep is a small price to pay for the stories they will reveal.*

Her hands reached for the journals, but a throat-clearing "ahem" from Dr. Miller halted her.

"You can examine those later. Now, I'd like to introduce you to more of our patients."

Ella rose. "Yes, doctor. Don't worry, reading your notes will not interfere with my duties. And I thank you for trusting me with your personal records. I will be most discreet and focus only on the medicine."

Dr. Miller gave her a nod and opened the door for her. "After you, Dr. Parker."

Chapter 22

Dr. Miller ushered Ella into the parlor. There, several women embroidered or knit while others simply sat, staring into space with vacant gazes. A swarthy woman in her fifties muttered to herself as she mended a sock. Constance sat among the patients, patching a dress.

"The one that's mumbling gibberish we call The Lost One." Dr. Miller led Ella closer. "We don't know her name or anything about her. She was one of the few survivors of the typhoid fever that swept through the public asylum she was confined to. My colleague described a hellish scene. Patients rolled in their own waste on the floor, moaning and weeping. The corpses lay unattended for hours, if not days. Most of the staff abandoned their jobs to save their own lives. And this woman, along with the few brave orderlies who remained, walked around the sick, bringing them water and washing their soiled clothing and sheets. When a patient she had tended to died, she fell on the floor and wept as if it were her own child. But then she got up and cared for other patients. I heard her story and gave her a place here. Unfortunately, her records have been lost."

Ella's eyes widened. "Is her speech ever sensible?"

"No." He shook his head. "What would you say she's suffering from?"

Ella straightened her spine. "A shock so great that it resulted in amnesia. The memories of how to do things remain intact, but most other faculties are gone, including intelligent speech."

"Yes, I agree. I keep hoping to see improvement, but at this point it's unlikely. Let me introduce you to the other patients."

He nodded to Constance, and she jumped up to offer her chair. Then she brought another one for Ella.

"Constance, would you bring us tea and some of those delicious biscuits Mrs. Landon sent?" Dr. Miller said as he took his seat. "And please try not to get distracted this time. I prefer my tea piping hot."

When Constance left, Dr. Miller introduced Ella to the patient she was sitting next to. "This is one of our East Wing patients, Mrs. Beth Lowe. Mrs. Lowe, please tell Dr. Parker how you came to be here."

Beth put down her knitting needles. "Please, Doctor. It's too sad to think about. Now I'm well again and soon can return to my husband."

"Now, Mrs. Lowe, I agree you are doing better, but you are not well yet. It's too early to think about returning home." Dr. Miller shook his head.

"But I miss my husband and children." Beth's face crumpled.

Ella shifted in her seat. *I wonder how many patients recover and go home to their families.*

"Your husband won't take you back." The woman sitting on Beth's other side chuckled. "If you truly believe that he wants you to return, you're mad beyond hope."

Beth's eyes filled with tears.

Harsh, but likely true.

Dr. Miller gave the woman who spoke a stern stare. "Mrs. Helen Thackery, when you are socializing with other patients you must show kindness. That's a rule of our sanctuary."

"Beth doesn't show kindness to me." Helen threw her head back. "She calls me—"

"Murderess." Beth pointed her finger at Helen. "You've poisoned your husband. You said so."

Helen smiled mysteriously. "Perhaps. Perhaps not. If I did, I had a good reason."

Ella angled her body away from Helen.

Dr. Miller clicked his tongue. "Mrs. Thackery has a new story every day. Today she's a mysterious poisoner. Yesterday, she was separated from her lover by her parents, who had a deathly feud with his. Last week, she was a spinster who lost all hope of marriage and fell into despair. But when her husband, who by the way is in perfect health, brought Mrs. Thackery here, he told me that his wife is a different person every week."

Constance set the tea and biscuits in front of them.

"Perhaps you should be more careful with your words, Doctor. Or with your tea. Who knows what's in it." Helen's dramatic laugh made the hair on Ella's arms stand up.

"I think I will be fine." Dr. Miller took a long sip.

Ella took a tiny test sip but tasted nothing except sweet honey and tangy lemon.

Miss Burke entered with Lillian, who dragged her left leg as she walked.

"I persuaded Miss Lillian to join us." Miss Burke smiled at the patients. "Miss Lillian, would you like to embroider with your new friends?"

Lillian pouted. "They are no friends of mine." But then her gaze stopped on Ella, and her eyes brightened. "Except for Ella. You've returned! Come, talk to me while I play scales."

Ella allowed Miss Burke to take her seat and sat next to Lillian on the piano bench.

Lillian played scales. "I'm happy you are visiting me," she said without pausing her warm-up.

"Dr. Miller offered me to work with him. I readily agreed."

"I'm glad. I had another fit yesterday, and Miss Burke took care of me. Perhaps this place isn't as bad as I feared. The pianoforte is in good condition. Do you play?"

"Poorly."

"I want to play a melody my mother taught me when I was a little girl. My earliest memories with my mother are of me in her lap as she taught me the pianoforte. It was bliss to lean against her soft belly with my head on her chest and listen to the sounds the pianoforte made." Lillian's smile was wistful and nostalgic. "I remember my father walked in, listened to our practice, and said something like, 'We are a family now.' I always wondered why he said such a thing, like we weren't a family before. Now it makes sense... For a short while I made them happy." Lillian's smile waned.

"I'm sure you continued to bring them joy." Ella rubbed Lillian's shoulder.

Lillian sniffled. "Learning the pianoforte in my mother's lap was my favorite part of the day. But one afternoon, when I was six years old, I leaned back against her belly, and she yelped and pushed me off herself. She told me I'd become too heavy for her lap and might squish the baby growing inside her. The next day, she hired a teacher for the pianoforte. Father said it was a needless expenditure, especially considering the expansion of the family, but Mother persuaded him by saying my skill could help them find a husband for me someday. Anyway, this is what my mother often played."

Lillian started playing an upbeat melody just as Ginny ran into the room holding her doll. With keen eyes, she stared at Ella and Lillian.

Ella grinned. "Your belly must be better."

"Do you like music, little girl?" Lillian asked.

"She's deaf and mute." Miss Burke approached and put her hand on Ginny's shoulder. "Child, don't bother the ladies. I'll take you to the garden to play."

"She doesn't bother me." Lillian stopped playing and smiled at Ginny. "I'm Lillian. What's your name?"

Ginny continued staring.

"Her name is Ginny," Miss Burke jumped in. "Like I said, she can't speak."

Lillian pointed to her lips and spoke slowly. "Ginny. Now you say it."

The child blinked, and her lips shook.

"Let's go, my sweet." Miss Burke led Ginny away to the garden.

"I remember speaking with a girl who was deaf," Lillian said. "I spoke slowly and pointed at my lips. It must be another memory from the orphanage."

She's right. I can try to teach Ginny to read lips.

Lillian started playing again but then abruptly stopped and stared at her hands. Her pupils were enlarged. "I can't recall what follows... And my left hand is weak."

"You dragged your left leg when you walked in." Ella frowned.

A gasp escaped Lillian's chest. "This sickness is worsening."

An attendant rushed to Lillian's side. "My dear, you are upset. Let's return to your room to rest. We don't want another fit."

"One moment." Dr. Miller walked over and bent to Lillian. "Please squeeze my hand with your right hand and then with your left."

Lillian did as he asked and then let the attendant lead her away. Ella pointed out to Dr. Miller how Lillian's leg dragged.

Dr. Miller exhaled audibly. "I don't want to be right about Miss Lillian's condition. She had suffered much already."

Ella's stomach lurched. "Have you seen this before?"

"Yes. The case I wrote about."

"I will look for it in your notes."

She bid the patients a good afternoon and hurried to Dr. Miller's office. When she stepped in, a plain-looking woman was there, putting the journals back on the shelf.

"Wait, I need those."

The attendant shrugged. "Well, go on and take them. I must dust here."

As Ella collected the journals, the woman eyed her with a judgmental expression.

"What? Dr. Miller has granted me permission to read his notes."

"It's none of my business as long as you stay out of my way."

"I'm Dr. Parker." Ella thrust out her hand. "What's your name?"

"Ursula." The woman held on to her duster and didn't take Ella's hand. Instead, she opened a drawer and gave her a stack of papers. "Take these as well."

Ella glanced over the papers, but Ursula groaned and tapped her foot. Under the attendant's frown, Ella grabbed the papers and marched to her room.

Later that evening, she combed through the pages of the doctor's elegantly penned notes. As fascinating as each case was, Ella had to keep digging. When she spied an account about a boy having a seizure from thirty years ago, she knew she had found the correct case.

05 April 1783, Churcham

A dreadful incident occurred today. As I was walking down Willow Street to the hospital for the morning shift, I heard a woman's frantic cry from a first-floor window, "Someone help my son!"

Along with several passersby, I rushed inside to investigate. There, surrounded by his brothers and sisters, a boy around ten years old lay on the dirt floor. His left arm and leg twitched, and his face tightened in a grimace. Froth poured from his mouth.

While I observed the seizure, two men who walked in with me declared that demons possessed the child. They frightened the mother so much that I feared she would swoon. When they left to fetch a priest, I spoke to her calmly and explained that I was a medical doctor and wanted to help her son.

When the boy stopped twitching and opened his eyes, the mother calmed and answered my questions. Her son, Archie Smith, had been complaining of headaches. No recent injuries to his head. He vomited several times this week. He dragged his left leg when he walked and often dropped things from his left hand.

Hearing the men returning with the priest, I lifted the boy off the floor and told her I was taking her son to the hospital. Then I carried the boy out through the back door, avoiding the spectators.

Thirty minutes later Dr. Norris examined the patient in the children's ward. His diagnosis: epilepsy. I disputed that, believing the patient was suffering from a brain tumor, most likely on the right side of his brain because his left limbs twitched during the seizure. Dr. Norris disagreed and discharged the boy.

How frustrating it is to argue with my colleagues! I must start my own practice as soon as possible. Unfortunately, the only way I can afford it is by marrying a woman with a large dowry like Miss Amy Arnold's, even if I find her unattractive and dull.

Ella leafed through the journal to search for any updates on Archie's case. After perusing several months of notes on other patients and learning of Dr. Miller's marriage to Miss Amy Arnold and the opening of his medical practice, she found another record pertaining to Archie Smith.

13 December 1783

I had to deal with the most despicable people to obtain the body of Archie Smith. My efforts proved worthwhile. The tumor, 1.5 inches in diameter, was exactly where I predicted, on the right side of the boy's brain. I can't describe the emotions I felt when I opened the skull and found it. I was right, but that did no one any good. Not to the advancement of medicine, not to the dead boy, not to my career. I can't even share my findings with my colleagues because I can't tell them how I got the body. This journal will be the only record of the case, and no one will know what killed Archie, who died after yet another of the many seizures he'd suffered.

A punch struck Ella's gut. Why didn't she realize this earlier? Lillian had a brain tumor. Her illness was progressing, a sign that the tumor was growing and pushing on her brain.

Unless Dr. Miller discovers a cure, Lillian will die in a few months.

Chapter 23

Ella knocked on the door of a new patient. "Miss Adelaide Jackson?"

"Go away! I won't take your calming potions," a young woman's voice shouted back.

"I only want to meet you and make sure you are comfortable." Ella cracked the door open. When she poked her head in, a shoe flew only a few inches above it.

"I will get out. And when I do, I will make my stepmother regret this."

She has healthy energy, Ella thought as she ducked the second shoe.

"Miss Adelaide, I want to help you. I'm a doctor." Ella crouched as the patient raised a book to throw next.

"I'm sane! Let me out of here!" The young woman aimed the book but then set it on the table. "Are you going to take my books away?"

"Why would I do that? If books give you pleasure, you should have them." Ella made a hesitant step inside the room.

The young woman studied Ella and spoke in a hushed voice. "Perhaps you can help me. I'm not a lunatic. Please get me out of here."

Humming a song, Miss Burke walked in, carrying a vial of a dark-green substance. Ella knew that this was the strongest sleeping potion Dr. Miller prescribed.

"Time for your medicine, dear. And I must take your book away. The doctor warned you."

Adelaide's lips shook as she hugged the book to her chest.

Why does Dr. Miller want her book taken away? Why such strong medicine?

"Let me confer with Dr. Miller about his instructions," Ella said.

"Yes, ma'am. But you will find that I'm following them exactly, as always. He's in the dining room speaking to dowager Mrs. Landon." Miss Burke winced as she said the name. "Oh, and Ginny had another bellyache this morning. Your worm medicine did not help at all. Dr. Miller gave her a purgative and ordered me to resume the prior treatment plan."

Satisfaction seeped from Miss Burke's lips, and Ella's spirits fell.

She found Dr. Miller stirring his tea, a solemn expression on his face, as Mrs. Landon's voice rang through the dining room. "A beautiful building will not be enough. Bedlam looks like a grand palace from the outside. And plenty of other places offer well-furnished rooms and decent food. You must offer treatments that no other asylums could boast."

"Are you referring to my experiments with electricity?" Dr. Miller rested his chin on his steepled palms.

"I'm speaking of every kind of cure. This place must be at the forefront of advancements." Her cheeks flushed as she swiveled her head toward Ella. "There's a sign of progress walking through the door. I'm happy to see you again, Dr. Parker. Ladies in my social circle have been interested in you. I expect that in the next few months you will have new patients asking to be treated by the lady doctor."

Despite her dislike of Mrs. Landon, Ella's heart fluttered. "You think so?"

Mrs. Landon nodded to the chair next to her. "I know so. Perhaps I could organize an evening for you to tell my friends about the excellent care offered by The Women's Sanctuary."

"Unfortunately, my schedule is extremely busy. I came to check with Dr. Miller about his orders for the new patient." Ella shifted her gaze to Dr. Miller.

"Is it Adelaide Jackson?" Mrs. Landon jumped in before Dr. Miller could answer. "What a shocking case. Her stepmother is my longtime friend. What have you prescribed?"

Ella bit her lip, unsure if she should discuss the patient with the dowager. Dr. Miller answered instead.

"I prescribed the strongest calming draught available and ordered the removal of all stimulation, such as books."

"But why?" Ella interjected.

Mrs. Landon's chest rose. "Excellent, doctor. I will reassure her family about the diligent care Miss Jackson is receiving. And if the current treatment is not enough, you will do more. Her family will pay a king's ransom to have her reason restored."

"But she seems completely sane!" Ella clenched her hands. "Angry and defiant, but not ill."

Dr. Miller and Mrs. Landon became still and their expressions soured.

"Insanity isn't always obvious," Dr. Miller said finally. "Only when I learned some disturbing facts from the family did I become convinced that the patient needs to be committed."

"I still cannot understand how this could happen in a proper family." Mrs. Landon's eyes shined. "Surely the girl's mother indulged her. Despite the kindness my friend showed her stepdaughter, Miss Adelaide responded with the most ungrateful and disrespectful behavior. When I found her an excellent suitor, she expressed her refusal in vulgar language. Her family suspected that the girl had a secret paramour. They had her followed, and she was caught in bed with her lover."

Ella bit the cuticle of her nail. "Her behavior may be immoral and unwise, but that's not insanity."

" a *woman*." Mrs. Landon grinned at Ella's gasp. She turned toward Dr. Miller. "Doctor, don't you see why you must return to your experiments with electricity? If rest and potions are not enough, you must offer more effective methods. I found your article from several years ago where you wrote about surgery for insanity. You must continue working on that operation as well."

A surgery on the brain? Ella shifted to the edge of her seat. *That would be extremely risky... but amazing.*

"I was speaking in theory." Dr. Miller pinched the bridge of his nose. "Let's give my usual methods a chance to work. Miss Burke is excellent at getting new patients adjusted."

"Yes, she runs a tight ship," Ella agreed.

Mrs. Landon pushed away her tea. "I don't like her. That ugly deformity on her face—I'm sure it's upsetting to the patients."

Ella's skin prickled. *What a despicable thing to say.*

Dr. Miller stood. "Mrs. Landon, I've told you before. Miss Burke carries scars on her skin and in her soul from a fire that engulfed her orphanage. She's excellent with the patients. Now if you have nothing else, I must return to my work."

"It's not just her face. I heard rumors..." Mrs. Landon rose, as did Ella.

A vein pulsed on Dr. Miller's forehead. "That gossip is all nonsense, as I told you. I knew her when she was a child. Even then she was intelligent and caring, a little star in that dreadful orphanage. If you will excuse me, I will return to my office. Dr. Parker can show you out."

He turned his back on her.

"No reason for anger, Doctor." Mrs. Landon clicked her tongue. "I will keep my reservations about Miss Burke to myself. But I will return soon to check on Lillian's progress. If it's a tumor, I want you to remove it."

Dr. Miller turned slowly. "You are speaking of an extremely complex operation."

"Which is why Lillian is so fortunate to be in your care. Care her husband and I are paying for." She raised her chin. "I must go. Another appointment with the lawyer. This annulment is such a laborious and expensive ordeal. Don't worry, I know my way out."

After the visitor left, Ella followed Dr. Miller to his office. She sat in the chair across from the doctor. "I read the case about Archie Smith and his brain tumor. Lillian has the same symptoms."

"That's what I believe. A tumor on the right side, triggering seizures and headaches. I didn't want to tell dowager Mrs. Landon yet, but she was terribly insistent with her questions." Dr. Miller stared at his desk. "I cannot afford to offend her, as it would put the financial health of this institution at risk."

Ella hugged herself. "Regardless of all her charity work, that woman is a bully. Why does she want Lillian to have surgery if she's working on an annulment?"

"Because she's always preparing an alternative. The annulment will be difficult to achieve and cost a fortune. Her son must petition the ecclesiastical courts of the Church of England, a procedure that is extremely complex and rarely succeeds. Thus, she's preparing for the possibility that Lillian will remain her son's wife. In that case, she wants her to get better. Keeping a family member confined to a private asylum is also costly. Besides, she's an avid supporter of medical progress."

Does she want Lillian to get better or die from the surgery? That horrible family may prefer Lillian's death.

Dr. Miller scratched the back of his neck. "In my entire career, I've performed only one successful brain surgery."

"You've removed a tumor?" Ella leaned forward.

His gaze became unfocused. "No, it was a pistol shot to the patient's head."

Ella gasped. "I must read that case."

"You will find plenty of information in my notes from twenty years ago. Mrs. Alexandra Fulton." He said the name slowly and closed his eyes. After a pause, he opened them and shook his shoulders. "Twenty years feel like yesterday. That case made me famous. But it came at the right time. I was still young but skillful and experienced. If only I could shed the years and have the same dexterity in my fingers and clarity in my head..."

A cold sensation traveled down Ella's spine. "You don't believe you can operate successfully? But if not you, who else? You are the greatest surgeon in England. When I was a student, I stood by your side as you performed a successful appendectomy, saving a little girl's life."

His posture slumped and his chin dipped to his chest. "That was my last successful surgery. I've dedicated the last few years to researching the most mysterious organ of the human body: the brain."

Ella stood and walked around the office. The skulls that sat on the doctor's shelf caught her eye. "Without surgery, Lillian will die. How long does she have? Eight months? Six?"

Dr. Miller rested his head in his hands. "Less, I believe. Her disease is progressing quickly."

Lillian has had so much misfortune. She hasn't lived.

"We should tell Lillian that she needs surgery." Ella faced him. "She must know she has a chance at a cure."

"It would be her husband's decision, because an insane person cannot decide for themselves. But he signed a document saying I'm permitted to treat his wife any way I choose, including surgery. And he'll likely agree with his mother." Dr. Miller tilted his head. "But just because we can operate, should we? Remember the Hippocratic oath: '*First, do no harm.*'"

Her shoulders slumped. "On the ship, the patients brought to me were severely hurt. I didn't have to consider my oath. But about six months ago, I suffered a severe disappointment and found myself unable to concentrate. That day, I asked my assistant to take over."

"That was a wise decision. I doubt I would've shown such sound judgment when I was a young and eager surgeon." Dr. Miller quieted and scratched his beard.

Ella's cheeks warmed.

"I have something else to ask you. Besides the journals, I have read the records of the current patients. Who is Cora Butler? I don't believe I've met her." A woman by that name was in the papers Ursula gave her.

Dr. Miller's lips tightened. "She keeps to her room."

"I visited all the rooms in both wings."

"You must've missed hers." Dr. Miller checked his pocket watch. "Is there anything else?"

"Mary Murray and Jane Bell—who are they?"

He clasped his hands in his lap. "Those women died."

"Only a few months ago. And both were young West Wing patients. What happened?"

"Miss Murray drowned herself in a well. Miss Burke found her and pulled her out, but it was too late. And Miss Bell found rat poison in the storage and ingested it. Since then, we've increased the staff and implemented preventive measures. But I must say that once a patient's mind becomes fixed on self-harm, it can show incredible ingenuity in finding a method. Please be vigilant."

Dr. Miller blinked rapidly and looked away. Ella felt a tightness in her throat. *These deaths weigh heavily on him.*

After a silent moment, he shook his shoulders. "Time doesn't stand still while we sit here. Some of our West Wing patients are receiving a cold bath. Please find Miss Burke and observe the treatment."

Chapter 24

When Ella came to the West Wing, Miss Burke greeted her in the corridor.

"How may I help you, Dr. Parker?"

"Dr. Miller asked me to observe the patients taking a cold bath."

Miss Burke led Ella into a patient's room, where a woman in her twenties was curled on her bed, crying. Ursula was there as well, filling up a tin bathtub.

"Good day, Kitty." Miss Burke touched the patient's arm. "It's time for your bath."

Kitty buried her face in the pillow. "Leave me alone!"

"No, dear. You are here to get better, and this bath will chase your misery away." Miss Burke undid the hooks on the patient's dress.

Ella studied Kitty's shaking shoulders. *She must be suffering from melancholy. Cold baths are supposed to restore humors and give the patients vigor.*

Miss Burke removed Kitty's dress, leaving her in a white chemise. Catching Ella's gaze, she pointed to the long white scars on the woman's wrists.

"Kitty was a maid in a nice home, but the work was too much. Her master found her in her room with her wrists lacerated. Saved her just in time."

"Why do you think he was going into my room?" Kitty wailed.

Ella shivered.

Miss Burke patted Kitty's back. "Thanks to Dr. Miller, your troubles are over. You will get better and start anew. Now, get into the tub."

"You get in." Kitty pulled a blanket over herself. "That water is like ice."

Ella put her hand in the water. The cold bit her, and she withdrew her hand with a yelp. "It's way too cold."

"That's why it works." Miss Burke grinned. "I've seen patients energized the entire day."

Ursula straightened her spine and peered at Ella. "At Mercy's Asylum, the patients were taken outside in their underclothes and barefoot. Usually at sunrise, when the breeze is coldest. I saw it myself when I worked there."

Good Lord. How many of those poor souls caught pneumonia?

"You see, other places do this." Miss Burke nodded to Ursula. "Dr. Miller prescribes cold baths to all patients suffering from melancholy."

"I'm not disputing that the cold bath energizes." Ella crossed her arms. "But the water must be warmer. If you disagree, I suggest you both try Kitty's suggestion and get in yourselves."

Miss Burke approached the tub and dipped her hands.

She shrieked, rubbing and blowing on her fingers. "Blimey! Ursula, what were you thinking? Warm some water immediately!"

Dr. Miller's voice echoed from the door. "How is it going, Miss Burke? Did Miss Kitty take her bath?"

Ella came out into the hallway. "Dr. Miller, we should speak privately."

She led him to the stairs, away from the patients' rooms.

"What's on your mind, Dr. Parker?"

"The water in Kitty's bath was extremely cold. This appears to be Ursula's fault. And I have an inkling that she did this on purpose."

"Why would she do that?" He leaned in.

"I'm not sure, but I thought I should warn you to keep an eye on her."

Dr. Miller exhaled. "Thank you. Please continue watching her closely and report any mistakes to me."

Rapid footfalls resonated from the East Wing corridor. Constance was running toward them, her skirts bunched in her hands.

"Miss Lillian is having a fit!"

Ella's heart thundered as she sped behind Constance. Dr. Miller's breaths wheezed behind her.

"I'm too old... to run like this," he croaked.

Not waiting for him, Ella rushed into the room. Lillian thrashed on the floor, a pillow under her head. Her left arm and leg twitched. Ella called her name, but Lillian did not respond.

"I f-found her like that..." Constance pressed her hand to her chest. "And I slipped the pillow under her head."

"You did right." Ella touched Constance's shoulder and turned to Dr. Miller, who staggered into the room. "The seizure is affecting her left side more than the right. It must be a tumor. On the right side of her brain. Like you saw with Archie."

"Yes." He stared up at the ceiling. "Why? Why did it have to be Lillian? Hasn't she suffered enough?"

Ella peered at him, frowning.

Meanwhile Lillian's thrashing stopped, and her lashes fluttered. "What? What happened?"

Ella knelt next to Lillian. "You had another seizure. Don't get up. Rest."

Once Lillian fully came to and allowed Constance and Ella to help her to her bed, Dr. Miller approached and lifted her wrist to count her pulse.

"The fits are becoming more frequent. Why am I getting worse?"

Dr. Miller patted her hand. "You must rest now." He turned to the attendant. "Constance, please bring the calming drops from the dispensary. If you are unsure of which one, ask Miss Burke."

The attendant rushed away.

Lillian grimaced. "No, I won't sleep. I must know what's wrong with me."

Ella exchanged glances with Dr. Miller. He shook his head.

"What? What are you hiding?" Lillian sat up despite their protests.

Bending down to meet Lillian's gaze, Ella took her friend's hand. "We first thought you were suffering from epilepsy, but now we believe you have a different malady. A brain tumor. And we are considering if we might be able to remove it."

Lillian's eyes bulged. "You would cut into my head? That will surely kill me. And if I don't die, which would be a blessing, what if I become a complete idiot? I thought you were my friend, Ella." She withdrew her hand and covered her face as she wept.

Miss Burke walked in with a bottle and shook her head. "Poor dear. I brought your medicine."

"I don't want any. If I sleep, they will cut into my head."

Miss Burke gaped. "Is she hallucinating?"

"No." Ella's shoulders fell. "I'm afraid I said things she wasn't ready to hear."

Dr. Miller's lips tightened as he measured the dose. "Miss Davis, please drink this. We'll talk about the surgery another day."

"No! I want all of you to leave!" The remains of Lillian's strength seemed to go into her cry.

"It's all right," Miss Burke said. "Leave me alone with her. I'll coax her into taking the medicine."

"Thank you." Dr. Miller passed the matron the vial of strong-smelling liquid and motioned for Ella to leave the room. "Come, Dr. Parker."

When they stepped into the corridor, Ella's hands hung at her sides. "I made a mistake. Now she won't trust us."

Dr. Miller's eyebrows came together. "My heart aches for her."

"How long have you known her? I mean, before she became Mrs. Landon and you were called to cure her headaches?"

He closed his eyes and exhaled. "Let's speak of that later. Right now, we have patients." He offered his arm to lead Ella to the next patient's room.

Chapter 25

The rest of Ella's day flew by. Under Dr. Miller's observant gaze, she examined patients, learned their histories, and discussed treatments. Many of the West Wing patients, most of whom had spent time in other institutions, suffered from physical ailments as well as mental breakdowns. Their skin revealed old scars from beatings, and their hair was cut short in an effort to deal with lice. Those who spoke complained of hearing voices in their heads or seeing faces on the walls.

By evening, Ella was too tired to search through the entries in Dr. Miller's journal for his successful brain surgery. But her curiosity awakened her in the night. After tossing and turning on her bed, she gave up on sleep and lit a candle. She leafed through the papers until the name Mrs. Alexandra Fulton caught her eye. She leaned back to read.

1 February 1793, Churcham

I finally have time to record the most important case of my career so far. Last Monday, I was awakened by my valet, who told me that a constable had come for me. His words made me bolt from my bed. But then the man added that the constable was here to take me to a patient who needed urgent attention. Not knowing what I would require, I grabbed almost everything in sight, including the trepanning kit. Then I dressed hastily and came downstairs. The young constable asked me to follow him.

"A terrible tragedy," he said as we sprinted down the street. "I can't imagine the poor woman will survive. I saw your sign from the front door and ran to fetch you."

Thus it was a coincidence that I, and not a less competent surgeon, was called to save the victim, Mrs. Alexandra Fulton. I've met her several times concerning a delicate matter. Our first meeting happened when Mr. Victor Fulton sent for me because his wife failed to conceive a child. I examined Mrs. Fulton, twenty-two-years-old, and suggested she should drink herbal teas and tonics to stimulate her womb. I visited her regularly for several months prescribing those remedies. When they didn't work, I suggested the couple should take a holiday to the seaside. They left four months ago, and I haven't seen or heard from them since. Apparently, they returned last week, and instead of a blissful homecoming, a heartbreaking tragedy played out.

We entered the house and walked into the parlor where only four months ago I sat on the white sofa and explained to Mrs. Fulton the health-giving benefits of sea bathing. Now the same sofa was crimson with the blood of the mistress of the house, who lay on it motionless. Her husband, a man twice her age and highly unpleasant in face and manner, was in the room as well, held by two constables. His palms and clothing were covered in blood, but it must've been her blood because he stood firmly and showed no signs of injury. As I began examining the victim, unsure if I would find signs of life, he broke from the guards' grip and dropped to his knees. I thought he would beg me to save her life.

Instead, he said, "If she dies, I'll be hanged. Heal her."

The man cared only for his skin. I was relieved when the constables took him away.

Meanwhile, I found an unsteady pulse at my patient's neck and observed her breathing. I proceeded to examine her head wound. The bullet entered the right side of the forehead half an inch above the eyebrow and lodged inside. Blood oozed from the wound. I lifted her eyelids and checked her pupils. Her right pupil was blown, a sign of pressure in the skull. I had only minutes to act.

I asked the two constables who remained in the room to clear the dining room table and put the patient on it. Once the patient lay before me, I cut away a chunk of her auburn hair. Then I opened the skin with the scalpel and drilled three holes with my trepanning saw. When I opened the skull, a large blood clot shot *out of her head and slid onto the floor. My patient's breathing became deeper and more audible. I cauterized the hemorrhage. Removing the bullet was too risky. Nor could I replace the bone because of the bulging that occurred as the result of the pressure produced by the blood clot. I sutured over the hollow spot. Then there was little to do but wait.*

As I kept vigil, Mrs. Fulton's housekeeper informed me that all the servants, including her, were leaving. I was vexed by their disloyalty, especially since I'd always observed Mrs. Fulton speaking to her servants with kindness and respect. I promptly sent a note to the hospital to request an experienced caregiver. A woman came at nine in the evening, and I gave her instructions. She seemed capable and intelligent, exactly what I needed for the patient. At the time of my departure, Mrs. Fulton remained unconscious but alive. A miracle, considering the severe injury.

6 February 1793

There has been no change in my patient's condition. Each time I visit, I am accosted by newspapermen looking for details to print. Today, when I was walking to see my patient, the newspaper seller caught my attention by shouting the day's headline: "Mr. Fulton confessed his motive for shooting his wife!" I bought the paper and took it with me.

After I examined Mrs. Fulton, who showed no improvement but no decline either, I sat down next to her and unrolled the paper. "Three lives hang in the balance!" the first line read. Confused by the statement, I read on and learned that Mr. Fulton had had his day in court. When the judge asked him why he shot his wife, he accused her of infidelity and of becoming pregnant with another man's child. The paper fell out of my hands.

Before this moment it did not occur to me to inspect Mrs. Fulton's abdomen for pregnancy. I checked her belly and found a small bulge, easily hidden by clothing. When I examined her four months ago, her stomach was flat. I sent a note to my colleague who specializes in midwifery, Dr. Keen.

As I waited for my colleague to arrive, I finished reading the paper. The judge ruled to keep Mr. Fulton in jail. If the victim dies, the murderer will be hanged. Thus, the headline referred to the lives of the husband, the wife, and the tiny fetus inside my patient's womb. The writer then speculated about Mrs. Fulton's unfaithfulness, and his nosiness made my blood boil.

Dr. Keen arrived an hour later and examined our patient. He confirmed that Mrs. Fulton was pregnant, about four months along. I asked Dr. Keen the vital question: Was the baby inside Mrs. Fulton's womb still living? Did that tiny life survive the mother's injury and the operation? Dr. Keen put his ear to the patient's abdomen several times but declined to give a conclusive answer. Time will tell.

7 March 1793

I've been so busy that I've neglected my writing routine. The papers credited me as being 'Mrs. Fulton's savior.' The fame I desired had come but that gives me little satisfaction. Mrs. Fulton is still in mortal danger, and I see her daily. Meanwhile, at the hospital, my colleagues are asking me to give a lecture on treating head wounds, and medical students follow me to ask questions. I'm being consulted for everything having to do with the head, from simple bumps to insanity.

Mrs. Fulton has shown improvement over the last few weeks. She moves her limbs on command and responds to voices. Today, when I pressed on her belly, I felt the slightest movement under my palm. I called on Dr. Keen, and he confirmed that despite the odds, the baby is alive. There's tiny hope for the mother and the baby to survive the whole ordeal.

My private practice is flourishing. While I've alleviated some suffering, too many of those visits have been to the houses of society ladies who, during their exam, would ask about 'dear Alex,' the true father of the baby, and other details. Even though I told them that Mrs. Fulton could benefit from company, no one has visited the patient.

To my frustration, my wife behaves similarly. While vacationing in London, she saw my name in the papers and returned home. Almost every night she goes to social gatherings where she basks in attention.

10 March 1793

For the first time in my career, I'm crying tears of joy for a patient. Today, when I squeezed Mrs. Fulton's hand, she opened her eyes. Her gaze was blank at first, but then it gained focus, and she stared at me as if trying to remember who I was. I asked her if she could tell me her name, and she whispered 'Alex.' Then she moved her legs and raised her right hand to her bandaged head. Then she touched her abdomen. I don't know if she remembered her condition, but I thought to keep quiet until she gets stronger. I instructed the caregiver to say nothing about the shooting. Evoking those memories could give my vulnerable patient a shock she may not survive.

17 March 1793

This morning, Mrs. Fulton greeted me with a smile. "I feel..." She touched her belly. "Baby?" I put my hand on her stomach, and a strong kick made me gasp.

After my exam, she caressed her belly and asked, one word at a time, "Where... my... husband?"

While in my mind I wished for her husband to rot in his jail cell, I reassured Mrs. Fulton that he was out of town on business but would return soon.

10 April 1793

Mrs. Fulton is getting stronger every day. She's speaking more and asking about the baby and her husband. I told her she'd fallen and hit her head. She responded, "Oh no!" and caressed her stomach, which seems to grow larger each day.

I called on Dr. Keen again. He marveled at the patient's progress and agreed that Mrs. Fulton and her baby have a decent chance of survival. The baby, by his guess, is six months along, an average size, and is head down. He gave instructions to the caregiver to feed the patient heartier meals to build strength for the pregnancy and birth.

3 May 1793

Today, ~~Alex~~ Mrs. Fulton stood up and, supported by the caregiver and me, walked around her room. She breathed heavily, as expected after being bedridden and at this stage of pregnancy, but her eyes shone. When she became tired and sat on the bed, she hugged her belly. "Soon I meet you."

Her speech is becoming clearer, and she's remembering more words and names. Her mind, however, must be protecting her from the memories of the tragedy. Again, I reminded the caregiver to say nothing of what occurred.

8 May 1793

What a folly! After all that progress, a terrible setback. I was away for one day, performing operations at the hospital. A drunk coachman ran over two people, and I removed mangled limbs and set broken bones.

When I finally returned home, my servant informed me that the caregiver came earlier, asking for me. Despite my exhaustion, I rushed to see Mrs. Fulton. To my shock, I found the patient in the parlor, on the same sofa where she lay bleeding three months ago. She was unresponsive, her breaths shallow and infrequent, her pulse unsteady. The baby inside, however, kicked vigorously.

While I poured stimulants into Mrs. Fulton's mouth, the caregiver told me what had occurred. After eating her breakfast and walking around her room, Mrs. Fulton sat down to rest and asked the caregiver the questions she's asked several times before: "Where my husband?"

The caregiver swore to me that she gave no hint of the tragedy and answered calmly that he was away on business. At first Mrs.

Fulton seemed satisfied, but then she felt her healing head wound and asked, "How I fall?"

The caregiver stuck to the story we agreed on and replied that Mrs. Fulton swooned and hit her head on a table with a sharp corner. ~~Alex~~ Mrs. Fulton frowned, as if trying to recall this, and asked where this happened. This wasn't a detail we had planned in our white lie. Thinking that a near truth was the best answer, the caregiver replied that the accident occurred in the parlor. Mrs. Fulton slowly stood and asked the caregiver to take her there.

The walk down the stairs was difficult for the patient, but she ignored the caregiver's plea to return to bed. When she came to the parlor, she froze and stared at the sofa, now covered to hide the blood stains. Mrs. Fulton's knees buckled, and she slid to the floor. When, with significant effort, the woman dragged the patient onto the sofa, Mrs. Fulton mumbled, "He shot me." Then her face contorted, and her eyes rolled back. This was three hours earlier, and when I examined her, her state was the same.

I spent the night at her side, giving her stimulants and massaging her heart. By morning, her breathing had deepened, and her pulse strengthened. I sent a message to Dr. Keen, and he arrived promptly.

We discussed how to proceed. I proposed to perform a cesarean section at the first sign of the patient's decline or labor. Timely surgery could save both the mother and the child. Doctor Keen argued that the cesarean section should be attempted only if the mother died. We left the patient where she was and moved the

long table from the dining room into the parlor. This way, we were
ready for an emergency operation.

Ella glanced through several entries. Mrs. Fulton remained unconscious. Her heart and lungs worked, but she no longer reacted to speech or touch. It took a careful effort to feed her. Despite her grave condition, her abdomen swelled more each week, and the kicks inside grew stronger. The baby was getting ready to come into the world.

5 June 1793

Late last night, when I finally went to bed after a long day
of caring for patients, my servant shook me awake. Downstairs,
a messenger boy, sweaty and breathless from a run, told me that
Mrs. Fulton was in trouble. Knowing what kind of trouble was
most likely, I sent him to fetch Dr. Keen and hastily got ready.

As I walked to the house, I silently prayed for a miracle. If
there's virtue and fairness in the world, Mrs. Fulton should awak-
en as she delivered her child. Alas, my patient lay in the same par-
lor where she was injured and was just as unresponsive. Instead
of blood, however, her nightgown was soaked with amniotic fluid.
Her breathing and heartbeat were rapid. I checked her cervix and
found it dilated. The labor had started. I asked the caregiver to

heat water and find warm blankets for the baby. The messenger boy returned and said that Dr. Keen was away tending to another patient. It would be up to me to deliver the baby.

The next eight hours were some of the hardest I have lived through in my career. A young woman was losing her battle with death as the life inside her was attempting to break through and live. Alex opened her eyes several times, but her gaze was blank. As hours passed, her pulse slowed, and her breaths became shallower and sparser. At six in the morning, her heart stopped. One life was lost, but another could still be saved.

With the caregiver's help, I carried her body to the operating table. As I sliced into the hard abdomen, I regretted listening to Dr. Keen. I should've performed the cesarean section while the mother was alive. Relieved of the fetus, she might've lived. Now the child, if it survived, would be an orphan.

A slice of my scalpel on the uterus revealed a fetus curled in the head-down position. Its face was slightly bluish, but after I blew a couple of breaths into the tiny mouth, the child gave a feeble cry. A small girl nestled in my arms, her shiny eyes gazing at the strange and cruel world. Her mother just expired, her father imprisoned and facing hanging. I knew that Mrs. Fulton's parents were dead, as were her siblings. From what I heard of Mr. Fulton's affairs, he had enormous debts, and all his assets would be seized by the authorities. All the newborn girl inherited at her birth was the name her mother gave her a few weeks ago. I made sure that the caregiver and the wet nurse, who took temporary charge of the child, knew that she was called Lillian Fulton.

Ella rubbed her eyes as the morning light bathed the room. Lillian was born under terrible circumstances she knew nothing about. Memories flooded her. Almost a year ago she delivered a baby by cesarean section. Jamie, who appeared at just the right moment, helped her bring that baby back to life. A warm feeling spread to her heart when an image of Jamie holding the newborn came to mind. It was one of those moments that bonded them deep in their souls.

She shook her head, chasing the memory away, and looked for more entries about Lillian.

8 June 1793

I visited the wet nurse's home and examined baby Lillian. She appeared healthy and cried vigorously during the exam. The wet nurse said the child ate and slept well, and she had no complaints. Her expression was serious, however, when she stated she would only care for her until she could be weaned. If no relatives came forward, she'd take her to the orphanage.

If my wife had shown any inclination to become a kind mother, I would have adopted Lillian. Alas, I'm working day and night at the hospital and in my private practice and have no time for a child. My wife is taking a holiday again and sends me bills for new dresses and jewelry. She could never be the mother that Lillian needs.

I pray that some kind soul steps in and raises Lillian. The innocent child has already suffered more than she deserves.

Further entries shed no light on Lillian's fate. Dr. Miller managed patients, gave lectures, and authored medical papers. There was no mention of Lillian for several months.

2 November 1793

I finally found a day to check on Lillian. The wet nurse greeted me coldly and informed me that she'd weaned the child and taken her to the orphanage a week ago. She demanded payment. After dealing with her I hailed a coach to the orphanage on the outskirts of town.

While I've never stepped into the place before, I've treated many young patients in the hospital who'd arrived from there with illnesses such as smallpox, whooping cough, and scarlet fever. I've also treated orphanage children who fell out of windows or suffered other accidents. Last week I saw a six-year-old girl named Constance who scared everyone by vomiting something black and chalky. After vomiting some more at the hospital, the girl confessed she had swallowed a chunk of coal. Obviously, I had much concern about Lillian growing up in a place where children are neglected and get hurt as a result.

The woman in charge, Mrs. Mulligan, confirmed that a baby girl named Lillian was brought in a week ago. When she asked my relationship, I said that I was the surgeon who'd delivered the baby and that the mother died. I pretended not to know the mother's name. The terrible history of Lillian's birth could hurt her chances of being adopted.

I made a generous donation and said that I wanted to visit Lillian often. Mrs. Mulligan rebutted that if I didn't intend to adopt her, then it's better if I don't. I understood that as the child grows, she might get attached. I must stay away. However, we arranged that if Lillian becomes ill, the staff would notify me immediately.

As she closed the journal, Ella's head swam. Dr. Miller knew Lillian from her first breath. He cared for her health while she lived in the orphanage, met her adopted parents, and even tried to intervene when her new mother's life was in danger from a difficult labor with twins. And watching Lillian suffer from the symptoms of the brain tumor must be heart-wrenching for him.

Together, we can save Lillian.

Chapter 26

Ella's next day started calmly, with breakfast in the dining room in the company of the East Wing ladies. She longed to speak to Dr. Miller about Lillian, but when she passed him in the hall, his bloodshot eyes told her he'd had little sleep. She encouraged him to rest while she took care of the patients.

Once again, the breakfast table impressed with its pearl-white tablecloth, the delicate cups and saucers, and the delicious spread of strong tea, fresh bread, and sweet tarts. The patients ate with nice manners, and if not for the fact that some of the women murmured to themselves and laughed without reason, she could imagine herself enjoying a tea party in a fine home. Lillian was absent, but Constance, who served breakfast, reassured her that Lillian was eating in her room.

Constance poured tea for Ella with a smile.

"Ginny is having a fine morning. Miss Burke said she ate everything on her plate."

"That's great. Although I wonder what helped." Ella scratched her chin. "Constance, can I ask you something? Did you swallow a piece of coal when you were little and lived in the orphanage?"

Constance's mouth rounded. "How did you know?"

"Dr. Miller's notes mentioned you."

Constance tapped her head. "I was a silly child. At least I didn't swallow a pin, like another girl."

"Oh dear. You were inadequately supervised. Dr. Miller mentioned other accidents, such as children falling out of windows."

"Yes, one boy fell." She frowned. "I don't remember him much. He was a quiet boy."

"Such terrible accidents. Did you know Lillian when she was at the same orphanage?"

Someone cleared their throat, and Ella's face snapped to Miss Burke, who approached the table.

"How nice to have that much time to chat, Constance. Why isn't Beth here?"

Constance grinned. "A letter came for her. I was able to read her name. When I gave it to her, she said it was her husband's handwriting, and she wanted to read it before breakfast."

"You just gave her the letter without consulting someone?" Miss Burke's mouth went slack. "What if that man wrote something cruel? Beth is fragile!"

"I-I was proud of myself for reading her name…" Constance's eyes brimmed with tears.

Ella stood. "I will go check on her."

The next several hours Ella spent caring for Beth, who rolled on her bed in hysterics.

"He doesn't want me anymore! He took on a mistress and the children think of her as their new mother!" She wailed, clutching the letter. It took a strong dose of laudanum to calm her down.

At the end of the day of treating patients, Ella found Dr. Miller in the dining room, drinking tea. Seeing Ella, he motioned for her to join him.

"Thank you for taking care of things today. I didn't sleep well last night and felt poorly. I'm much better now. I heard Beth Lowe had a difficult day?"

Ella sat with her back straight. "Beth was hysterical after receiving a letter from her husband. From what I understood, his choice of words was extremely harsh. His letter snatched away her hopes of returning to him and their children."

"Unfortunately, her husband has the power to take the children away from her. How is Ginny today?"

"She surprised me today by saying my name. She's learning to read lips." Ella clenched her fists. "She's intelligent and doesn't belong in a mental asylum."

"I'm afraid an orphanage would be an even worse environment for her. Children can be mean and the staff uncaring." Dr.

Miller's shoulders fell. "I've made many visits to the orphanage where Lillian lived. Speaking of Lillian, how is she today? I heard her playing the pianoforte earlier."

Ella steepled her hands and rested her chin on them. "Lillian refused to speak to me. Thankfully, she's receptive to Miss Burke's diligent care. Dr. Miller, is Lillian the baby you saved?"

"Yes." Dr. Miller rubbed his chest, as if relieving tightness. "The tiny infant I removed from the womb after her mother died."

"All this time you kept track of her? You care that much for Lillian?"

Dr. Miller loosened his cravat. "I can't help it. I owe it to her mother. If my wife had any inclination toward motherhood, we could've become Lillian's guardians, and eventually her parents, after her father died in jail. But she wouldn't hear of it. Instead, Lillian spent her early years miserable in the orphanage. After her adoption, I tried to convince myself that she was happy, but a persistent unease gnawed at me. In every little girl I treated, I saw Lillian. I had dreams of her falling from a tree branch, of dogs biting her, of her contracting malaria. Insomnia plagued me so much that I required a holiday to restore my health. I chose the town near Lillian's new home, hoping that a glimpse of her would put my mind at ease."

His eyes clouded. "That's when I befriended Mr. Davis, her adoptive father, and examined his wife, pregnant with twins. Lillian became scared of me and wouldn't show herself during my visits. I stayed in touch with her father. He mentioned in his letters his wife's friendship with Mrs. Landon and their plan to send Lillian to Plymouth when she was of marriageable age. Occasionally he mentioned Lillian's headaches. But I didn't realize the severity of her illness until I saw her in Mrs. Landon's home."

"You are her guardian angel. You were meant to save her."

"If only I could believe that." A weak smile touched his lips. "I couldn't sleep last night for wondering what's best for our patient: a surgery that could go terribly wrong or letting nature take its course. In my younger years, I always advocated for surgery. But now I'm not so sure of myself. And it's hard for me to stay objective when it comes to Lillian."

Ella touched his hand. "I know what it's like to feel powerless, to doubt your skills. That hesitation cost me my job as a ship surgeon. But I believe in you and will do all I can to help. There's much from the two cases you had me read—Archie's brain tumor and Mrs. Fulton's head wound—that we can learn from. Let's discuss the surgery, at least in theory."

With quiet steps, Miss Burke entered the room. Ella raised a finger, warning the matron not to interrupt them.

The doctor's eyes were fixed on Ella's face. "Yes. It would greatly help if we had a cadaver for a dissection, but we'll have to do with books and previous cases. And there's something else that may aid us. I recently received a letter from a surgeon-dentist I know. We met eight years ago, when he pestered me during my holiday in Dorset to examine his son. What he writes is that he found some substance that makes patients oblivious to pain. He's been utilizing it during tooth extractions. He wants my advice on using it in surgery."

"This substance makes people oblivious to pain as he pulls out teeth?" Ella gaped. "That's impossible!"

"I have doubts as well. But to learn more, I've written back and invited him to come here and demonstrate his discovery. If what he wrote is true, the surgery could be longer and have a better chance of success. Now let's speak of how to remove the tumor." Dr. Miller drained his tea. His neck snapped to the matron. "Oh, Miss Burke. I didn't see you standing there. Do you require anything?"

Miss Burke grinned. "I came to report that all patients are asleep. Would you like more tea?"

Dr. Miller rubbed his eyes. "Yes, please. Dr. Parker and I will stay up late, planning the operation."

"To remove Lillian's tumor?" The matron beamed and stood on her toes. "Oh, Dr. Miller, this will be your greatest triumph."

"More likely my biggest defeat. Please, not a word to anyone, including the patient. It's a theoretical exercise for now."

"If anyone can do it, it's you, sir. What luck for Dr. Parker to learn from you." She grinned at Ella. "I will make that tea extra strong. It's a small part I can play in this grandiose plan."

When she swept out of the room, Dr. Miller exhaled a long breath. "Miss Burke is too kind."

Ella opened her palms. "I agree with her. It is a great privilege to be working by your side and learning from you. And I believe you can save Lillian's life."

With my help.

Chapter 27

Bright June sunlight streamed through the window, and the coach rumbled over the unpaved road, rocking Jamie. Conor, seated across from him, clutched a simple wooden cross, one of the few things he had of his mother's. Conor's eyes were red-rimmed, telling Jamie that his friend had slept poorly again.

"What's the place called again? The one we are going to?" They had visited so many Jamie'd lost track.

"The Women's Sanctuary. It's a private asylum for rich ladies. That's why I didn't think of visiting it before. But apparently they take charity cases as well. That could be my mother."

"Didn't Mrs. Landon collect donations for it at her ball?"

"I think so. It's our last lead. Either my mother is there, or she died from typhoid in that last place we saw. It's all my fault." He blinked hard and averted his eyes.

Jamie bit his lip. "Don't do this to yourself. You'll find her alive, remove her from the asylum, and care for her."

Conor nodded but stayed silent the rest of the journey.

The coach stopped by the tall gates. A man approached the window.

"Gentlemen, I'm afraid you won't be allowed in. Visiting day is Wednesday. Please come back then at noon."

Conor's face flushed and his fists balled. "Is that the only day you feed your patients decent food and give them clean clothes? We've visited a dozen asylums and know such tricks. If you don't let us in, I'll break the door."

He jumped out of the coach and stepped toward the guard.

The man retreated with his hands up. "I'll get the matron. She may allow an exception."

Soon he returned with a young woman with dark scars on her face. She gave them a curt nod. "I'm Lavinia Burke, the matron. Whom are you visiting?"

"My mother," Conor replied. "I've been searching for her. If she's alive, she must be here. Her name is Marie-Louise Leach."

Miss Burke gave him a sympathetic look. "We have no patient by that name. I'm sorry."

Conor's shoulders shook.

"What if she doesn't remember her name?" Jamie asked. "Do you have a patient who's forgotten who she is? Or speaks a different language?"

"Is she your mother as well?" The young woman studied him.

"No, I'm here with my friend."

Miss Burke frowned and shifted her feet. "There are several patients who suffer from amnesia or whose real names we don't know. Even though today isn't a visiting day, I will make an exception and let you see them."

She led them into the stately building that had bright flowers in front. There were no broken windows, as they saw in a few other places, and more surprisingly, no bars.

"I'll go prepare the patients," Miss Burke said when they came inside. "Some of them have never had visitors, and seeing you may agitate them. Please wait in the parlor down the hall. Most of the patients are outside, enjoying this glorious weather."

They found the parlor, a comfortable-looking room with sofas and chairs. One woman was there, sitting with her back to them at the pianoforte bench. She didn't turn as they came in. Quiet sobs shook her shoulders and back. Then she sighed and started playing a quiet melody.

Jamie sat on the sofa and spoke quietly to Conor to avoid disturbing the musician. "This place is much cleaner and nicer than others. If your mother is here, I'm sure she's treated well."

Conor remained standing. His gaze stayed on the young woman at the instrument.

Is that Lillian Landon, Arthur's wife? Oh no.

The way Conor watched, seemingly without breathing, told him it was her. Jamie's stomach tightened.

For a minute, she played, with the music flowing from her fingers like waves beating against the shore. Her long chestnut hair swayed as she reached for the keys. But when the melody grew more intense, like a warning of a forthcoming storm, the woman dropped her head into her hands and broke down weeping.

"Lillian! I mean, Mrs. Landon!" Conor rushed to her. "What are you doing here?"

She raised her head. Her face was even paler than before.

"Mr. Leach! I…" Her legs shook as she stood. She reminded Jamie of a sick bird he'd found as a child.

Jamie rose and stepped to his friend. "We didn't mean to frighten you, madam. Are you all right? Do you want us to call someone to help you?"

A grunt escaped Conor's throat, and his fingers flexed. "Did your husband send you to this place against your will? Is he hiding you away from the world?"

Her palm went to her forehead, and she quivered. "Please. Leave me alone."

Conor stepped closer. "He disposed of you like a broken trinket. He won't get away with this."

Miss Burke entered the room with another woman, likely an attendant judging by the uniform dress. The matron crossed her arms as she took in the scene and turned to her subordinate. "Constance, you left Miss Lillian here by herself? What if she had fallen off the bench? Take her back to her room and call Dr. Miller or Dr. Parker. Tell them that Miss Lillian needs her calming draught. And then check on Beth."

Jamie's ears pricked. *Did she say Dr. Parker? That can't be Ella. She returned to her home in Newcastle. And Dr. Miller... That was the name of the doctor who diagnosed me with a deadly heart defect when I was a boy. His words took my family's happiness away.* Beads of sweat formed on his forehead.

Lillian leaned on Constance as she hobbled away. When they left, Miss Burke studied Conor and Jamie. "You mustn't speak to patients without my permission. They are easily disturbed. Now, Mr. Leach, come with me." She gestured to Conor, then shifted her gaze to Jamie. "And you stay here, please. I'll send someone to bring refreshments. But please don't speak to any of our patients."

When Conor left, Jamie reclined on the sofa. After a few minutes his eyelids grew heavy. His daydream took him to the night in the woods in France when Ella rescued him. That night he let himself pretend he was healthy and that they had all the time in the world to love and cherish each other. They shared words of love and their first kisses.

If every day could be like those few hours...

A yelp woke him from his reminiscing. Constance was running through the hall, shrieking and waving her hands as if a wolf chased her.

Jamie sprang after her. "What's happening?"

The young woman turned and put her hand on her heart.

"If Beth jumps it's all my fault. I gave her that letter."

"I don't understand. Who's Beth? Jumping from where?"

"The roof! Dr. Parker said she'll try to climb up there and talk her out of it. But what if Beth doesn't listen? Miss Burke ordered that I take the patients inside from the garden. If they see Beth jump to her death... Oh, dear God!" Constance said all this in one breath.

Jamie's heart skipped a beat. "Dr. Parker? Ella? She went to the roof?"

Constance put her hand over her mouth. "I was told not to speak to anyone and not get distracted. Please, sir, I must go."

He grabbed her arm. "How do I get to the roof?"

"I don't know!" Constance tried to pull away, but he held her firmly. She exhaled and frowned in thought. "Beth probably snuck up to the top floor and found the stairwell to the roof. There's a locked door there, but perhaps Beth opened it somehow. You could try the same."

He sprinted to the staircase.

***

Ella forced her legs to stop shaking as she crept to the figure at the edge of the sloped roof. The surface was slightly wet from the morning rain. Her eyes caught a glimpse of the ground, and her stomach flipped.

Never look down! You learned that when you climbed the rigging!

She forced her breathing to slow and made her voice gentle. "Beth, please come away from the edge. Give me your hand."

Beth, barefoot and in her white nightdress, snapped her head around. Her pupils were enlarged, her mouth gaping.

"Why live? My husband doesn't want me. My children have a new mother."

Ella tiptoed closer. "No, you can't believe that. They still love you." There was some commotion behind her and someone gasped her name, but she didn't dare take her eyes off her patient.

With her body trembling, Beth faced the brink. "She told me I must jump. Then everyone will love me again."

Beth must be hearing voices that tell her to harm herself. Her illness has progressed to a new stage.

"Don't listen to that voice. You'll be terribly hurt or dead if you jump."

Beth tensed like a cat readying for a leap. Holding her breath, Ella lunged to grab Beth's arm. At that moment, Beth pushed off and jumped. Ella stumbled forward, grasping air. Screams and the thud of something hitting the ground came from below.

Ella bobbed at the very edge of the roof, waving her hands. She bent her knees and dug her feet into the wet, slanted surface. For a heartbeat, she caught her balance. But then, her shoe slipped, tipping her body over. By some miracle, her fingers found purchase on the edge. Someone cried her name.

This is how I die. Jamie, I love you. Those two thoughts flashed in her mind as her fingers numbed and her nails chipped.

Strong hands gripped her wrists. "Ella, hold on. I've got you." *Jamie!*

With a grunt and a groan, he heaved her upward, his breath ragged.

"Jamie, be careful. You may slip like I did," Ella cried as he gripped her right elbow.

"No. I'm on my belly and have my leg around the chimney. I won't slip. Grab hold of me with your other hand. You are almost safe, my love."

Ella's heart squeezed at his words. His head loomed above her. Staring into his blue eyes, she pushed her panic away and reached for him, grabbing his shoulder. Inch by inch, he pulled her up and dragged her away from the edge.

For a minute or two, Ella lay on her belly, waiting for her heart to stop racing. Wails from below reached her ears.

"Dr. Miller! Look, Beth is dead! Broke her neck." Miss Burke's declaration sank like a stone inside Ella's chest. Her throat constricted with the force of her silent weeping. Her teeth chattered despite the sun's heat.

Jamie's hands caressed her back. "Ella, you did all you could."

"I should've grabbed her earlier. I wasted time listening to her raving about a voice that told her to jump."

"Don't blame yourself." Jamie's kisses covered her hair and then her neck.

She turned onto her back and wrapped her arms around his shoulders.

"Jamie, how did you know I was here?" His heartbeat hammered under her ear.

"Later. Let me kiss you some more." He cupped her face and leaned to kiss her on the lips. She let go of her grief for Beth and the questions she had for Jamie and melted in his arms.

***

Jamie held Ella's hand as they descended the stairs and went outside. Beth's body was no longer there, and the front yard was empty of patients and staff. Once again, Ella was thankful for Miss Burke's efficiency. Only trampled grass and bloodstains on the pebbles revealed the tragedy that occurred minutes ago. With a lump in her throat, she led Jamie away from the spot and faced him.

"I must go to my patients. Hopefully no one saw Beth jump. The news of her death will upset them, and I'll need to comfort them."

Jamie's arms hugged her shoulders. "Ella, I understand, but please stay with me a moment longer. For heaven's sake, why did you tell me that you were going home to Newcastle when you were here, a short ride away?"

Ella locked eyes with him. "I found a place where I can heal minds and learn from a teacher I admire. But also... I'm here to get over you."

He pulled her so close that their hearts beat next to each other.

"Would it help you heal to know I love you with all my soul and I always will?"

But if you love me, why won't you marry me?

Before she could ask this aloud, his lips found hers. A thrilling warmth spread through her veins at his kiss.

The door opened with a screech. Dr. Miller was staring at her with his face flushed and his eyebrows furrowed so deeply there was no break between them. "Dr. Parker? What are you allowing yourself? The patients can see you from their windows."

Ella tensed and leaned away from Jamie, who flinched as he studied the older doctor.

It took a moment for her to find her voice. "I'm sorry, sir. I... didn't think."

Jamie took her hand. "Sir, Dr. Parker faced terrible danger up on the roof."

"And Mr. Flowers saved my life," Ella added.

Dr. Miller offered his hand for Jamie to shake. "Then we owe you thanks, young man. I'm grateful Dr. Parker is unharmed. But with the patient's death, this sanctuary has suffered a terrible blow. I must ask you and your friend to leave for today. Dr. Parker and I must care for our distraught patients. Your friend is waiting in the parlor." He turned but then spun around. "Have I met you before?"

Jamie stared at the ground and shook his head.

"Please let me say goodbye to Mr. Flowers. I will be quick," Ella pleaded.

Dr. Miller nodded and closed the door behind him.

"Thank you for saving my life..." Ella touched Jamie's hand and met his eyes. "If you want to give our love another chance, come back to speak with me. I'll be waiting." She stood on her toes and gave him a quick kiss. Then she rushed inside to find Dr. Miller.

As she climbed the stairs, a thought made her pause. *How did Jamie know to look for me here?*

***

Jamie lingered at the door, savoring the sensation of Ella's kiss on his lips.

Tomorrow, I will return, tell her about my heart defect, and let her decide if she wants to marry me. In the brief time I have left, we may find more happiness than some couples do in a lifetime of marriage.

He found Conor pacing the parlor. His friend wiped sweat off his forehead with his sleeve.

"What happened? I heard something about a woman jumping off the roof and that you were up there as well with Ella. Before I sorted out what was happening, Miss Burke said it's all over."

"Yes. The woman jumped despite Ella's efforts to save her, but thankfully Ella's safe. Did you find your mother?"

He closed his eyes and shook his head. "No. Miss Burke showed me several patients, but none of them is my mother. She must be dead. Strange, but I'm relieved. I was so afraid to find her among the helpless wretches, completely out of her wits." He shuddered. "But thanks to our search we found Lillian. Did you see how pale and thin she was, how she was crying at the pianoforte? I swear Arthur will pay for locking her away."

"You can't get involved."

When Conor thrust out his lower lip, Jamie ushered his friend outside. "This day was eventful for us both. Let's get some food to help us digest all we've seen."

I should tell Conor about my heart defect. But not today. He's coming to terms with his mother's death and the shock of finding Lillian in a mental asylum, Jamie thought as he climbed into the coach to take them back to the Cooked Goose.

Chapter 28

"Jamie, wake up!"

Jamie's eyes fluttered open. Conor was shaking him awake.

"What time is it? What's happening?" Jamie yawned.

"I need you to be my second." Conor averted his eyes.

Jamie blinked, forcing his sluggish mind to remember the events of the past day. After they'd returned from the asylum, they consumed a large dinner at the Cooked Goose, both ravenous after the eventful morning. He had thought Conor wanted to talk about his mother and was ready to comfort his friend, but Conor changed the subject each time he started the conversation. Later in the evening, Conor announced he was going out to play cards and replenish their savings. A noisy tavern or a smoke-filled card room were the last places Jamie wanted to spend the evening. He yearned for solitude to find words for his confession to Ella. Sleep must have overtaken him before Conor returned.

As the meaning of Conor's words reached him, Jamie bolted from his bed. "Your second? Did you quarrel with someone over cards last night?"

Conor, already fully dressed, picked up a shaving razor.

"Something like that. And we must hurry or they'll think that I'm a coward."

Jamie staggered to the basin and splashed water on his face. He was planning to speak to Ella today, but Conor's duel would have to come first. "I knew I should have gone with you last night. Whom are you fighting?"

"Arthur Landon. I asked around and learned that he and his brother frequent The Devil's Anchor. I went there and relieved several sailors of their coins. Then Arthur and Drake stumbled in with two drunk whores. When Arthur put a tart on his lap and kissed her on the lips, I confronted him about locking away his wife so he could tickle loose women. Then I challenged him."

Jamie's neck heated. "Good Lord. You went looking for trouble and found it. What were you thinking?" He grabbed his clothes from the trunk.

"I will kill that scoundrel and free Lillian from the asylum." Conor's eyes were wide and full of determination.

Jamie touched Conor's elbow and chose his words carefully. "You are pursuing a dangerous fantasy to avoid grief for your mother. Let me talk to Arthur and stop the duel. I've managed that once before."

Conor stomped his foot. "Absolutely not! I'm fighting for the woman I love."

"Come to your senses. You don't love Lillian Landon." Jamie rubbed his forehead.

"I will defend her honor and win her freedom." Conor pointed his finger at Jamie's chest. "Don't speak to me about love, Jamie. You're not the one to lecture me on the subject. I kept my mouth shut, but I will say this to you now. Your rejection of Ella's marriage proposal was a cowardly act. I know you are capable of courage in battle, but your fear of commitment broke her heart. I love you like a brother, but when it comes to Lillian, I will trust my heart and not your warnings."

He's right about Ella. I should've married her when she asked and made her happy every day I have left. When I see her, I will tell her that.

Jamie put his arm on his friend's shoulder. "I see talking you out of this is useless. I'll check if Oli is awake and will provide his services as a surgeon."

An hour later, Jamie, Conor, and Oli stepped into the meadow beyond the town wall. Despite the early hour, the air was warm. White daisies and pink clover covered the grass; the bees' buzzing and the birds' chirping sounded the summer morning melody.

The Landon brothers stood by the hedgerow. Drake approached with a swagger. His eyes, almost black, pierced Jamie's. "We won't accept any apologies from Mr. Leach. He preyed on my brother's wife while she was under treatment in a mental asylum. Perhaps it's the only place he can find a lady's affection." He curled his lips.

Conor's nostrils flared. "Shut your mouth, Drake. Confining a helpless woman to an asylum and then finding pleasure in the arms of a whore is despicable."

Oli's cheeks flushed, and his hands curled around his middle.

"He's provoking you on purpose." Jamie grabbed Conor's arm, then glared at Drake. "Let's get on with it then."

Drake flashed a mean grin. "While we waited, I thought to save us time by measuring the distance and loading the pistols."

"That's not how it should be done," Oli piped. "Mr. Flowers should verify that both parties have equal chances of hitting the target."

Drake rounded on him. "Who asked you? You are paid to care for the wounded. Stay out of things that are not your concern."

Jamie stepped in front of Oli, shielding him from Drake. "Dr. Higgins is correct. Code Duello requires that the second inspect the dueling ground and the weapons."

Drake's mouth turned downward, and he stepped back to his brother, who watched the scene pacing back and forth.

"I cared for a man wounded in a duel by Drake Landon." Oli stared at the grass. "He was sure that Drake cheated."

"Did he say how?" Jamie asked.

Oli shivered. "He died before he could tell me."

Good thing Conor is dueling Arthur, not Drake. But Drake will do everything to help his brother.

Biting the inside of his cheek, Jamie counted the paces between the marks, finding no fault. Then he dropped to his knees and inspected the spot where Conor would stand. He pressed on the patch of grass, and his hand dropped into a small hole.

"Why are you crawling around there?" Drake's voice taunted him. "Are you picking some flowers for Mr. Leach's grave?"

Jamie raised his head. "You dug a hole and concealed it with grass, hoping Mr. Leach would trip as he aimed at your brother. Dr. Higgins, I want you to see this."

Oli and Conor raced to view Jamie's discovery. The young surgeon raised his chin. "This cavity was created on purpose to make Mr. Leach trip or fall."

While the brothers denied their cheating with mock outrage, Conor shook from fury. "You have no honor, either of you."

Jamie marked new spots for the principals to stand. Then he walked up to Drake.

"Now, let me inspect the pistols."

He used the ramrod to ensure that both pistols were loaded, then carefully weighed them in each hand. "One feels heavier to me than the other. I suspect there's some trick with the powder, possibly one is double charged to inflict more damage. I won't let Mr. Leach use these pistols. You can watch me prepare the set I've brought."

"Again, I don't understand your meaning," Drake said. "You are using tricks to help your friend, but it won't work."

Conor kicked the ground, sending pebbles flying. Oli reminded him to keep his composure, but his words made Conor's face turn beet red. Determined to keep his wits about him, Jamie loaded both pistols and offered them for Drake to inspect.

Drake did a quick check with the ramrod and nodded. Before Conor and Arthur took the pistols, Jamie raised his hand. "I implore one last time to settle this without bloodshed." He locked eyes with Conor.

Please, please reconsider.

Conor and Arthur shook their heads and took their positions.

Jamie raised a handkerchief. His heart slammed so hard against his rib cage he could barely breathe. When he counted, the voice that came out of his throat seemed to belong to another person.

"One. Two. THREE!"

He dropped the handkerchief. Before it reached the ground, two shots boomed. A cloud of smoke irritated Jamie's vision. When he blinked it away, giddiness spread in his chest. Conor was standing with no visible injuries. Arthur was on the ground. Oli sped toward him with his medical bag.

Once he confirmed Conor was unhurt, Jamie said a silent prayer of thanks. They approached Oli and Drake, who were on their knees beside Arthur.

"Will he live?" Jamie asked Oli.

"I don't see bleeding anywhere," Oli answered as he held a small jar under Arthur's nose.

Jamie looked about. A trampled patch of grass caught his eye. He bent to investigate and ran his hands through the green strands. A hot ball rolled from his fingers.

"What are you doing?" Drake bellowed at the surgeon.

"Administering smelling salts. He's not hurt. He fainted," Oli answered.

"What?" Conor chortled, throwing his head back and laughing. "Did Arthur swoon from fright?"

Drake growled and his face darkened. "Be quiet, you fool."

Arthur opened his eyes and moved his limbs.

Jamie approached and showed the bullet. "I found it in the grass. No blood."

"I will be sure it's known that Arthur Landon fainted from fear for his life." Conor doubled over. "Doctor, please check if he soiled himself."

"Rest your tongue, Conor," Jamie said. "You've survived; that's enough."

Conor was wheezing, unable to stop laughing.

He's hysterical. Jamie flexed and unflexed his fingers.

"I will make you choke on your words." Drake lunged at Conor and slapped him on the cheek.

Conor's laughter died at once. "How dare you?"

"I'm challenging you to duel, right here and now."

No. Jamie wanted to kick the ground.

Drake stepped toward Conor. "I see no reason to delay. Let's reload the pistols. You've escaped one death this morning, but you won't escape two."

"I'm ready." Conor tossed his head back. "Finally, I will punish you for what you did to Olson."

"This is madness. Please calm yourselves and set another day to settle this affair." Jamie waved his hands. When Drake and Conor ignored him, he grabbed Conor's arm. "He just wants to save his brother's honor and change the outcome of the duel."

"The outcome is that one brother is revealed a coward, and another will die for his dishonor." Conor squared his shoulders. "I'm ready."

Sighing, Jamie loaded the pistols and offered them to the principals. Conor and Drake took their positions.

Drake is known as an experienced duelist. Conor has bravado but little skill. He'll kill Conor.

A daze clouded Jamie's vision.

Oli came to stand by him. "Are you all right, Jamie?"

"Count already," Drake said through clenched teeth.

If I stay silent, perhaps they will reconsider.

"If you won't perform your duties as a second, the doctor can take over."

"Why are you delaying?" Conor flexed his shoulders and shifted his feet.

To save your life.

Oli tapped him on the back. "What do you want me to do? I can count if you prefer."

Jamie didn't answer. His heartbeat was louder than the thoughts in his head. Louder than Oli's voice as he counted. Louder than the shot that whistled through the air and broke the wild rose hedge behind Drake. Rose petals spilled to the ground.

"A miss!" Oli gasped.

Jamie exhaled but then his breath caught.

Drake didn't shoot yet.

Drake closed one eye as he aimed. A sneer curved his lips.

"You are a poor shot, Conor. I saw how you aimed at my brother and knew I could kill you. Will you beg me for mercy?"

"Get on with it." Conor's face was ashen.

He's mad enough to shoot Conor. My life is nearly over, and I accomplished what I wanted. Ella, my love, I'm so sorry.

Jamie directed all his strength into his legs. As Drake's fingers touched the trigger, he reached Conor and pushed him away. Time stood still for a moment. Then a terrible force threw him to the ground.

Chapter 29

As Ella neared Dr. Miller's office, raised voices echoed. Then the door swung open, and Ursula stumbled out. She approached Ella and grabbed her by the hand.

"Dr. Parker, listen to me, please."

Miss Burke appeared in the doorway with her arms crossed. "Ursula, you must leave immediately. Your things will be sent to you."

"I know what you are up to! The truth will come out," Ursula vowed, but a guard stepped out of the office. He took Ursula by the shoulder and led her away.

"What was that about?" Ella asked as she stepped into the office.

Dr. Miller, sitting at this desk, shook his head. "Thank you for warning me about Ursula. I'm still shaken by what I've discovered."

Ella stepped back. "What did she do?"

"She was the one who left the door to the roof open. The door Beth used to get onto the roof and jump. Then Miss Burke discovered something even more disturbing. She caught Ursula adding milk to a bowl of porridge meant for Ginny, something she specifically told her not to do."

"You believe Ginny's stomachaches were caused by milk in her porridge? But doesn't Miss Burke always feed her?"

Miss Burke bobbed her head. "I often asked Ursula to prepare the porridge. She must've added a small amount; too little for me to notice but enough to sicken Ginny. That was the cause of her illness."

"I want to believe that Ursula misunderstood the instructions about the milk and left the door open by accident, but both of these incidents led to unfortunate consequences. Miss Burke recalled that the deaths of Mary Murray and Jane Bell also occurred because someone left a door unlocked. It might've been Ursula." Dr. Miller slouched. "She has been let go."

Ella exhaled a sigh of relief. "Good."

Dr. Miller rose. "And now we will learn what we can from the corpse of poor Mrs. Lowe. Perhaps her death can save Lillian's life."

In the cold basement, Beth's naked body lay on the dissection table. The odors of blood and decay pressed on Ella. She took in the grayish face and the shaved head. The thin hands of a woman who was still young. Her flabby belly was covered with stretch marks from several pregnancies.

Ella's throat squeezed. *Oh Beth… I tried to save you. Thank God Jamie was there to catch me, or my body would lie here as well. Why didn't he come to speak to me? I waited all day.*

"Is there anything else you need me to do? I can stay and help." Miss Burke's gaze moved between Ella and Dr. Miller. Earlier, she had performed all the preparations, showing no fear as she undressed the corpse, cut and shaved the thick hair, and laid out the instruments.

"You've been incredibly useful, as always," Dr. Miller answered. "Please ensure all our patients are asleep and get some rest."

"I won't be able to sleep, thinking of poor Beth." She sighed as her gaze lingered on the body and the surgical instruments. "I'll stop by later to clean up."

When Miss Burke left, Dr. Miller pointed at the broken neck. "Instant death. At least she didn't suffer… from the fall. Unfortunately, she hurt too much from her melancholy and her husband's betrayal. We did all we could to restore her mind, but when she learned the news from her husband, it broke her. And then she found the open door to the roof."

Ella's eyes widened. "I just remembered. Before leaping off the roof, Beth said, 'She told me I must jump.' What if she meant Ursula?"

Dr. Miller jerked back. "You cannot think… Most likely Beth was hallucinating."

We'll never know for sure.

He cleared his throat. "We must get started. Dr. Parker, have you ever trepanned the skull of a living patient?"

"Once." Ella swallowed. "A sailor fell off the rigging. He died during the operation."

"Show me what you've done."

Ella gripped a scalpel and separated the skin. "He died while I was drilling the hole."

"You must drill far enough but not make contact with the brain matter. You also must be fast. Would you like to try?"

Nodding, Ella raised the trepanning saw.

Dr. Miller placed his finger against Beth's skull, just above her right temple. "Here. Lillian drags her left foot and has trouble with her left hand—the growth lies on this side."

Putting strength into her arms, she bore a hole at the place he'd indicated. When she finished, she looked up at the doctor. "How did I do?"

His eyebrows drew together. "Despite your small hands, you are strong. But if you take that long, the patient is unlikely to survive. You must work faster."

Ella wiped her hands on her apron. "Would you like to show me your technique?"

"No, I want you to keep practicing until I see you can operate without killing the patient."

Ella's lips tightened, and she bore another hole. A loud crack made her curse under her breath. "I broke the bone and drilled into the brain, didn't I?"

"I'm afraid you've killed your patient for the second time with this surgery. This time you were too forceful and too fast." Dr. Miller clicked his tongue. "Good thing trepanning wasn't on your final exam. You impressed the committee with your thesis and correct answers to their questions. But if they had witnessed this..."

"And a male student would have done better?" Anger flowed into Ella's hands. She gritted her teeth and bore a third hole. This time she was quick and stopped in time to avoid the brain matter. "I believe that one was successful." She raised her eyes to Dr. Miller's.

His grin was one of the widest she had seen from him. "It seems this has a chance after all."

Heat rushed to Ella's cheeks. "You vexed me on purpose, didn't you?"

"It worked. You now have a sense for how it must be done. The surgeon-dentist I mentioned should be here tomorrow, and we shall learn about his find. But now, please give me a chance to do some exploring of my own."

Ella passed him a scalpel. "What is it you're trying to study, Doctor?"

Dr. Miller rocked in place. "Why was Beth afflicted with melancholy? Hippocrates blamed the womb. Other early doctors believed a worm travels around the abdominal cavity and rules moods. We now know that the brain handles actions and thoughts. What was wrong with Beth's brain that caused her illness?"

"Do you believe her brain had a deformity that we can see?"

"Yes. Perhaps some time soon, an insane person will be able to go under the knife, and a surgeon could fix an anomaly in their brain. The other owner of The Women's Sanctuary is a proponent of such a surgery and wants to offer it as an experimental treatment." The doctor lifted the dura and pointed. "This is the prefrontal cortex. Severing connections to it may make the patient calm and obedient. At least, that's my theory."

A cool sensation traveled through Ella's veins. She was amazed and terrified.

"It sounds... like a revolutionary treatment."

"Exactly."

Chapter 30

Lillian's sobs sounded through the door as Ella knocked. "Lillian, can we talk, please?"

"Come in." Lillian's voice was just above a whisper.

When Ella entered, Lillian was sitting at the table with her breakfast untouched before her. Tears streamed down her cheeks.

Ella sat down on the bed. "How are you?"

"Ill. Lonely. And the last two days, sick to my stomach. Poor Beth." She moved the plate with eggs further away.

"Oh dear, did you see her jump?" Ella leaned in.

"I saw her body carried inside... She was covered by a sheet, but there was blood, and for a moment her face came uncovered. Those dead eyes. I can't shake it off." Lillian stood up and paced the chamber, dragging her left leg. "I heard you were on the roof as well and almost fell."

Ella shuddered as the view from the edge came to her mind. *Jamie, where are you? It's been three days. You saved me from falling to my death and disappeared again.*

"I did all I could to save her. But it wasn't enough."

Lillian stopped pacing and faced Ella. "I'm sorry for treating you so poorly the last couple weeks. You are a hero for risking your own life for Beth. And my only friend. Are you sure I can trust Dr. Miller and let him operate on my brain?"

Ella gestured for Lillian to sit next to her and took her hand. "I'm more sure than ever. Last night we worked out a detailed plan for the surgery. Dr. Miller taught me a great deal about trepanning, which is how he'll get to the tumor. We guess that it's on the right side because your left limbs are affected. It's risky surgery, but it gives you a chance to be cured. If you don't have surgery, you will die."

"Once again, I don't have any good choices." Lillian dropped her head. "Letting the disease kill me or undergoing a surgery that has a miniscule chance of success. I was thinking of taking my own life. After seeing Beth's body, I don't want to die like her. I want to live. I will have to take my only chance at getting better." She straightened and wiped her tears

Ella peered into her friend's eyes. "Beth's suicide awakened your will to fight?"

"Not exactly. Do you remember Mr. Leach from the ball?"

"I know him well. We served on the same ship and are good friends. Why?"

A faint blush bloomed on Lillian's cheeks. "He was here yesterday. I think he's infatuated with me. I know this is silly, but after seeing him I spent much of the night thinking of a future I could have if I recover. My marriage to Arthur will be annulled. And I could build a new life. I don't know Mr. Leach, but both times I saw him, I've trembled from head to toe and my heart danced. My own reaction scared me yesterday, yet it made me feel alive. Despite all I've been through, I'm still capable of love. I'm not saying that I love him. What I want is a chance at a future where I love someone and am loved."

"I didn't know he was here yesterday. You and Conor would make a lovely couple." Ella grinned. "I'm glad he inspired you to fight for your life. So you've decided on surgery?"

"I have one reservation. Can I trust Dr. Miller? It's so unsettling to me that he was the same surgeon who was going to operate on my mother when she carried twins. At times I get the feeling that I saw him even before that. I remember being a little girl, ill with a fever, and him feeling my forehead and giving me some medicine to drink. I thought it was a dream, but perhaps not. If he visited me in the orphanage, it can't be a coincidence. He followed me from one place to another since I was a child. Why? He must have some kind of sinister motive."

I must tell her. It's the only way to build her trust.

Ella filled her lungs. "Lillian, it's true what you've suspected. Dr. Miller has followed you all your life to be near when you needed him. He cared for you since the first moments of your birth. He performed brilliant surgery on your mother, Mrs. Alexandra Fulton, who was shot in the head."

Lillian jerked away. "What? By whom?"

Ella decided to be truthful. After all, Lillian didn't remember her parents. "By your father."

"In some sort of an accident?" Lillian covered her mouth.

"No. In a fit of rage and jealousy. He died in prison."

"What about my mother?"

"She survived for several months after the injury, thanks to the diligent care of Dr. Miller. Long enough to give you life. When she died, Dr. Miller delivered you."

Lillian sat spellbound as Ella retold the details in the doctor's journal. When Ella finished, her friend continued sitting for a few minutes without moving a muscle. Finally, Lillian rose, her legs wobbling.

"I must speak to Dr. Miller."

Ella hesitated, but seeing Lillian's burning eyes and shaking lips, she offered her arm to take her to Dr. Miller.

They found Dr. Miller at the foot of the stairs. He was holding his case.

"I was on my way to do rounds of the West Wing patients." He bowed to Lillian. "How are you this morning?"

Lillian stepped closer. "Dr. Miller, now I know how much you care about me. You tried to save my mother and saved my life during my birth. Please save me again. Remove the tumor and heal me. I want to live."

Tears glistened in Dr. Miller's eyes.

"You are as strong and brave as your mother."

Lillian joined hands with Dr. Miller and Ella. Dr. Miller's grip squeezed Ella's left hand, while Lillian clasped Ella's right like a child holding on for balance.

This will be a radical surgery. But if there's a surgeon who can save Lillian, it's Dr. Miller.

"Oh my, what's happening?" Miss Burke floated in from the corridor in her noiseless manner. "I believe I can guess. Miss Lillian decided to undergo surgery. It will be an incredible success, I'm sure."

"Yes, let's hope it will be a success." Dr. Miller wiped sweat off his forehead. "Did the surgeon-dentist arrive?"

"No, but you have a visitor. A young woman by the name of Miss Caroline Flowers. I showed her to your office."

Ella's breath caught as a grin spread on her lips. "Did you say Miss Flowers?"

"Flowers?" Dr. Miller frowned. "That's the name of the surgeon-dentist who claimed he could put patients to sleep. Why is she here?"

"She's the surgeon's daughter. Said her father couldn't travel," Miss Burke replied.

Jamie's older sister! Ella's heart fluttered from memories of playing and conversing with the witty girl who was slightly older than her.

Dr. Miller glanced at his pocket watch. "I must tend to a couple of patients. Please ask her to wait. And please take Miss Lillian to her room and make sure she eats her breakfast." He nodded to Lillian. "We need you strong for the surgery."

When Lillian left with Miss Burke, Ella turned to Dr. Miller. "Why don't I speak to Miss Flowers while you do the rounds?"

"I would appreciate it. I'm confused as to why this young lady is here. I hope she didn't travel from Dorset just to say that her father is indisposed."

Constance approached, breathing hard. "Dr. Miller, Mrs. Landon is here. Not Lillian. You know the one."

Dr. Miller grunted. "She'll want an update about Lillian's surgery. All right, I shall go meet her. I cannot ask her to wait."

While he left to greet the dowager, Ella sped to his office and threw open the door. A brown-haired young woman was peering at a skull in her hands. She almost dropped it when she turned.

"Caroline Flowers, what in the world are you doing here, my friend?"

"Ella Parker?" Caroline returned the skull to the shelf and wrapped Ella in her embrace. They shrieked with delight like little girls.

Caroline stepped back, studying Ella. "You promised to become a beauty, but you've surpassed the expectation. Don't bother with returning the compliment because I know the truth. I'm not the pretty sister. I'm the bookish and peculiar one. But what are *you* doing here?"

"I work here. As a physician and a surgeon."

Caroline gaped. "But how?"

"I disguised myself as a man and studied in medical school. Then my mentor, Dr. Joseph Pesce, invited me to be his assistant on a Royal Navy ship. When he became injured, the captain promoted me to ship surgeon. And now my medical school professor, Dr. Miller, hired me to collaborate with him in this marvelous institution."

"Incredible! Since Dr. Miller accepted you as a fellow doctor, perhaps..." Caroline rubbed the back of her neck. "Perhaps he won't mind that I've come instead of my father. He's become frail lately, and we feared the journey would make him worse. Then, a week ago, he twisted his ankle, and that sealed my decision to come without him."

"I hope he recovers quickly. So... you are here alone?" Ella leaned on the desk.

"Oh no, my mother would never allow that." Caroline giggled. "I've come with my old nurse, Mrs. Armstrong. She's nearby, likely hiding in the hedge. She vowed that if I didn't come out by noon, she'd find constables to tell them I'm being committed to the asylum against my will."

"No need for such precautions. But we require your father because he wrote he puts his patients into a deep sleep for painful procedures. There's a patient here with a brain tumor, and we must operate to remove it. We had much hope that your father would help us save this woman's life."

Caroline threw her shoulders back. "I was the one who discovered how ether works during one of my chemistry experiments. I distilled alcohol with acids and didn't take precautions; I inhaled a whiff. I heard my parents speaking, but I didn't feel them dragging me to the couch and loosening my corset."

"You are the inventor!" Ella clapped her hands.

Caroline gave a dismissive wave. "It's not so much an invention as applying what was known in a new way. I was following an experiment from William Nicholson's *A Dictionary of Chemistry*. My parents forbid further experiments, but I've worked while they slept and enlisted my sisters for help. I would administer different doses and methods, and they would poke me or yell into my ears. After waking, I would record my sensations. My first patient was our dog, Lucy. A thorn became stuck deep in her paw. I put Lucy to sleep, and my father removed the thorn. When she woke up and barked, father allowed me to show him all I've learned about ether and administer it to him. Soon, he let me work on his patients who were willing. Most don't want to be put to sleep and even think that it's the devil's work. But I believe my discovery has potential, especially in the hands of a great surgeon like Dr. Miller."

"Absolutely! It was a good thing that your father wrote to him."

Caroline's cheeks reddened. "It was my letter. I signed the letter as C.J. Flowers. J for Jamie, in his honor." A shadow crossed her face.

"When did you arrive?" Ella asked.

"Just this morning; I came straight here. The woman who met me, Miss Burke, brought me breakfast. She asked many great questions about how ether works."

"And I have many more." Dr. Miller entered the room with Miss Burke and dowager Mrs. Landon. "Except I'd planned on asking Mr. Flowers, the surgeon-dentist I met eight years ago. Unless my eyes deceive me, you are not he."

"May I present his daughter, Miss Caroline Flowers. She has the knowledge we need." Ella gestured to Caroline, who curt-sied. "She anesthetizes patients while her father extracts their teeth."

Dr. Miller raised an eyebrow. "In that case, I'd like to see you demonstrate how it works."

"Oh, me too. This is fascinating. May I stay to watch?" Miss Burke pleaded.

"If your duties allow," Dr. Miller replied.

"I will watch as well." Mrs. Landon said. "I want to see what you are planning for Lillian's surgery."

Dr. Miller frowned but then addressed Caroline. "Miss Flowers, what do you require for the demonstration?"

Caroline lifted her case. "I need a table or a bed and a volun-teer."

Chapter 31

D r. Miller led them into the room behind his office, which had a long table as its only furniture. The immaculate room was a stark contrast to the operating room in the medical school, where blood seeped through the linens and floor and which reeked of sweat, alcohol, and body humors that made new students cover their noses.

Ella's heart sped up. *In this operating room, Dr. Miller will perform a brilliant surgery. And I will be at his side. Just like I dreamed when I was a student in medical school.*

"Miss Burke, would you please help me with the demonstration?" Caroline asked the matron.

"Oh, I'd love to." Miss Burke beamed. "What must I do?"

"I need you to be the patient. Please climb onto the table."

The matron's shoulders fell. "But then I won't see what you are doing."

"Miss Burke, don't waste everyone's time." Mrs. Landon glowered at her. "Do what Miss Flowers says."

With a crushed expression, the matron lay on the table, folding her hands on her abdomen. "What do I do next?"

Caroline lifted her bag and retrieved a cloth and a small vial. "Close your eyes. Talk about something. For example, tell me about your family."

The matron bolted up. "Why do you ask of my family? My parents are long dead."

"Oh dear, I didn't mean to upset you. I'm so sorry." Caroline stepped back. "I need you to think of something nice. What do you enjoy doing?"

Miss Burke frowned. "How about I count to ten?"

"Yes, good idea." Caroline exhaled loudly. "Please lie down, close your eyes, and count slowly."

As Miss Burke counted, Caroline put several drops on the cloth and held it away from her face. A sweet but unpleasant smell wafted in the air, making Ella nauseous.

"This is how much I use when my father extracts someone's tooth. The patient sleeps for two to three minutes. If the tooth is difficult to remove, I apply more," Caroline explained.

She placed the cloth over Miss Burke's nose and mouth. "Please keep counting, Miss Burke."

"Five... six... eight..." Miss Burke's voice sounded more sluggish with each count. She stopped after nine.

Dr. Miller brought a candle closer to Miss Burke's face, but Caroline stopped him with her hand. "Be careful. Ether is highly flammable."

"Can she hear us?" Mrs. Landon asked.

Caroline shook her head. "Probably not. Why don't you try to call her name?"

"Miss Burke! Lavinia!" Dr. Miller bellowed, but the woman didn't stir.

"You can tickle or pinch her."

Ella gently pinched Miss Burke's ribs and tickled her hands and feet. Then she put her ear to her chest. The woman's heart beat evenly, and her breaths were deep.

"This is remarkable. She truly doesn't sense what I'm doing?"

"When I administered it on myself and asked my sisters to pinch me, I felt nothing. But they must've tried hard because my hands and neck were blue the next day," Caroline replied.

After a couple minutes, Miss Burke stirred.

Constance shuffled in. "Dr. Miller, I can't find—"

Dr. Miller shushed her.

Miss Burke's lashes fluttered, and she mumbled under her breath. Ella bent to listen.

"One. Tom Williams. Two. Jolly Molly. Three. Peter Harris."

Each name she said louder and more clearly. Constance's mouth gaped.

"What does that mean?" Ella asked Caroline.

Caroline put away the vial with ether into her case. "Some patients speak as they wake up. Usually it's nonsense. One woman sang a song in another language. When I asked her about it, she said that her grandmother used to sing to her in Welsh, but she couldn't remember the words when she was awake."

"Four. Mrs. Simmons. Five. Deaf Fannie," Miss Burke mumbled, then opened her eyes.

She looked about, as if woken up from a long dream. Constance backed away and slipped from the room.

"What did you feel, Miss Burke?" Dr. Miller asked.

"Feel?" She blinked. "I was counting, like Miss Flowers asked me. I think I got to ten and started over. Is she starting?"

"We're all done." Caroline gave her a hand to sit up. "I take it you didn't hear your name called or feel anyone pinching you."

Miss Burke slid off the table. Her eyes gained their usual sharpness. "No. I was counting, and then Dr. Miller asked what I felt."

"And you don't remember the names you were saying?" Ella asked.

She leaned away. "Names? I didn't say any names."

"It's nothing to pay attention to." Caroline waved her hand in dismissal. "So, what do you think?"

Mrs. Landon raised her hand. "This is extraordinary! Lillian is incredibly lucky to be here. Her surgery must be done with ether. Not only will she sleep like a princess from a tale, but this operation will also bring fame and profit to The Women's Sanctuary."

Caroline shifted her feet and stared at Dr. Miller. "I thought you'd want to perform more experiments before using ether in surgery, especially as complex a surgery as removing a brain tumor."

Dr. Miller stroked his beard. "Where are you staying, Miss Flowers?"

"I've just arrived with my nurse. We haven't found a place to stay."

"You can stay here." Dr. Miller turned to the matron. "Miss Burke, you seem well enough to attend to your duties. Please prepare a room for Miss Flowers and her chaperone."

Miss Burke lifted Caroline's bag. "I'll put this to your room."

"It's all settled then." Mrs. Landon threw her shoulders back. "When is the surgery planned?"

"Two weeks from today," Dr. Miller answered. "That should give us enough time to prepare. I also would like the patient to get stronger."

"Excellent. I will let Arthur know. I don't want to distract you from your duties any longer." Mrs. Landon left humming a melody.

Dr. Miller massaged his forehead and addressed Ella. "I must get back to the rounds. Dr. Parker, would you be so kind as to show Miss Flowers around the Sanctuary?"

"With pleasure." Ella grinned, excited to catch up with her friend.

They locked hands as they strolled through the blooming garden. White hydrangeas, pink foxgloves, and purple sweet peas flaunted their vibrant colors and sweet aromas.

"What's this way?" Caroline pointed to the narrow path that wove to the back of the building.

Ella shrugged. "I've never had a chance to explore. Do you want to see?"

They followed the path and came out at a cemetery with five graves.

"I didn't know about this place," Ella murmured, reading the names. "I suppose if the deceased patients have no family, they are buried here."

She found the simple graves of Mary Murray and Jane Bell, whose deaths were described as accidents in Dr. Miller's records. Two more graves were next to them of patients who died in old age. But the most noticeable grave was marked with a tall stone cross and was some distance from the others. White flowers blanketed the ground around it.

Caroline reached it first and peered at the headstone. "Amy Miller. Was she Dr. Miller's wife?"

"Yes." Ella read the inscription. "Where the surgeon erred, God made whole."

She died during surgery? Dr. Miller never mentioned it.

"Look. She died one year and four days ago." Caroline pointed to the date.

While the flowers bloomed, perfuming the air, the grass bore the imprints from repeated kneeling. Ella's imagination conjured Dr. Miller praying next to his wife's grave.

"He never mentioned his wife's death. Not even in his journal," Ella said.

"Sometimes the pain goes so deep there are no words to describe." Caroline's voice rang with profound grief, and her eyes became unfocused. Ella wondered whose death she was mourning. Before she could ask, Caroline turned. "Let's return to the garden."

They came to the flower beds, where patients, wearing wide hats, watered the sweet peas.

Ella stopped a short distance from the women. "The patients maintain the garden. The young blond woman hears voices and sees faces on walls. Next to her is the woman we call The Lost One because she can't tell us her name or where she's from. And the tall one is convinced she's made of glass and if she falls, she would shatter like a broken mirror. The mind is fascinating, isn't it?"

Caroline's head dipped. "My mother says she hears Jamie's voice. Sometimes she sees his shadow or reflection in the glass. Father hopes this will pass with time."

"What are you talking about?" Ella stepped back and gaped. "You make it sound like your brother is dead."

Tears glistened in Caroline's brown eyes. "I thought you knew. Jamie left home a year and a half ago. He wanted to find adventure, and... This will sound strange, but he wanted to find you. We never heard from him again, but we read an account in the naval paper of sailors captured by the French. Jamie's name was among them. We've made inquiries to the Admiralty and learned that he was held at a prison called Verdot. After a benevolent act by the inmates, all living prisoners were released to travel back to England. Since Jamie never returned or wrote home, we had to accept that he died in prison."

"He most certainly did not die!" Ella grabbed Caroline's wrists. "I saw him alive and well three days ago."

Caroline's knees buckled and hit the gravel. "Where? Where is he? Our father became weak. Our mother is going insane. My sisters and I cry into our pillows. And you say he's alive and here in Plymouth? I will kill him myself. After I give him a million kisses."

"I believe he stays in a tavern called the Cooked Goose. It's well known." Ella helped Caroline stand. "Caroline, you've gone so pale. Perhaps you should rest first."

Caroline shook her head. "I can't rest until I see Jamie. I'm collecting Mrs. Armstrong and going to see my brother and stay with him. I'll send a note to Dr. Miller telling him where to find me. I will help with the surgery, of course. But now, I must go."

Despite Ella's warnings to watch her step, Caroline flew to the gate. Ella found a bench and sat.

Jamie, what does this all mean? You rejected my proposal. You let your family believe you were dead. You said you would come to explain, and you didn't. Why?

Chapter 32

"**J**amie. Jamie, do you hear me?"

The voice was Caroline's. It took him back to their childhood, playing in the woods or perusing books.

She's home in Seatown with our parents.

Pain surged. It pushed on his chest, constricted his breathing. A cough racked his body.

"I think he's waking up. But he looks to be in a lot of pain." Caroline's voice quivered.

"I'll do all I can to make him comfortable," Oli's voice replied.

A hot drop landed on Jamie's cheek.

"Miss Caroline, please don't cry. It's a miracle that the ball missed his heart and lungs. I very much hope Jamie will recover."

His desk and the window appeared in Jamie's vision. He was in his room at the Cooked Goose, lying in bed. The sounds of dinner patrons resonated from downstairs. His older sister sat on a chair next to him. Oli was standing by her, watching him intently.

No, this is not how it should be. I should've died quickly, either from the fatal wound or from my heart finally breaking. Caroline, you shouldn't watch me die. Is the rest of my family here as well? Is Ella here? Please, let this be a dream.

Pain seared his left shoulder, waking him more. Details became sharper. Oli's face was flushed and sweaty. Tears streamed down Caroline's cheeks.

"Caroline, why are you here? I don't want you watching me die."

"Don't you dare speak of dying, Jamie. You will get better." Caroline clasped his hand. "I'm not going anywhere. Our parents and sisters will come and help me care for you. Your friend Conor Leach will bring them from Seatown."

"No. Don't summon them here. Please." Jamie winced in pain.

"We'll nurse you back to health."

"Miss Caroline is right, Jamie." Oli stepped closer. "The ball is lodged just below the left clavicle, between the ribs. If it had entered a little lower, you'd have bled to death. You are extremely lucky, but it's a severe injury. You will need your family to take care of you for a while. Eventually you'll be well enough to travel home."

Jamie cringed. "And die there. No, thank you. It's too bad Drake didn't shoot lower."

Caroline sobbed.

"Stop upsetting your sister." Oli's eyes shot arrows at him. "We'll keep the wound clean, watch for bleeding and inflammation, and help you regain your strength. Men live out the rest of their lives with a bullet lodged in the chest. With care and nursing, you can survive this."

Caroline wiped her tears. "Dr. Higgins, are you sure it's better to leave the ball inside? What if it moves?"

Oli stared at her a moment too long before answering. "I shouldn't attempt to remove the ball so near the heart and major arteries. The wound will heal over time. Jamie must be careful not to fall or get hit, or the bullet may shift closer to his heart. You hear me, Jamie? No more duels."

Jamie sighed; a wave of pain washed over him. Not from his wound, but from knowing that his sister and his friend would have their hopes shattered.

"I won't survive. Caroline knows this."

"What does he mean?" Oli asked.

Caroline's hands dropped by her sides. "Eight years ago, Dr. Miller diagnosed Jamie with a heart defect and said that patients with such a condition don't live long. The oldest one was twenty when he died."

"My twentieth birthday is in a month," Jamie added.

Oli crossed his arms. "You could've told me. Does Ella know?"

"I was going to tell her. But then the duel happened."

"Then you should've brought it up earlier. I'd set you straight, and I believe Ella would've as well."

"Dr. Higgins…" Caroline put her palm to her chest. "Are you saying you don't believe that Jamie's heart is damaged?"

"Please call me Oli. Dr. Higgins sounds so formal. I consider Jamie my friend…" His eyes fell on her hand, pressed to her bosom, and he averted his eyes. "No, I don't believe it, even if Dr. Miller thinks otherwise. How did he determine his diagnosis?"

"I wasn't in the room. I was upstairs, reading to my little sisters," Caroline replied. "But I believe he listened to Jamie's heart."

Jamie saw that day in his mind so many times, each detail was clear, as if it had happened yesterday and not eight years ago. "Yes, he listened to my chest. Then he asked Mother if she'd had any illnesses during her pregnancy. She said she had German measles, and Dr. Miller said he'd suspected that. He also became concerned when he heard I had a poor appetite, cough often, and catch colds."

"We all caught colds while living in London, but much fewer once we moved to Dorset," Caroline said. "We moved for Jamie, but the whole family became healthier."

Jamie continued. "He also asked about my feet swelling. My father thought it was from tight shoes, but the doctor seemed to think otherwise. And finally, he asked if there were moments when my heart beat too fast or skipped a beat. I told him that sometimes my heart beat like it wanted to jump out of my chest and run on its own. I have such heart palpitations often. Each time I think that my heart will explode. Even now it's racing."

"So is mine," Caroline said.

Jamie gaped. "You can't have a heart defect."

"Not according to Dr. Miller, or I would've been dead by now at my old age of twenty-two." She shrugged.

Oli ran his fingers through his hair. "Jamie, everyone's hearts beat faster when they are anxious or frightened or in... in happy times as well. And from physical exertion. When doctors ask that question, they mean when you are at rest and not feeling strong emotions. You didn't know that?"

"No... I was afraid to upset my parents, so I kept quiet about how I was feeling. But what about all those other things Dr. Miller confirmed?"

"None of them prove you have a heart defect. Your mother had German measles when she was pregnant? That could affect the baby's heart development but not necessarily. Poor appetite and colds? Sounds like London air made your whole family sickly, and you all got better after moving near the sea. Feet swelling? Perhaps your father was right and the shoes were to blame. Now answer this. If your heart is as weak as you believe, how did you survive your service at Royal Navy? I can tell by your muscles that you did plenty of physical work."

Jamie's lips tightened. "I had to work my hardest."

"And how did you survive the French prison?" Caroline asked. "Harsh conditions killed many of our men."

"Conditions were dismal at first, but I worked with the men to clean our cells and build an infirmary."

Caroline hid her face with her hands and sobbed.

Oli stared at her. "Please don't cry, Miss Caroline. All this points to one conclusion: Your brother doesn't have a heart defect."

Her shoulders shook. "He left us because he didn't want us to watch him die. When we learned of his imprisonment and didn't receive any letters, we assumed he was dead. Our parents became ill from grief."

Pain stabbed Jamie in the shoulder. "No… I didn't want you to mourn me." He looked up at Oli, who was watching Caroline's trembling shoulders. Catching his gaze, Oli hid his hands behind his back.

Jamie bit the inside of his cheek until it bled. "After the exam, Dr. Miller said that he heard a distinct murmur when he listened to my heart. Oli, you can't tell me that I've devastated my family by leaving them, risked my life to protect others since mine was nearly over, and rejected my chance at happiness, hurting the woman I love. You can't tell me that I did all that for nothing, that the great Dr. Miller made a mistake. Many other doctors confirmed his diagnosis. So you can't tell this to my sister and me… unless you are sure without any doubt."

"Without any doubt," Oli echoed. "It's hard to speak that way. Yes, I believe Dr. Miller erred. I don't know what he heard when he listened to your heart, but he seemed to build his case by focusing on various symptoms that weren't necessarily related. And I'm not surprised that other physicians and surgeons parroted him. When I was his student, I saw intelligent, innovative people give their opinions and immediately change them if Dr. Miller disagreed. I'll listen to your heart again."

Caroline let Oli sit on her chair and stepped behind it. Oli put his ear on Jamie's chest and listened. Then he asked Jamie to hold his breath. "No murmur that I can hear," he said when Jamie exhaled. "A strong, steady rhythm. As long as the ball doesn't shift, we can be hopeful of your recovery."

"Are you sure?" Caroline's hands gripped the chair so hard that her knuckles turned white.

Oli stood and paced through the small room. "You are asking much from me. Dr. Miller was my instructor in medical school, and I'm not impervious to the weight of his opinion. It's human nature to doubt ourselves. I don't hear a murmur. That's all I can say."

I must speak to Ella and tell her everything.

Jamie attempted to sit, but the pain seared him like a wall of fire. His sister eased him back on the pillows.

Oli measured a dose of laudanum and gave it to Jamie. "Don't even try getting up yet. Miss Caroline, why don't you make yourself comfortable in the room next door," Oli said. "I'll bring my things in here. The proprietor should be able to find another bed for your servant."

"Oh, I completely forgot about Mrs. Armstrong. I've sent her to buy meat for the broth and more bandages. She should return soon."

"Very thoughtful of you."

She sat on the chair. "I think I'll stay with Jamie some more. It's been so long. You don't mind, Jamie, do you?"

"Not at all. I've missed you too." He smiled, looking up at her face.

"Ah, he's smiling. Laudanum must be working," Oli said, smiling as well. "I'll go pack my things to move them here."

Caroline waved in objection "Please, you shouldn't have to change rooms for us. I'm sure I can find a place to sleep somewhere else."

"Absolutely not. I'll sleep in the same room as Jamie, and you'll be next door with Mrs. Armstrong. This is the best arrangement to keep an eye on your brother."

When Oli left, Jamie murmured. "He likes you."

She burst out in giggles. "That's laudanum talking."

"I think it's nice."

Her hands covered her rosy cheeks. "Even if he likes me now, he'll forget about me when our sisters get here. The moment Julia and Audrey bat their eyelashes at him or pout their lips, I will become invisible."

"Not this time. I think he sees how intelligent you are. And pretty."

"Oh, please. Only you see that." She kissed him on the cheek, then put her ear on his chest.

"What are you doing?"

"I'm listening to your heart, although I don't know what to listen for." She was still for a good while. "Hmm."

"Yes, Doctor?"

"Now I understand why he wasn't sure." She straightened. "It's hard to hear. I imagine there's room for mistake, even for a trained ear. It's something to think on. But later. I should write to Ella and let her know what happened to you."

"I must write her myself." Jamie swallowed. "I told her I would come and explain everything, and then Conor got involved in the duel... Where is he?"

"On the way to Dorset. He very much wanted to do something for you. I asked him to bring my letter to our parents. There was also a boy here, Tobby. He was inconsolable until I promised him you would be well soon. So don't make me a liar to your young friend."

The pain dulled as he thought of his friends. "Conor and Tobby survived French jail with me. We are like brothers."

She took his hand. "I'm glad you've found what you wanted. Adventure. Brothers in arms. Ella. You've grown much from the overprotected boy I knew. Our parents will hardly recognize you. What shall I write Ella?"

He closed his eyes. "The things I want to say... I can't put in a letter. But please ask her to come."

Chapter 33

Late in the evening, Ella was in her room, reading Dr. Miller's journal. Lillian's name caught her eye.

23 December 1795

I visited Lillian in the morning, before work, and was pleased to see that her fever broke. A nine-year-old girl named Lavinia Burke was sitting by her bedside and told me that she gave Lillian water several times that night. I complimented Lavinia on her nursing. She then took me to the bed of another child, a two-year-old named Molly, or Jolly Molly, as the children called her. The child doesn't speak but is known for her cheerfulness. Not today. Molly was hugging her belly and crying. Lavinia informed me that Molly vomited earlier and there was blood. As I examined the girl, Mrs. Mulligan came by and asked if Jolly Molly had influenza, like Lillian. At her words, Lavinia stomped her foot. "Doctor, Mrs. Mulligan won't listen to me. I counted the sewing pins, and one is missing. Jolly Molly must've swallowed it when we made Christmas decorations."

I proceeded to examine the patient and found that Molly's skin was warm and damp, and she cried out when I pressed below her navel. Her pulse was rapid. I told Mrs. Mulligan that I would take the child to the hospital.

When I was about to carry Jolly Molly into my carriage, Lavinia surprised me with several medical questions, showing unusual knowledge of the digestive system for a young girl. When I commended her, she puffed her chest and said, "I want to be a surgeon. Perhaps by the time I'm grown, women will be allowed in medical schools." There was something comical about the way she said it, full of self-importance. I patted her head and said that this could never be, but she would make a great caregiver.

In the hospital, Molly's abdominal pain became severe, her fever rose, and there was blood in her feces. Lavinia's guess about the pin was likely correct; I expect it perforated an intestine. I'm outraged at the negligence that led to this accident and pray Lillian will be adopted and taken away from the orphanage.

There's little chance to save Molly, but I'm determined to try. I won't get any sleep tonight, as I plan to operate in the morning, before sepsis steals the child's life.

"Jolly Molly," Ella repeated the name. It was one of the names Miss Burke had murmured when she woke up from the ether demonstration. Perhaps she had been counting her friends from the orphanage.

The door squeaked, and Constance shuffled into the room, holding a large sack.

"Constance, what are you doing up? I was about to read about Molly's operation. Did you know her? She swallowed a pin."

"Jolly Molly, yes." Constance stared at her wool dress. "I remember that day. We were all so worried about her, and even Lavinia was crying. I've never seen Lavinia cry and asked if she thought Jolly Molly would die. She said, 'No, you fool. Dr. Miller will save her. But he said I could never be a medical student.' I told her she was being silly to cry over that, and she called me some mean names. But then we made up. Later we heard that Dr. Miller had opened Molly's belly and removed the pin, but Molly died from a fever the day after."

Ella touched her face. "How sad. But this happens often after surgery."

Constance went to the door and looked out. Then she closed it and came close to Ella. "Did you hear Miss Burke mutter names as she was waking up?" she whispered.

"Yes, Jolly Molly and some other names. Were they her friends in the orphanage?"

Constance shook her head. "I was her only friend. She liked to supervise the little ones, to run errands for teachers, to care for the children in the sickroom, but she always said that they weren't her friends, only me. She made me feel good. People always laughed at me because I forgot things and couldn't finish tasks. But she would tell me it wasn't my fault. She'd also tell me nice stories. I loved her so much, I'd do anything for her. But when I heard her say those names today, I became afraid."

"Why?" Ella studied the young woman's face. Her pupils were wide, and her lips bled from her biting them.

"Tom Williams fell out of a top-floor window. He broke many bones in his back and his legs and arms. We heard he had surgery and died during it. You already know what happened to Jolly Molly. Do you remember the third name?"

"Peter, I think."

"Oh yes. That was a few years later. His tongue would swell up. Dr. Miller said to be watchful and never give him anything with milk, yet it happened a few times. Then one day, during evening prayers, Peter grabbed his throat and made a sound like he was choking. Then he dropped onto the floor. Lavinia shouted to call the doctor, but Peter died before anyone moved. Dr. Miller was so angry. We all heard him yell at Mrs. Mulligan that Peter's stomach was full of pudding that was surely made with milk. And then, only a month later, Mrs. Simmons died in her sleep."

"That was another name Miss Burke mumbled." Ella shuddered from a sudden chill. "Are you saying Miss Burke named everyone who died during her time in the orphanage? Perhaps she still mourns those deaths."

"Oh no, many more died. From coughs in the winter or stomach maladies in the summer. One child would break out in red blisters, and then all the children sleeping nearby would become ill. But there were accidents as well. Someone would climb a tree and fall. Someone would cut themselves with scissors. Perhaps that's what happens when you have a building full of children and not enough adults. Nurses often asked Lavinia to help them look after the little ones because she was the oldest and the brightest."

Ella clenched her hands. "Are you saying those deadly or nearly deadly accidents happened on her watch?"

Constance shifted her feet. "No, it was never on her watch. Lavinia was often the first one to see someone hurt and rush to help. All the teachers and nurses loved her except for Mrs. Simmons. Only she didn't praise Lavinia's helpfulness. After Peter died, she seemed to watch Lavinia's every move. Lavinia hated that and called her names behind her back. Mrs. Simmons took a medication every night. But it must've stopped working. She massaged her chest often and complained of pain. Then one day, she didn't wake up in the morning. Lavinia was the first to notice her absence and find her dead."

"And the last one? I think she said Deaf Fannie?"

"Deaf Fannie was deaf, as you can guess. She didn't hear when the teachers screamed that there was a fire. Lavinia led me out, as well as many other children. When we came out, we realized Fannie wasn't with us. Lavinia rushed back inside. I thought she was searching for Fannie, but she went back for the books. The bookcase fell on her and she almost died. That's how she got her scars. Fannie's body was found later in the closet, where teachers would lock us for being naughty. But no one remembered locking Fannie in."

Ella stood. "What are you trying to say, Constance?"

Constance grabbed her belly, as if it hurt. "It may be that Lavinia caused those deaths... on purpose," she whispered. "I didn't think of it. I'm not that clever and I loved her as a friend. It was Ursula who said this."

"Ursula? But she's gone."

"She wanted to know about the orphanage. Her questions made me remember those deaths and other accidents. I recalled how Lavinia told me a story about a girl who swallowed a magic piece of coal that always brought her luck. The next day there was a piece of coal in my pocket. When we went to bed, Lavinia told me the story again and said, 'Oh how I wish to have that magic coal. It's not just any ordinary coal. It must appear by itself in your shoe or your pocket. And one must never talk about it, or it won't work. If I had it, I'd eat it at once so I could leave this orphanage.' I waited for her to fall asleep, broke off a piece as big as I could swallow, and got it down my throat. When

I felt sick, Lavinia was the first to help me. I asked her about the luck I was supposed to receive. She made her eyes wide like she had no idea what I was talking about. So I thought I hadn't understood the story and had only myself to blame."

"Do you think she meant to kill you? I'm sure you felt terrible, but swallowing a piece of coal wouldn't be deadly."

"Perhaps she was punishing me for something. Ursula said that she noticed that Ginny's stomachaches would happen after she'd bite or hit Lavinia." Constance shuddered.

"Constance! Are you here? I need you at once!" Miss Burke's voice sounded from the corridor.

Ella and Constance froze, holding their breath. The steps grew louder, stopped, then receded.

Constance put her hands on Ella's shoulders. "I must leave. Lavinia may use me for one of her tricks or hurt me. That's what Ursula said. She gave me the address of a woman I could go to and be safe."

She gave Ella a quick hug and crept out of the room with her bag.

Ella stared at the door left half open by Constance. *Lavinia is behind Beth's death and other so-called accidents. I must warn Dr. Miller now. Wake him up if he's asleep.*

Squinting in the darkness, Ella mounted the stairs to the third floor. Dr. Miller's bedroom door was wide open, and candlelight streamed from the room. As she neared it, the boom of something heavy falling and smashing made her jump.

"Alex! Alex... don't die! Don't leave me!" Dr. Miller's voice bellowed.

"Please, doctor. Calm down. Drink this," Miss Burke said in a pleading tone.

Ella tamed her fear and ran into the bedroom.

Shards from a broken vase, an overturned chair, and scattered papers littered the floor. Dr. Miller, dressed in a robe, was sitting on the rug by his bed. His forehead was sweaty and his beard disheveled. Miss Burke and another attendant hovered over him.

"What are you giving him to drink?" Ella demanded.

"Calming drops. The same ones we give to the patients." Miss Burke poured a spoonful from a bottle.

Ella hit the woman's hand, making her spill the medicine, and shoved her out of the way. Then she knelt to view Dr. Miller's eyes, which were bloodshot and unfocused, with enlarged pupils. "Dr. Miller, what's wrong?"

"Alex... Noo!" The doctor covered his head with his hands and wept.

"Dr. Miller?" Ella tried again. Her heart was in the pit of her stomach.

"He needs a strong dose of a sedative and some uninterrupted sleep," Lavinia said. "He hasn't slept for five nights, planning Lillian's surgery. Insomnia can cause him to become like this, but he recovers quickly enough. Help us get him into bed."

With the same efficiency that Lavinia used to quiet the patients, she helped the doctor off the floor and made him sit on the bed. Then she grabbed his hands.

"I'll hold him. Give him the medicine."

Ella poured the medicine on the spoon and smelled it. It was the usual mix of opium, alcohol, and herbs that many patients took each night before sleep.

When Ella brought the spoon to his lips, he turned his head away.

"Tell him that Alex wants him to take his medicine. That often works," Lavinia suggested.

Alex. Lillian's mother. Perhaps their relationship was more than that of a patient and their doctor.

Ella made her voice gentle. "Dr. Miller, Alex wishes for you to take your medicine and sleep. You must rest."

The doctor rocked in his seat. "I can't rest. Lillian needs me."

"Lillian needs you to have a good night of sleep, so you can do your brilliant surgery and save her life." Ella caressed his cheek as he opened his mouth and drank the medicine.

Lavinia and her assistant made him lie down and covered him with a blanket. The doctor's face relaxed and his eyes closed. The attendant bent down to straighten the chair and collect the scattered papers.

Ella crossed her arms. "Why didn't you tell me that he's ill?"

The matron, who was sliding a pillow under the doctor's head, turned and came face-to-face with her. "He's a great man.

If rumors of his condition spread, he'll lose everything he's worked for. He'll be barred from practicing medicine and won't perform surgeries that only he can. We must be quiet and help him. He's even more brilliant when he doesn't sleep for several nights. That's when he gets his best ideas. But when he gets exhausted, he needs a bit of time to recover. Only a few of his most trusted staff know this. Can you keep your beloved teacher's secret, Dr. Parker? You won't betray him, will you?"

"No, I won't betray him." Ella exhaled. "I just wish he'd told me."

Lavinia snuffed out a candle by the bed, then peered at Ella. "Why did you come to him so late at night?"

Ella fidgeted. "I... I had an idea to discuss with him. About the surgery. I was so excited about it, I couldn't sleep. I hoped he would be up as well."

"You couldn't sleep?" Lavinia frowned. "Do you want some calming drops?"

"I'm fine." *Would you give me medicine or poison?*

Dr. Miller snored and turned in his sleep.

"He'll sleep for a long time," Lavinia said. "You should go to bed, Dr. Parker."

Ella stared at her teacher. *When you wake up, I'll tell you all that Constance revealed to me. Lavinia Burke cannot be trusted.*

Chapter 34

E lla paced her room, still reeling from Dr. Miller's episode. The chaotic scene and the doctor's wild stare chilled her blood.

What should I do? Patients who suffer such fits are committed to their homes or asylums. But... he was well until last night. Lavinia said that such episodes are infrequent and go away. Should I listen to her and keep his secret?

Her gaze fell on the journal. She leafed through it and found a note in a crooked handwriting very different from the doctor's usual penmanship.

20 July 1797

By now Lillian should be home with her new family. Mrs. Mulligan reassures me that the couple who adopted her are good people. She says it's great luck Lillian was adopted. Yet I suspect that someone plotted to keep the child away from me. One in-

sufferable teacher, Mrs. Simmons, recently dared to question my motives for visiting Lillian.

It took some silver to persuade Mrs. Mulligan to give me the names of Lillian's adoptive parents. My little girl is now Miss Lillian Davis, living in a small town in Cornwall. Will her new parents love her and keep her from harm? I haven't slept in three nights, thinking of her.

It's fortunate that she's away from that terrible orphanage. After I spoke to Mrs. Mulligan, I treated a two-year-old girl who cut her feet on broken glass earlier that day. As usual, no one knew how the accident happened, why there was broken glass and a shoeless child. The wounds were well cleaned, and the dressing was done expertly. When I asked who took care of the child, it turned out to be Lavinia Burke. That girl is more able and intelligent than any of her teachers and nurses.

I should be happy about Lillian's adoption. But I can't sleep. When I medicate my insomnia, I dream of Lillian getting hurt and crying out for me. Better to pour my energy into work. There's always so much to do.

The next note was so hard to read, Ella couldn't make it out. After that, there were missing pages, their jagged remains just visible. Dr. Miller must've ripped them out. The note after that was dated six months later.

28 January 1798

Tomorrow will be my first day back to work. I'm still weak and must start slowly. The illness and the treatments I've received depleted my energy. It will take time to gain my full strength.

My wife did not greet me on my return. She's away in London, enjoying herself. Instead of her letters, I've received bills for extravagant expenditures.

The person I crave to see is Lillian. Some days, the thought of her gives me the will to rise from my bed. Other days, I can't bring myself to eat in my despair. I may never see her again. What if she's ill or hurt? I'm too far away to help.

Perhaps seeing her in good health and embraced by her new family will lead to my improvement.

Ella closed the journal.

What was Dr. Miller doing during the six months between notes? Why were some pages ripped out?

Perhaps he'd worked himself into a state of exhaustion, weighed down by anxieties about Lillian, which now struck Ella as an unhealthy obsession. He likely suffered an episode like this night and required treatment. His next few notes were evidence of his illness and he destroyed them later.

And Lavinia Burke? The journal revealed another example of her being a supposed savior to an injured child who was hurt in a preventable accident. Did she cause the child to be injured and then swoop in to treat her?

I will be with the patients, caring for them while Dr. Miller recovers. He's Lillian's only hope, and I will keep his secret. But Miss Burke is dangerous, and I won't let her hurt another patient.

Next day, when Dr. Miller failed to appear at breakfast and for patient rounds, Ella marched into his room. Dr. Miller was still in bed, and Miss Burke was coaxing him to drink his tea.

"It's almost noon, sir. You should administer treatments." Ella opened the velvet curtains.

"Leave me alone." Dr. Miller shielded his eyes from the sunlight and turned onto his side. "I have no strength."

"Your patients are asking about you." Ella touched his sweaty forehead.

Miss Burke, who stood on the other side of his four-poster bed, smoothed her apron. "They miss you, doctor, but while you recover, we have everything under control. You can rest all you need while the patients are in our able hands."

"Thank you, Miss Burke," he muttered. "You are an angel."

Ella narrowed her eyes. *What a perfect opportunity for you to cause an accident while the doctor is indisposed. I won't allow it.*

"Yes, we have things under control." Ella widened her stance and crossed her arms. "I will be in charge while Dr. Miller recovers. Please have all the patients and staff gather in the dining room."

"What for?" Miss Burke frowned. "Many of the patients want their meals in their rooms. And Dr. Miller didn't agree to let you take charge. With all respect, Dr. Parker, you are still relatively new here. I've been running this place from the first day."

"But you are not a medical doctor. It's obvious—"

"Must you fight?" Dr. Miller mumbled, massaging his temples. "Dr. Parker is in charge for now. Miss Burke, please assist her. Now, let me sleep."

Ella took Miss Burke's wrist and escorted her out of the room. In the corridor, she faced her. "For the benefit and safety of our patients, I'm changing some rules. All patients will eat in the dining room, together with the staff. Ginny, of course, will be given a separate meal, and I will supervise it being made."

Lavinia opened and closed her mouth like a fish. "I don't understand. Do you think the staff will poison the patients?"

Ella raised her hand to halt her. "I'm not done. From now on I will administer all the medicines."

"But that will slow down our morning and evening routines." Miss Burke wrung her hands.

"And I will routinely check all doors and windows to make sure no one is able to escape the building or climb to the roof."

Miss Burke's shoulders fell. "I think I understand. Someone set you against me. I have been nothing but loyal, hardworking, and compassionate to the patients."

"Good." Ella raised her chin. "Then while Dr. Miller recovers, we should have no mistakes or unfortunate accidents."

***

Oli undressed Jamie's wound. Despite his slow movements, each touch shot pain through Jamie's chest and shoulder. He suppressed a moan, afraid to scare Caroline.

As Oli inspected the bandages, Caroline, who stood next to him, clenched her hands.

"No green pus or putrid stench. The discharge is thin and clear." With a finger, he pressed near the wound, making Jamie groan. "And no swelling or other signs of inflammation. Sorry, Jamie; I've tried to be gentle."

Caroline folded her hands in a silent prayer of thanks. Oli's gaze lingered on her before he turned back to Jamie.

"Have you tried to sit up?"

Jamie cringed. "It hurt too much."

Oli spread ointment on the wound. "Wounds like this take time to heal. It's only been a week. Miss Caroline, would you hand me some clean bandages from my bag?"

Caroline retrieved the linens and passed them to Oli. Their fingers met for a moment, and they both blushed and looked away. Watching his sister and friend's subtle infatuation while they worked hard to hide it amused Jamie, keeping his mind off his pain and worries about Ella.

Why didn't she come after receiving Caroline's letter? Yesterday I sent another one.

When he finished changing the dressing, Oli put his ear to Jamie's chest and listened for a moment. "A strong and steady heartbeat. Clear lungs. No murmur or other problems that I can hear."

"May I ask..." Caroline rocked on her feet. "What do you listen for? How would you know if there's a disease?"

"I listen to the heart rhythm, which should be steady, not too fast or too slow. A swooshing sound is a murmur; that indicates a valve problem. Then in the lungs, I listen for rales, which sound like crackles. Those mean that there's fluid in the lungs." Oli's palm went to his cravat, perhaps to loosen it, but then he folded his hands on his middle instead.

"And you can detect all those sounds clearly? I've tried to listen myself. It's hard to hear."

"You should've become a physician, Caroline," Jamie said. "Should've put on men's clothes, like Ella, and run off to the medical school. Perhaps you could still do that."

Caroline swatted away the idea like a fly. "Stop it. I could never leave our parents, especially after their health has worsened. I'm Father's assistant, remember? But perhaps I can learn something useful."

Oli stared at his shoes. "It takes training. And there are limitations. For example, I've been treating a seven-year-old boy with a moderate fever and only a slight cough. I wasn't too concerned and predicted a quick recovery. Then, last night, his fever intensified, and he could hardly breathe. When I listened to his chest, he had a bubbling sound in both lungs. Pneumonia, and I missed it until it became severe. I'm going to visit the patient tonight and see how he's faring after the medications I administered."

"Then we shouldn't keep you away." Caroline's eyebrows drew together. "I remember Jamie having pneumonia when he was little. He had a fever, and his cough rattled through the house. Our parents forbade me and my sisters from going into his room, but when they slept, I sat by his bed."

"When I had a bad dream and was scared, you climbed into the bed to hold me," Jamie remembered. "In the morning, I was sweaty and hungry, with my fever finally broken. And you were hot and shaking. By afternoon, you were sick in bed, and I was begging to visit you."

"I have no regrets." Caroline grinned. "You carved a whistle for me. Remember, you shaped it like a nightingale?"

"I *tried* to shape it like a nightingale. It looked like a duck at best. And sounded like a mouse being squished." Jamie chuckled.

Oli lifted his case. "It's good to hear you laugh, Jamie. A patient who laughs is well on their way to recovery. I'm leaving you to your sister's excellent nursing. By the time I return, I want you to eat the soup Mrs. Armstrong made for you."

"Should I save some soup for you, Dr. Higgins?" Caroline asked. "I can keep it warm. The beef was very fresh when Mrs. Armstrong bought it at the market this morning. Much better than the fried meats they serve downstairs."

Oli shook his head with pretend seriousness. "Don't criticize the tavern cooking in front of Miss Jenny or she'll take offense. But I would love some beef soup when I return. And please, call me Oli."

A few minutes after he left, a thin voice rang from behind the door. "Miss Caroline, there's a letter for you."

"Is it from Ella?" Jamie beamed. "Come in, Tobby."

The boy gave Caroline the letter and stared at Jamie's bandages. "Does it still hurt?"

"The wound is healing, thanks to everyone's kind care." Jamie winked at Tobby and turned to his sister. "What does Ella write?"

"Actually, most of the letter is written by Miss Burke, the matron." A shadow passed over Caroline's features. "She writes that there's a smallpox outbreak at the asylum. No one may enter or leave The Women's Sanctuary. Ella wrote a short note at the end: 'Unfortunately, I cannot see you as my duty is to my patients. I wish your brother a speedy recovery.'"

Jamie's shoulders stiffened. "That's all she wrote?"

She must be angry with me.

"I'm sure she's busy with patients. Likely she'll write more in a couple of days." Her voice trailed off, and she stared out the window.

"What are you thinking about?" Jamie asked.

"She's thinking of Oli." Tobby snickered into his fist. "The cooks were talking about it downstairs. He fancies her."

Caroline blushed and tousled Tobby's hair. "That's silly. If you must know, I was thinking of the whistle Jamie made for me."

"Why? It was a clumsy toy." Jamie frowned.

Tobby raised his head. "I can make a whistle. Or a reed pipe. I have one that's very loud. You can have it if you want."

"Yes, I'd like to see it," Caroline replied.

Tobby rushed out of the room and brought back a wooden pipe. He put it to his lips and made a shrieking, piercing sound.

"Ah!" Jamie plugged his ears with his fingers. "That's worse than my whistle."

"Impressive." Caroline stooped to study the pipe. "Such a simple and narrow tube, yet so loud when you blow into it. If only..."

"If only what?" Tobby raised an eyebrow.

"Um... nothing. A peculiar idea I had for a moment."

Chapter 35

In Ginny's room, Ella brought her young patient to the window and pointed to the dark clouds. Then she pointed to her mouth. "Clouds." The girl touched her own lips and copied the movement. Ella then pointed to the drops knocking on the window. "Rain." Ginny copied her lips, then grinned, and her eyes shone. "Ginny likes rain." She said this in an almost inaudible whisper.

Since Ella began her work with Ginny, it became obvious that someone taught Ginny to speak. The child was remembering words at a rapid pace and sometimes said words and phrases out loud.

Ginny picked up a book with illustrations that Ella had brought to her and studied the pictures. The sky grew dark, and rain poured. As Ella lit a candle, she wondered if it would be an ordinary summer rain or a storm with thunder and lightning that would frighten the patients.

Leafing through the pages, Ginny found an illustration and pointed to it. Ella smiled and brought her finger to her own lips. "Shell." Ginny mimicked the word several times while tracing the picture with her finger.

The shell, like the one she found with Jamie on the day they first met, shifted her thoughts to him. *Jamie, where are you? Once again, you lit my soul and then disappeared. It's been two weeks, and you didn't visit or write, not even in response to my letter. And Caroline should've replied to my letter as well and confirmed where she's staying. We'll need her for the surgery soon enough, when Dr. Miller is better. He's finally up and about in his room.*

Ginny closed the book and reached for her doll.

"Yes, I know you want to play with your doll. But let's repeat your most important lesson." Ella touched Ginny's face and made her look at Ella's lips. "No milk."

Ginny repeated it with her lips and rubbed her belly.

"Yes. Milk makes your stomach hurt."

The clamor of several women's voices sounded from the hall. "Dr. Parker! You must come quickly! Help!"

Here's that storm. What did Lavinia do?

"You stay here." Ella pointed to her lips even though she hadn't taught this phrase to Ginny. "Trouble."

Ella went into the corridor, where three attendants surrounded her and shouted all at once.

"She was on the stairs when she grabbed her belly and vomited."

"She's lying there, moaning from pain."

"Who? Who are you talking about? Where's Miss Burke?" Ella hastened toward the stairs, with the distraught attendants following. Moans and shrieks resonated from somewhere below, loud enough to reach the floor above and still Ella's breath.

"It *is* Miss Burke!" the youngest of the attendants cried. "She's dying."

A stone fell off Ella's chest. "Nonsense."

Ella reached the top of the stairs. At the bottom step lay Miss Burke, covered in vomit and clutching her belly. Two attendants were cleaning her face with a wet cloth as she wailed. The stench of stomach acid and half-digested food made Ella nauseous. Ten or so patients, Lillian among them, stood by the banisters and stared down with horrified expressions.

"Where's Dr. Parker? I'm dying!" Miss Burke cried out in a strong voice that indicated to Ella that the woman was far from death's door.

"Ella, what's wrong with her?" Lillian's face was as white as the banister she was clutching. "She's so sick."

The Lost One stepped onto the stairs and wobbled. Ella caught her arm and pulled her back to the landing. Then she knelt and touched the stairs. They were slippery with soap and Lavinia's vomit. The railings glistened, and when Ella touched them, her hand came away covered with oil.

"No one go to her." Ella yelled to the patients. "Look what she did. Wet staircase. Oily railings. She even forced herself to retch on the stairs. And then she lay down at the bottom, waiting for someone to run to her and slip. She stages tricks like that, hoping someone will get hurt. After that, she'll find strength in herself to stand and heroically administer aid."

The attendants and the patients stared at Ella with their mouths open. One of the attendants stepped away from Ella. "You make no sense. She'd hurt no one."

"She's severely ill. Look at her." Another attendant pointed to Miss Burke, who had turned onto her hand and knees and was expelling puddles of vomit. "You must do something."

"Don't worry about her. She's fine." Ella touched the hand of the third attendant, who jerked back. "Take all the patients to their rooms."

"There's blood! I've been poisoned!" Miss Burke let out a chilling scream.

The attendants collectively gasped. A patient named Winnifred, who suffered from paranoia, fell to her knees. "I'm poisoned as well. All of us are poisoned. We'll be dead by tomorrow." The faces of the other patients turned green, and a couple grabbed their bellies.

"Take them to their rooms!" Ella waved her hands before the attendants. "Observe them for stomach pains. Most likely they are only frightened."

The attendants shepherded the stunned and anxious patients away from the stairs and into the corridor. Ella was hoisting half-conscious Winnifred when Lillian touched her shoulder. "What about Miss Burke? When are you going to help her?"

Heavy Winnifred was a deadweight in Ella's arms. "Forget about Miss Burke. I'm sure she'll miraculously get better once she realizes her trick didn't work. Go to your room, Lillian, and stay there. Miss Burke is dangerous and may try something else."

"Ella, you are confused." Lillian's hands touched her trembling neck. "I've remembered more recently. Miss Burke was once a girl in my orphanage, an angel loved by everyone. She stayed at my bedside when I was sick. And here she's been nothing but kind to me and the other patients. You are a doctor. Help her!"

"Lillian, get into your bed before you work yourself into another fit." Ella pointed to the attendants. "Someone take Lillian to her room. And help me with Winnifred."

With the help of another attendant, Ella dragged Winnifred to her room. When the patient was settled in bed, Ella inspected her tongue and throat and palpated her abdomen. "You are completely fine, Winnifred."

"Then what's wrong with our dear Miss Burke? Who could've poisoned her?" Winnifred's right eye blinked from a nervous tic.

An attendant was at the door. The young woman panted as if she'd run. "Dr. Parker! We need you to help us with Miss Burke. She's getting worse."

"Not in front of the patient!" She led the attendant out of the room and grabbed her by the shoulders. "What?"

"Miss Burke vomited more, and there are streaks of blood. She says her throat feels like it's on fire and her stomach aches like someone punched it."

She must've taken an emetic or a small dose of some poison. Did she overdo it? Or am I wrong and someone else poisoned her?

Wails pierced Ella's ears as she neared the staircase. "Help me! The poison is killing me!"

Ella descended slowly, careful not to slip, and bent over Miss Burke. "What did you ingest? If you want my help, you must tell me what you did."

Miss Burke clenched her abdomen and moaned.

One of the attendants, who fanned Miss Burke with her apron, raised her head. "How can you think she's done this on purpose?"

"She's been mean to Miss Burke for no reason. Now she's letting the poor woman die!" another said with a glare.

Ella knelt next to the matron and raised Miss Burke's head, making the woman look at her. "You wanted a patient to slip on those stairs. It's just like many other mysterious and tragic accidents you've staged. You need to be committed, and to a stricter place than The Women's Sanctuary. Somewhere where there will be bars and straitjackets. Now tell me what you've taken and how much."

"Someone poisoned me..." Miss Burke's eyes closed. "Please. Give me egg whites and milk. Perhaps that will save me."

"Of course. You know an antidote."

The two attendants were already running to the stairs that led to the kitchen.

Left alone with Miss Burke, Ella shook her. "You stay awake. And tell me exactly what you've planned."

"Miss Burke! Dear God!" Dr. Miller's exclamation made Ella startle. His beard was untrimmed and his face haggard, but he was dressed in his usual suit and carried his medical case. He was coming down from the third floor, with Lillian holding onto his arm.

"Please help her. I know you can." Lillian looked up at him with reverence.

Didn't I say to keep her in her room? Yet, in these ten minutes she got Dr. Miller to do more than I have in the last couple weeks.

They were near the second floor, where the stairs were slick and soapy.

"No! Stop!" Ella shouted.

Lavinia writhed with her whole body; a stream of bile poured from her mouth.

Before Ella could shout another warning, Dr. Miller stepped down. His legs shot from under him, and he crashed backward. His weight pulled Lillian, and she fell forward, her arms flailing.

They both slid down, the doctor groaning and cursing as his back and head hit one stair after another. Lillian flew headfirst, hit her head on the floor, and collapsed atop the doctor in a tangled heap.

Ella gaped. "Did you plan this?" she shouted into Miss Burke's ear. "Did you plan to hurt Dr. Miller or Lillian?"

"No. Leave me. Save them."

The two attendants returned with glasses of milk and egg whites. Ella left Miss Burke in their care and rushed to Lillian and the doctor. Dr. Miller sat upright and pressed his hand to the back of his head. Blood trickled between his fingers. Ella bent to see the wound, but he pointed at Lillian's closed eyes. "Did she hit her head?"

Blood pooled at Lillian's temple. Dr. Miller shouted in her ear, but she didn't move or speak. With bated breath, Ella pressed around her skull and found a bulge on the right side. She pointed it out to Dr. Miller. "Depressed skull fracture." Dr. Miller checked her pulse at her neck. "Pulse is unsteady, and her breaths are irregular." He lifted her eyelids and pointed at her fixed right eye. "She's bleeding into her brain. It's the same side where we expect to find the tumor. I must operate immediately. If I'm lucky, I will stop the hemorrhage and remove the tumor in one surgery."

Ella studied his widened pupils. "But... Are you sure you are well enough? You were ill. And you hit your head falling."

The doctor moved Lillian off his legs and stood. "I'm perfectly fine. There's no time to send for Miss Flowers, so we'll have to do without ether. Please prepare everything for the surgery."

Chapter 36

Ella shouted commands for the attendants to bring the stretcher and prepare the operating room. The staff rushed to obey. Lavinia was still on the floor, but her eyes were alert, and she was drinking a second glass of milk and raw eggs.

When attendants lifted Lillian onto the stretcher, Lavinia stood on shaking legs and approached Dr. Miller.

"Please, allow me to help with the surgery."

"Well, that was a quick recovery." Ella's remark was barbed. "You are so intrigued by the procedure, even supposed poison can't keep you away. But no, I won't allow you in the operating room."

Lavinia's lips trembled as if Ella had slapped her. "I don't know why you hate me. I only want to help."

"I'm puzzled by Dr. Parker's choice of words, but I believe she means you are unwell. It's encouraging to see you on your feet, but you must rest," Dr. Miller said in a pacifying tone.

Lavinia caressed her belly. "That awful pain is passing. I can help you by administering ether. When Miss Flowers rushed away from here, she left her bag with her supplies, the chemistry book that she followed for her research, and her notes on dosages and reactions. I've read them all and performed a few experiments."

"On whom?" Ella crossed her arms.

"We don't have time for these questions, Dr. Parker." Dr. Miller rolled up his sleeves. "Miss Burke, you are a brave woman, and your help is most welcome. Let's hurry."

Dr. Miller and Lavinia held onto each other as they staggered toward the operating room. Ella ran ahead of them. The attendants hovered over Lillian, who lay on the operating table, her body secured by restraints. One attendant was covering her clothing with a sheet, and another was cutting off her long hair.

"Shave it all off and wash the skin with vinegar," Ella instructed the woman who was cutting hair. "Heat the cautery iron," she ordered another attendant. Then she asked the others to spread sand on the floor to absorb the blood. After donning an apron, she placed her hand on Lillian's neck. The pulse ebbed under her fingers.

Ella cupped Lillian's ashen face. "Hold on, Lillian. You said you wanted a future where you will love and be loved. Fight for it."

When Dr. Miller and Lavinia walked in, Ella and the attendants were laying out the surgical instruments: trepanning saws, scalpel, needles and thread, and others. Dr. Miller put on an apron and gave one to Lavinia. He sent all but one attendant out of the room.

"All is ready," Ella said. She stood on the right side of the table, next to the instruments, and Lavinia took a place opposite her. The matron opened Caroline's bag and removed the vial with ether and the cloth. Dr. Miller took his position by Lillian's head and studied her shaved right side.

"Administer the ether, Miss Burke. The patient mustn't move her head."

Lavinia poured a generous measure on the cloth and pressed it over Lillian's nose and mouth. The sweet fumes filled the air.

"Scalpel," Dr. Miller commanded.

Ella passed him the sharpest blade. He made a deep incision into the scalp. Ella reached for a sponge, dabbing away the blood.

"Forceps."

After Ella passed the instrument, he peeled away the skin, exposing the smooth skull. Lillian's chest undulated, but there was no other movement or sound.

Dr. Miller took a long breath. "Trepanning saw."

His right hand reached out, and Ella lifted the saw to pass it to him. His fingers touched the instrument, but then he dropped his hand and gripped the table instead.

"Dr. Miller, are you all right?" She peered at the doctor, whose face grew pale.

"I... of course..." He grabbed the saw and placed it against Lillian's skull. Held it there for three agonizing seconds and laid it down. "I'm dizzy."

His legs swayed, and he might've fallen if Miss Burke hadn't grabbed his arm and wrapped it over her shoulder, supporting him.

Ice gripped Ella's insides. *He must've suffered a concussion when he fell.*

"Fetch him a chair!" Lavinia yelled to the attendant.

Ella gripped the trepanning saw. "I'm taking over. Miss Burke, help Dr. Miller to the chair and come stand by the instruments. You will assist."

Lavinia led the doctor away from the table.

"Lillian..." Dr. Miller muttered as he limped to the chair. "Why Lillian? She's my daughter. Mine and Alex's daughter."

Confusion, as a result of a concussion? Ella wondered. *No, it must be the truth. Alex was shot by her husband in his jealous rage when he learned the baby wasn't his. Dr. Miller is Lillian's father. He could never bear to be away from her too long.*

There was no time to contemplate the revelation. Ella positioned the trepanning saw and turned the crank, reminding herself of the practice Dr. Miller forced her to do. The grinding sound of the blade drilling through the bone resonated in the room. Telling herself to breathe calmly, she extended the cut with careful strokes, enough to lift away a wedge of bone without piercing the brain beneath.

A soft pop sounded. The moment she lifted the wedge of the bulged bone, a sizable blood clot shot out of Lillian's head, just missing Ella. Blood hit the wall and slid down like a crimson slug. A metallic smell hit Ella's nose.

"No! Alex, no. Don't die," Dr. Miller moaned. Ella willed herself not to listen and stayed focused.

"Cautery iron, Miss Burke. Careful. It's burning hot."

"I'm not a fool." Lavinia handed her the glowing red iron. The acrid smell of burning tissue mixed with the stench of blood as Ella cauterized the artery. The blood stopped pouring. Between each stroke of the iron, she pressed a lint sponge soaked in vinegar to hold back the oozing. Relief washed over Ella, and she allowed Miss Burke to sponge the blood. Lavinia's eyes shone brighter than the instruments laid out before her.

The blood clot was dealt with. Ella observed the rise and fall of Lillian's ribs and braced herself for the next part of the plan Dr. Miller had discussed with her.

He couldn't predict the fall, but he knew that his illness could prevent him from operating. He was preparing me for this possibility.

"Scalpel." She took the instrument from Miss Burke and sliced into the membrane. A swollen, gray mass became visible under her blade.

"Dr. Miller," Ella exclaimed, though she doubted the doctor would comprehend her. "You were right. The tumor is exactly where you said it would be, on the right side, between the thickest part of the dura and the lining of the brain."

He continued muttering about Alex.

The tumor, however, was significantly larger than they predicted. Lillian must've been sick for years, her illness taken for female complaints, then a shocking pregnancy, and finally, the falling sickness. All that suffering from a cauliflower-shaped mass that was about two inches across and pushed on her brain.

Dr. Miller planned to remove the tumor with his fingers, but seeing the size of it, Ella decided to use an instrument. She selected a hooked probe and inserted it beneath the tumor's edge.

"As I lift the mass away, you sponge the blood," she told Lavinia.

The tumor resisted Ella's tug; its tendrils were lodged deep in the membrane. Blood welled, and Lavinia sponged it as Ella cut some of the tissue to clear the way. More blood pooled, swiftly cleaned by Miss Burke.

She'd be an excellent medical student. If she weren't insane.

Finally, the tumor came free. Ella dropped it into a basin, planning to preserve it in alcohol and study later. Immediately, she had to reach for the cautery iron again to stop the bleeding. As Lavinia applied more ether, Ella braced herself for suturing. When they were practicing on Beth's skull, Dr. Miller told her he wouldn't replace the bone because of the swelling. Following his plan, she drew the scalp together over the hollow. Eventually,

Lillian's hair would grow and cover the soft spot where only scalp and scar tissue covered the brain. If Lillian survived the treacherous postoperative period.

When Ella made the last stitch, she couldn't contain her grin. Lillian's breathing was deep and audible, and when Ella put her ear to her heart, the beat was steady.

Lillian, you've made it through the surgery. I will pray that inflammation and fever will not claim you.

Ella knew it was too early to celebrate, yet her feet felt ready to dance.

Dr. Miller gripped his head. "What's happening?"

"The greatest surgery of my career so far. The blood clot and the tumor removed. The patient alive."

"Lillian?" His hands folded in prayer. "She lives?"

"Yes. Her heartbeat is strong. And she slept through the surgery. The ether worked well."

"And it will work well on you!" Miss Burke laughed with glee.

Before Ella could blink, a rag covered her face. The sweet smell of ether rushed into her nostrils. Her scream stilled in her throat.

Lavinia's voice sounded far away. "From the night you became ill, Dr. Parker attacked me several times. Today she mixed poison into my tea. The woman is dangerously mad."

Colors swirled in front of Ella's eyes, and the world spun at a sickening pace. Then all went still.

Chapter 37

Ella's hands were numb from being tied behind her back by the straitjacket sleeves. Her shoulders ached. So much for "inhumane use of restraints." It turned out that The Women's Sanctuary had all the measures needed to contain a dangerous patient. Straitjackets. A room with bars on the tiny window that let in the eerie morning light.

To relieve tightness in her back, Ella wiggled herself into a sitting position on her narrow bed and watched her roommate. The old woman with long gray hair and a hooked nose stared at the ceiling. She had never seen her before she woke up in this room five days ago. From what Ella observed, the woman's legs were paralyzed and she couldn't speak. Lavinia changed her soiled clothing and sheets. Not often enough, though, as the room stank of urine and feces.

I must escape, or I will end up like her. The thought made the hair on the back of Ella's neck stand up. But before she could plan how to save herself, she needed to empty her bladder. And for that she needed Lavinia, the only person who came here to care for her and the other woman.

Is that how Ginny felt, depending on Lavinia for everything and unable to complain about abuse?

Hoping that the matron was within earshot, Ella yelled, "Please! Let me use the chamber pot!"

"Haven't you realized Miss Burke avoids coming when you call her?"

The sharp voice startled Ella so much she barely managed to lock her knees and not wet herself. The old woman craned her neck toward Ella but didn't rise from her bed. "If you keep quiet, she may get worried and check on you."

"Who are you? Can you help me?"

"Can't you see I can't move my legs?" The woman snorted. "I'm Cora Butler. And if you tell anyone that I can speak, they'll say you've lost your mind."

Ice flowed through Ella's veins. "Were you a victim of an accident staged by Miss Burke? Is she hiding you from Dr. Miller?"

"Hiding me from Dr. Miller? No. Dr. Miller himself put me in this room. He couldn't bear to look at me. Since that day, he's only come in once, and that was to bring in a woman who lay where you are now. She never woke up, died the next day."

A cold hand squeezed Ella's heart. "What did he do to you and her?"

"I don't know what he did to her. As for me, I found a bottle of wine, just standing there on the dining room table, and gulped it down. Drunkenness was my disease, you see. I don't much remember what I did afterward, but I must've caused some mischief. Then that grand lady appeared, the one who collects charity for the poor patients. She shouted at me because the wine was hers, and then she shouted at Dr. Miller to treat me with something effective. I remember feeling horrible pain everywhere. When I woke up, my legs no longer worked."

What had they done?

Light steps and a soft hum sounded from beyond the door. Cora lowered her voice.

"Here comes Miss Burke. I keep quiet so she thinks I'm too broken for her tricks. It's the only way to stay alive around here." Cora turned her head away from Ella.

A key clicked in the lock, and Lavinia walked in, holding a tray with food. The matron set the tray on a chair and grinned at Ella.

"Are you talking to yourself? You must be lonely here, with mute Cora for your roommate. But now you have me for company."

Ella grunted. "Blast you! Untie me and let me take a piss."

"There's no need to untie you for that. Here."

Lavinia retrieved a pot from under the bed, helped Ella stand over it, and lifted her underclothes. Ella winced from the indignity and cold air. But when her bladder was finally blessedly empty, she felt giddy with relief.

When Ella was done, Lavinia pushed her down to sit on the bed and sat next to her with the food tray.

"Untie me and let me eat myself."

"So you can attack me and run? No, I can't let you do that. For your own good and everyone else's. Two physicians signed a declaration that you are raving mad and need treatment." Lavinia patted Ella's shoulder.

"Two? Dr. Quail asked me only two questions. That was enough for him to establish my insanity?"

Lavinia filled the spoon with porridge and glided it into Ella's mouth. "He learned all about your long illness from me. About your dangerous obsession with medicine. How you disguised yourself as a man so you could view surgeries and dissections. How you've attacked me verbally and physically, accused me of horrible deeds, and then poisoned me by slipping tartar emetic into my tea. You suffer from paranoia and delusions."

"I can prove my sanity. I am a surgeon." Ella swallowed the lumpy porridge. At least Lavinia didn't use starvation as treatment or punishment.

Lavinia sighed. "Are you going to claim again that you performed a great operation, removed a brain tumor?"

"You and Dr. Miller know the truth. And one attendant was there as well. I believe her name is Mary Ann. Let's ask her who operated on Lillian."

"Ah, right, you don't know." Lavinia shoved another spoonful into Ella's mouth and blinked away an invisible tear. "Mary

Ann is dead. Choked on a piece of meat. I tried to get it out of her throat, but it was stuck deep in there. By the time Dr. Miller rushed in with his instruments, she was dead. And speaking of Dr. Miller, he doesn't remember what happened during surgery. Poor dear, he had a concussion earlier in the day. But I've reminded him that he performed a groundbreaking operation, with me at his side, and together we saved his daughter's life. Did you know Lillian is his daughter? I knew even at the orphanage and watched over her."

The porridge turned bitter in Ella's mouth. "You killed Mary Ann. You had to get rid of the witness so Dr. Miller could claim credit for the surgery. What was wrong with her meat? Did you shove it down her throat and strangle her?"

Lavinia rolled her eyes. "Not that again. Mary Ann didn't chew well and choked. But her death won't be in vain. Dr. Miller is dissecting her skull and studying her brain. He's allowing me to help. It's exciting work! Not sure how much intelligence we'll find in her gray matter, but one has to do with what's available for learning. Eat, Ella. We must keep you strong." She fed Ella another spoonful.

Porridge got stuck in Ella's throat, and she cleared it with coughs. "With what's available. Like helpless orphans. You studied what happens when a child falls out of a window or swallows a pin."

"Ah, Constance must've talked." Lavinia raised an eyebrow. "Did she make you feel sorry for poor Tom or Jolly Molly?

They were slow, foolish, and at times, unbearable. Common brats. But when Dr. Miller and other surgeons gathered to heal them, those orphans became valuable. How much blood they vomited, how many times their bowels opened, all was recorded and published in medical journals. I used to steal those from Mrs. Simmons and read about the surgeries they underwent. When they died, students learned important lessons from dissecting their corpses. Their deaths brought more benefit than their pitiful lives ever could." Lavinia's eyes twinkled and her cheeks flushed as she talked. "But I'm talking too much while the doctor is waiting for you to administer a new treatment. And I still must feed your neighbor."

What are they planning to do to me?!

Lavinia walked over to Cora and slid a few spoonfuls into the woman's mouth. "See, Ella, you think badly of me. But look how good I am to Mrs. Butler."

Ella raised an eyebrow. "Because she already served her purpose? What happened to her?"

"Dr. Miller cured her of alcoholism."

"Cured her? I'm sure it's hard to fetch a bottle when your legs no longer work." Ella's jaw tensed.

Lavinia's head snapped to Ella. "The experiment was going well at first, if you must know. Dr. Miller was trying to cure her permanently. He overdid it with the dose in his excitement."

Ella's eyes widened. "The dose of what? What kind of medicine did he give her that would disable her in this way? And if he knew the dosage, how come the other woman who was here never woke up?"

"You mean Mrs. Amy Miller, his wife? Wait, how can you know she lay here?"

Cora's eyes shot daggers at her, and Ella's mouth dried. "I... I saw the words on the grave and assumed. What did he do to her?"

Lavinia spat onto the floor. "What did she do to him, you should ask. She was married to the most incredible doctor in England, yet she distressed and shamed him with her affairs and frivolous spending. Dr. Miller tried to fix her, and she failed him again. Didn't wake up after the surgery. Because of her, he lost faith in himself."

Ella trembled. *When we dissected Beth's skull, he spoke of the prefrontal cortex, how it controls emotions. Did he operate on his wife to make her submissive and apathetic? Is that what he wants to do to me?*

"What is he planning now? Why are you taking me to him?"

The matron yanked her to her feet. "You will find out. Don't scream or make any other noise. I have a rag and a bottle of ether ready to silence you. Such a handy discovery, ether. Your friend Miss Flowers left all the instructions and notes. I've learned how to produce it."

Ella spurred herself not to lose hope. *Caroline and Jamie will find me.*

"Are you thinking someone will come to your rescue, like that young man who saved you on the roof?" Lavinia said, as if reading her thoughts. "Miss Flowers believes you are fighting a smallpox outbreak. I've written to her in response to her letter. I'm sure she'll read my reply to her brother. Jamie, is it? Or perhaps it's too late to read my letter to him. She wrote that he'd been hurt in a duel, and his condition is grave. He's probably dead by now."

Ella kicked her ankle. "I don't believe a word you say. Show me the letter, thief."

Lavinia's fist punched Ella's ear, making it ring. "That was a warning. If you don't keep quiet and behave, I'll punish you. You understand?"

The matron led her out into the hallway, holding her by the shoulders. She opened a door, and they walked into another hallway. The simple rug, the wooden doors, and the view from the window were familiar to Ella.

The West Wing corridor. The room she's holding me in is just beyond it.

"You recognize where you are, of course," Lavinia said, leading her down the corridor. "But that information is little use to you. You won't escape with your arms tied up."

A door opened, and Ginny stepped out. She gaped, staring at Ella.

Ella mouthed the words "help me."

Lavinia waved her finger near the girl's nose. "Get back inside, you little rat. Or I will add some milk to your porridge, and you'll spend the night rolling with stomach pains."

She pushed the girl back into the room. Just before Lavinia closed the door, Ella mouthed, "No milk."

Lavinia threw her head back in laughter, and the menacing ring echoed through the corridor. She pushed Ella to keep going and whispered in her ear. "Too bad she can't tell anyone. Deaf. Mute. Stupid. And so easy to keep in line. A spoonful of milk mixed in her porridge makes her whimper and hold her knees. Three spoons make her toss and turn on her bed. Five make her belly bulge with air. How many should I add tonight? Perhaps I will give her some pudding instead. There was a boy in the orphanage who could only have pudding made with flour and water because milk would make his tongue and throat swell. I always brought him the treat he was allowed. But then I gave him pudding from the common table. Now I wonder what would happen if Ginny ate that much pudding baked with milk. It's interesting to compare the two cases. Why does Ginny's stomach ache, but Peter's throat swelled? That's what I'd love to know."

"You monster! Children and patients are not subjects for your sick experiments."

Lavinia slapped her on the lips. "Be quiet."

She thinks Ginny is stupid, but she's not. If only I could talk to her.

They approached the staircase where Dr. Miller and Lillian fell. Ella timidly put her leg on the top step.

"Don't worry, it's dry now," Lavinia said, leading her down. "You are too careful. Why didn't you run to me when I moaned in pain? Couldn't you bring me some water and charcoal to absorb the poison? You were heartless."

"So the accident was meant for me? Why?"

Lavinia hit Ella on the back. "Blame yourself. You became watchful and acted like you were in charge. I couldn't have that. Too bad Lillian and Dr. Miller got hurt, but it all worked out in the end. Lillian is speaking more and getting stronger each day. No more fits."

Thank God for that. Now if I could get out of here with her, Ginny, and the other patients.

They walked through the empty parlor. Ella listened for the clatter of plates and silverware from the dining room, but all was quiet.

"Where are the patients?"

"Don't you know? We have an outbreak of smallpox." Lavinia sighed dramatically. "Everyone must stay in their rooms. No visitors. This gives Dr. Miller the privacy needed for his work."

They stepped into the corridor that led to Dr. Miller's office and the operating room. A bloodcurdling scream came from there.

"Ah, that's Joanna. Dr. Miller mustn't be ready for you yet. But perhaps he'll let us watch." She poked Ella in her side. "This should be fun!"

When Joanna's scream subsided, Lavinia knocked. "Dr. Miller, I'm here with Ella. May we come in?"

"Absolutely!" Dr. Miller's voice rang with vigor. "I'm getting remarkable results. You should see this, Miss Burke. And let's let Ella observe so she understands the treatment."

Now I'm just Ella to them, like one of the poor patients.

Lavinia brought Ella into the room and pushed her onto a chair. On the operating table lay Joanna, one of the West Wing patients. Her eyes were large with fear. Restraints bound her to the table. A strange contraption of metal plates, glass jars, and wires was on a cart next to the doctor. Wires coming from it were tied around Joanna's head, wrists, and back. A burning smell filled the room.

"You remember Joanna," Dr. Miller said to Ella. "Since the death of her husband she heard voices in her head. Most days, she's sad and lethargic. Let me show what the treatment does to her."

"Please, no more," Joanna cried. "Let me be!"

Dr. Miller ignored her plea and asked Lavinia to turn the crank. A strangled shriek escaped Joanna's lips, and her body jolted, limbs jerking as if responding to an unseen puppeteer.

Ella watched, frozen with horror. "She's in pain. She doesn't want this treatment."

"She will be thankful later. This is the power of electricity harnessed to restore the mind and bring vigor to the body," Dr. Miller said with his arms folded. "I've implemented Luigi Galvani's ideas, using a Leyden jar and copper wires. An innovation I can show as proof of the progress this institution is making."

Lavinia bobbed her head. "This is only the beginning. Soon you will offer surgery to treat the most difficult patients. With me administering ether, you will be able to operate more safely and successfully than ever before. Your scalpel will restore minds."

A stone sank in Ella's chest. *With Caroline's invention, they will turn this place into a house of horrors.*

Joanna's shrieks became louder. Her eyes bulged and her face was a grimace of anguish.

"Stop it, please," Ella pleaded.

"We are about to make a breakthrough." Dr. Miller gestured wildly. "Go ahead and turn the crank one more time, Miss Burke. Only one more time, mind you. Not to repeat what happened to Mrs. Butler."

Is that how Cora lost control of her legs?

"Stop! What if you hurt Joanna permanently?" Ella cried, but no one paid any attention.

After another crank, Joanna's back arched and fell, and her eyes rolled into the back of her head. Ella hoped that the woman had found relief in unconsciousness.

"Dr. Miller!" Ella made her voice low. "You took the Hippocratic Oath. You taught it to your students, including me. First, do no harm. Don't you see that this supposed medicine violates your oath? You've harmed Cora Butler with your experiments. You are torturing Joanna. And what did you do to your wife?"

"Don't listen to her!" Lavinia bellowed. "Scientific progress requires sacrifices so others can benefit. You are a hypocrite, Ella. Wasn't your surgery on Lillian an experiment? Dr. Miller said many times that it was risky. And what about Miss Caroline's experiments with ether?"

Ella stared at Joanna's face, scrunched into a grimace. *Where is the boundary? Lillian could've died on the operating table. She may never recover from her surgery. How do I know that what I did to Lillian is ethical and what Dr. Miller is doing to Joanna is wrong?*

"Lillian... she gave permission. That's the difference. Dr. Miller, did Joanna allow you to give her this treatment? If not, this is cruelty, not medicine."

Dr. Miller stared at Ella, his expression vague. "*Primum non nocere,*" he muttered.

The burning smell became stronger. Then a spark, red and sizzling, jumped on Joanna's hair. Flames sprang up and danced.

"Fire!" Ella bellowed.

Miss Burke grabbed an apron, and the doctor removed his jacket, the two using the clothing to beat down the flames.

I can't help Joanna. I must save myself. And then I will save Ginny and others.

Ella ran as fast as her legs carried her.

Chapter 38

Running as fast as she could with her hands tied, Ella sped through the halls and up the stairs. She threw the weight of her body to open the door to Ginny's room. Ginny rushed to her and untied the sleeves of the straitjacket. Ella rubbed her hands to stimulate the circulation as she paced to the window. Not high at all, and there were no bars. She pushed, and the window squeaked and opened.

"Attendants, Ella's gone! Check the yard! Warn the guards. She couldn't get far." Lavinia's voice shouted through the halls.

It was broad daylight, and the guards walked below. An escape attempt now would be sheer madness. Ella closed the window.

Facing Ginny, Ella pointed to her lips. "Early in the morning, when everyone still sleeps, you must open the window and jump out." Ella pointed at the window and hopped.

Ginny stared with wide eyes. Then she shook her head no.

"You can do it. It only looks scary. There are bushes to break your fall."

With her mouth taut, Ginny hit herself with her hand. Then she brought her hand to her mouth and mimicked swallowing. Her knees hit the floor, and she hugged her belly, cringing.

"Is that how Miss Burke punishes you? She hits you, then forces you to eat foods made with milk?" Ella's heart squeezed. "I know you are scared to be caught. But it's the chance you must take, or she'll torture you and me until we die." Ella lay down on the bed and flailed her hands and legs like Joanna did during the electricity "treatment." She hoped Ginny would understand that the punishments would only become more horrible if she stayed. When Ella pointed to the window again, Ginny nodded.

Ella pointed to her lips. "You must follow the road. Remember the word *road* from your book?"

Cries of attendants echoed through the halls.

"Road," Ginny mouthed.

"It will lead you to the city. Plymouth. You remember Plymouth?"

The girl stepped back.

"You won't go to the asylum. Go to the Cooked Goose. You know the word *goose*. But I'm not talking of a bird, but of a tavern. There, ask for Jamie Flowers."

She'll never find it herself, but perhaps someone will help her.

She practiced the words *Cooked Goose* and *Jamie Flowers* with Ginny several times. Afraid to wait longer, Ella looked out into the corridor. Finding it empty, she dashed to her room and jumped onto the bed.

Cora turned her head to her. "I didn't think I would see you again, except in the same condition as me. What is Dr. Miller doing?"

"He used electricity. The woman was screaming, then lost consciousness. I got away when her hair caught fire."

"Then he's at it again. Doing his experiments in the name of medical progress. And wealth."

Ella's lungs contracted from a painful pressure building in her chest. "Is this about money? Dr. Miller never mentions it."

"There's that grand lady who always talks about profits. Quiet."

The door swung open, and Lavinia appeared on the threshold.

"There she is! I found her," she yelled to someone in the hall. Two attendants walked in and tied Ella's hands behind her.

When they walked out, Lavinia brought her fist to Ella's nose. "You will pay dearly for your little escape."

"Escape? All I did was return to my room. Couldn't stand to watch what you've done with poor Joanna. Is she dead?"

"None of your business." Lavinia folded her arms.

"She is." Bile crept up Ella's throat. "To think that I revered Dr. Miller and admired you. Two great minds turning the practice of medicine into cruelty and torture."

"Cruelty? It's not cruel if it can lead to discoveries that benefit others. Joanna is not anyone important. We've learned from today's mistake. Once we perfect the procedure, we'll use it on the East Wing patients. All that melancholy from unrequited love and reading too many novels will be cured with a charge of electricity or a slice of a scalpel. How their fathers and husbands will thank us!" She threw her head back laughing. "We'll continue the experiments tomorrow. First on Ginny, and then on you."

Ella spit into Lavinia's face. "You evil witch! You won't get away with this."

Her mouth twitching, Lavinia punched Ella in her middle, making her double over with pain, and pushed her onto the bed. Ella howled, and tears of pain burst from her eyes.

Lavinia bent down and caressed Ella's cheek. "Yes, you already said. I must be committed to an asylum, with bars and straitjackets. But look, you are tied up for your own safety, and I'm helping Dr. Miller change the future of medicine. Which one of us is mad?"

Chapter 39

Propped up by pillows, Jamie was sitting up and reading in his bed when Oli knocked on the door. When he walked in and scanned the room, the smile fell from his face.

Jamie lowered his book. "Were you hoping to see Miss Caroline? She went to the coach station about an hour ago. We received a letter from my parents, and she must urgently return home to Dorset. She left me in the care of Mrs. Armstrong."

"Oh." Oli's shoulders fell. "That's too bad. I mean, Mrs. Armstrong is an excellent cook and caretaker. But Miss Caroline... Well, I hope she has a comfortable journey home."

"You don't want to run after her and tell her how you feel? You may still catch her."

Oli's eyes dashed between the door and Jamie's face. "I shouldn't. Even if I want to with all my heart."

Jamie winked. "You passed my test. She's nearby, working on something with Tobby. Probably helping him with multiplication tables."

Oli gaped. "Why did you pull a trick like that? Are you hinting that I behave improperly with your sister?"

"You've been so proper I couldn't stand it anymore. Caroline is one in a million. Don't let her slip away."

The young surgeon blushed from his neck to his hairline. "It's not so simple."

"Are you married? If that's the case, you should've said something." Jamie crossed his arms.

"No. My parents pester me to choose a bride, but I keep frustrating them."

"Then perhaps you can surprise them with the happy news they've been hoping for. When my parents arrive, speak with my father. After you declare your feelings to Caroline, of course."

A sigh rocked Oli's chest. "Like I said. It's not so simple. Please say nothing to Miss Caroline."

"All right. I'll keep quiet."

Oli opened his bag and removed a jar with ointment. Lifting Jamie's shirt, he undid the dressing and examined the wound, pressing on the edges. "Does it hurt when I press on it?"

"A little. I think it's better."

"Yes, it's healing nicely. Some color has returned to your cheeks. Are you eating well?"

Jamie patted his belly. "Mrs. Armstrong had been stuffing me like a Christmas goose. First, I could barely stand all that food, but now I look forward to her meals."

"Healthy appetite is another good sign." Oli grinned. "Soon enough you'll have the strength to stand. Don't try that on your own or you could fall. But overall, you've done wonderfully so far. I give the credit to your sister."

"All the credit? You deserve more thanks than I could ever say." Jamie clasped Oli's hand. "But tell me. Do you still think that Dr. Miller was wrong when he diagnosed me with a fatal heart defect? Please understand. My parents and younger sisters will be here any day. They will be overjoyed with my recovery. But what if their joy will be short-lived and my heart gives out, as he predicted? Caroline told me that our mother's reason is slipping. I mustn't give her a shock."

Oli, who was spreading the ointment on Jamie's wound, halted. "That's something I was going to talk to you about. And I hoped Miss Caroline would be here to hear it as well."

By the time Oli had finished doctoring Jamie's wound and applying a new dressing, Caroline had returned with Tobby. The duo's eyes twinkled, and they grinned at each other.

"Oli, did you listen to Jamie's heart?" Caroline asked.

"I was just about to. Would you like to observe?"

Caroline removed a small wooden tube from her satchel that resembled the reed pipe that Tobby played. "Would you mind using this instrument of my design and Tobby's making?"

Oli frowned. "I don't follow. What would you like me to do with this? Play it like a shepherd's pipe?"

"No. Allow me to demonstrate."

She put one end of the tube to her ear and the other to Jamie's chest. After a few breaths, she straightened. "I heard Jamie's heartbeat and breathing more clearly. I've tried on Tobby as well and compared how his heart sounds with and without this tube. This aid amplifies the sound. The design can be improved upon, but this is promising."

Oli took the tube from her and listened. His eyes widened. When he rose, a grin spread on his lips. "This is incredible, Miss Caroline. My compliments on your brilliant invention. You must patent it."

"Oh, please." Caroline blushed and waved her hand in dismissal. "You are being too kind. Nobody will take seriously a tube created by a woman and a boy. But please tell me how Jamie's heart sounds."

"I hear more clearly. And I can say with more confidence than before that Jamie's heart doesn't have a murmur."

"Hurray!" Tobby cheered.

"Hurray indeed." Caroline hugged Jamie and cupped his cheeks. "Do you believe it now, brother?"

A wave of emotion hit Jamie, and he couldn't answer. Tears threatened to spill from his eyes.

Oli stepped closer to them. His hand reached for Caroline but stopped short of touching her. "I have something else to share regarding the heart defect."

All eyes went to him as he retrieved two newssheets from his case. "Jamie, you mentioned Dr. Miller saying that the oldest of his patients with a heart defect died at twenty. And you concluded that you would die at that age or earlier. Correct?"

"I realized it could be a few months more. But yes, that's what Dr. Miller said."

Oli held up one of the papers he was holding. "This is *Medical Essays and Observations*, a journal in which Dr. Miller regularly publishes. In this article he recounts inborn heart defects, mentioning several patients, particularly seventeen-year-old Charles McMurray. I've learned that poor Charles died three years later."

"What you found confirms Dr. Miller's words." Jamie knitted his brow. "His oldest patient died at twenty."

Oli put the paper on Jamie's lap. "This is an account of his death in the newssheet. Read it."

"I'd rather spare myself the dreadful details." Jamie cringed.

Caroline snatched the paper and brought it to her face. Her jaw fell open, and she threw the paper on the floor. "This is outrageous. Shame on him."

"Now I must know what it says." Jamie leaned forward.

Tobby tugged Caroline's skirt. "What did it say? I want to know."

"I don't have the words for this." Caroline's face reddened, and she wiped a bead of sweat off her forehead. "Dr. Miller is a scoundrel."

Oli passed her a handkerchief. "Your reaction is completely appropriate, Miss Caroline. I was just as incensed on behalf of your brother and your family."

"Tobby, give me the paper," Jamie said.

The boy lifted the paper off the floor and started reading. "What does that say about a cow?"

"A cow? You must not have read that right. Give it here." Jamie reached for the paper. His eyes darted over the print. "Charles McMurray died at his home three days after sustaining a kick to his chest from Fiona, his dairy cow."

Caroline crossed her arms. "In other words, who knows how long this man would've lived if not for a tragic accident. Dr. Miller had no right to tell our parents that you wouldn't live past the age of twenty. Why would he make such an ominous claim?"

"I believe he concluded that a heart defect always means an early death and ignored important details that weakened his assertion," Oli said. "While we don't know how long Charles would've lived if not for the accident, till twenty-one or till old age, we can say one thing for sure. Dr. Miller's words should not be believed without skepticism."

Jamie put the paper down and collapsed on his pillows. The tears that had pricked his eyes when Oli used Caroline's invention and confirmed that there was no heart murmur now poured down his cheeks.

Oli clapped him on the shoulder. "Promise me you'll stay away from dairy cows. Especially ones named Fiona."

"I can't laugh at this." A lump in Jamie's throat made it hard to speak. "I risked my life, thinking that it was almost over anyway. I left my family. I rejected the happiness I could've had with Ella. And I have a ball stuck near my heart that could still kill me. All this because of Dr. Miller's arrogance and carelessness. I can forgive an honest mistake, but your discovery proves that he lied or misrepresented the facts."

Caroline took Jamie's hand. "All will be well, Jamie. You will recover, lift our parents' spirits, and confide in Ella why you rejected her. I'm sure she will forgive you."

"Where is Ella?" Oli asked. "Did she visit?"

"No." Caroline shifted her feet. "But I received a letter from the matron of The Women's Sanctuary, Miss Burke. She wrote that Ella is treating smallpox cases. A quarantine has been imposed, and no one can enter or leave the premises. Miss Burke also said that my expertise with ether, the original reason I visited, won't be required and sent back my things."

Oli scratched his chin. "Strange. Why did Ella have someone write this letter for her?"

"Ella added a few lines. I understand she's extremely busy fighting the outbreak," Caroline offered.

Jamie bit his lip. "I wrote several more times. What if she's sick?"

"She wouldn't catch the pox." Oli crossed his arms. "All medical students were inoculated against it in our medical school, and I believe her mother inoculated her even earlier. But only one short letter? That doesn't seem like her. She'd want to know every detail of Jamie's recovery. Something isn't right."

Tobby's eyes opened wide. "What could have happened to Dr. Ella?"

"I should go see her. I promised." Jamie's hands were damp with sweat.

Oli put a hand on his shoulder. "Not yet. You need more time to recover. But I can go."

"Or I," Caroline added.

Before Jamie could respond, Miss Jenny's voice sounded from the door.

"Dr. Higgins! Are you here?"

"Yes, ma'am. How may I be of service?"

She opened the door but stayed on the threshold. "Honestly, I'm not sure. There's a girl downstairs. She's shaking and crying. Her dress is ripped and has thorns stuck to it. I thought she might be hungry and offered her food and warm milk, but she's staring at it like it could bite her."

"What is she saying?"

"That's the thing. She's just grunting or moaning. Apparently, she was found by a coachman on the road. It took him a while to understand where she wanted to go, but he made out the word *goose*. Not knowing what to do with her, he took her along with him to Plymouth. When they passed by here, he said to her, 'I can't find the goose you want, but here's the Cooked Goose. I like to eat there.' The girl waved her hands for him to stop, and he brought her in. I don't know what to do with her. She seems not right in the head. I thought of fetching a constable but then wondered if you might want to see her." Miss Jenny's gaze shifted to Tobby. "You are supposed to be helping in the kitchen. It's almost dinnertime."

"Can I see the girl? Please?" Tobby whined.

"No. She's not for you to gawk at or mock. Go!"

With his head down, the boy flew from the room.

Oli grabbed his bag. "The mind is not my area of expertise, but I'll see if I can help."

Chapter 40

Jamie was drinking a meaty broth under Caroline's watchful eye when Oli returned. A thin girl of twelve or so with disheveled ginger hair and large, tear-filled eyes followed him in. In her arms, she clutched a ragged doll. With her chin trembling, she stared at Caroline and Jamie.

Caroline smiled at the girl. "I'm Caroline. Do you need help?"

The girl indicated her lips, opening and closing them several times.

"You are hungry? Thirsty?"

The girl touched her lips again.

Frowning, Caroline glanced at Oli.

"It took me a few minutes, but I finally realized that she's mouthing words. She must be deaf, but someone taught her to speak," Oli said. "And it seems to me that she's saying *Jamie Flowers*."

"What?" Jamie put down the bowl. "I don't know her."

Caroline bent down to have her eyes at the same level as the girl's. She moved her lips slowly. "Are you looking for Jamie Flowers? That's him." She pointed to Jamie.

A smile lit up the girl's face, and she came to Jamie's bed.

Unsure what to say, Jamie offered her his hand. "I'm Jamie Flowers. How may I help you, Miss?"

The girl pointed to her lips and mouthed something.

"I'm sorry I don't understand." Then a guess hit him like a chilly draft. "Are you from that place where Ella works? What's it called?"

"The Women's Sanctuary." Caroline clenched her hands. "Oh dear. I think you are right. I saw patients there dressed like her. She must be a runaway."

"But she knows my name. Did Ella tell you to come here?" Jamie leaned in.

She took a breath, as if preparing for a difficult task. "Ella. Trouble," she whispered.

"Ella is in trouble?" Jamie touched the girl's elbow. His heart hammered, but he no longer worried about that. "What's wrong? Is she sick?"

The girl mouthed some words he couldn't understand. Then she repeated, "Ella. Trouble."

Jamie caught Oli's arm. "Oli, give me my clothes and your hand to help me stand."

"No! It's too early for that, Jamie. You haven't built up the strength." Oli shook off his arm and gestured to Caroline.

"Please reason with your brother. He can't go. A fall could kill him."

"I'm not staying in bed if Ella needs help!"

"Oli is right." Caroline rested her hands on Jamie's shoulders. "I'll go to The Women's Sanctuary and demand to see Ella. If I'm refused entry, I'll fetch a constable."

"I will come with you." Oli lifted his bag. But then he froze. "What do we do about the girl?"

"Let's bring her downstairs to the kitchen," Caroline suggested. "The cooks will keep an eye on her. When she feels safe, she'll eat and sleep."

Caroline put on a bonnet, took the girl by the hand, and led her out of the room.

Oli took a step after them, then turned on his heel and shook his finger at Jamie. "Don't even think of leaving that bed."

"Keep my sister safe and get Ella out of there," Jamie answered. "Godspeed."

When the door closed behind Oli, Jamie collapsed on his pillows. It dawned on him that Caroline should've taken her chaperone, Mrs. Armstrong, but he trusted Oli with his sister. It was the thought of Ella that made him unable to keep still.

Something's happening to Ella, and I lie here like a log. This is not a time to be weak. If Caroline and Oli don't return, I must go myself.

He chugged the rest of his broth, lukewarm but hearty, and swung his legs over the side of the bed. His feet touched the wooden floor. He grabbed the chair, tested his weight on his feet, and stood. Pain shot into his shoulder. His vision blurred for a moment, but his legs held steady.

Holding onto the chair, Jamie straightened and braced himself to take a step. A voice sounded from the corridor.

Oli and Caroline can't be back already. They must've forgotten something.

He sat down on the bed.

"Jamie, it's Tobby. Ginny told me something. Can we come in?"

"Who's Ginny?" Jamie got under the covers. "Do you mean the girl? All right, come in."

Tobby and the girl walked in, holding hands. "This is Ginny. We were in the orphanage together, before the Marine Society took me to be a shipboy and the orphanage director sent her to the lunatic asylum," the boy explained.

"Don't tell me, she's your long-lost sister." Jamie grinned.

"Sister? No! Although, I know nothing about my family. Mayhap she is. If so, I don't mind because she's clever and funny. We played together all the time."

Jamie furrowed his brow. "But from what I can tell, Ginny is deaf and mute."

"So what?" Tobby shrugged. "She was still a great playmate. I taught her many words that she repeated with her lips. Sometimes she would even speak. Ginny, remember what you would say when it rained?"

"Ginny likes rain." Her voice was the softest whisper.

"That's all great." Jamie raised his hand. "Now what did she tell you about The Women's Sanctuary?"

"Show him." Tobby nodded to Ginny.

The girl raised her doll. Then she folded the doll's sewn-on arms behind the doll's back.

"What does that mean?" Jamie frowned.

Tobby threw up his hands. "Don't you understand? Ella's imprisoned! The asylum workers tied her hands behind her back, like she's a lunatic. Instead of a doctor, she's now a patient or a prisoner."

Jamie's insides quivered.

If this is true, Ella will be guarded. I must have some idea where she's held.

"Tobby, I need you to speak to Ginny. Have her tell you all she can about that place. Where are the patient rooms? Who works there? Where are the guards, and how are they armed? Where's Ella's room? If you two can draw me a map of the place, I'll give you any reward you want. You can use Miss Caroline's room to work. There you should find drawing paper, pens, and other things you need. Meanwhile, I also have something to work on."

Tobby took Ginny's hand, and the children ran out of the room.

Again, he swung his legs to the floor, grabbed the chair for support, and stood. Then he let go of the chair and took several steps around the room. Pain burned his shoulder, but he willed himself to ignore it.

Three hours later he stood over his desk, fully dressed, his pistol at his belt. The map Tobby and Ginny drew was spread before him.

Tobby rocked on his heels. "Are you sure you can be out of bed?"

"Absolutely. Oli was just being cautious." Jamie waved his hand. "Now tell me what that is." He pointed at the drawing.

Ginny moved her lips.

"That's the parlor." Tobby translated.

"Good, I remember the parlor. Is that the staircase to the second floor?"

Tobby nodded.

"Excellent. And these are the patient rooms in two wings. You even drew the beds."

Tobby pointed. "This is where Ginny's room was. And that's where Ginny saw Ella."

"What was happening when she saw her?"

"She was led down the hall by the evil woman. I think her name is Miss Burn."

"Do you mean Miss Burke? I've met her. Why is she an evil woman?"

"She hit Ginny and made her eat foods that gave Ginny a stomachache. If Ginny refused, she forced her."

"Good Lord!"

The door flew open, and Conor appeared on the threshold.

"Jamie! You are on your feet!" Conor whooped and rushed to Jamie. "Thank God!" He wrapped Jamie in an embrace, sending bolts of pain through Jamie's chest.

"I think you're hurting him!" Tobby exclaimed, and Conor let go.

"Got too excited. I'm sorry."

Jamie rubbed his wound. "I'm much better, but not ready for such a mighty hug. How are my parents and sisters?"

"They are well. I've brought them to a nearby inn to change clothes and eat, and then they will come here. I'm so glad that they will see you up and about. Although I tried to deliver the news gently, as Miss Caroline instructed, I still gave them a shock. Your mother swooned into your sisters' arms. Your father, who has a sprained ankle, rushed to her and aggravated his injury. It took several days for them to recover and arrange for the trip. We've traveled at a slow pace, with frequent stops, because of your father's leg and your mother's frailty. Such delay drove me mad at first, but I stayed with them in case they needed help. Your parents were extremely kind to me, and your sisters were lovely conversationists. I told them all about our adventures, and I now know every story of your childhood. Which begs another question. Why didn't you tell me you had a heart defect that could kill you? How could you keep such a thing a secret from me?"

Jamie's head dipped. "When people learned about my heart, they would look at me with pity. I didn't want my friends to treat me that way. But it doesn't matter now. Oli convinced me that my heart is healthy." *Except for the ball lodged near it.*

Conor fisted his good shoulder. "Hurray! We must celebrate."

"Forget the celebration. Ella is in trouble, likely held prisoner in the asylum where she worked. We must rescue her."

"What?" Conor jerked back. "But your parents and sisters are coming to see you. They've traveled all this way."

"The reunion must wait. Caroline and Oli went ahead, but I won't stay back."

Conor's eyes bulged. "What are you planning?"

"I'm planning to gather our ship's crew and storm the place."

Chapter 41

Disturbed by a thunderstorm during the night, Ella didn't sleep. Her roommate shrieked from the bolts of lightning, keeping Ella awake and anxious.

Did Ginny get out yesterday morning? What if she got lost in the woods and is still out there in this horrible weather? And can it be true what Lavinia said about Jamie being injured?

All day yesterday Ella heard commotion in the halls. Lavinia eyed her with suspicion when feeding her, but she didn't fetch her for the experiments with Dr. Miller as she'd threatened. Ella assumed the delay happened because of Ginny's escape.

The rain finally subsided in the morning. Ella badly wanted to stand from the bed and stretch her limbs. Her hands were still tied in knots that cut into her skin. But when the lock on the door turned, Ella shut her eyes, faking sleep. If Lavinia had come to take her to Dr. Miller, she hoped to delay her even a couple of minutes. Anything to disrupt their plan, no matter how futile her attempt may be.

"Ella, get up and talk some sense into Dr. Miller"

Ella's eyes snapped open. Lavinia stood over her.

"Excuse me?"

Lavinia paced the room. "Mrs. Landon and her sons are here. They visited Lillian, and now they insist on speaking to Dr. Miller. But after your little speech about 'do no harm,' he locked himself in his bedroom. Tell him you didn't mean that nonsense you said. He must come out to speak to dowager Mrs. Landon, or she may get offended and stop her donations. Dr. Miller knows he cannot afford to frustrate her."

"So why aren't you telling him this?"

"Do you think I would be here if I hadn't tried everything I could think of?" Lavinia groaned.

The matron dragged Ella to the third floor. The door to Dr. Miller's bedroom was locked. The doctor's muttering resonated from inside.

"That boy... I told his parents... he would die by age twenty. But I didn't hear—"

Lavinia grabbed Ella's shoulders, causing her pain. "Speak to him!"

"Dr. Miller!" Ella called. "Dowager Mrs. Landon is here. She wants to talk to you about Lillian's surgery."

"I was supposed to do something for him. I wrote it down somewhere. Where?" Dr. Miller's voice wheezed.

"He's delirious." Ella's eyes widened.

"Keep trying!" Lavinia dug her fingers into her hair. "The Landons are too high and mighty to speak to me. The dowager had the nerve to say that the burns on my face disturb the patients and that I should wear a veil. They will only speak to the doctor."

I must use this chance.

Ella locked eyes with Lavinia. "Dr. Miller is clearly not himself and likely won't recover for a while. Untie my hands, dress me in my clothes, and let me speak to them as Dr. Parker. Mrs. Landon is my supporter."

"Do you take me for a fool? You are planning an escape." Lavinia shook her finger.

"Then you go speak to them, explain what's wrong with Dr. Miller, and listen to more insults about your face."

Lavinia swung her palm to slap Ella but stopped her hand in midair.

"One wrong word from you, and a patient will die. Two words, two patients. And I'll try the electric machine on you. You understand me?" she hissed into Ella's ear. When Ella nodded, she added in her normal voice. "They want to know how fast you can get Lillian back on her feet and make her presentable again."

Ella froze and her jaw dropped. "Presentable? She underwent surgery on her brain! Even if her recovery goes well, it may take months or years. Besides, I haven't seen the patient since the surgery."

"Tell them what they'd like to hear. They want her to recover but be out of their way. I overheard them saying that they cannot get an annulment for the marriage. They are stuck with Lillian as Arthur's wife."

Or Lillian is stuck with them. Ella sighed.

Twenty minutes later, Ella was dressed in her old clothes. Lavinia regarded her with a discerning gaze.

"You look and smell like you were dragged through a fishwife's stalls, but it will have to do. After all, you work in a lunatic asylum. Now, let's go. They are waiting in the parlor. And I remind you, every word you say should be in praise of Dr. Miller and this sanctuary. You know what will happen if you cross me. And don't even think of running. There are guards all around the building, ordered to detain you."

Lavinia brought Ella to the parlor, where dowager Mrs. Landon, Arthur, and Drake sat on the large sofa, sipping tea from porcelain cups. They ogled her from head to toe.

"What questions can I answer?" Ella sat down on the chair across from Mrs. Landon. Lavinia stood behind her. Her hot breath blew on the back of Ella's neck.

Mrs. Landon took a long sip of her tea. "I'm disappointed Dr. Miller is still not here, but we can't wait for him forever. What can you say about my daughter-in-law's recovery?"

Feeling Lavinia's stare, Ella replied, "It's going as well as we could hope for."

If Lillian is speaking and hasn't had a seizure since the surgery, then that's the truth.

"She only speaks a few words and even those are slurred. When will she converse normally?" Drake asked.

"And when will her hair grow back? That bald head is atrocious," Arthur added, sipping his tea.

"That we can fix with a wig," Mrs. Landon replied to him. "The most important question is, when can we expect a full recovery?"

"I cannot give you a concrete answer. She's unlikely to ever be the same. In the very best case it would be a year, and only if she receives careful nursing."

"A year?" Mrs. Landon exchanged glances with her sons.

"It will be too expensive to keep her here that long." Drake scowled. "But we can't send her to a public institution either. People will say we don't treat her well."

Arthur curled his lip. "I don't want to see her again until her looks and speech improve." He glanced at Lavinia. "Good tea. Not the bergamot I asked for, but whatever you've used is flavorful."

Mrs. Landon drained her cup. "I found the tea only tolerable, Miss Burke. Next time, add more sugar. And wear a veil, as I asked. The dreadful burns on your face are upsetting my digestion."

Lavinia flushed from ear to ear.

The dowager cleared her throat. "If it's as Dr. Parker says, we should accept the proposal from Mr. and Mrs. Davis and send Lillian to them. There, she'll recover away from the gaze of society. And our gazes."

"Her parents wrote to you? They want Lillian to return to them?" Ella asked, afraid to hope for good news.

"Yes. Although our relationship will never be the same because of their deceit about Lillian's adoption, we are still corresponding. I've informed them of Lillian's illness and her confinement to The Women's Sanctuary. Her father thought she should remain here until she's well enough to return to Arthur, but Mrs. Davis wants a chance to make things right with her and nurse her back to health."

Her adoptive mother's love will be the best medicine for Lillian.

A commotion came from a distance. Then an attendant rushed in.

"Miss Burke, there's someone asking for you."

"Who is it?" Lavinia demanded. "We are not supposed to have visitors."

Ella held her breath. *If she leaves, it will be my chance to act.*

Mrs. Landon curled her lip. "Go answer the door, Miss Burke. That's your job."

Once Lavinia disappeared, Ella assessed if she could run. She could see a guard from the window, posted in the garden. And Lavinia just went to answer the door, where there likely would be another guard or two.

The guards can catch me and then Lavinia may take revenge on the patients. Instead of running, I must convince the Landons to help.

She rose and scanned their faces. They stared back with coolness.

"I must tell you what's happening here. Dr. Miller is doing horrible experiments."

"Experiments?" Mrs. Landon's mouth rounded. "Are you speaking of his groundbreaking work with electricity? I fully support it. It's the future of medicine. I even hoped he would give a demonstration today."

"You don't understand. A patient died."

"Who?" Drake frowned.

"Mrs. Joanna Lyons. Her hair caught fire during the experiment. And Mrs. Cora Butler lost control of her legs some time ago."

"Well, that's unfortunate." Mrs. Landon sighed. "But I'm sure such accidents will be prevented in the future. This institution must offer effective cures. Some lunatics must be shocked to regain their reason."

"Would the magistrate investigate?" Arthur clicked his tongue. "I hope our family name won't be dragged into the papers."

"What's to investigate? Joanna was a charity case, a nobody. And Mrs. Butler was so grateful to The Women's Sanctuary she left it all her assets. Dr. Miller has all the proper documents." Mrs. Landon shrugged.

Ella stumbled back. "You can't approve of this. This nightmarish treatment is forced on the patients. And Miss Burke is insane. She manipulates and tortures her charges. Bring the magistrate here. He must investigate."

They all stared at her with jaws hanging open. Finally, the dowager folded her hand on her belly and spoke. "Obviously, Dr. Miller made a mistake hiring you. I'm extremely disappointed that you don't see the great potential of his research and the innovations this sanctuary offers."

This is useless. I should run.

Ella dashed to the door.

"Grab her! She'll go to Magistrate Harrow!" Mrs. Landon's voice barked behind her.

Before Ella reached the hallway, four muscular arms seized her and pushed her down to the floor. As she wiggled like a worm and screamed at the top of her lungs, many pairs of boots and shoes entered the room.

"What are you doing? Release her at once!" a male voice commanded.

The weight of her assailants' bodies lifted off her.

"We were... helping Dr. Parker." Drake offered her a hand to stand.

Ella scrambled to her feet and scanned the room. Caroline and Oli regarded her with relieved expressions. Next to them was a tall, gray-haired gentleman wearing an immaculate black coat and leaning on a walking stick. On his other side was... Ursula, barely recognizable in a burgundy dress and a matching hat. She was holding a pocket notebook. A man, slightly older than her but with the same long nose and sandy hair, was beside her. Two constables stood in the back.

"Magistrate Harrow, what's happening here?" Mrs. Landon rose and crossed her arms, addressing the gentleman with the walking stick. Her sons flanked her. "I'm the benefactress of this sanctuary. Why did you bring the constables?"

"Their first order of business was to arrest Miss Lavinia Burke. She's been taken to the carriage," Magistrate Harrow said. "Their colleagues are currently arresting Dr. Miller and collecting his documents in his study."

"What charges are you bringing against the brilliant doctor whose research will change the world?" Mrs. Landon's forehead became soaked with sweat. "Surely not patient abuse or cruelty. Compared to other institutions, this place is wonderfully humane."

She has a point. An experienced lawyer will paint the Woman's Sanctuary in the best light and say that everything was done for the good of the patients.

Magistrate Harrow raised an eyebrow. "Yes, proving abuse would be difficult. But financial manipulation is another matter. Patients are confined here for profit and not released when they or their families want them home. And sometimes, they are pressured to will their entire fortunes to the Sanctuary."

Mrs. Landon grabbed her chest and blanched. Her sons watched her with concern.

Ursula squared her shoulders. "We also plan on exposing all of Miss Burke's crimes, from killing her parents and endangering children in the orphanage to abusing patients in Mercy's Asylum and here. My brother and I spent years working on this grim story."

"You are writers?" Ella gaped.

Ursula extended her hand for a handshake. "Pleased to officially meet you, Dr. Parker. My name is May Ursula Collins, and this is my brother, Jack Collins. My brother is famous for stories exposing various places for unsafe and harsh conditions. Few people know, however, that I've gotten jobs to witness the abuses firsthand. This story has a personal connection for us, however. Our younger sister died at Mercy's Asylum, and we believe Miss Burke was responsible. Now that I've followed Miss Burke for almost three years, I'm convinced it's true. And we now have witnesses such as Constance and you to confirm my accounts. I must say, you were a bright spark in this place, and our story will praise your efforts to help the vulnerable patients."

Arthur cringed. "A scandal in the papers? Mother, let's go. We don't want our name connected to this."

"Not a penny of our family money shall go to this place from now on. Do you understand, Mother?" Drake added, offering his hand to Mrs. Landon. "Find yourself another charity to throw your money at."

Mrs. Landon's face turned white and sweat poured from her forehead. "Yes. We are leaving. Now."

The magistrate stepped up to her. "Are you in a hurry? I'm afraid there's something I must show you. These are papers for the arrest of Mrs. Georginia Landon."

The dowager moaned and shielded her face with her hands.

Drake stepped toward the magistrate. "How could you arrest our mother? She's a lady. If something criminal has happened in this asylum, she cannot be held responsible."

"Mrs. Landon, would you like to explain to your sons, or should I?" Magistrate Harrow asked.

"I'm under arrest because I own The Women's Sanctuary." Mrs. Landon dipped her head. "You both own it as well. I don't know if you remember signing the papers because you were drunk more than usual."

Arthur's eyes bulged. "Why, Mother? You waste your time and money on charities, but this is beyond my comprehension."

"Don't look at me like that. I did it for you as much as for me." She threw her shoulders back. "The Women's Sanctuary is a business I've built. I've doubled the money left to me by my husband. And you've profited as well. How do you think your frivolous spending and your gambling debts are covered? And how much have we paid the lawyers thanks to Arthur's elopement? Your earnings as officers don't cover even a third of what you spend, and your inheritance is long gone. Of course, being a woman in society, I had to pretend that I'm the benefactress of a charity."

Ella's jaw fell. *All that talk of doing good for others and her Christian duty. The dowager profited from confining women, promising breakthrough treatments, and having the families foot the bill. And to cover up her motives, she took on charity cases, making them first in line for medical experiments.*

"Wait, if we are the owners, that means we..." Drake rubbed his forehead.

"Yes, I have the papers to arrest you, Mr. Drake Landon, and your brother, Mr. Arthur Landon, as well." Magistrate Harrow showed them the documents. "I was at your residence earlier but learned from your servants that you were here. How nice of you to come to the asylum, where I was headed as well."

Mrs. Landon made a choking noise in her throat. "Do you mean to take us in the same carriage that you've hired for Miss Burke? I'm a lady, sir. I can't be transported with a common criminal."

The magistrate scratched his chin. "Out of respect for your family I will allow you and your sons to return home in your carriage. Accompanied by a constable, of course. You all are under house arrest."

"Outrageous. We'll appeal," Drake and Arthur grumbled, following their dejected mother and the constable out of the building.

"We are so glad you are safe, Ella," Caroline said with her hand on her heart. "That poor child found us, but all she could say was *Ella* and *trouble*."

"It's a miracle Ginny found you. How did you decide to bring the magistrate as well as Ursula?"

Oli spoke. "Miss Caroline and I came here and asked for you. An attendant told us about an outbreak of smallpox and that we could not see you. We informed her that we are a doctor and a caregiver, but even then she refused us entrance and called the guards. We visited the magistrate to confirm if he was aware of the outbreak and told him of the message the runaway child brought."

"I should've looked into The Women's Sanctuary earlier, when Miss and Mr. Collins told me of the horrors happening here." Magistrate Harrow's face tensed. "I refused to believe them, thinking they were exaggerating for a scandalous story. But the visit from Miss Flowers and Dr. Higgins, the claim of a smallpox outbreak, and the story about a deaf girl made me suspicious. I sent for Miss Collins."

Ursula spoke. "I brought Constance, who told us chilling tales of Miss Burke staging accidents in the orphanage and the asylum. The pattern was obvious. With time, her schemes became more elaborate and shocking."

Magistrate Harrow loosened his cravat. "When we spoke of Mrs. Beth Lowe's tragic death, I remembered a complaint I'd received from her husband. Shortly before his wife's fatal jump, Mr. Lowe had written her a letter, saying that he and the children could no longer stand being apart from her and would make arrangements for her care at home. Her death was a great shock to him, and he urged me to investigate it. Miss Constance said that the letter Mrs. Lowe read was of a different nature: cold and cruel, telling her that her husband had found a new wife and mother for her children. The accounts of two different letters made me conclude that someone forged the husband's letter to drive poor Mrs. Lowe to suicide."

"Miss Burke's talents include forgery," Ursula said.

Ella felt a lump in her throat. "I was with Beth on the roof. Someone told her she must jump in order to be loved by her family again. I thought she was hallucinating, but Constance opened my eyes."

Jamie was there too. Why isn't he here?

"But why did she drive that poor woman to suicide?" Caroline cupped her cheeks in her hands.

"Miss Burke overheard that Dr. Miller and I needed a skull to dissect so we could prepare for an extremely complex surgery. I think she sacrificed Beth to help us." Ella bit her cheek.

Magistrate Harrow spoke again. "And another letter came to my mind. A woman named Mrs. Pamela Cline was looking for her twelve-year-old sister, Justine. Ten years ago, when Miss

Pamela was only fourteen, a terrible fever killed both of her parents and left Justine deaf. The neighbors convinced her that caring for her deaf two-year-old sister would be too big of a burden. The older sister gave the child to a clergyman who promised to place her with a good family. He left the parish unexpectedly, without telling Miss Pamela what happened to Justine. Since then, the older sister has had a change of fortune and married. She told the story of her sister to her husband, and they combed orphanages and asylums, looking for the girl. Several places had records of a deaf and mute girl named Ginny who suffered frequent and painful bellyaches. Mrs. Cline was convinced that Ginny must be her sister Justine. Mrs. Cline herself suffers from an affliction brought on by the ingestion of milk, a condition her mother had as well. The records pointed to The Women's Sanctuary as the place where the girl was currently confined. Mr. and Mrs. Cline visited and were greeted by Miss Burke, who swore that no such patient was living here. The couple asked me for help in their search for Justine."

"Ginny must be the child they are searching for. Miss Burke kept her away from her family." Ella swallowed.

Ursula set her jaw. "Miss Burke enjoyed her experiments on Ginny's stomach too much to let her go. It makes me wonder if there are other patients here who have relatives searching for them. And while looking into financial statements, I found enormous fortunes were being paid for some patients and inheritances turned over to the Sanctuary."

"There were patients who wanted to return home, but Dr. Miller insisted they must stay. Mrs. Landon likely pressured him to keep the wealthy patients as long as possible. But what will happen to the patients now that Dr. Miller and Miss Burke have been arrested?"

The magistrate spoke. "I've arranged for them to be taken to other asylums and hospitals. Their relatives will be notified. The carriages should arrive in a few hours to transfer them. But where is Dr. Miller? I want him to answer my questions before I send him to the holding quarters."

Pressure squeezed Ella's chest. *Dr. Miller's experiments went too far. But he had also done so much good. What will his punishment be?*

"Do you smell something?" Oli said. "Smells like... smoke."

"Yes, I smell it too." Caroline waved her hand in front of her nose.

The magistrate coughed, and Ella's throat tingled.

Ursula ran to the window. "Did the witch escape the constables and start a fire? Arson is one of her alleged crimes. She burned her parents' house and the orphanage."

"Where is it coming from?" Ella's pulse drummed in her ears. "Let's go in different directions and look for the source."

If this is Lavinia's doing, she'll likely want to burn the patients' records.

Ella ran toward Dr. Miller's office. The air thickened as she neared the room, making Ella's eyes itch and water. Still, she made out a body in a constable's uniform lying by the door. "The fire is in the study! And the constable is unconscious," she cried, hoping someone would hear. The smoke clawed at her throat, and she doubled over, coughing. A sweet-smelling rag covered her nose and mouth, and the world dissolved into a haze.

Chapter 42

Jamie's shoulder stabbed with agonizing pain, but he didn't dare to slow his horse. The black geldings they'd borrowed from Miss Jenny were sturdy and fast, just what they needed to ride through the woods and fields on a muddy road. But the haste came with a price. Each hoofbeat seemed to echo in the ball lodged in Jamie's wound.

Conor rode beside Jamie, glancing at him every few minutes. "Jamie, let's stop and give the horses a drink. Why such haste? We are well ahead of the men."

"Haste? I wanted us to go last night." He would've ridden in the dark, if not for a thunderstorm so strong that Miss Jenny said that riding through the woods in it would kill them and the horses. Instead, they trudged through the downpour, combing the taverns and inns, looking for familiar faces. Despite the storm, they found a good number of seamen who knew Ella and volunteered to participate in the rescue. The group gathered crowbars, axes, and ropes, as well as cutlasses and daggers, and set out to march toward The Women's Sanctuary at dawn. Jamie and Conor, riding fresh horses, were well ahead of them.

"If you don't want to stop for the horses' sake, stop to give yourself some rest. Your face is whiter than the morning mist."

If I get off the horse and lie down in the soft grass, I may not find the strength to get back up again.

"We must be close. Once we see the gates, we'll take a short rest."

Jamie soon learned that he underestimated how long it would take them to ride on the unfamiliar and muddy road. They took a couple of wrong turns and needed to turn around. By the time the iron gates appeared on the horizon, the sun was nearly at its peak. They dismounted their horses and tied them to a tree. Jamie gulped water from his flask.

"Why don't I go first and learn what's happening while you rest? You are wincing in pain." Conor offered him a sip of his brandy.

Agony was a more fitting word, but Jamie forced a smile. "Diplomacy was never your strong point. I should do the talking." He gave Conor back his brandy and labored toward the gates.

"I don't even see a guard. And the gates are wide open." Conor said, catching up to him in two strides.

"That's strange. Convenient, but strange." He glanced around, but no one seemed to be rushing to meet them.

The smell of smoke reached his nostrils. Jamie peered at the stately building. The front doors flew open, and people rushed out, bumping into each other. Something red flashed in a window on the first floor. Black smoke curled, and the curtains were ablaze. Jamie's legs weakened, and he gripped the gate to prevent a fall.

"Fire. What if Ella is locked inside?"

"And Lillian."

Putting all his remaining strength into his legs, Jamie rushed to the building, Conor next to him.

A gaggle of women emerged as they approached the open doors. Some had eyes wide with fright; others wore passive expressions, as if they didn't comprehend they were in danger. One laughed with her head tilted back.

A calm voice sounded behind them. "Keep moving, ladies. Step away from the building and find a place in the shade. If you are hurt or feeling poorly, let me know. I will bring Dr. Higgins to you."

"Caroline, thank God," Jamie cried as his sister appeared, her dress black with soot. "What's happening?"

She gasped. "Jamie, what are you doing here? You belong in bed. Mr. Leach, how could you let him come?" she added, shaking her head at Conor.

Jamie grabbed her hand. "No time for that. Where's the fire? Where's Ella?"

"The smoke came from the study. Mr. and Miss Collins and Magistrate Harrow tried to put it out, while Oli and I went to the second floor, where the bedrooms are located. Some of the corridors were thick with smoke. We are leading the patients to safety, and Oli is treating those who need aid. Mostly smoke sickness, not serious burns."

"Where should I go?" Conor bent to her.

She coughed and spit before answering. "If you have the strength to break down doors, go to the second floor. There are some patients locked in their rooms. We've been trying to free them." She took a gulp of water Jamie offered her.

Conor rushed inside. A woman in a brown dress, likely an attendant, led out a couple of crying and shivering patients in nightgowns.

"Where's Ella?" Jamie's palms gripped his sister's shoulders.

"She was with us earlier, in the parlor, before we noticed the fire. She's probably helping the patients who can't walk on their own."

"Have you seen her since the fire broke out?"

Caroline blinked. "I don't think so."

A man and a woman carried out an unconscious person in their arms. Caroline sped after them. "Did you see Ella after the fire started?"

The man shook his head, and the woman frowned.

"She wasn't on the second floor with us," the woman answered.

Jamie ran inside. Thick smoke stung his eyes, making it impossible to see his way. His chest burned. He shuffled forward but bumped into a man with a face black with soot, carrying someone in his arms.

"Conor!" Jamie exclaimed when he recognized his friend's clothing, if not his face.

"My mother," Conor rasped, coughing. "Help me."

Jamie grabbed the shoulders of the woman his friend carried. He moaned at the pain in his chest as they brought her outside. After they laid her on the grass, they waved to Oli to attend to her. The woman's chest didn't rise.

"This is your mother?" Jamie asked Conor, who trembled despite the sweat rolling from his forehead.

"Yes. Why didn't I see her that day we came looking? And now it may be too late." His voice quivered.

Caroline ran over to them. "Do you know who this is, The Lost One or Lillian? Those are the last two patients Miss Collins hadn't accounted for."

"This is my mother, Marie-Louise Leach."

"Oli! Over here!" Caroline knelt and put her ear to the woman's chest.

Jamie's heart pounded like a drum as he scanned the faces around him. *Ella isn't here. Where is she?*

"Is she breathing?" Conor knelt by Caroline.

Caroline dipped her hand into her pocket and removed the wooden tube. After listening through it, she nodded. "She's alive."

She said something else to Conor, but Jamie wasn't listening anymore. His hand on his aching shoulder, he pushed inside the burning building again.

The map sketched by Tobby and Ginny unrolled in his mind.

I'll check the basement first.

He stumbled through the smoke toward the corridor that would lead to the basement stairs.

Someone grabbed his arm and pulled him in a different direction.

"What are you doing?" he choked out.

Conor's voice shouted into his ear. "Third floor. That's where Dr. Miller's private quarters are. He didn't come out. Ella and Lillian must be there with him."

"Shouldn't you be with your mother?"

Conor coughed. "Oli said she will be fine. I must find Lillian."

Leaning on Conor, Jamie staggered up the stairs.

Chapter 43

*W*here am I?

Ella woke up seated on a chair with her hands tied behind her back. Her feet, also tied together, rested on a stone floor. Crackling and muffled shouts came from somewhere nearby. Windows were up high and let in little light. For a moment Ella thought herself to be in the orlop, where she cared for the wounded during battles. There were barrels and crates of various sizes, broken furniture, and a table by the wall with something—or someone—lying on it. A rotten stench came from there. But the air was thick with other smells: turpentine, alcohol, and smoke. Each breath burned Ella's lungs.

I'm in the basement where Dr. Miller did dissections. The body on the table is likely Joanna's. The fire is burning above.

She pulled on the cords that restrained her arms, trying to loosen them, and grunted with the effort. Lavinia, her nose and mouth covered by a scarf, approached.

"Ah, you are awake." Lavinia's voice was menacing. "Not for long."

Despite the rising heat, Ella's blood went cold.

"What have you done?"

Lavinia coughed. "Things usually end the same way: with a fire. When this is over, Joanna will be barely more than ash, and everyone will think she burned alive. Like my parents. Or Deaf Fannie. The coroner declared they died in the fire, but they were dead before the fire started."

She poured something on the floor and retreated to a corner hidden in darkness.

Did she pour something flammable, like alcohol or turpentine? She means to start another fire.

"Help! I'm in the basement!" Ella yelled with all her might. Her voice was hoarse, and the effort caused her to break into a coughing fit.

"Your friends can't hear you from here. And they are busy saving the patients," Lavinia said, moving a crate out of her way to approach the dissection table, where Joanna's body lay. "A lifetime of Dr. Miller's priceless records could burn, but they are rescuing the lunatics. Good thing I've saved the records and journals in a metal chest that will withstand fire."

With her teeth gritted, Ella rubbed the cords on her arms against the chair. "You will not escape justice."

"There's no proof against me. Only you and Dr. Miller saw how Joanna died. Dr. Miller won't tell. And you will not come out of here alive. You can stop pulling on your cords. Unlike those empty-headed constables who thought me harmless and only loosely tied my hands in the front, I've secured you properly." Her chilling laugh made Ella shrink inside.

A floorboard above them creaked and sagged. Sparks flew but died in the air.

Continuing to rub the cords on the chair, Ella said, "Lavinia, it's not too late to stop this. Untie me and come out with me. I will say that I was trapped in the basement, and you've saved my life. Don't you want to be a hero and be praised?"

Lavinia, who was pouring liquid over Joanna's body, abandoned what she was doing and came to stand in front of Ella. Her palm caressed Ella's cheek, making Ella's muscles lock and her breath still. "You know me well because we are so much alike. We are both brilliant, both love science and medicine. But neither of us could walk into the medical school as women. We chose different paths to pursue our goals, but at our cores, we are the same. It's a shame to lose such a great mind as yours."

I'm nothing like you. I studied medicine to help people. You staged cruel experiments that hurt the most vulnerable. That's not science. That's evil.

Biting back retorts, Ella babbled, hoping to win some time as she rubbed the cords on her wrists. "It's true what you say... There are many mysteries in medicine. We can research together. I can teach you."

The first lesson would be medical ethics.

The air was now thick with fumes of turpentine and alcohol. The sparks were crackling. Any minute the fire would start here on its own.

Lavinia's hand squeezed Ella's shoulder. "Perhaps in another life. I can't let you go, not with all that you know about my past. But I will be good to you. I'll dose you with ether before I burn this place and you."

She dipped her hand into her pocket and removed a bottle and a rag. There must have been little left, because she tilted the bottle upside down and shook it. Ella worked feverishly to free her hands. The cords loosened.

The ceiling cracked with a loud pop. A beam fell in the far corner. The ether bottle slipped from Lavinia's hands and broke on the stone floor.

"Blast it, it splashed on my dress! But that's all right. I've made more." She walked to a shelf and reached for a large bottle. As she opened it, Ella twisted her wrists, and the cords loosened more, enough for Ella's right hand to come free. Holding her breath, she worked to free her left hand.

Lavinia turned with a bottle in one hand and a rag in the other. The fire from the lantern reflected in her wide, crazed eyes. With slow, deliberate movements, she wetted the rag.

"Your friend Miss Flowers wrote about the different stages of anesthesia. Which one would you prefer? I could give you a whiff of ether, reducing pain but allowing you to scream. Inhaling more would put you into the second stage; you would hear and see but not respond. I've been favoring stage three. It puts a patient or an opponent into instant sleep, and they feel nothing. That worked for Lillian's surgery, but I also found it handy to overpower the constables and you. Finally, there's stage four... death."

A burning beam caved in from the ceiling and fell, hitting Lavinia on the head and landing at her feet. Her dress caught fire. Screaming, Lavinia tossed on the floor. Flames rose from the puddles of ether and turpentine. They engulfed her and spread through the cramped space. She rolled to beat the blaze off her, but the fire burned brighter. Lavinia's bloodcurdling screeches were silenced by the roaring flames.

What a horrible death.

Ella's hands were free, and she untied her legs. The fire was nearing her. Each breath scorched her with heat and fumes. Blinded by smoke, she stumbled as she searched for the stairs.

Chapter 44

Smoke covered the stairs as Jamie and Conor ascended to the third floor. Each step sent a wave of pain into Jamie's chest. They stumbled into two men who were coming down the stairs, coughing profusely. One of them wore a constable's uniform. The other Jamie guessed to be Magistrate Harrow.

"Are you coming from Dr. Miller's rooms? What's happening there?" Jamie yelled.

The magistrate coughed before speaking. "The doctor locked himself in his bedroom, and he's taken a woman hostage. Threatens to shoot her first and then himself if anyone opens the door." He paused and coughed some more. "We've pleaded with him to let the woman go, told him that the fire will kill them both, but he seems determined to die with her. We must get some air and find help." They pushed past Jamie and Conor.

Covering their mouths with their sleeves, Jamie and Conor continued upstairs. On the third floor, smoke poured through the hallways. The one to their left was impenetrable with smoke, but the one to their right seemed passable. Jamie checked his mental map. This was the way to Dr. Miller's bedroom. He pointed to Conor to proceed in that direction.

Conor shouted in Jamie's ear, "I will break down the door."

Before Jamie could stop him, Conor ran up to the door and gave it a powerful kick and a shove. The hinges squeaked, but the heavy door held.

"I warned you. You will not arrest me and separate me from Lillian, my beloved daughter." A deep male voice came from the room.

"Lillian." Conor's lips trembled.

Jamie's heart dropped. *Where's Ella?*

"Help," a weak woman's voice pleaded.

"My child, don't be scared. Your death will be easy, and you will finally be with the two people who love you the most. Your mother will welcome you into her arms. And then I will follow."

"He means to murder her," Conor mouthed. "Let's ram the door."

"No." Jamie's grabbed Conor's shoulder and spoke through the door. "Dr. Miller, I'm Jamie Flowers. Do you remember me? I want to help you."

"Help? How? Aren't you here to arrest me?"

"No. I..."

Conor punched the door. "You do with yourself whatever you want, old lunatic, but don't you dare hurt Lillian!"

Despite the heat, a chill ran under Jamie's skin. *No! He'll shoot her!*

The door creaked and opened. Dr. Miller stood there with his pistol pointed at Conor. On the floor behind the doctor, Lillian, with her head bandaged, lay on the rug.

"Please put away your pistol and come with us." Jamie choked on the smoke as he spoke. "We'll take you and Lillian to safety."

Dr. Miller stared at him. "I want to die with my creations: my sanctuary and my daughter."

"Die with your blasted sanctuary, but leave her out of this." Conor lunged at him. Dr. Miller lost his footing and fell back on the rug. A shot boomed, and something whistled over Jamie's head. The wall behind him cracked as the bullet hit it.

With Lillian in his arms, Conor disappeared into the smoke. The doctor made no move to get off the floor. He sat there, as if there weren't smoke covering his feet.

Jamie walked to the door to check if the corridor was still passable.

"That man who took Lillian, does he love her? She wanted to be loved."

Halted by Dr. Miller's question, Jamie turned.

"He will save her, even at the peril of his own life," Jamie answered, looking between the doctor and the door. "Is Dr. Parker here?"

"No, I haven't seen her today. Although I wish to speak to her. She asked me a great question I've been pondering the last couple of days."

Ella spoke of him with reverence, even after he wanted to remove her from medical school. She'd be horrified at me leaving him to die.

Something exploded in the hallway, and the blast resonated through Jamie's body.

Jamie drew a long breath and offered the doctor a hand to stand. "Let's go before it's too late."

"Do you know your shoulder is bleeding?" the doctor asked as evenly as if speaking to a patient during an exam.

Jamie glanced down and touched his wound. Blood covered his hand.

The ball. It must've shifted.

"Forget it. I'm offering you one last time, go with me or die here."

Dr. Miller broke into a cough. "Why do you want to save my life?"

"Why are you wasting time on talking?" Jamie cut his arm through the air. "The building is burning. Are you mad?"

A chuckle escaped the doctor's throat. "That's a question I've wrestled with for years, and I still don't have the answer. Usually not, but at times, very likely. Yet most people don't notice my insanity and praise my mind, so perhaps I'm sane and they are mad."

Jamie's fists clenched. "I must be mad as well, wasting precious time on you. You've ruined my life. And yet I want to save you. You mean a lot to Ella. She'd want you to come with me and live."

"All night I've been thinking how many people I must've harmed. The botched surgeries. The mistakes in diagnosis. Those horrible experiments with electricity." He blinked and wiped his face. "You are Jamie Flowers, son of a dental-surgeon?"

"Yes." Jamie bent down and put his hand around Dr. Miller's waist.

"When I have recalled my mistakes, I've remembered you. I must tell you everything."

"Not with the fire about to burn us." Jamie pulled the doctor to stand and ushered him into the hallway. The hot smoke almost knocked him off his feet. His eyes burned.

He guided the doctor back to the room and scanned his surroundings. "The balcony. We must jump."

"You do what you must to save yourself." Dr. Miller sighed. "I had a vision of The Men's Sanctuary, but I didn't get a chance to build it. I don't want to spend my remaining days in prison or some dreadful asylum."

The door to the balcony was stuck. Jamie pushed with his weight. More blood gushed from his shoulder, wetting his jacket. The world reeled.

"Jamie! Dr. Miller!"

Ella, covered in soot from her hair to her shoes, ran to them. At the sight of her, Jamie wanted to drop to his knees and give a prayer of thanks.

Her hands reached for Jamie's shoulders. Jamie braced for pain but didn't want to stop her. "Jamie, you came. Lavinia said—"

"Dr. Parker, I was hoping to speak to you," Dr. Miller interrupted. "Will you tell people I wasn't a monster? As you have probably suspected, I have an illness of the mind. When it takes hold of me, my judgment is poor. I'm afraid Mrs. Landon and Miss Burke exploited my weakness for their goals."

Ella took his hand. "I know. But now you must get out. The stairs caught fire just after I climbed up here. Let's go to the balcony."

"The door is stuck," Jamie said, coughing.

"Let's push on it together. Dr. Miller, you try as well."

With their collective effort, the door relented, and they stepped onto the narrow balcony. Jamie grabbed the railing and yelped from a burn to his hands. A hot draft, thick with soot, hit his face. Bitter ash filled his mouth, making him cough. But then a gust of fresh air ran through his hair and cooled his sweaty forehead.

People were moving below, rushing away from the building. There were women in blackened dresses and soiled nightgowns and a group of sailors with a cart. A few people administered aid to someone lying on the grass.

The height from the balcony to the ground was significant, and most likely a jump would cause injury. In his case, an injury would likely be fatal. The ball would shift to his heart and kill him.

It doesn't matter. Ella must be safe.

Tears streamed down Dr. Miller's face. "I wonder if my soul will meet Alex's or my wife Amy's. They both died after I operated on them. Alex died from her wound, birthing our baby. And Amy... I tried to save her when a vessel in her brain ruptured. But I botched that surgery and killed her."

Ella wrapped her arm around him. "Lavinia told a different story about your wife. I believe you, Dr. Miller. You will not die. Let's join hands and jump together."

Dr. Miller turned away from her. His eyes were wide, and his lips muttered something. A prayer, perhaps?

A boom came from the floors below, and the balcony shook.

Jamie locked eyes with Ella. "You jump first," they said at the same time.

"I will use treatment to help the sick... to help..." Dr. Miller rasped, his voice breaking. "Not... to harm. My art... pure and holy..."

Caroline's voice rang from below. "Can you reach that tree branch and climb down? That should be safer than jumping."

"Ella, you do it. I'll help Dr. Miller," Jamie said. When Ella climbed onto the railing and leaped into the tree, he tugged on

Dr. Miller's sleeve. "Sir, can you stand on the railing and jump with me? This way you are more likely to avoid an injury."

"*Primum non nocere.* First, do no harm," Dr. Miller mumbled.

"Jamie, get off the balcony for heaven's sake." That was Conor, standing next to Caroline.

Dr. Miller pointed to Ella. "Make sure she's safe. She's the best student I ever had. Go ahead, Mr. Flowers. I will follow you."

Jamie climbed onto the hot railing, holding on with his fingertips. He leaped and grabbed onto a thick branch. His shoulder was engulfed with pain, but he held on. His feet found a sturdy branch for him to stand on. Cheers from his friends sounded below.

He turned toward the balcony. Dr. Miller was still standing there, staring up into the gray-orange sky. As Ella yelled for him to jump, he tensed, ready to leap. But then he sped inside. A crack sounded, whether of a beam falling or a pistol shot.

"No!" Ella screamed. Tears streamed down her face, washing the soot off her cheeks.

A moment later, a window exploded with a deafening boom. Glass rained down to the ground.

This building will collapse.

The realization hit like a club to Jamie's gut.

He reached for Ella. "Give me your hand. We'll jump down together and run."

Ella stretched her hand toward him.

A blast split the air, followed by screams. Windows shattered. The ground shook.

An invisible force threw Jamie out of the tree. He landed on his wounded shoulder. Deafening sounds and extreme pain flooded his senses and then ceased.

Ella, my love. Be safe.

Chapter 45

A gust of cool air awakened Ella. Her eyes opened to the gray-orange sky, a shade that was beautiful and menacing at the same time. It took her a moment to wiggle her fingers and toes. Groaning from pain all over her body, she sat up. What had been the stately building housing The Women's Sanctuary only this morning was now nothing but rubble. Somewhere inside were the bodies of Joanna, Lavinia Burke, and Dr. Miller.

For a moment, there was silence. But then sights and sounds came from all directions, making her head pound. The snakes of fire crackling. Patients wailing. Attendants shouting, leading them away from the smoldering remains of the building, Magistrate Harrow, Ursula, and her brother helping them. Moans from two women prostrated on the ground, Conor kneeling next to them, and Oli alternately turning between them, giving aid. Among that chaos, a rustle of leaves on a nearby tree, the only unaffected witness of the fire. The tree that Jamie and she had climbed into before the explosion.

Jamie! Where is he?

He wasn't among the people rushing about her or the injured limping about. Nor was he among the patients that Oli was assisting. A foreboding feeling clenched her gut.

"Ella! We were worried about you, but Oli said you would wake up soon." Conor limped to her and handed her a flask. She expected it to be water and took a greedy gulp. Brandy burned her tongue and throat but also gave her vigor.

"Have you seen Jamie? After the explosion, I mean."

Conor coughed into his fist. "His wound reopened, and the ball shifted. Oli said that could be terrible."

Ella's breath caught. *Did Lavinia tell the truth that Jamie was hurt in a duel?*

"Oli halted the bleeding. Our ship's crew brought a cart, and Oli asked them to take Jamie to a roadside inn a couple of miles away. Caroline went with them. I'd have gone too, but my mother and Lillian need help." He gestured toward the two women on the ground. Both were now sitting up. Oli was unwrapping Lillian's bandage.

"Your mother?"

Conor approached The Lost One, who was now sitting up and mumbling. Or was she speaking? She called Conor by name.

Ella's mouth dried. "Does she speak another language?"

Conor bent his head. "Yes. She should've never been taken to an asylum. It's my fault, and I will do whatever it takes to make it up to her."

Oli gestured to Ella, and she approached. He was changing the dressing on Lillian's head. "Jamie had a ball lodged near his left clavicle. When the explosion blew him off that tree and he hit the ground, that ball likely shifted. I stopped the bleeding, but his breathing was failing."

Dizziness overcame Ella. If the ball damaged major blood vessels or the pericardium, Jamie would die.

"How do I find him?"

"Are you able to ride?" Conor asked. "Our horses are tied to the tree by the gates. If you follow the road, you'll find the inn."

Ella hurried to the gates. Her lungs burned as she gulped the heavy air. A cold drizzle began, spattering her face and soaking her filthy dress.

Jamie, please be alive when I find you.

Coaches and wagons jostled toward her on the road, coming to a stop at the gates. These must've been arranged by Magistrate Harrow to transport the patients to other asylums and lodgings. The drivers exchanged gasps and exclamations, pointing at the ruins.

"Please go to Dr. Higgins in the yard," Ella shouted to them. "He'll help you find your passengers."

While the drivers yelled questions about the fire, she took the reins of one of the horses and mounted it. Following Conor's directions, she spurred it down the road, which was already becoming muddy from the increasingly heavy rain. Each clop of the hooves thudded in Ella's chest.

Jamie, please hold on.

Thirty minutes later, the rain had soaked her through and blurred her vision. But then, as she rode over a hill, a light glowed in the distance. Ella drove her horse faster. Soon, the hazy light became a lantern carried by a man who walked next to a cart. More lights shone beyond it from the windows of a wooden home, which Ella hoped was the inn Conor told her to find.

She caught up to the cart and the men who walked next to it. The man holding the lantern was Mr. Morgan, a coxswain from the *Neptune*'s crew. She recognized the other sailors as well.

"Dr. Parker, it's good to see you safe and sound," Morgan greeted her with a solemn expression instead of his usual rough humor and grin. "I'm afraid Mr. Flowers is not long for this world."

The other men sighed or averted their faces. These men had seen the deaths of many crewmates.

With her chest pinched, Ella craned her neck inside the cart. Squeezed in there, Caroline held Jamie, her body pressed to his. Jamie's eyes were closed, his face bloodless.

"Ella!" Caroline's face was wet with tears. "I'm trying to keep him warm and shelter him from the bumps. I think he's struggling to breathe. He's been unconscious throughout this ride, but he moaned when the wheel hit a rock. I have your medical bag. I found it in your room."

The battered bag Caroline lifted was as welcome a sight as an old friend. Squeezing her calves, Ella prompted the horse to run forward toward the inn.

A stable boy met her, and she passed the reins to him and dismounted. A cheerful blaze in the hearth and a bearded innkeeper greeted her inside an empty dining room with only a couple of tables. Ella's clothes dripped on the wooden floor.

"Would you like to dry your clothes by the fire, madam, while I pour you a warming drink?" The elderly innkeeper pulled a chair to the fireplace. For a moment, the image of Lavinia engulfed in flames appeared to Ella, making her shudder.

How easily the things that serve us can transform into a force of destruction.

"Thank you, sir, but later. We have a wounded man with us. Will you allow us to tend to him here?"

The proprietor straightened. "An injured man will always find shelter and aid in my inn. I will send my son to fetch a surgeon. Unfortunately, with the rain, it will take many hours for him to get here."

"Don't worry about that. What I need is one of these tables." She checked the table for sturdiness, asked the man to wipe it, and rushed outside to show the way to the men.

The sailors were lifting Jamie from the cart, Caroline begging them to be careful. When they brought Jamie inside, Ella had them lay him on the table. She gestured for Mr. Morgan to bring his lantern close and for Caroline to give her the medical bag. The innkeeper muttered that he'd fetch vinegar from the kitchen. He also brought Ella a basin with water to wash the soot and grime from her face and hands, and a towel to pat dry her dripping dress.

Ella wasted little time on getting herself dry. With her scissors, she cut Jamie's shirt and peeled away the bloody bandages. The entry wound revealed itself— torn at the edges, with angry red skin surrounding it. Fresh blood seeped from it.

A stifled gasp from Caroline reached Ella's ears.

"It's not as bad as it looks," Ella said to comfort her friend and herself. "The wound has reopened and is irritated but not festering."

A bulge rose just beneath the collarbone. Could that be it, the ball? Her fingers pressed on the warm skin and found something hard and smooth underneath.

Ella opened her bag and spread her instruments on the table: a scalpel, forceps, needles, and more. "Please help me wipe them," she told Caroline, passing her a cloth.

"Do you mean to remove the ball?" Caroline's voice shook as she worked. "Dr. Higgins said it's too dangerous."

"Not when it's so close to the surface I can grasp it. His wound healed well, and then, when Jamie fell, the ball shifted in a fortunate way."

She asked the men to hold Jamie while she washed the wound. Then she made a small incision right above it and slipped the forceps inside. Guided by her touch, and then by the sound of metal clinking, she grasped the ball. With steady movements, she slid it free and brought it out.

"You did it," Caroline exclaimed, and Ella passed her the ball. A tiny patch of fabric was stuck to it. Once again Ella marveled at Jamie's constitution. It was a miracle the wound hadn't festered and his body had healed as well as it had. She checked for any remaining fabric and poured vinegar on the wound. Satisfied, she washed away the blood and threaded her needle with a silk thread. With confident movements, she sutured the wound.

"I think he's breathing easier," Mr. Price, a sailor who'd survived the French prison with Jamie, said.

Ella bent down to listen to Jamie's heart and lungs.

"Here, use this." Caroline reached into her pocket and passed Ella a small, wooden tube. "Put it to your ear."

Puzzled, Ella did as Caroline suggested. The rhythm of Jamie's heart was steady and strong, and Ella heard it more clearly than without the instrument. She shifted the tube to hear Jamie's lungs and detected a slight wheeze. Caroline's simple instrument amplified the sound, helping Ella distinguish the problem.

"The smoke has inflamed his lungs. We all likely suffer the same and must drink a coughing tincture." Her own chest constricted, and she hacked. "But nothing alarming."

Caroline brushed away the tears that clung to her lashes and kissed Jamie on the forehead. "He feels warm."

"We'll watch for a fever." Ella nodded. "The next few days will be critical."

The innkeeper approached and addressed Ella. "I've prepared a bed for the wounded gentleman and warmed it with a heated pan. I've also prepared a room for you ladies. I'm afraid the other rooms are occupied, but the rest of you can find shelter in the village. The rain has thankfully passed. I must say, I've seen much in the thirty years I've owned this inn, but I've never seen a woman surgeon." He scratched his almost bald head.

"We've been lucky to have her," Mr. Price answered.

Mr. Morgan clapped Ella on the back. "To think that once we took bets on how soon you'd beg the captain to send you home. We've missed you, Dr. Parker. We came to rescue you, but you saved yourself and then you saved Mr. Flowers."

"I've missed you too, my friends," Ella said, wrapping the large man in a hug. She addressed the innkeeper. "Thank you so much for your help. I must send for my belongings that my friend Matilda Pesce is keeping safe for me in Plymouth. Then I will pay you handsomely for your hospitality. And for a supper and drinks for all of us." Ella's stomach rumbled, reminding her she hadn't eaten yet today.

Caroline touched her lips. "Look, he's waking up."

Jamie's eyes fluttered, and he mumbled. "Caroline, I'm dying. Tell Ella that I love her."

"I hear you, Jamie." Ella cupped his face. "But no talk of dying. You are going to recover."

"If I do, I'll marry you, Ella. If you will still have me."

Ella's cheeks became hot, and the men chuckled.

Caroline tilted her head. "I don't think this proposal counts, little brother. You'll need to ask Ella properly when you've recovered."

Ella squeezed Jamie's hand. "Caroline is right. First, you must heal. When you are better, I'll be waiting for a proper proposal. And a full account of why you didn't marry me when I asked you to. Then I will give you my answer."

Chapter 46

Sitting next to Caroline, Ella watched the dawn kiss the clouds with scarlet hues. From the open window came the aromas of hay and summer flowers, chasing away the heavy smells of medicines. After a fever that lasted several days, Jamie was finally sleeping with a restful expression, his deep breathing occasionally interrupted by coughs. Despite spending the entire night on the chair by Jamie's bed, Ella didn't feel like sleeping, and Caroline seemed alert as well.

After another of Jamie's coughing fits, Ella asked Caroline to let her use her tube and listened to his heart and lungs. When she finished, she whispered to Caroline.

"Once again, Jamie's lucky. His fever is broken. The irritation caused by the smoke is improving. And his heart sounds fine. I don't understand why Dr. Miller said he heard a heart murmur."

Caroline sighed. "Other doctors agreed with him. Oli said they were afraid to give an opposing opinion."

Ella raised the tube. "And they didn't have this little device you invented. You must patent it. If Sarah Guppy was awarded a patent for a bridge design two years ago, why shouldn't you try?"

"Please, I didn't invent a new kind of bridge. A child made this." Caroline took the newssheets she was reading earlier from her lap and rolled them into a tube. "Look, these papers rolled up will have a similar effect."

"How would you feel then if someone else got all the credit? And for ether as well?"

Caroline slouched, her shoulders rolling forward. "Oli thinks more testing should be done before administering it to a patient during surgery. A mistake in dosage could be deadly. He suggested more experiments I hadn't thought of before."

"You and Oli should work together." Ella smiled. "And you must write to a medical journal."

Caroline unrolled the papers. "Speaking of medical journals, I was just reading in *Medical Essays and Observations* the story from Mr. and Miss Collins. Other papers printed it as well. Their account contains disturbing details of abuse and carelessness happening in asylums, things only someone with inside access could witness. They expose Lavinia Burke and her crimes. And they call for change and accountability."

"What about Dr. Miller? What did they write about him?"

"The article gives credit to Dr. Miller and the Sanctuary for providing patients with comfort, curing their physical ailments, and treating them with dignity. But then Dr. Miller's accomplishments were tarnished by turning a blind eye to Miss Burke's abuses and Mrs. Landon's financial schemes and by his experiments that resulted in harm to patients and were done without consent. His legacy will likely be that of a genius who fought for progress but at times overstepped the bounds of morality. And of someone who fought his own demons. The article mentions he had secretly sought treatment in several private asylums, staying there for months."

A lump formed in Ella's throat. "I'm glad they wrote about the good he did and not just the bad. But you may disagree."

Caroline smoothed Jamie's blanket that had bunched as he turned in his sleep. "Dr. Miller's diagnosis was a catalyst that changed our lives. But perhaps Jamie became a stronger and a better person for it. And I'm thankful for the things Dr. Miller taught you and Oli in medical school that allowed you to save my brother. Today is his twentieth birthday. And he's alive. Despite it all."

"I didn't realize..."

Jamie, you didn't think you would live to this day. But you are here. And so am I.

The high-pitched babbling of several women rose from downstairs, followed by two men's voices.

"I believe my parents and sisters have arrived. I sent them a note asking them to stay in Plymouth until Jamie is well enough to travel, but likely they could wait no more. And I hear Oli as well." Caroline's cheeks turned rosy.

Ella stood. "I'll leave you to have some private time with your family."

Ignoring Caroline's protest, she slid out of the room. On the stairs she met Jamie's mother, thinner-faced and with more wrinkles than she remembered from meeting her eight years ago. Her younger daughters, Julia and Audrey, now eighteen and sixteen, blond and blue-eyed like Jamie, greeted Ella with wide grins. Jamie's father limped behind them, leaning on his walking stick and Oli's arm. Tobby, with a downcast expression, brought up the rear.

"Jamie is sleeping, with Caroline watching over him," Ella spoke quietly to them. "His fever broke just two hours ago. Please try not to wake him."

Mrs. Flowers swiveled to her daughters with a strict expression. "If you wake Jamie with your chatter, you won't have dessert for a week."

Audrey pouted, which somehow made her even prettier, while Julia scoffed. "Most likely *you* will wake him, Mother."

Pressing a finger to his lips, Mr. Flowers hushed them. "We all will be quiet as mice and wait for Jamie to awaken. But we can't postpone seeing him any longer."

"Please go to him. I will speak to Ella downstairs and then come up to check on Jamie," Oli said and turned to Tobby. "You go downstairs as well. Let Jamie's family savor the moment in privacy."

While Oli spoke to the innkeeper and ordered breakfast, Ella opened her arms to hug Tobby. "Why do you look so sad?"

"I miss Ginny. Her older sister took her away. I know it's a good thing, but... I wish she didn't leave."

Jamie and I were about the same age as Tobby and Ginny when we first met. How much has happened since then.

"If it's meant to be, you will see her again," Ella replied and gave him a few coins for breakfast. Then she joined Oli at the table, where he was nursing a cup of coffee.

"Did you find out where the patients have been placed?" Ella asked after a warm greeting.

"Yes, I have a list for you if you want to visit anyone. Some were claimed by their relatives, but most were taken to private asylums with good reputations. Magistrate Harrow promised to inspect those asylums and ensure the patients are getting proper care."

Oli passed her the list and Ella scanned it.

"I'm glad to see Cora Butler's name here. I was afraid she got left behind. But I don't see Lillian's. Where is she?"

"Lillian and Conor's mother are both being cared for by Captain Grey's family until they are well enough to be moved. I understand Lillian will be living with her parents, and Conor will find a place to live with his mother." He sipped his coffee.

Ella beamed. "It's kind of the Greys to shelter them."

"They are wonderful people. They nursed Owen Olson back to sanity."

Ella clapped with joy. "I'm so glad."

The server brought them plates of kippers, boiled eggs, and bacon. Appetizing smells wafted in the air, and Ella dug into the food. It was salty but good when chased down with the strong coffee.

"Have you heard what happened to the Landons?" Oli tilted his head.

Ella's mouth twisted. "I know they were placed under arrest in their grand house, where they are quite comfortable, I'm sure. And they are likely using all their connections to escape justice."

"Well, they didn't escape a mysterious malady that took Mrs. Landon when she got home. I know the doctor who attended her. He found the lady severely ill with burning pain in her stomach, vomiting, and muscle cramps. The sons ran away from the arrest upon arrival to their home but didn't make it far. The constables caught them in the woods just beyond the city gates. Both were too sick to continue running. They were taken to jail, where a surgeon attended them and noted the same symptoms their mother experienced. But all three are now recovering. What do you make of that?"

Ella winced as the food took on a bitter taste in her mouth. "They insulted Lavinia, then drank the tea she made them. I assume she used rat poison—white arsenic—and masked the taste with honey and herbs. I must say, though, I'm not too sad about the Landons. But I'm grateful that Lavinia can no longer harm anyone."

Oli chewed his egg thoughtfully. "Me too. And I'm also glad she saved Dr. Miller's journals. She hid them in a metal chest before starting the fire. Magistrate Harrow let me have them."

Bacon lay untouched on Oli's plate, and Ella helped herself to it. "He was a great surgeon, and I'm glad his notes will be preserved. And perhaps his journal will shed light on his illness. He had periods of mania, when he would work tirelessly day and night and, at times, suffer hallucinations or delusions, followed by profound melancholia, when he wouldn't rise from his bed."

Oli opened his medical bag and passed her a yellowed journal. "There's an entry at the end that will be especially interesting to Jamie and his family."

Ella pushed away her plate and read.

8 July 1806, Seatown

Today marks a week I've spent at Seatown, Dorset. The village is tranquil and quiet, exactly what I craved for my holiday. Yet I haven't slept in several nights. Thoughts about Lillian are pursuing me like hounds. Is she healthy? Do her adoptive parents treat her well? Her cries follow me everywhere.

Mr. Flowers sent me another note, his fourth or fifth. He was apologetic about bothering me on my holiday, but this note seeped with despair. "I plead as a father. I don't know if you have children, Dr. Miller, but please understand the anguish of a family that has been told that their beloved son may be seriously ill. You are most qualified to give the diagnosis." I could no longer ignore the man. Besides, it occurred to me that I've read his publications and was impressed by his work.

When I came to see the patient in the evening, I immediately regretted it. The air was humid and heavy before the rain, and my headache started on the way. Instead of the esteemed colleague I expected to see, I was greeted by a man in an old suit whom I mistook for a butler. It turned out that this Mr. Flowers was a different man than I expected, a surgeon-dentist. The mistake vexed me, and that made my headache worse. I was eager to leave. I should've left, but how could I have explained my abrupt exit? How could I tell them of the feeling of hopelessness that bounds my chest? Of my weariness from insomnia and the nightmares that come when I finally sleep? I composed myself and proceeded to examine the twelve-year-old boy.

As I listened to the boy's heart, a cry sounded as loud as if the weeping child were in the room. But there was no other child but the boy, who was calmly lying on the bed. I recognized Lillian's cry. It filled my ears, and I couldn't hear the boy's heartbeat no matter how hard I tried. Panic crept up my throat. What will these people think of me? Word of my illness may get around, and I will find myself committed to another asylum.

I proceeded with an assumption that there must be something wrong with the boy. He was pale and thin. His mother had German measles when she was pregnant with him. His feet swelled at times. The family physician was concerned about the frequent lung illnesses the boy caught. And most importantly, the boy himself admitted that his heart frequently palpitates. I no longer needed to hear his heart to know that he suffered from a fatal heart defect. Just recently I did a postmortem on the body of a thirteen-year-old girl with the same disease: She died of apoplexy. The oldest of my patients with this illness lived to be twenty. My headache pounded and Lillian's voice wept with fear and woe, making it hard for me to hear the worried parents and the boy. I gave my diagnosis, answered a couple questions, and left.

When I returned home, I went to bed, but sleep eluded me again. The rain started, and the drops drummed on my nerves. I shouldn't have come to Dorset. I don't need sea air and swims. I need to see Lillian, to know why she cried.

It would be prudent to examine the young Jamie Flowers again in a year or two to monitor how his illness progresses. I'm confident of my diagnosis, but still, I should see him when my own health is better and I can listen to his heart again. I will keep this entry as a reminder to follow up, and then destroy it.

Spots flew in Ella's vision. She locked gazes with Oli, who sat with his head resting on his fists, his fingers scratching the stubble on his cheeks.

"He was hallucinating! And he was too proud to admit that he wasn't fit to examine a patient that evening. Poor Jamie and his family!"

"Good thing he forgot to destroy this page. Now we know what happened. Even though there are many ripped-out pages, there's enough to see that Dr. Miller suffered from an illness of the mind. Yet, he saved lives, made great advances in surgery, and taught students like us. I'm glad he survived."

Ella jerked her head back. "What? But he ran back inside before the building collapsed."

"One of your crew heard his moans and pulled him from under the rubble. From what I heard he has severe amnesia and will be committed to an asylum."

Ella's ribs grew tight, restricting her breath. "I wonder if he knew that would be his fate. Perhaps that's why he wanted to study the mind and build a sanctuary for the insane."

Caroline came down the stairs. Her eyes gleamed as they lingered on Oli. "Jamie woke up and said he's hungry. What should we let him eat?"

"That's excellent news, Miss Caroline. He can have meat to rebuild his strength." Oli's cheeks glowed as he grinned at the young woman.

Ella narrowed her eyes. *I hope there's something between them, because they would make a lovely couple.*

"Ah, excellent. We'll feed him our mother's famous ham. I'm sure he missed it. I'll bring you some as well. It's delicious." She sped back upstairs.

Oli's face fell, as if all happiness walked out of the room. "How can I tell her?"

"Tell her what?" Ella raised her eyebrow. "That you don't eat pork because it's against your religion? That you are Jewish?"

"That she and I cannot be together. Even if I love her, I'm forbidden from marrying outside of my faith."

Ella's jaw fell. "Tell her. You two will find a solution."

He shook his head. "It's better that she returns home with her family. She'll forget me soon enough."

"And you? Will you forget her?"

With his lips turned down, he pushed his plate away. "I will try."

"Why? She's truly special. At least write to her. You write lovely letters that I always love to receive. And you can guide her further research with ether."

"That I can do." A smile bloomed on Oli's face.

Chapter 47

Jamie was getting weary from his family's fussing. They were all speaking at once, asking him if he was hurting, if he wanted breakfast or more water. The wound was throbbing, and he was doused with sweat. But this was the best he had been feeling since the fire and the bullet's removal.

His father propped his pillows to help him sit. A tear glistened on his lashes. "My boy... I can't even express how I feel. We were in despair when we read you were imprisoned in France. When you didn't write, we lost all hope and thought you were dead. Then your friend Mr. Leach brought news that you were alive but dangerously wounded. When we arrived to nurse you, you'd disappeared, and we didn't know what to think. And then, finally, Caroline wrote you are here, ill with a fever, but we should hope you will make a full recovery. And that you never had a fatal heart defect. All this was enough to make our heads reel."

His father's wrinkled hand rested on Jamie's knee. Jamie squeezed it. "I'm sorry, Father."

"Now that's the hand of a man," his father said, studying Jamie's palm. "Calluses. Blisters. Burns."

"I had to toil my hardest on the ship, and in prison. The burns are from the asylum fire."

He broke into a cough. Immediately, his mother brought a cup of water to his lips and sniffled.

"You should've stayed home, like I begged you to. Instead, you embarked on your foolish adventure. Mr. Leach told us of the horrors you survived during ship battles and in France. And then you've dueled! You've put yourself in mortal danger repeatedly. Will you listen to your parents now?"

Jamie reached for her, and she bent down to let him kiss her cheek, salty from tears. "Mother, you know I didn't leave to seek fun. I didn't want you to see me dying because you said you would die with me. I chose to make the little time I had left meaningful. And I hoped to die in such a way that it saved someone else. I'm extremely lucky and thankful that I've made it through it all. But my journey changed me. I've faced death, and I've also experienced great joy. I've learned who I am. Yes, I will appreciate your well-meaning advice, but I must listen to my heart, even if it leads me to danger. Some things are worth fighting for."

Caroline put her hand on his good shoulder. "I always said that the doctors don't know how strong and kind your heart is. But please don't get hurt again."

"We've missed you. I want our home to be happy again," Julia said.

He grinned at his sisters. "You've all become so lovely. I've missed you as well, more than you can ever know."

Audrey, the youngest sister, smiled through tears. "I've found so many new shells for your collection. I brought them with me. Here." She passed him her satchel. "Happy Birthday."

Jamie blinked as he accepted it. "My birthday? Is it today? I lost track..."

After years of dreading this day like a death warrant, I forgot about it.

"Happy Birthday, son. We'll celebrate later, when you are well," his father said.

Caroline bent down to kiss him on the cheek. "Happy Birthday, and many more. What do you want to do, now that you know it's not your last?"

He took in her chestnut eyes, wise beyond her years. "If you are asking what I want to do with my life, I can't say yet. Besides, life is too unpredictable to make long-term plans. But I know what I want today."

Everyone leaned in, but then a quiet knock came from the door. "How's Jamie feeling?" Oli's voice called.

"Come in, Oli," Jamie said. "I'm feeling a lot better."

Oli walked in. His eyes lingered on Caroline, and his smile waned. But then he turned to Jamie and grinned again. "That's great. But don't exhaust yourself."

"Jamie, you said you wanted something for your birthday," Julia reminded him.

He looked up at Oli. "Is Ella downstairs?"

"Yes, she just finished breakfast and plans to go to the market. Some medicinal herbs she wants to purchase."

"Dear sisters, please prevent her from leaving. Keep her downstairs." He winked at Caroline, and she answered with a knowing grin.

"Julia, Audrey, you hear that? We have a mission." She ushered the younger girls from the room.

"What's this, Jamie?" His mother wrung her hands. "Surely, she will be back soon."

His father stood. "Jamie, I think I know what you want to do. But it would be wiser for you to fully recover first."

"Father, my heart says differently. I can't wait any longer."

"Then it's fortunate that we brought you some clean clothes." His father gave his arm to Jamie's mother. "Come, sweetheart. When a man's about to make a fool of himself out of love, the decent thing is to let him do so without his parents watching."

When the door closed, Oli crossed his arms. "Are you thinking of getting out of bed? As a doctor, I advise against it. You just started feeling better. I'll bring Ella here."

Jamie lowered his voice. "You are an excellent doctor, but you are also my friend and Ella's. I'm asking as a friend. Help me get dressed and shave. Then I will go to Ella."

Oli grunted, then offered his arm in support. "It may be a good thing I have smelling salts in my pocket. Take your time getting up."

***

Jamie's sisters were ushering Ella up the stairs and into the room she was sharing with Caroline.

Julia studied her with a critical eye. "Do you have a prettier dress you can change into?"

"Can I do your hair? I'm very good at that," Audrey added.

She glanced down at the sturdy gray dress she was wearing. "I was about to go to the market. I don't see why I should change."

"You can go with us later." Caroline's eye shone like gems. "Please let my sisters dress you up."

"But what are we doing?"

"Oh. We are..." Julia chewed her lip.

Audrey burst out in giggles. "Yes, what are we doing?"

Caroline threw up her hands. "Did you forget? We are celebrating Jamie's birthday."

"Even though he's not well?" Ella scanned the sisters' eager faces. "Although, I suppose a little celebration will cheer him up. My friend Matilda sent me some of my clothes."

Ella indicated a trunk, and Julia knelt to peruse its contents.

"Not that. Definitely not that. What are trousers doing in here?" Julia muttered, tossing the garment on the floor. "Oh, that's perfect." She lifted a violet gown.

"No." Ella's shoulders fell. "I wore it when… when I proposed to Jamie."

The sisters exchanged glances.

"Proposed marriage? I didn't know a woman could do that," Audrey said, wide-eyed.

Caroline tilted her head. "Ella, if people deserve second chances, so should dresses. Don't you think?"

"Besides, you have nothing else to wear," Julia added, throwing the discarded clothes back in the trunk.

They're right. This dress was made by my dear friends, and it's lovely. It's not the dress's fault that Jamie rejected me that day. And now I know he acted out of love.

She nodded, and the sisters cheerfully dressed her and styled her hair.

Ten minutes later, Ella was back in the dining room. The innkeeper was wiping tables. Seeing Ella and Jamie's sisters, he bowed. "How fortunate that Mr. Flowers was brought here. With so many fine ladies about, the whole place is brighter. I will fetch you some of my best cider as a thanks for gracing my modest inn."

Julia and Audrey beamed and sat by the fire.

Ella moved to join them, but Caroline pointed to the stairs. "Go to Jamie before he falls."

With slow and careful steps, and holding the railing, Jamie was descending the stairs. His lips were tight, but he seemed determined to push through the pain. Oli stood back at the top, leaning on the banister, shaking his head. Tobby was next to him, bouncing from foot to foot. Caroline wrapped her arms around her sisters.

Her heart in her throat, Ella ran to the foot of the stairs. "Jamie, you shouldn't!"

"Yes, I should. You are worth this and more." Breathing heavily, he got down a couple more stairs.

"No, you wait for me." Ella flew up the stairs as he labored down.

They met halfway, on a broad landing, both breathing hard.

"Jamie, you can't—" Ella's voice caught as Jamie grabbed the railing and lowered himself on one knee. Ella's palms went to her mouth.

"Ella, I blundered once, but today is my chance to get it right. I thought that my heart had a fatal flaw, and I wouldn't live long. But it wasn't my illness that tore us apart. It was my lack of trust in myself and in you. I want to spend all our days together, however many there may be. Would you make me the happiest man in the world and be my wife?"

Ella's heart danced so fast that she also needed to hold the railing.

I haven't even told him the truth about my inheritance. He's in for a surprise.

"Jamie, I didn't think I could forgive you. But I'm glad that we didn't get married when I asked you. Because now I love you even more. Yes, I will be your wife."

He tried to stand but grabbed his shoulder. "I think I need your help."

"Here, lean on me."

Once he was standing, he pulled her into an embrace, and his lips found hers. It seemed to Ella that their hearts beat in perfect unison.

Chapter 48

Plymouth, May 1814

As they stepped out of the packed church, Ella held Jamie's hand. Her bridal veil fell on her light blue dress, the shade of the cloudless sky over the sea. Jamie wore his midshipman's uniform, and to Ella, he had never looked more handsome. Most importantly, he looked healthy, fully recovered from his injury.

Neptune's officers, including Conor Leach and Jack Wyse, stood in front of them. With elegant movements, they raised their swords, forming an arch. The swords fell as the newly married couple passed under them. The peal of church bells and the chirping of birds filled the air.

Weapons of war give way to love. Here, and in the world around us. Napoleon abdicated and is exiled to Elba. After long and turbulent years of war, we finally have peace.

When the last sword was sheathed, a great roar erupted from the crowd that spilled out of the church. Caroline, Julia, and

Audrey Flowers, Bella and Cecilia Grey with their mother, Ella's childhood friends Veronica Allen, Marietta Wyse, and Henrietta Fillips, among other women, were clapping and waving. Mrs. Flowers, standing next to her husband and Conor's mother, wiped happy tears, while Matilda Pesce winked at Ella with a wise smile.

"Men, three cheers for our brave midshipman and our skillful surgeon!" Captain Grey bellowed, and the *Neptune's* crew shouted and stomped their feet. Retired Lieutenant Wyse and carpenter Owen Olson cheered the loudest. Ella's assistants Tyler and Sully and all the shipboys hoorayed. Tobby blew into a pipe that made an earsplitting sound.

Jamie drew Ella to him. "Must we go to the wedding breakfast? Let our family and friends eat and chat so we can finally be alone."

"I'm afraid we must mingle with the guests, at least for a little while," she said, caressing his cheek.

They walked slowly, holding hands, and were among the last to arrive at the Cooked Goose. Ella could hardly recognize the dining room decorated for the occasion. Tables boasted white linens, candles in brass holders, and vases with fresh flowers. Garlands of ivy hung along the railing. At a table designated for the bride and groom, Jamie's sisters were putting final touches on a centerpiece made of primroses and violets.

Mr. Williams, the fiddler from the *Neptune*, played cheerful music as Ella and Jamie greeted their guests. While Jamie went to show his parents to their seats, Ella received hugs from each of Jamie's sisters. Caroline was the last to embrace her. She dipped into her satchel and removed a small shell on a cord, like one she had on her own wrist. "My sisters and I love to collect shells on the beach. We want to give you a matching bracelet as a symbol of our sisterhood. Not only do you and Jamie love the sea, but you've embraced the changes it brought you. Shells are left behind by creatures who have grown too large for them. You too are leaving behind your past because you are ready for a new chapter as husband and wife." Caroline tied the bracelet on Ella's wrist and kissed her cheek.

Tears welled in Ella's eyes. "Thank you. I couldn't dream of better sisters than you all."

"I want my wedding to be just like yours," Audrey said with sparkling eyes. "But Mother said my sisters must get married first." She gave Caroline an accusing look.

Caroline blushed and her gaze shifted across the room, where Oli and Conor were filling their glasses.

"Is Oli writing to you?" Ella asked Caroline.

"Yes, he writes often, and his letters are wonderfully amusing and helpful, with advice for my experiments. But he has declined all invitations to visit us. Mother says I must stop hoping and accept the attention of other suitors." Her shoulders fell.

Oli, what are you doing? How can you let Caroline go? But I can't fix your life for you.

Julia cleared her throat. "How soon can we visit you in New-castle? Jamie said your estate has a grand ballroom."

Ella smiled, thinking of Jamie's face when she revealed she'd inherited all her family's money and property, which by law, would go to her husband. Jamie insisted on seeing a lawyer and ensuring that most of the riches stayed with Ella.

"Actually, we are thinking of turning that wing into a clinic. The patients' beds would be in that room." She'd long thought that her father's estate, the place of her lonely childhood, should be transformed for good use. But she didn't know how to start such a project until she discussed it with Jamie. Sharing ideas and making decisions together helped them turn an over-whelming idea into a manageable plan.

Julia gaped. "You will still be a surgeon? What about when you have children?"

The thought of children still gave Ella heart palpitations. Not so much the children, whom she imagined to be lovely, but childbirth.

I've learned to be calm when helping other women give birth. When my time comes, Matilda will keep me and the baby safe.

"Yes, I want to continue healing patients. I also want to build a wing for the sufferers of mental illness where everyone will be treated with respect and dignity."

Caroline grinned. "Since our father extracted teeth with four children running through the house, I see no reason you cannot be a mother and a healer."

Ella's heart squeezed, but the sensation was more pleasant than painful. "My mother was a noblewoman, but she learned to administer smallpox inoculations and traveled to orphanages to save poor children. I'm continuing her legacy."

How I miss her today. But I know she's with me.

The door opened, and Lillian walked in, leaning on the hand of an older woman. Her wig suited her, and she was no longer painfully thin, but her hesitant gait and paleness spoke of the ordeal she had survived.

Ella hastened to them. "Lillian, I didn't expect you to come. How are you feeling?"

"Every day better." Lillian gave her a weak smile. "Thank you for your letters. They help me remember."

The older woman shook Ella's hand. "I'm Lillian's mother, Mrs. Davis. I long wanted to thank you in person for saving Lillian's life. And congratulations on your wedding."

This woman's heart was stronger than her husband's indifference. She welcomed back her adoptive daughter and nursed her back to health.

A glass shattered, and all gazes went to Conor, who wiped spilled wine from his uniform.

"Mother, can we sit there?" Lillian pointed to the two empty chairs near Conor. "I think that's him. The man who saved me from the fire."

Mrs. Davis put her hand on Lillian's back. "No, my dear. You may not remember your husband, but in the eyes of the law, you are a married woman."

How sad that the church court refused to annul her marriage.

Ella showed them to the table with Captain Grey and his family, who greeted Lillian with great enthusiasm.

The guests were helping themselves to pigeon pie, roast beef, cheeses, and tarts and chasing them down with spiced ale and wine. Ravenous from inhaling the delicious smells, Ella sat next to Jamie on a tall chair decorated with ribbons. As she buttered a crust of bread, Jamie's father stood.

"To the happy couple. We once thought Jamie's heart was broken. Turns out, it was just waiting for Ella to heal it. While I no longer worry about his illness, I worry about his wit, because my son looks entirely mad with love."

Laughter and cheers erupted. Jamie took Ella's hand and kissed it. "It's true. You saved my life several times. But our love makes me happy for each new day."

Lost for words, Ella beamed at him.

Captain Grey raised his glass. "I also want to toast the newlyweds. No two people ever surprised me more than Ella Parker and Jamie Flowers. I thought that Dr. Parker would beg me to take her home. She proved to everyone that she belonged on the ship, saving the wounded. I was sure Jamie would make a mess of every order I gave him. He learned the ropes and then emerged as a leader who got the men home from captivity. To fair winds and calm seas on your voyage together."

Ella clinked glasses with Jamie. Like rain clouds, the memories of those who were absent came to Ella's mind. The captain stood in for Dr. Pesce, her beloved mentor. Matilda, his sister, must've been thinking of him as well. Wiping a rare tear, she raised her voice over the music and chatter.

"My brother Joseph would've loved to see this day. He was extremely proud of Ella, of her achievements as a surgeon. I wanted to make Ella a midwife and an herbal healer and pass my craft to her. But Ella forged her own path. Compared to that, marriage should be easy. Ella doesn't need a knight to save her. She deserves a man who'll walk beside her and not run away at the sight of blood—or brilliance."

"Hear, hear!" Oli cried in support.

Ella stood and embraced Matilda in a tight hug.

A spirited jig sounded, and the guests indulged in sweets and punch. Ella took a bite of the wedding cake: a spiced fruitcake with a sugar glaze.

"Too sweet for me. I think I prefer the sailor duff," she confessed.

"I'm happy to make it for you whenever you want it," Jamie replied. "I baked it for Captain Grey."

What will my old servants think if my husband enters the kitchen and starts cooking? But then, there will be a great deal for them to get used to. We are not my father and mother.

"How about a dance for our bride and groom?" the fiddler yelled over the noise. A tender melody flowed, and Jamie bowed before Ella. They waltzed through the room, and it seemed to Ella that they floated on air. She didn't want the music to stop.

Jamie sighed when it finally did. "I spent my life thinking about what would happen when the music stopped instead of treasuring every dance step. I won't make that mistake again. And thanks to you, I have that chance."

"Thanks to you as well," Ella answered.

After the dancing, the wedding party promenaded through decorated streets. Fresh wind blew from the harbor, making the banners and ribbons dance. Music flowed from all directions, and people danced by the bonfires.

Tobby caught up to Ella and Jamie. "Is all this for you? How do you know so many people?"

"It's not for us." Jamie chuckled. "Plymouth is celebrating Napoleon's abdication. We have won the war."

"Hurray!" Tobby threw his hat into the air.

Indeed. Let there be peace. Instead of suturing wounds, I can focus on curing illnesses. Perhaps I'll be able to help Dr. Miller.

They came to the port, where vessels, including the *Neptune*, heaved on bobbing waves. The gun salute boomed, making the spectators gasp and cover their ears. Jamie pulled Ella into his embrace, and their kiss lasted throughout the cannonade.

She caught her breath and waited for her pulse to slow. "I'm glad that these guns are shooting in celebration, not in battle.

Although I'm a little sad that our voyages are over. I loved watching the sunsets over the sea."

"Don't you want to be home, fixing it to your taste and organizing the clinic?"

"I do. But..." She tasted sea salt on her tongue. A taste she would dearly miss.

"The adventure doesn't have to be over because we are married. We could take a holiday before we settle at the estate." His eyes were shining like the silver glimmers on the water. "What do you think of that brig? It can take us wherever we want."

Ella stepped back. "That ship... you bought it?"

"You don't like it?"

She shuffled her feet. "It's lovely, but I thought... that a purchase like that we would make together. But I suppose as the husband you may spend our money as you wish, except for the portion set aside for me..."

"Of course we would make it together." Jamie put his arm around her. "I wouldn't make such a decision without you. I've made inquiries, and I know that it's available for purchase. Captain Grey says it's in excellent condition, and Conor already asked if he could be the captain. But you must want it as much as I do."

Her heart buoyed.

"Well, then... I love it. We'll hire men from our former crew who need jobs and want to sail. And make sure the shipboys are cared for and come sailing with us. We can take a sea holiday each year."

"Then it's settled." Jamie took her hand. "Soon we'll be sailing to another adventure. And then we'll return to Newcastle and fill that abandoned estate with purpose, life, and eventually the laughter of children. When you are ready." He added the last quickly.

She took his hand. "When *we* are ready. Whatever lies ahead, we choose together."

The sails of the ships went taut and whistled in the wind as Jamie's and Ella's hearts set their course for what lay beyond the blue horizon.

***

While Ella and Jamie are sailing toward their new adventure, will Oli find happiness with Caroline despite his family's objections? Read their story in Abigail's Song.

Jamie's and Ella's first meeting happens in the prequel Hearts by the Sea. Read a free book!

Ella's and Jamie's first meeting occurs in the prequel novella

Hearts by the Sea

Read for free!

An innocent game brings unforeseen consequences

In the idyllic setting of the English coast in 1800s, Jamie Flowers experiences his first infatuation when he meets Ella Parker, a mysterious girl with a troubled past. As the two rehearse *Romeo and Juliet* together, they decide to sneak out for a midnight swim. But their plans are abruptly halted by a shocking revelation, and Ella is soon gone. Left with a broken heart, Jamie searches for her... and himself. With unexpected twists and turns, Hearts by the Sea is a story of first love, secret codes, and self-discovery.

Read for Free!

Historical Notes

In the early 1970s, Stanford psychologist David Rosenhan wanted to know: Can the staff of a mental hospital truly tell if someone is insane? He created an experiment in which he sent eight sane people complaining that they could hear voices to different mental institutions. They mentioned those voices only during the initial assessment, and all eight were admitted. During their hospital stays, they never mentioned those voices again, took notes about their daily experiences, and told the doctors that they were sane. In all cases, the doctors continued with the confinement and medications and even found their journaling to be a symptom of insanity. Eventually, they were released when they admitted they were mentally ill.

While this experiment underlined several issues with mental institutions, Rosenhan concluded that once someone is labeled insane, others responded to the label more than to their own observations of the patient. If doctors in the 1970s couldn't identify a sane person among their patients, one cannot blame my fictional characters for making similar mistakes.

My research into mental health, brain surgery, and the history of asylums in England uncovered great surprises. I expected chains, starvation, and neglect. Some asylums, especially public institutions, were awful, but by the early nineteenth century, physicians believed patients should not be restrained and could benefit from a pleasant atmosphere. London's Bedlam boasted grounds for walking, music, and cleanliness. A patient could insist on their sanity and gain freedom. The insane who needed treatment, however, often became subjects of experiments.

One of the most influential books in my research was *Ten Days in a Mad-House*. In 1880s New York, Nellie Bly pretended to lose her mind and was committed to the insane ward at Blackwell's Island. Her account inspired some of my scenes and characters, including Ursula, a journalist investigating patient abuse. References to wrongly committed non–English-speaking patients especially moved me.

The secrets of the mind intrigued doctors, and they proposed unconventional theories and treatments. I wove several into the story. In 1917, Dr. Cotton believed mental illness came from an infection. He removed teeth, the gall bladder, stomach, uterus, ovaries, testicles, and parts of the colon as a means of treating mental illness. Despite the high mortality rate and lack of consent from patients or their families, he continued practicing his methods for thirteen years. Other doctors experimented with electricity, risking electrocuting the patient and themselves, trying to treat sexual deviance among other conditions.

Brain surgery was extremely risky in the early nineteenth century and performed only in emergency cases. The doctor who revolutionized neurosurgery was Harvey Cushing, born in 1869. His biographer Michael Bliss wrote: "Harvey Cushing became the father of effective neurosurgery. Ineffective neurosurgery had many fathers." The story of the pregnant woman shot in the head by her husband was based on a real case Cushing treated. All three lives were lost. I changed the outcome in my fictional story and created characters Alexandra Fulton and Lillian.

Ether was first discovered in the sixteenth century but first used in surgery in 1846 by dental surgeon William Thomas Green Morton. The operating room at the Massachusetts General Hospital, where he anesthetized a patient to remove a neck tumor, became known as Ether Dome. Morton's discovery revolutionized surgery, relieving patient suffering and allowing surgeons to perform longer and more complex procedures.

French physician René-Théophile-Hyacinthe Laennec invented the first stethoscope in 1816. He was a musician and had a keen understanding of sound. Supposedly, he felt uncomfortable putting his ear to the chest of a female patient, and he created the stethoscope as a solution. The female patients were surely grateful; other doctors, maybe less so.

Mental illness carried a stigma in the nineteenth century and still does in 2025. Yet it can strike like any other illness. It's not a failing of character or a weakness. Please get help if you need it. I wish all my readers the best of health.

Also by Alina Rubin

Grand Prize Winner of the Goethe Award in Late Historical Fiction 2024

Abigail's Song—Hearts and Harmony Book 1

Can music heal a broken soul?

Cast out from her home after her mother's death, orphan Abigail Jones wanders around her English town on Christmas Eve of 1809. Desperately trying to suppress her cough—the same that killed her mother—Abigail begs for coins on the freezing cold streets. With the help of the medical student, Oli Higgins, she recovers and avoids being sent to the cruel orphanage. Oli then reveals his secret: he is hiding his Jewish identity and his birth name, David Fridman, to pursue his chosen profession. He brings her into his devout, loving Jewish home. Over time, she embraces her found family and discovers her talent for music.

When she grows up, Abigail is caught between two worlds; not Christian enough for the Gentiles, but as a non-Jew, she has no hope of marrying David, the man she dreams of. While she is recovering from a deadly illness, David's brother Moishe inspires her with music to rise from her sickbed and to begin her journey of converting to Judaism.

Her attempt to capture David's heart fails when his true love appears in town. Heartbroken, Abigail hastily accepts another man's marriage proposal and plans a double wedding with David's bride. On the big day, guilt and misery drive her to take drastic actions.

Can her family save her?

***

Winner of Illinois Soon to be Famous Author Award!

A Girl with a Knife—Hearts and Sails Book 1

Women could not be surgeons. She did it anyway.

After the heartbreaking loss of her mother and a cruel attack by her drunken father, Ella Parker decides that dishonesty is fine when it serves her needs. At a time when wealthy young ladies do little more than embroidery, Ella escapes her luxurious but lonely life, disguises herself as a male medical student, and finds her footing in the university.

But when she brilliantly saves a patient and gains the approval of a famed professor, she must choose between truth and lies, and distinguish between real and false friends, before her pretense is discovered.

Read the Hearts and Sails series!

Friends Don't Let Friends Read Boring Books!

Thank you for reading A Woman on the Knife's Edge!
Leaving a review is like recommending a book to hundreds of friends. Please share your thoughts at:

Amazon

Goodreads

BookBub

Join the crew! Be the first to know of new adventures by subscribing to the newsletter at alinarubinauthor.com
I love hearing from my readers! Please connect with me!
Instagram: Alina.Rubin.Author
Facebook: Alina Rubin Author

Acknowledgements

First, I want to thank my wonderful readers, especially those who read A Surgeon and Spy when it came out and waited a year for this book. I hope I fulfilled your expectations and rewarded your patience. Thank you to everyone who posted thoughtful reviews, invited me to their book clubs, and recommended my books to their friends and family. Your support means the world to me.

Next, my gratitude goes to my amazing beta readers, who offered critique and made this book better. Thank you Michelle Ross, Rosemary O'Brien, Lisa Gavin, and Lindsey Fera.

No matter what tools become available to writers, nothing can replace an experienced editor. Thank you to Carrie Krause of Get Carried Away Editing for helping my story become more organized and meaningful. Thank you to Betsy Judkins of Maine Woods Editing for your eagle eyes and for finding problems I've missed.

Teachers are never thanked enough. Thank you, Mr. Kevin Hickey, Mrs. Barbara Fryzel-Marquette, and Mrs. Barbara Schuman, among many other wonderful teachers from Prospect High School.

Thank you to my dearest Elanna, who inspires me every day. And thank you to my husband, Vitaly, for his love and support. Special thanks to Inessa Levina and Michael, Jamie, and Karina Rubinshteyn for being my loyal readers.

As I'm writing these words in October 2025, the world around me feels full of anger and division. I hope my stories bring a little joy.

Alina

About the Author

Alina Rubin was once a writer of heart wrenching IT compliance documents. Now she is an award-winning historical fiction author who celebrates heroines with strong voices and able hands. Her characters took her on a journey beyond her wildest dreams. She's an accomplished speaker, book coach, and an owner of Hearts and Sails Author Services.

Alina obtained a B.S. and M.S. degrees in Business and Information Technology from DePaul University. She lives in Chicago with her husband and daughter. She enjoys yoga, hiking, and traveling.

Follow her blog and sign up for her newsletter on her website alinarubinauthor.com